When a Sparrow Falls

Adriene Russell

Martha,
Thanks for your friendship!
Adriene

PUBLISH AMERICA

PublishAmerica
Baltimore

First printing

ISBN: 978-1-4489-5373-8
PUBLISHED BY PUBLISHAMERICA, LLLP
www.publishamerica.com
Baltimore

Printed in the United States of America

This book is dedicated to the men and women who, in the midst of abuse, found a way out through dissociation. And to those who provide tireless emotional and spiritual support to them.

May you each find grace, peace, and hope as you walk on your healing journey together. Be fearless in forgiving others, and find comfort in the love offered to us all through Jesus Christ.

Acknowledgments

Special thanks to my friend Paula and my mom. Without your help and encouragement over the years, this book would not exist.

To my friends and family, thank you for your support in this process.

Chapter One

Distancing herself from the immense pain, Amanda drifts swiftly into the scene of sunshine and soft breezes that begins to take shape in her young mind. The warm, safe, summer wind drifts off the ocean. The smell of sand and sea mingles with the scent of day lilies. The sounds of seagulls and rushing waves are everywhere.

Amanda, walks along the beach, feeling as if everything is finally right with the world. She no longer senses a connection to the family's horrifying secret. The cold, damp basement she had just been locked in seems so far away. Here, on her beach, she is surrounded by a wondrous peace and calm that is so real she can almost reach out and touch it.

Sparky, her hyper cocker spaniel, runs along beside her chasing birds that fly down to snatch a bit of food. He likes to run after sticks that Amanda throws into the water. Jumping waves seems to be his favorite pastime. Sparky is Amanda's best friend in the world. He listens to her tell about her wonderful dreams and goals. He understands when she is sad. He seems to always know when it is time to jump in her lap and comfort her.

Today is no different. Walking with him by the shore makes Amanda feel so happy. She is safe, warm and smiling. She is no longer aware of the pain and fear her body is experiencing. "If she only knew," Carol thought, "who it is that lets her off the hook."

Carol is strong, much stronger than Amanda. *Carol* can take the abuse and hold onto those feelings for her. That's all *Carol* has to do. Amanda has to go to school and look happy when guests come to visit. *Carol* can hide away with her thoughts and memories where no one can see her. *Carol* does her job well. Amanda isn't even aware of the horror or secrets that *Carol* holds. She's enjoying her time away from it all.

The sun feels so soothing. Finding a blanket, Amanda lies down, marveling at how close the fluffy clouds look. She thinks of how neat it would be to just reach up and touch one. Relaxed and comforted, here on the secret beach within her mind, Amanda drifts into sleep.

Absent from the security and safety of the internal world that Amanda gets to enjoy, *Carol* is forced to deal with a painful reality. Dad has commanded her presence for their special games—the ones reserved for just the two of them. He does so like the games they play together. Explained as an opportunity to bond with his young daughter, the secret event is played out nightly on his favorite couch in the basement while his dutiful and loving wife cleans the dishes from dinner.

Silently, *Carol* endures his violent intrusion. Fear, shame and love intermingle to form a confusing, yet compelling motivation for *Carol's* speechless compliance. Too young to understand and too obligated to consider acting any other way, *Carol* selflessly bears the unwanted touches. Survival depends on it. Not just her survival, but the survival of her dad, her friends, her mom, and most important of all, her secrets: these secrets she keeps locked close to her heart; these secrets that can destroy; these secrets that keep her alive. No one must ever know what a bad girl she is.

With the 'bonding time' completed for another night, *Carol* is allowed to return to the bedroom. Tears are not shed. Cries are not heard. No one must know what happens in the basement. This is the rule *Carol* knows must never be broken. *Carol* must be quiet, and above all else, she must remain hidden. Slowly, quietly, painfully, she drifts into a deep sleep.

Amanda awakes to the sound of the alarm clock. She feels a little sore, but rested. She is ready to face another day. The wonderful dream she had the night before has put her in a good mood. Nothing can beat a dream about the beach.

She has been to the beach three times in her short life that she can remember. Each of those times, she was allowed to spend a week during the summer at her grandmother's summer house on the beach—just the two of them. Her grandmother is such a sweet and loving person. She spends the weeks making sure that Amanda is happy and enjoying herself. What a safe feeling it is to be near her.

As Amanda reminisces, her thoughts are interrupted by the sound of her mother coming down the hall. The footsteps seem heavy, very heavy. That can only mean one thing—Mom is not happy. In a panic, Amanda jumps from her bed. She quickly pulls her covers back to make her bed as presentable as possible, knowing that is the first thing her mother will check. Bracing for her mother's wrath, Amanda absent-mindedly begins to brush her hair using the wrong side of the brush.

As the door flies open, Amanda can not help but notice the new bruise under her mom's right eye. "Mommy!" she cries, "What happened to you? Are you okay?"

"Yes, it's nothing that you need to concern yourself with. What you do need to be concerned about is the number of times I've told you that breakfast is served promptly at 6:00 a.m. You're doing this on purpose! You know that you're to be dressed and your room cleaned before you eat! How dare you think you deserve to sleep late! You are not some kind of princess that can lay around all day! It's well past time for you to get yourself going. I swear I've never seen a child that's so useless!"

As her mother rants, Amanda feels herself going farther and farther away. She begins thinking about that dream, the beach, the warmth, and the safety. She just can't handle her Mother's outburst this morning. Amanda never knows how to please her mother, though she really wants to. She has tried everything she can think of, but nothing seems to work.

To dramatically demonstrate her point about Amanda's lack of organization, her mother opens the first two drawers in her dresser and dumps the contents onto her bed. "These drawers are a mess! Just like you are a mess! Now I want you to fold these clothes up neatly and place them back in the drawers. You better be quick about it too! You will be skipping breakfast this morning. Someone as lazy as you doesn't deserve to eat!" With that announcement her mother turns on her heel and stomps from the room, slamming the door behind her.

Without hesitation, *Marie* begins to fold the clothes that were thrown on her bed. As quickly and neatly as possible, she places them in perfect rows in their respective drawers. Once completed, she turns her attention to the sheets and blanket that need to be smoothed and tucked.

The next order of business—to get herself dressed for school. A quick feel of the window pane tells *Marie* that a sweater is needed. Carefully rubbing her fingerprints off the glass, she moves to the closet to find that cute little green sweater that her mother likes so much.

While looking in the closet, she notices that her shoes are just piled in the corner. This will never do! Mother will be so upset if she sees her closet in such disarray. Meticulously, *Marie* arranges her shoes into one perfect row. Now a quick check to make sure the spacing between hangers is right—two fingers worth, no more and no less.

Always at the forefront of her mind, *Marie* is aware of how well known the Clarks are in their small urban town. Everett Clark, the most successful general insurance agent around, is actively involved in many community and church activities. Having served as First Church's head deacon for several years, he is well respected and trusted by many. His wife, Victoria, is known for her charitable works, dinner parties and a green thumb, which she uses to grow her exquisite rose garden. Her garden, beautiful and tranquil, serves as a place of safe solitude and sanctuary for both Victoria and Amanda. Victoria spends hours pruning and nurturing the prize winning roses while Amanda silently watches from her bedroom window. Although perfect to the outside world, the Clarks' life is nothing like it seems.

Her parents began with very little but Amanda is given much. She knows that both of her parents hope their daughter will eventually extend their social standing within the community. They carefully monitor her posture and her use of proper etiquette. To maintain the highest level of behavior, her actions are critiqued constantly, even when it is just the three of them. Fully aware of her parents' expectations, she never feels like she is quite good enough to please them and always strives to move closer to perfection—closer to being the child with whom both parents can be pleased.

Having finished her chores, *Marie* quietly goes downstairs to sit on the couch and wait for the arrival of the school bus. The plan is to stay out of sight until the appropriate time to avoid causing any further irritation to her mother. She completes her careful dissent just as her mother turns the corner with her lunch bag. Hoping to find a pleasant reaction to the selected outfit and the completed tasks, *Marie* is disappointed to hear her mother continue the berating she had begun earlier.

"Victoria," came her father's calm voice as he moves toward the pair from the living room. "Let the girl breathe for a minute. I honestly don't know why you are so hard on her all of the time. A girl of her age needs to have a few minutes a day that she can relax. Just look at her! Why she looks just like a beautiful princess this morning. And that sweater...it makes her look so grown up."

"Well," Victoria shot back at him, "Why can't she act grown up?"

Ignoring this irreverent outburst from his wife, Everett lightly kisses the back of his daughter's small hand and bows. "May I have the honor of taking my princess to school today? One as lovely as you should not have to wait for a stinky old school bus. Please, my lady, your chariot waits."

"Just make sure the chariot arrives on time today," Victoria shouted after them.

Escorting Amanda with all the proper pomp and circumstance due a child of royalty, Everett pretends that he doesn't hear his wife's last comment. The first order of business is to take care of his precious Amanda. This morning, she gets treated to breakfast of cream-filled donuts and chocolate milk.

With a full stomach, the first part of Amanda's day at school is going well. She got an "A" on her penmanship assignment and had the neatest item for show-and-tell. After all, what can beat a seashell that makes the sound of the ocean?

Just before lunch, Amanda's teacher approaches her with a message that she is to go to the principal's office. After gathering her things she walks down the long hallway to the front of the school. Her stomach starts to feel funny as she ponders what she's done wrong.

Finding her mother standing in the school office, the feelings get worse. She silently wonders if her mother is there to tattle on her for something or if the principal was mad and called her. She certainly doesn't look happy. Her expression—what Amanda can see of it behind the dark sunglasses—is unusual, almost like anger, but not exactly. There seems to be some sadness or fear mixed in as well. Amanda can't be sure how to interpret this expression. One thing she does know, whatever it means, it can't be good.

The principal, Mr. Sanders, is standing with her mother. He looks worried. "Amanda, your mother has come to take you home. She has some very sad news for you", he says softly.

Looking to her mother, Amanda fears what she might say. Unsure of how she is supposed to respond, she looks back to her principal for another hint. Before he can continue, before any reassurance or direction can be given, her mother thanks him and excuses herself. A firm grip on Amanda's arm, she quickly moves toward the exit, practically dragging Amanda along.

Amanda waits for some sign, some gesture from her mother that will give her a clue about what she should say. In spite of her careful observation, she is unable to detect a single indication of the behavior that is expected of her. There is nothing but silence, and a sense of irritation.

Once in the car, her mother finally speaks. Her voice fluctuates between loud and soft. "Amanda, Grandma Clark has died. We have to go to South Beach for the funeral—as if I need any more complications in my life." Aware again of her daughter, she adds, "Anyway, your father is very upset and I don't want you to make things worse. When we get home you are to put some clothes on your bed for me to pack in the suitcase. They better match and you better do it quietly! I don't need you getting your father angry. Do you understand?"

The news hit Amanda like a shock wave. Surely she could not mean that Grandma Clark is dead! But that is what she said. But it can't be! Not the one person in the whole world that she can trust. How could she be dead? As she stares out the window, Amanda can feel the tears beginning to rush to her eyes and a sob escapes her throat.

"Now you stop that Amanda! You have no reason to cry! Think about your father and how he feels right now. I'm not happy about this trip, but I know that your father needs us to be strong. I'm sure I'm asking too much from such a selfish child, but you have got to do exactly as I say. I will not tolerate your tears! You just better stop feeling sorry for yourself for once and think about others around you."

Victoria feels bad having snapped at her daughter, but she just does not know the danger of not heeding her mother's every word. If everyday life with Everett was a time bomb, this new event meant a possible nuclear meltdown.

"Yes Momma", is all Amanda can say. It is time to put on the smiling face and be a happy, obedient child. There is no room for sorrow or grief. These feelings will not be allowed.

Amanda wishes that she knew what to do, how to act and feel. An older person would know. Someone caring and wise. Someone just like Grandma Clark that is strong and able to take away the confusion and sadness that Amanda feels. Effortlessly, Amanda begins to imagine just such a friend. Lost in her imagination, Amanda's new, older friend and grandmother figure gently puts her arms around her. The closer her new friend gets, the more real she feels.

Softly she hears her friend say that she understands and can help her with all the sadness she feels. Amanda imagines a big basket, like the one she uses to collect seashells with her grandmother. In this basket she is able to place all of the yucky stuff that she is feeling, along with the wishes of spending time with her grandmother again. Her new friend carefully takes the basket and pulls it into herself. As *she* does, *she* begins to feel the depth of pain from the loss of a wonderful grandmother that showed her such friendship and protection.

Gerald shakes his head sadly and names the new friend *Agnes* as a tribute to the lost grandmother. Once the transfer of emotions is completed, *Gerald* escorts *Agnes* from Amanda's side, leading her to *Mitch* for direction. *Mitch* tells *Agnes* that she will now be the grandmother to them all. She can provide direction and guidance as she is able, but the one thing she must keep a tight hold of is the feelings of pain she is now experiencing. He will teach her to hold her feelings inside and to carry the burden of heartache for them all.

Pulling into the driveway, Amanda's mother gives her some final instructions. She is to lay out enough clothes for a week, but she is not to pull out everything in her closet. *Marie* nods and says, "Yes Momma", as she exits the car.

Gerald tells *Carol* to stand close by. *Gerald*'s job is to make sure the right person is at the right place at the right time. He is concerned that the father might need some "special attention"—he usually does when he is upset.

While *Marie* neatly stacks folded clothes on the bed to be packed, *Carol* is hoping that *Gerald* is wrong. Though they all feel some sadness, there was no time to show their emotions. The parents have to be appeased. Everyone has to do their part and play their role and *Gerald* sees to it that their roles are played to perfection. He suggests that everyone take a few minutes to visit *Agnes*, and if they happen to leave their grief behind, all the better for the whole.

The trip to South Beach goes by quickly for Amanda. It seems as if she had just settled in good when her father pulls up at her Grandmother's house. It must have been a long journey though because it looks as if the sun is rising. She doesn't even remember the sun setting. She must have slept through most of the drive, she reasons.

The sight of her grandmother's house brings feelings of happiness. "This is a good place," Amanda remembers. Her grandmother is...was a good person. This will be a good visit, even if her grandmother isn't here.

Amanda's aunt, Libby, was the first to emerge from the house, greeting the family with hugs and room assignment instructions. Amanda's parents are to sleep in the guest room, and Amanda will be sleeping in the third room. Libby and her husband are already settled in the master bedroom. Everett notes that his sister-in-law makes sure that her needs are met first, as usual. The sleeping arrangements don't matter much to Amanda, she is just happy to be at the beach, at her grandmother's safe house.

Without saying much, Everett takes the luggage into the house. Victoria and Aunt Libby walk together to the large porch that overlooks the beach. There they will sit and visit over coffee for several hours.

An unexpected feeling of dread suddenly overtakes Amanda as her father gives her a little wink and says, "Baby girl, you go wait for me in the room. I'll bring your clothes from the suitcase in just a minute." *Carol* immediately does as instructed. She alone will know what happens next and grandmother's house will remain safe for the others. Willingly she submits as another one of her dreams is shattered, another place of safety is desecrated.

****

These memories are as fresh for *Carol* as if they had just happened. She has been carrying them for years: never allowed to just be a kid; always expected to act as an adult wife; always keeping the secrets. When will Amanda be ready to hear the truth about her past? When will *Carol* be able to share some of this pain with the others and at long last, find some happiness for herself? These questions have filled *Carol's* thoughts for over twenty years with no hope for an answer in sight.

Chapter Two

Just before the clock strikes 4:00 a.m., Amanda suddenly awakes sitting straight up in her bed. Sweating, finding it hard to breathe, and shaking in fear, she tries desperately to escape her nightmare, searching for some thread of the present, some link to reality.

Through her bedroom window, the street lights provide just enough illumination to cast shadows of strange and frightening figures on the walls. Amanda hesitates to turn on the lamp, wanting to be sure she is alone first. As quietly as her panicked and rapid breathing will allow her, she slowly scans the rest of the room. Her ears feel as if they will burst from the strain of listening so intently for any unusual sound—hearing only her own heart beat as it pounds out a quick and steady rhythm.

In spite of the fact that everything appears to be in order, Amanda still doesn't feel right. She reaches out and flips on the light. Gradually she begins to acclimate to her surroundings, finally recognizing her new apartment.

Whispers of, "God help me," was sufficient to express her fear and confusion in genuine prayer. With the passing of the latest adrenaline rush, her breathing begins to slow down, and her legs stop shaking enough to walk.

Pulling herself together, Amanda cautiously makes her way to the bathroom to splash some water on her face. As she glances up in the mirror, reflections of a younger girl mix with the adult signs of sleepless nights and the pressures of being on her own. How much longer can she continue? During the day, she feels nothing. Empty and numb, she goes through the motions of living. At night, while she tries to sleep, endless emotions flood through her restless mind. She attributes these bouts to the stress of independent living and an exhausting waitress job that barely pays the bills.

Her parents definitely don't approve of her "career" choice. But even with the disapproval of her parents, she must find a balance—she has to make this work. These long nights don't make it any easier. She's torn between the security of living at home and the freedom of being alone. Compelled by a deep, inward motivation, she continues to strive toward some proof that she is worth something.

As if planted in her mind expressly to cause her failure, Amanda finds herself battling the same horrid dream, night after night. Although it is powerful enough to drain her emotions and energy, she is never able to remember any details of the dream. Instead, she is left with flashes of nonsensical images of her parent's basement, and feelings of terror and shame.

Drying her face and returning to bed, Amanda debates her options of staying awake or trying to get a few more hours of sleep. There certainly are some things she can do around the apartment. The kitchen needs to be cleaned, and some laundry waits for her in the bathroom. As these thoughts fill her mind, she drifts into a dreamless sleep.

Awaking a few hours later, Amanda begins her day with only a vague recollection of the night before. Today Amanda has an interview with an accounting firm downtown. It's time for the struggles of college to pay off.

Four years of work and thousands of her parent's dollars spent obtaining a business degree, made her mom seethe and her dad proud. In her mom's day, women were expected to marry after high school. But, oh no! Not little Miss Princess-Amanda-Know-It-All! She had to always make her mother look like an uneducated, unreasonable, ancient fool. Victoria would be overtaken by headaches with just the thought of it. Everett however, was busting his buttons with pride at what his sweet Baby Girl had accomplished. Now she could take care of herself and would not need a husband to take care of her. The thought of a strange man with his darling Baby Girl filled his mind with dark thoughts.

As for Amanda, the degree was neither a victory nor defeat. With her parents she never knew what to do. The saying goes, "You can please some of the people some of the time, but you can't please all of the people all of the time." In Amanda's house you could please none of the people none of the time. But if all goes well at 10:00 a.m., she can please herself by hanging up her waitress uniform and kissing those long hours and low pay good-bye.

First things first: Amanda walks into the kitchen to start coffee and is astonished to see it so spotless. "Ha!" Amanda chuckles, "the kitchen fairies Mom sarcastically referred to do exist!" She decides that she must have taken care of that before going to bed and dismisses it.

After her coffee and toast, Amanda brushes her teeth, checks her hair and make-up and looks over her blue suit one more time. "Thanks Mom for sending the laundry elves too," Amanda giggles as she grabs her keys. This could be the break she has been waiting for at long last.

Standing at the large mahogany reception desk waiting to be announced for her interview, Amanda realizes that time has passed. Interviews aren't easy for most people. For Amanda, interviews seem to be incredibly difficult. She has succeeded in arriving for her appointment on time. If she can just hold it together, she might actually make it through the interview without throwing up. Feeling ridiculous for her fears, Amanda quietly fortifies herself with the thoughts of larger paychecks and less dependence on Mom and Dad. If given a chance, she is sure that she will prove to everyone, herself included, that she can do the job and do it well.

Noticing the receptionist's glances, Amanda wonders if her expressions are portraying her secret internal struggles to the world. Forcefully smiling back at the receptionist she is suddenly aware that she has been unconsciously swinging her briefcase in front of her. In an attempt to cover her 'less than professional' actions, she follows through on a swing, turning herself toward a set of chairs. Just as she takes a seat, the voice of her mother begins to resonate through her ears, "You are worthless and will never amount to anything! You sloppy, messy child!" The sound is so clear and loud that Amanda feels compelled to look around to be sure her mother isn't sitting there with her.

"What makes her think she can ever do this? Her mother is right, she is worthless," Amanda begins to concede. Looking around, the professionalism displayed through the spotless decor in the office adds to the intimidation she feels. She begins to sink deeper and deeper into the chair as her mind starts swimming. Messages of doom from her mother mix with visions of the polished brass accents on the rich mahogany reception desk to form a spinning kaleidoscope of inadequacy and fear.

Gerald immediately calls for *Sabrina*. Amanda isn't up to the challenge, she is going to blow it. *Sabrina*, quickly makes her way forward. *Gerald* instructs her on the interviewer's name, the job description and the salary requirements. *Sabrina* is great at handling social interactions. She is never uncomfortable meeting new people and is a master at getting them to talk about themselves instead of her. She's perfect for this job.

"Mr. Morris will see you now," the receptionist announces just as *Sabrina* is gaining her bearings. Poised and confident, *Sabrina* practically floats toward the office door marked "Tom Morris, CEO". *Sabrina* politely introduces herself to her potential boss, offers an appropriate handshake, and gracefully settles into the chair opposite his desk. While Mr. Morris quietly scans Amanda's resume, *Sabrina* discretely scans him, being careful not to be obvious with her interest. Of all of the people she's met with, he most certainly is the most handsome. Even if they don't get the job, this has the potential to be a fun interview for *Sabrina* anyway.

After quiet consideration, he begins, "Well, I only have one question for you…When can you start?"

"Excuse me?" *Sabrina* asks, not sure she heard correctly. She didn't even have a chance to lay on the charm!

Gerald, hearing this quick transition makes things ready to bring Amanda back. She needs to know that she has a job!

"Everything I need to know about your technical skills is right here on your resume."

As Mr. Morris continues his explanation, *Sabrina* makes a quick retreat, being careful to make the switch with Amanda as smooth as possible.

"You will be on a 30-day probationary period," Mr. Morris continues. "If all goes well, you'll be hired with full benefits at the end of the probationary period. So…when can you start?"

Elated, Amanda quickly searches her mind for an answer. "Will Monday be okay?" she asks timidly.

"Great, I'll see you Monday morning at 8:00. Welcome aboard," Mr. Morris adds as he offers a strong handshake to symbolize their agreement. Responding in kind, Amanda smiles at her new employer. Unsure of how she managed to snag the job, she is grateful for the opportunity.

Filled with a new sense of pride and belonging, Amanda turns to leave. Even though she is anxious to share the good news with her parents, she determines to wait a few weeks before telling them. This will give her the chance to make sure it is going to work, just in case something goes wrong.

Turning her attention to her last week of working at the restaurant, and unsure of the condition of her waitress outfit, Amanda goes straight home. Mentally she begins to craft her resignation speech. It isn't like she has to put it in writing. Waitresses have come and gone so often that she's seen how it's done there. But she doesn't want to be mean or hateful like some of the others she's watched. She wants to be fair to Warren, her manager, just as he has been fair to her.

Her mental preoccupation allows *Marie* to emerge and finish her cleaning chores. The others inside don't seem to appreciate the need for cleanliness and order. *Marie* on the other hand is driven by her need for order, even perfection. It's not really that *Marie* likes it so much as that she has learned how pleasing it can be to their mother and society in general. "Nobody likes a messy house," her mother always said.

Victoria was never so pleased as when Amanda, her room already spotless, helped her remove the specks of dust around the house. It was one of those rare times when mother and daughter shared an activity with full devotion and passion. It's an activity that usually brought peace and harmony to the house. It's a good thing and *Marie* intends to keep it up even though they no longer live at home.

Her tasks complete and the time for Amanda to leave for work drawing close, *Marie* signals that she is ready to go back in. *Brooke*—full of anger and disgust for the way *Marie* works so hard to please their mother—jumps at the chance to express her feelings once more.

Taking only a few minutes to make her mark, *Brooke* moves from room to room making a mess as she goes. Starting in the bedroom, she begins pulling on the covers like a cat who is fluffing up a pillow to find a comfortable place to sleep. Satisfied with the mound of sheets and blanket in the center of the bed, she moves on to the closet. Pulling dresses and shirts off the hangers and rearranging pairs of shoes, she moves from left to right, disturbing the carefully arranged items until it looks as if they were just thrown into the closet without care.

Before she has a chance to do much more damage, which could interrupt their ability to make it to work on time, *Gerald* manages to pull her back inside. But he doesn't let *Marie* back out either. *Mitch* can deal with the two of them internally. But for now, someone has to get them to work.

Thinking quickly, he calls for *Dana*. She will have no problem telling Warren that she quits but will still be nice with how she says it. The switch complete, *Dana* dons the waitress outfit and heads out the door.

****

Deciding to move out on her own after college was the first time she had directly gone against her parents' wishes. On the outside, her parents seem mildly supportive. Through their actions, Amanda is constantly aware of their disapproval. Trying not to be paranoid, she sometimes wonders if her parents would be happiest to see her fail or succeed. Tonight is her first opportunity to show them both that she has the real potential to make it on her own, without their help or influence. Breaking away isn't easy.

Sitting at the dinner table, Amanda nervously fidgets with the new dress she bought with her first real paycheck. Her mother sets out the salads and rolls for the first course while her father begins the polite inquisition. "So, a new job! Are you sure this company is going to be around for a while? You should be looking for a long-term career you know. Are you making enough money? I mean—is it going to be enough to support you without the second job?"

"Yes Daddy, it will be enough. I'm making some good money now and the company seems to be doing very well," Amanda replies, trying to hold onto the fleeting feelings of confidence.

"I'm sure that's true Honey. You've always been so good at what you do. It's just that I want to make sure they aren't taking advantage of you. Will you have medical benefits and dental?"

"Yes Daddy, the medical benefits are included with the salary. It's really a good job."

"I knew you could do it Amanda. Let's just hope you can hold onto this job," came the words of encouragement and despair from Amanda's mother.

"Yes Momma."

"Well, let's eat. Baby Girl finally has her a respectable job. It's time to celebrate!" Amanda's dad never failed to make Amanda feel like a little child again. For some reason, she just hates it when he calls her 'Baby Girl'.

As the after-dinner-coffee is being served, Amanda's father asks her to step outside with him while he smokes his cigar. Her mother naturally takes her place in the kitchen to clean the dishes as Amanda and her father walk to the swing in the rose garden. Her parent's house can feel so suffocating at times, making the walk outside all the more inviting to Amanda. Her sweater wrapped around her shoulder makes the cool night air the perfect temperature. As they both sit down on the swing, Amanda looks up at the bright stars and dreams of floating gently to some peaceful place far away from the family-imposed pressures.

Everett takes several big puffs off his cigar, making sure it is well lit. "Amanda," he begins between inhalations, "you know that your mother and I worry about you. But, I'm sure you will do well at this new job of yours." Convinced that his cigar is fully lit, Everett puts away his lighter then adds with a grin, "It looks like you've already been able to get you a new dress. It sure is a pretty dress too."

"Thank you Daddy. I'm sure I'll do fine. It really is a great job and there are opportunities for me to advance in the company. Mr. Morris seems to be very encouraged by the work I've done so far," Amanda says without really looking at her father.

The two continue to swing together, looking out into the night. Putting his arm around Amanda, Everett adds to his previous observation. "You know, you sure are looking all grown up in that dress. I sure have been missing my Baby Girl since you moved out. You really should visit with us more often."

A feeling from deep inside Amanda begins urging her to get out, run, move, leave…as in NOW! Confused by the feelings of panic, Amanda at first tries to ignore it. The urgings grow stronger and more desperate. "Daddy," Amanda begins, standing up so abruptly that she almost swings her father onto the ground, "I need to get home so I can get some sleep before work tomorrow. It was great having dinner with you and Momma tonight."

"What's gotten into you Amanda? You can spare a few more minutes here with your Dad." He reaches up and takes her hand, giving her a quick wink and saying, "Come on Baby Girl, sit down beside me."

The feelings of panic and urgency are overtaken by dizziness and nausea. The ground begins to spin as her father seems to move farther and farther away until she can no longer see him. Amanda, feeling as if she has fainted, has fallen back into her sub-consciousness, into the dark, hidden places of safety and secrecy within her mind.

"I really must be going now. I'll say goodbye to Mother on my way out. Good night Father." *Dana* was not going to have any of his non-sense tonight! This was a time for celebration, but not the type of celebration he wanted. Shaking his hand firmly, then quickly releasing it, *Dana* turns to go inside the house.

"Mother, thank you very much for an interesting evening. The dinner was very good but I must be going home now. I'll give you a call later. Good night."

The cordial exit complete and the keys in her hand, she was out the door before her father even made it back in the house. "Good night Honey," her mother calls after her.

When Amanda finally comes to herself, she is sitting at a table with Mr. Morris. A menu in her hand, Amanda looks around self-consciously trying to ascertain the time of day. The bright sun shining through the restaurant windows and the hurried looks on the other patrons' faces indicate lunch time. She quickly reviews the menu and decides on a chicken salad sandwich.

Tom Morris is halfway through his sentence when Amanda realizes that he is talking to her. "...and he is very impressed with how quickly you are picking things up around the office. I have to agree with him. You are doing quite well. I just wanted the opportunity to touch base with you and see if you have any questions about your benefits now that you are a permanent employee."

He had such a quiet and gentle expression on his face. But there was something else in his eyes that Amanda could see, but didn't recognize. It's a look with which she wasn't familiar. He seemed to be staring right through her, looking deep into her soul.

"Well yes Mr. Morris. Thank you very much. I do have a question."

"You can call me Tom if you like and I will try to answer your question as thoroughly as I can."

"Okay, thank you. I appreciate you giving me a chance with this job. I was wondering why you hired me after such a short interview. To some that's a little unorthodox."

"Well Amanda, my approach could seem that way to some. I don't know where you stand on the subject of faith, but since you asked, I'll be honest with you. I pray over every resume that comes across my desk. After praying over your resume the Holy Spirit confirmed that I was supposed to make you part of the company.

"Does that sound strange to you?," Tom asks.

"No, that's a refreshing approach to business and I'm thrilled to work for someone who takes his faith so seriously," Amanda assures.

"Great. Is there any other question you have for me?" Tom asks.

"No, that was the main question."

Amanda's response serves to assure that Tom once again has heard correctly from the Lord. Pleased with the honest discussion that has started their lunch, he asks, "So what would you like for lunch? I hear their chili is good."

He had a way of making her feel comfortable and at ease. Without realizing it, Amanda sighs from the release of tension she initially felt. A smile dares to creep onto her face as she answers, "A chicken salad sandwich sounds good to me."

What is it about Tom that makes her feel so good? Can it be as simple as the fact that he recognized her accomplishments? Is it something deeper? Sneaking another look at his face, she notices how softly his hair sweeps across his forehead. It isn't a messy look, but a relaxed style. It serves his personality well.

As they sit, talking about work, Amanda tries to remember the last time she felt this good. Tom is quickly becoming a good friend. She ponders how easy it would be to spend time with him. Careful not to overstep the professional boundaries, Amanda does her best to hide her feelings of admiration that are quickly growing inside.

Suddenly realizing the restaurant is almost empty, Tom announces that it's definitely time to go back to work. "Don't worry about the extended lunch period, I'll clear it with your boss," Tom says with a chuckle. Amanda smiles back, grateful for the experience and hoping it wouldn't be the last time she will be able to talk with him.

"You know, I really enjoyed our lunch. If you are not doing anything this Saturday, how would you like to come to a cookout at my sister's house? Your boyfriend is welcome to join us as well, of course," Tom adds, hoping that no such boyfriend exists.

Complete shock is all Amanda can feel. Can this really be happening? Tom is interested in spending time with her as well? "That sounds lovely Tom. I would like that very much, thank you. But…I don't currently have a boyfriend so it will just be me."

"Good, it's settled then. Hey, does a movie sound better? I've been trying to come up with an excuse to miss Rick's attempt at barbeque," Tom says with a smile.

"That sounds wonderful," Amanda responds.

"Perfect. I'll pick you up at 11:00 Saturday so we can get some lunch and then see a matinee. Now I think we had better get back to the office otherwise we are likely to talk until closing."

Chapter Three

It's hard for Amanda to believe that she has been dating Tom for four months. Enjoying a quiet lunch at the quaint little café where they have now shared several meals, she finds herself just watching him. He is such a gentlemen; always opening the door for her and pulling out her chair. He makes her feel so special.

Towards the end of their lunch, a small sparrow hops over to their table, hoping for a crumb from the sandwiches. Grinning, Tom throws some crumbs to the bird. "I can't help but to think of a Bible verse every time I see a sparrow. Are you familiar with the scripture that talks about God knowing when even a sparrow falls to the ground?" Tom asks.

Amanda nods in confirmation, "It is one of my favorite verses. I find a lot of comfort in knowing that God watches the birds and knows what happens to them. He must certainly think that humans are more important than birds; at least this way I know that someone cares when I fall down." Not wanting to sound pitiful, she adds, "That must be very comforting to a lot of people."

Tom sends Amanda a smile of validation and assurance. "It certainly must be. Are you ready to go see a movie?"

Amanda nods and gracefully stands to be by Tom's side. Leaving the cafe, hand-in-hand, they stroll a few yards down the river, to the shopping mall. The cinema, located at the west end of the mall, is offering several matinees. Once they agreed on which movie to watch, Tom purchases the tickets. "Would you like some popcorn and soda?" Tom asks as they enter the theater.

Amanda still relishes the moments of someone so kind attending to her every need as if she were a queen. "That would be wonderful," she replies. Then, as if an afterthought, she adds with a playful shrug, "Can I have some candy too?"

"Well of course you can," Tom said. What a breath of fresh air Amanda has been to Tom's life. His routine, monotonous days are now filled with excitement and expectation.

Arms full of treats, Tom and Amanda begin to look for appropriate seats; nothing too close to the screen, but not too far in the back. Fortunately, the theater isn't too crowded and there are plenty of seats available right in the middle. They choose their seats and get settled in just as the movie starts.

Throughout the movie, Tom and Amanda sit quietly, sharing popcorn and laughs. Amanda, pretending not to notice how Tom is staring at her, looks straight ahead, trying to keep up with the movie. Secretly, she absorbs each and every turn of his eyes. Every smile he makes when looking her way increases her confidence and hope that their relationship will be one that will last for a long time.

At the end of the movie, they begin a walk through the shopping mall that will last for hours. Laughing at the changing fashions, they tease each other with how a particular style might look on them. Go-go boots on Amanda and ripped up jeans for Tom.

The lunch and movie they had planned is quickly turning into dinner, as usual. Amanda considers how they should just agree to turn their lunches into a lunch-afternoon-dinner outing.

They talk non-stop the whole way there. The moments at dinner are filled with laughter, conversation and quiet reflection. Amanda and Tom both feel good to be with someone who doesn't require constant dialogue. The silence is comfortable, even welcomed at times.

The date finally comes to an end as Tom drives Amanda home around 10:00. She offers him a cup of coffee before he heads home. He politely declines and thanks her for a marvelous day. "It's me that should thank you," Amanda replied. "I really enjoyed myself, more than I can say."

"I'm very glad to hear it Amanda. I'll see you tomorrow at church," Tom says as he reaches over and gently kisses her check. "Have a good night." As he turns to leave, Tom stops and spins back in Amanda's direction. "Oh, and by the way. When God told me to hire you, he told me something else."

"Oh?" Amanda inquires, her curiosity peaked.

"Yeah, He told me that you are going to be more than just an employee." Tom teases with just a bit of information.

"So, what did He say?"

"He told me that you will one day be my wife," Tom announces. "Just something to think about." With that, Tom sprints off jumping and clicking his heels together as if he were playing the lead role in "Singing in the Rain".

Chuckling at his display of joy, while sorting through the news, Amanda feels as if she is floating on air as she turns toward her apartment. Tom's announcement couldn't have made her feel better if he had said that she had won a million dollar prize.

Opening the door to her apartment, she notices a faint scent of 'Old Spice' cologne in the air. The smell nauseates her. Looking up, she sees her father sitting in the recliner, waiting for her. Then…the feared greeting: "Hello Baby Girl. Where have you been? I've been waiting for you for almost two hours now. Come on over here and give your daddy a kiss. I want to hear about your day. Tell me what you have been up to."

The smile on Amanda's face quickly vanishes, as does Amanda. "Where's Mother?" *Dana* asks.

"She's at home. She sent me with some left-over cake. It is our anniversary you know. I've been married to your mother for 28 years now. Can you believe that?"

"Thank you for bringing the cake Father. I hate to be rude, but I've had a very long day and I'm tired. You need to get home now. Please convey my appreciation for the cake to Mother."

"Can't we talk for a few minutes? I've been waiting a very long time for you to come home. Is there something wrong with you Baby Girl? Come on over here and talk to me."

Dana steps aside to be sure he sees the open door and replies, "No Father, not tonight. It is time for you to leave. I insist."

"Amanda, what is wrong with you? Can't you see that I'm needing some attention? It's my wedding anniversary. I want to celebrate."

"Then go celebrate with your wife. I am tired and you need to go. I'm quite certain you don't want Mother to know your real intention here. You and I both know what you are expecting and it isn't going to happen. Now I really must insist that you leave."

"Amanda, I don't know what you are talking about. I simply came over to bring you a piece of cake and make sure you were okay. I can see that you are tired. I'll head on home and check back with you later. Maybe you and I should schedule some time for dinner together, just the two of us. It's been a long time since I took my baby girl out on a date."

Her father slowly stands up and walks toward the door. As he gets closer, *Dana* moves out of his path so there would be no risk of an "accidental" brush up against her. Closing the door behind him, she scribbles a note on the message pad by the phone. *Change the locks and don't give Father a key.*

That night, Amanda's dreams are mixed with feelings of joy and fear. Flashes of Tom and her father combine to create a twisted, confusing picture of love, desire and fear. Perhaps these are feelings best worked out during the day when she can clearly think through what is happening. Unfortunately, dreams don't always give you the choice. One thing that stands out clearly is that Tom doesn't belong in the basement where fear and hatred live. He fits much better in the bright sunshine, glowing with compassion, walking beside Amanda on the shores of South Beach.

****

As the days go by, Tom and Amanda's relationship grows stronger. Even if Tom had considered writing a company policy prohibiting dating amongst the associates, he certainly wasn't going to now. Amanda has a unique ability to keep her personal and professional life separate. This just added to the long list of characteristics Tom finds so appealing about her.

The few times they had disagreements, it always ended with both Tom and Amanda feeling like winners. The beautiful thing is that Amanda never brought past issues up to Tom. It is as if she doesn't even remember the argument.

Not only is their friendship growing, but they are developing a relationship on a spiritual level. They attend Tom's church on a regular basis. They are present for the worship services, and participate in the weekly prayer meeting. This is a special time for Tom and Amanda, deepening their bond with each other as they grow stronger in their love for God.

Expanding her contacts to include the couples at church and her co-workers, Amanda finds the communication with her parents decreasing steadily. A quick call to let her parents know she is doing well is the extent of their dialogue. She has mentioned Tom a few times, but wanting to avoid the game of 20 questions, she always keeps those conversations short.

Freedom and independence is a glorious feeling. Amanda's nightmares seem to have stopped. She no longer feels as if she is mindlessly walking through life. God truly blessed her and Tom both when He brought them together.

Chapter Four

"Hello Mr. Clark, it's very nice to finally meet you. Mrs. Clark, these are for you," Tom said as he hands a bouquet of flowers to Amanda's mother.

"Thank you. How thoughtful of you. You can call us Everett and Victoria," her mother responds, instantly receiving a look of disapproval from her husband. Quickly changing the focus of conversation, she continues, "Please come in and make yourself at home. I'll get some water for these flowers."

Tom and Amanda walk into the house together, exchanging a smile of comfort with each other. Her mother leads the way to the living room and offers them a seat.

Amanda's father follows along quietly, staring holes in the back of Tom's head. Usually the silence with Tom was so comforting, but this feeling is making Amanda uneasy. She delicately guides Tom over to the sofa, making sure he doesn't sit in her father's favorite chair.

"I've heard so many good things about you both. It's very nice to finally meet you," Tom says, realizing instantly that he is repeating himself. Amanda's father sits down cautiously in his chair, giving Tom no sign of relief from the tension in the air. Her mother returns without the flowers and takes a seat opposite her husband.

All eyes seem to be glued on Tom, as if waiting for some move, that glaring—yet unnamed—mistake that will inevitability come from any man Amanda would have chosen. Desperately needing to be rescued from the silence, Amanda asks her mother about the new flower arrangement on the coffee table. Her mother takes Amanda's cue and begins to explain how she purchased the arrangement at a church bizarre the week before. Poor, old Mrs. Bikel has nothing to do with her time since the death of her husband, except making flower arrangements. Now she is doing this for extra money because, of course, Mr. Bikel didn't leave her with much to live on. Trying to fit into the conversation, Tom remarks on how hard that must be for Mrs. Bikel.

"Well, what more could she expect marrying into such a family? Mr. Bikel never really did do right by her," Amanda's mother retorts quickly. The response wouldn't have been as uncomfortable if it had not been accompanied by a condescending sneer from Everett.

The room returns to a state of utter stillness as it begins to take on that hazing look which has become all too familiar to Amanda. Breaking through the cold silence, *Sabrina* proclaims with a mirthful lilt to her voice, "Well they all can't be like Dad; can they? Dad, why don't you give Tom a tour of your trophy room while Mom and I get us some coffee." Jumping out of her seat to overcome any hesitancy from the others, she turns and walks straight into the kitchen. Tom will be on his own for a few minutes, but Dad will get a chance to brag. There's nothing Dad likes better than to show off his trophies.

Amanda's father begins the tour of the house. He takes Tom to the trophy room where several animals were stuffed and mounted, showing to the world just how brave he is. He begins telling Tom of how he tracked the big buck, now hanging over the fireplace, through hills and valleys for more than two days before he finally was able to snag him. The story continues while he walks through the rest of the house, showing Tom all the wonderful things he has provided for his family.

As they approach the door to the basement, he explains to Tom, "I've saved the best for last. It's not much to look at, but it's my favorite room in the house. I've spent many hours down here. Of course, I haven't been down here in quite some time, but you know, a man needs to have a place that isn't disturbed by the glitter of fanciful female decor." Chuckling at his own comment, he leads Tom down to the special room.

Looking around, Tom can't understand why anyone would want to spend time here, not even a man wanting to have his own space. The room feels damp and empty. Lack of sufficient lighting makes the details of the furnishings hard to discern. A couch and a few bean bag chairs, an old television set, a wet bar, and what looked to be a small half-bath. Certainly not what Tom considered to be a special room.

At the sight of the basement door being open, *Sabrina* feels a rush of adrenaline accompanied by a need to act quickly. She immediately calls for them to join her and Mother in the garden. Enough brag time for Dad! It's

Mom's turn now. She can show off her prize winning roses and Tom can escape from that horrible place.

Before long, the four of them are talking up a storm. Returning to the house, it is now time to brag on Tom. *Sabrina* begins with how Tom built his company from the ground up and now employees over 50 people full-time. In fact, she was the 50th person hired. At that comment Tom looks over adoringly at Amanda, "Yes. The best hire I've ever made."

Amazing how a single comment and glance can put a chill on a room. It is time to get to business, the purpose of their visit. *Sabrina* nods knowingly at Tom.

"Mr. and Mrs. Clark, I've come to know your daughter very well. Over the last six months we have spent many hours together. As a result, my life has been changed dramatically. I couldn't think of spending another day without her. Amanda and I have talked about this in detail and we would like to get your blessing for us to get married."

The air quickly turns suffocating and heavy as Amanda's parents just look at each other. Her father's face begins to evolve into a bright shade of red, although he maintains his quiet, calm expression. Her mother quickly takes a seat as her knees turn to Jell-O. Tom's grip on *Sabrina's* hand begins to cut off her circulation as she stills herself for the fallout.

"Amanda honey, don't you think this is moving a little too fast?" comes the first question from her mother. "I don't even know what kind of family this boy comes from. Does he attend church? Have you really considered everything involved?"

Everett quickly interrupts, "Vicky, let's not be rude. You remember what it was like to be young and to think you are in love. It's such a confusing matter and Amanda does change her mind so often.

"Amanda, let's just slow things down some now. I know that this boy has been treating you nice and you think you're in love with him. You know as well as I do that this relationship isn't going to last."

Sabrina, feeling somewhat indignant and definitely in strange water, attempts to find an appropriate response. "Dad, I don't know that this relationship will not last. You don't know it either. After all, your relationship with Mom has lasted so I have a wonderful pair of role models to show me how it's to be done."

Victoria, bound to try and resolve this horror, struggles to know when to talk and when to remain silent. Currently, silence is the only option. Even if her husband would allow a response, her daughter's comment has caught her by surprise. Through all the years of pain and secret battles with Everett; the dreams of Amanda making something of herself and finding a wonderful, rich husband; and hours of worry and prayer she has spent over Amanda—she never thought of herself as a role model. "What kind of example has she been to Amanda?" she wonders. "Does she really want the same for Amanda that she now has?"

As lost for words as Victoria is, Everett is full of them. Moving to his next quiet firing of questions, he hopes to quickly move in for a kill. "Amanda, you can't be as serious about this young man as all of that. Do you realize that this is the first time you have brought him to meet us? If you were so serious about him, I'm sure you would have brought him by sooner."

Without taking a breath or allowing any time for interruption, he immediately turns to Tom and adds, "No offense Tom, it is nothing against you personally. You see, our daughter is well known for her off-the-wall and spur-of-the-moment ideas, which she always regrets later. As her father, it's my responsibility to protect Amanda from herself. If you do care about her, then you will appreciate that I have spared her and you from this life-changing mistake."

Sabrina is dumb-founded. Her role is to make people feel comfortable at gatherings, to get along with everyone and to smile. She is not prepared to handle this complex situation of delicate interactions. She could crack a joke to make everyone laugh, but that would probably just make everyone mad right now. Desperate for help, she calls on *Gerald* to do something, to help her or tell her what to say.

Gerald, through his role as a gate-keeper and watcher, has spent his life observing the games Everett plays in order to anticipate the next move. He has also been watching Tom's reactions and interactions with Amanda and others. Armed with this information, *Gerald* decides that it is time for him to take some control over the situation.

This is not his normal role, and the transition into the "presenter" position proves to be a little difficult for him. As usual, *Sabrina* steps back so he can move forward. Having never practiced this part of the switching routine, *Gerald* is a little slow in taking control of the body, leaving a momentary vacancy. The body unable to control itself, goes limp and falls back, creating the effect of a fainting spell.

As *Gerald* "comes to", he is greeted with the panicked reaction of Tom, Everett and Victoria all trying to fan Amanda back to life. Having never "worked" the body before, it takes him a few seconds to figure out how to make everything work, adding to the onlookers' concern.

"I'm okay…really," *Gerald* protests with embarrassment while trying to look as normal as possible under the circumstances. Hearing his own voice coming out of Amanda's mouth, he instantly remembers that he must not only act like Amanda, he must sound like her as well.

Things are not going as he expected. This will require some quick talking to get through without further incidences. "I'm so sorry, I think in all of the excitement of the day I forgot to eat lunch. Mom, do you think I can have a few crackers and some orange-juice?" *Gerald* quickly lies.

Everett, now sitting back in his chair, lights up a cigar and stares helplessly as Tom comforts his daughter. Touching her face and brushing her hair out of her eyes, Tom whispers questions of concerns that only *Gerald* can hear. Attempting to maintain the appearance of being Amanda, *Gerald* forces himself to look softly into Tom's eyes while reassuring him that everything is okay.

Unable to watch this any longer, Everett again speaks up, causing the two of them to look in his direction. "Do you see Tom? Amanda is a handful and committing your life to her is more than anyone should be asked to do. What you have just seen is the onset of a change of heart. Mark my words; I've seen it happen before."

Gerald reaches over and pats the top of Tom's hand, Amanda's typical expression of quiet affection and assurance. She would usually follow such a move with a loving glance or by leaning on his shoulder. *Gerald*, having taken care of Tom's concerns momentarily, skips the intimate part so he can quickly move on to Everett's games. "Dad, this is not the beginning of a change of heart. It's just that I skipped lunch. I know you are concerned and I appreciate the protection that you have always given me. But Dad, I'm not a child any longer and…"

Before *Gerald* could finish the sentence, Victoria returns to the room and interrupts the conversation with some crackers, cheese and juice. Practically sitting on the coffee table between Amanda and Everett, Victoria moves into her motherly role of taking care of her daughter. This is definitely not the effect

Gerald had intended. Quietly, hoping to keep Everett from hearing, Victoria asks, "Amanda, are you pregnant?"

"What?" comes Everett's reaction. "Are you?" Not wanting to wait for the answer, he begins to bounce up and down in his chair, half leaving and then sitting back down again. His thoughts become obvious to everyone in the room as he considers what Tom had done to his daughter to even create the possibility of her being pregnant, followed by the options that lay before him of the many ways he can terminate Tom's life. As Victoria spins around, to avoid having her back to Everett during one of his fits, she explains pitifully, "I was just asking."

"No!" *Gerald* responds indignantly. "Of course I'm not pregnant. Dad, please calm down. You raised me better than that, didn't you?"

"Well I thought I did. But obviously I was wrong!"

"You weren't wrong Dad. I'm not pregnant, and it's not even a possibility." *Gerald* reassures.

Unwilling to let this go, Everett asks, "Why, are you taking the pill or something? You know those things aren't always reliable. Just when you think you are going to get away with something, that's when they will not work, you know."

That last dig was more than *Gerald* had anticipated, but he is able to recover quickly and respond with calmness and control. "Dad, it is not a possibility, period! I know better than to rely on such things to hide my secrets but secrets are something I don't have right now. Tom has been a perfect gentlemen and, as if this is an appropriate topic of discussion, Tom and I are waiting until we are married before we have sex." *Gerald* ignores Victoria's exaggerated exhalation of breath, showing that she is incensed with her daughter's participation in such an inappropriate discussion. Such talk is expected from men, but should never be heard coming from a lady's mouth.

Not wanting Everett to get the upper hand in the conversation again, *Gerald* immediately moves to his next approach, hoping this will work better than the last. "Dad, I do need to apologize to the three of you for not arranging an introduction earlier. I know this must have come as a surprise to the both of you and that is my fault. I have been so busy with things at work and church that I haven't been keeping you in the loop with the things happening in my life."

Seeing the calmness begin to return to the room, *Gerald* dares to take a quick breath before proceeding in a more relaxed tone of voice. "I will not presume to speak for Tom but I do appreciate your concern and recognize that this is a life-changing decision. It is something that we have not decided without long hours of discussion and prayer."

Tom nods his agreement but considers it best to remain silent. Amanda seems to have the room under control and he isn't going to interfere. *Gerald* continues, "I am sure that as you get to know Tom, you will see that he has been sent into my life from God. He and I are in love and have been in love for quite some time now. To try to make up for the lack of contact, I'd like for us to get together for dinner sometime next week. Maybe that way you and Mom can get to know him better. You'll see Dad, he really isn't bad." *Gerald* finishes with a smile.

"It isn't about him Amanda, it's about making sure that you aren't going to make a wreck of your life. I guess I just never thought of the day when another man would take my Baby Girl away from me." Everett pauses for a moment. If he is going to put an end to this madness, it will have to be through showing Amanda just how badly she is hurting him. Attempting to pronounce his painful resignation to the marriage, he adds, "It looks as if you two have made up your mind already. I suppose there is no talking you out of this."

Tom takes the opportunity to join the conversation on a positive note, "Mr. Clark, we do respect your opinion and would like to have your blessing."

As if a dagger had just been thrust into his heart, Everett stares back at Tom through narrowed eyes. With his teeth clinched tightly together, he practically hisses his disapproval that seems to extend to Tom's very presence. "My blessing? You might do what you want, but my blessing is something you will get over my dead body. If you really wanted my blessing, I would have been consulted before the decision was made."

As if challenged to show some fortitude, Tom straightens his posture, takes a deep breath and responds, "Your blessing is truly important, Mr. Clark. But you are right, we have decided that we are meant for each other and we want to spend the rest of our lives together. God has brought us together, but your approval is important to Amanda...to us both."

"So? Then go, get married. But I'll tell you one thing young man," Amanda's father says as his voice grows loud and his face turns darker, "If you ever hurt my daughter, I will have a new trophy to hang on my wall! Do we have an understanding?"

Attempting to maintain some form of courtesy, Tom consciously takes a breath before responding. "Yes sir, I believe we are beginning to understand each other very clearly. It was nice to meet you both. Amanda and I have reservations tonight and need to get on our way," Tom says as he takes *Gerald's* hand and stands to leave.

As if the surrounding circumstances weren't tense enough, *Gerald* is suddenly forced to walk, fairly quickly, while wearing high heels. He had known of the problem that others had faced, but never before had he been faced with the added stress of learning to make the body do as it is supposed to do. Using Tom's hand as a support, *Gerald* is able to pull off a fairly graceful learning curve within just a few steps. Having conquered the walking task, *Gerald* determines that switching with another is best left for a time when he is sitting down.

Feeling the control over her daughter's wedding will leave with them, Amanda's mother frantically begins an attempt to talk about dates, and getting together to arrange colors and bridesmaid selections. Tom barely slows his pace as *Gerald* politely promises to call her later when they would have time to discuss it in detail.

Tom gently puts his arm around *Gerald* as they walk to his car. "I love you very much," he whispers in her ear. "It's going to be okay. Everything will work out fine, you just wait and see."

Without thinking, *Gerald* responds with a laugh, "Yes Tom, it will be okay just as soon as I can sit down! Just don't take your arm away or I'm sure I'll fall, these shoes are likely to be the death of me yet." Out of immediate danger, *Gerald* begins to revel in the humor in the situation. Knowing that Tom can not fully appreciate the comedy of the moment, he tries to maintain himself long enough to sit down and allow for a planned switch. With a chuckle, *Gerald* makes a mental note to practice the art of switching while inwardly scolding himself for not previously preparing for such an event.

Back inside the house, Amanda's father turns his attention to his wife's inadequate handling of the situation. Someone has taken away his Baby Girl, and it must be Victoria's fault because it certainly wasn't his. She was always so jealous of his relationship with Amanda, she undoubtedly pushed Amanda into this decision. And this pregnancy business is something else that he must get to the bottom of. Surely Victoria knows better than to keep something like that from him. If she does know something, she is going to tell him and then pay for keeping the secret.

As his frustrations give way to rage, his wife begins to feel the full impact of the situation. Yelling quickly turns into slamming doors, broken crystal and smashing fists. The resulting bruises that Victoria will suffer can not compare to the emotional scars the beating leaves behind.

Chapter Five

Tom reassuringly touches Amanda to gently smooth away any lingering feelings of misgivings from the encounter with her parents. As empathetic and supportive as he is trying to be, he is not aware of the complexity involved in the struggle now going on inside Amanda's mind.

Gerald has successfully retreated to the more familiar inside world while bringing Amanda back into control. Although she has experienced time lapses frequently in her life, she is unsure how to handle this one. Amanda wonders how she is now back in the car and why they haven't told her parents about the wedding. Or perhaps, she considers, we did tell them and I just don't remember.

Drawing from her past experiences, Amanda contemplates the best method for uncovering what has happened during her most recent block of missing time. "Tom," Amanda begins thoughtfully, "I want you to be honest with me...What do you think of my parents?"

"Well, my love," Tom starts off cautiously, "I can tell you one thing that I am grateful for; I am grateful that your parents met and decided to have a baby because I don't know what I'd do without you."

As clever and as sweet as Tom's response is, Amanda's question is still unanswered. She decides to try one more question to see if she can get some more information. She learned a long time ago to avoid discussions about the time she misses through tactful queries and monitoring responses. "Did you feel comfortable around them?" she pursues.

"I don't know if I can say that they made me feel comfortable, necessarily. But I don't know that any man can feel comfortable when asking a person for his daughter's hand in marriage. I think it's just one of those rites of passage that someone dreamed up a long time ago to determine the fortitude and stamina of a man…to see if he is ready to stand up to the world and make something of himself," Tom explains, hoping to put a light-hearted spin on the last few hours.

Amanda, content with the information she now has, decides to let the questions drop for now. Sometimes the details of missed time just naturally seem to be filled in through silent visions played at later times. Based on Tom's answers, she is confident in waiting for the replay until a later time.

Thankful for the opportunity to change the subject and give Amanda something else to consider, Tom smiles as he pulls into the parking lot of the little Italian restaurant they went to on their first date. Looking over at the love of his life, Tom offers some assurance, "Let's have a pleasant night. Don't you worry about your parents' reaction. They'll adjust in time. Meanwhile, I want to see that pretty little smile that warms my heart so much."

Amanda quickly responds with a heart-felt smile. Although his words brought new concern about the lost time, Tom's touch and loving expression always makes her feel secure and safe. Hand in hand, they stroll to the restaurant entrance, oblivious to the world around them. Seeing only love in each other's eyes, Tom and Amanda peacefully share their thoughts and feelings over dinner. Reminiscing over pleasures shared and dreaming of things to come, the evening passes quickly.

As the waiter brings out the covered dishes containing their dessert, he nods briefly at Tom. Tom looks deeply into Amanda's eyes and takes her hand. "Amanda, I know we have talked about this before, but I want to officially ask you." Tom pauses long enough to move from his chair onto one knee. "Will you give me the privilege of being your husband?"

Tears begin to fill her eyes as the waiter lifts the cover from her dessert dish. Sitting on the dish is a sparkling ring with a large marquee cut diamond surrounded by perfectly formed baguettes. It feels to Amanda as if the sights and sounds were being replayed a thousand times in her mind. Finally conscious of Tom's anxious expression, she blurts out, "Yes! Did I say yes yet? Yes, Tom, I'll marry you!"

Pleased beyond words, Tom takes the ring and carefully places it on Amanda's finger. "Thank you," was all he could think of to say.

Sounds of applause fill the restaurant as waiters and customers alike, wish the couple well. Immersed in their own thoughts of happiness, Tom and Amanda are not even aware of the acts of kindness going on around them.

Admiring the beautiful shine in Amanda's eyes, Tom just sits silently, holding her hand. Her father's bizarre behavior is the furthermost thing from his mind. This moment is perfect. They truly are meant for each other. They share friendship, love, laughter, and a love for God. Life can't get any better.

Tom paid the dinner check and blissfully escorted Amanda to the car. Finally away from the eyes of the world, Tom whispers to Amanda, "You have made me the happiest man alive." Sealing the bond of love, he tenderly kisses her, caressing her long blonde hair.

As their solitude is disturbed by the blaring lights of a car entering the parking lot, Tom decides that his physical expressions of love are best left for later. He opens the car door for Amanda and helps her into her seat. Driving toward her apartment, Tom watches Amanda admire the ring in the street lights. How could such a sweet, caring woman come from such overbearing, seemingly loveless people? Tom looks forward to his life with Amanda and the opportunity to show her a home where true love resides.

He reaches over and gently brushes the hair from her face. Sometimes she just looks so young and innocent, almost childlike. Other times, she is nothing short of a full-fledged woman that is beautiful enough to bring any man to his knees. He loved that about her, so unpredictable, but so dependable. Humbly he utters a silent prayer of thanksgiving for the gift of love God has brought into his life.

Turning the corner into the parking garage, Amanda timidly asks Tom to come up to her apartment for some coffee and a movie. Neither one of them are wanting the night to end.

Tom parks his car and rushes to open her door. Reaching out his hand to help her from the car, he is mystified by the expression on her face. She looked almost hateful. "Amanda, are you okay?" Tom asks cautiously.

"I'm just fine Deary," *Agnes* says with a slight rattle in her voice. "I'm just waiting for you to help this old lady from the car."

"Old lady?" Tom chuckles. "You are definitely not an old lady. A beautiful young woman is more like it. Here you go my dear, take my hand and I'll help you to your apartment." This is a new one for him. Amanda is always coming up with something different. He decides to play along. These little games always serve to create an interesting time. "She really is good at acting out these other parts," he thinks to himself as he escorts her from the car.

Agnes feels the blush rushing to her cheeks in response to being treated so kindly, "Well you do know how to flatter a lady. How about I make you some nice hot tea? It's been a long, confusing night and I want to make sure you are able to relax properly. Some tea will help to relax your mind from all of the pressures of the evening. Which, by the way, you have handled very nicely."

Amanda was really playing this one up; she was even walking a little like an old woman. Tom loves her playful side and relishes the compliments she is paying him. "Why don't we take the elevator tonight, I don't want you to have to strain yourself going up the stairs," Tom says with a devilish grin.

"What a splendid idea, Deary, so thoughtful of you," *Agnes* responds.

As Tom calls the elevator, he looks down at the ring adorning Amanda's hand. "You sure do make that ring look pretty Amanda." Waiting patently for the elevator doors to open, *Agnes* doesn't respond to Tom's comment but acts as if she doesn't even hear him.

Once inside the apartment, *Agnes* invites Tom to take a seat while she puts some water on to boil. She fills the kettle with water and places it on the heated burner. Feeling uncomfortable in the dress, she excuses herself to change clothes. Tom is such a nice young man, she regrets not having all of the ingredients needed to bake him some cookies to go with his tea.

Though not the strongest of the insiders, *Agnes* usually has no trouble remaining in control of the body. Tonight however, Amanda's emotions will not be easily contained. Amanda's need to experience her excitement and joy to the fullest gradually wins out over *Agnes's* need to care for Tom as a grandmother would. Forced to resign temporarily, *Agnes* gives way to Amanda's unconscious struggle to be present.

The sound of a tea kettle ready to explode grabs Amanda's attention. Now dressed in sweats and socks, she races to the kitchen to free the kettle from the hot burner. With no thought of being observed, she steals another look at the incredible ring on her finger. Mindlessly, she reaches in the cabinet for a cup, places the tea bag in the cup and begins to pour the hot water.

"I would like coffee if you don't mind Honey," Tom's voice breaks through the silence.

"Tom! You...You scared me! I'm sorry Honey; I was off in my own little world there for a minute." Amanda quickly recovers from his unexpected presence. While preparing him a cup of instant coffee she makes sure to stir with the hand that bears her ring. Not sure exactly what time it is, she offers Tom something to eat. He politely declines as he moves closer to her, looking deep into her eyes.

"Amanda, you are an amazing and mysterious woman. Would you be upset if we just sit together and listen to music tonight instead of watching a movie? I just want to hold you in my arms and spend some quiet time with you. Would that be okay?"

"Nothing could possibly sound better Tom," Amanda softly replies. "I'll let you pick out the music while I finish up in here."

Chapter Six

Mrs. Amanda Marie Morris. Stretched out across her bed, Amanda practices her soon-to-be signature on a notepad. Between each attempt, she takes a minute to admire the picture taken for their engagement announcement in the newspaper. She had spent the entire morning getting ready for that picture. Her hair, incredibly enough, was perfect. Tom looked positively dashing. *Mrs. Amanda Marie Morris*, she carefully scribes again.

Deep in her thoughts of wedded bliss, she is startled back to reality by the ringing of the phone. Half in excited anticipation and half in dread, Amanda picks up the receiver. "Hello?"

"Hello, Amanda. It's Jessica, Tom's sister. I hope I'm not disturbing you," she says politely.

"Not at all. How are you doing today?" Amanda is relieved to hear her voice. From the moment Tom introduced them, she has been welcomed into his family with open arms. Jessica has been particularly kind, quickly becoming the sister Amanda never had. Strangely, she feels more at home with his family than she does with her own.

"I'm doing good, thanks. I'm calling to see if you want to go shopping with me today. I need to buy Tom a birthday present and I'm sure there are things you will need for the wedding. We can make a day of it, that is, if you don't have anything else already planned."

"I'd love to! Do you want to come over here, or should I meet you somewhere?"

"I'll come over there. I can't wait to see the patterns you have picked out for your dress!"

"Great! I can't wait to show you either. I'll see you in a little bit then."

As Amanda hangs up, she whispers a '*thank you*' to God for the people

He has put in her life, especially Tom and his family. She practices her signature one more time before jumping in the shower. *Mrs. Amanda Marie Morris.*

"Mrs. Amanda Marie Morris! It's never going to happen. You know that boy is after only one thing and I will not have it!" the voice of *Everett* comes through from deep inside. "This marriage is not permitted. I will show you just how much he loves you. How much do you think he will tolerate? You belong to me, not him. Your loyalty to me is being tested and you are failing. Do I need to punish you? No…I think I'll just make an example of this creep. You'll see how much he really loves you, and then you'll come crawling back to me, begging for my forgiveness."

Amanda turns the water on for the shower, hoping to drown out the voice. Still hearing the mocking tongue from inside, she adds the sound of music from the AM/FM radio by her sink. Twinges of guilt and fear begin to well up. Amanda undresses and steps under the water, desperately trying to feel clean again. Not realizing how strongly she is scrubbing, Amanda's washcloth begins burning her skin. "It's Tom that you are trying to be cleaned from. He is poison to you," *Everett* suggests as he develops his plot to destroy their relationship. Even though her father had even agreed to pay for the wedding, *Everett* can't believe that it is truly acceptable.

Amanda takes a deep breath and allows the water to flow over her hair. Unable to make sense of the message and her feelings, but determined to quiet the voices inside, she sings along with the song on the radio. As her resolve grows stronger, her singing gets louder. The voices have been silenced, for now. She can turn her attention toward the day that lay ahead of her.

Quickly drying herself, she begins the process of dressing for a day of shopping. Scanning her closet, she notices several new items, or perhaps they were so old that she doesn't remember them. But none the less, she hasn't worn them recently to be sure. She puts on a pair of caprices and a matching top, some sandals and a belt. While it seemed like a good idea at first, the feeling doesn't last. She'll need to find something different, besides, it's probably a little cool outside for such an outfit.

Several outfits later, she decides that jeans with a white buccaneer style shirt will be comfortable and fun. About the time she is putting on her shoes, Jessica knocks on the door. Excited, Amanda runs to welcome her. "Hello Jessica! Come in, I just need to finish up my hair and make-up, and then I'll be ready to go. Would you like a cup of coffee?"

"Yes, I'd love a cup. Then you must show me the pattern you chose for your dress." Jessica follows Amanda into the kitchen where she pours two cups of coffee. With the coffee served, they retreat to Amanda's living room to begin the dreaming of the wedding day.

"Jessica, there's something I've been wanting to ask you," Amanda says as she hands Jessica the picture of a Victorian styled wedding dress. "Would you consider being my matron of honor?"

"I'd be thrilled! Thank you Amanda! This is exciting. You know, you and Tom are really meant for each other," Jessica says smiling. "You fit in so well with our family and you definitely make Tom happy. I've never seen him so full of life."

"Well, I can't tell you how happy I have been lately. Seeing his family, I can understand how Tom turned out so great. There is so much love."

"Amanda, we feel the same way about you. It's like you're part of the family already, like you have been around all my life. I always wanted a sister and now I have one. We all love you very much," Jessica says as she reaches over and gives Amanda a hug.

After a few seconds, Jessica begins to pull away, but *Everett* doesn't let her go so quickly. "You know, we are like family. In my family we have a great way of showing love to each other," *Everett* says as he gently strokes her hair. "Would you like me to show you?"

Pulling away forcefully, Jessica scans Amanda's face for a hint of what she could possibly mean. Amanda's voice is almost frightening to Jessica. If she didn't know any better, she would say it was a man talking, not Amanda. Her eyes definitely look different too, almost sinister. "What's wrong Jessica, you aren't afraid are you?," *Everett* asks. "I'm sure it's nothing you haven't already experienced, being married and all."

With that clarification, Jessica abruptly stands to her feet. Not wanting to create any problems or confusion in their relationship, she feels the need to set the record straight. "I'm not sure exactly what you are referring to, but I don't like what you are implying. Are you okay? You seem, well, different."

The knocking on the door startles them both. Entering without waiting for an answer, Tom walks into the tension filled room. "Hi there! What have you two been doing?," Tom inquires.

"We were just looking at wedding dresses," Amanda responds. "What are you doing?," she continues as she stands to greet him with a hug and kiss.

"I was just coming to see if my beautiful bride-to-be would like to join me for some lunch."

Jessica, jumping on the opportunity to escape this strange situation offers, "You know Amanda, that's a great idea. You two go have lunch and I'll catch up with you later."

"Are you sure? You don't mind?" Amanda asks. "Oh Tom, Jessica has said yes to being my matron of honor!"

"Yes, I'm sure. There are some errands I need to run anyway. You two go and have some fun," Jessica says as she quickly makes her way to the door.

Feeling his sister's awkwardness, Tom offers, "You could join us if you would like."

"No, that's okay. You go and have fun. I'll give you a call later." With that, Jessica makes her get-away; feeling confused, almost violated.

"That's unusual," Tom observes. "She seemed pre-occupied or disturbed about something. Do you know what's going on?"

"No, I don't have a clue," Amanda responds honestly. "So, where are you going to take me for lunch? I still need to finish up my hair and make-up before we go anywhere."

"You look great to me, but if you insist on getting all fancied up, you go ahead. I was thinking of going to that cafe by the mall. I'm feeling a little nostalgic," Tom explains. "I tell you what, you go finish fixing yourself up, and I'll see if I can catch Jessica. I'm concerned about her."

"Okay Baby," Amanda agrees and kisses Tom on the cheek before going to her bathroom to dry her hair.

As Tom gets outside, he sees Jessica standing at her car as she is looking for her keys. "Jessica, wait!" Tom half-screams, not wanting to miss her. Running to her car, he notices that Jessica seems to be shaking. "Are you okay?"

"Yes, I think so. Tom, I'm just a little confused right now," Jessica responds not looking at Tom.

"Why, what's wrong? Did something happen?" Tom asks.

"I'm not sure. I mean…oh, I must sound like a fool. I'm sorry Tom, I'm just not sure how to interpret something that Amanda did, well not did, but said. Well, no it was more than what she said, it was the way she said it."

"What are you talking about Jessica? Now I'm confused," Tom says with a slight chuckle in his voice, trying to put Jessica at ease.

"Well…Amanda and I were talking about how much she feels part of the family. I gave her a hug, you know, just a friendly hug. Tom, the way she hugged me back, it was strange. Like the hug lasted longer than it should have and she wouldn't let me go. Then…well, I'm sure I'm just being silly, but I think she made a pass at me." Jessica looks up at Tom to see his reaction to such an incredible story.

"She made a pass at you? What do you mean? What exactly did she say?" Tom asks, being careful not to doubt his sister, but confused by what she is saying. Perhaps Jessica just misinterpreted the whole situation.

"Well, she said that in her family they have a special way of showing love to each other. She started rubbing my hair and offered to show me what they do." Jessica searches her brother's eyes, hoping he has a reasonable explanation for Amanda's behavior. "It was the tone in her voice too, that's what really got to me. Tom, she sounded like a man."

Not knowing what to say, Tom just put his arms around Jessica. Seeing how upset she was, he offered to drive her home. That would give him a chance to think about what he should do next.

Tom runs back upstairs to Amanda's apartment long enough to explain that he is driving Jessica home. He asks Amanda to meet him at Jessica's house when she is ready.

Back at Jessica's car, Tom tries to understand the situation better. "Is there anything else you noticed? Do you think she was just joking perhaps?"

"Tom, I don't know, honestly. I've never seen Amanda act like this. She had a strange look in her eyes, like she was up to no good. Then when you came in, her expressions change completely, like turning on a light switch or something," Jessica recalls.

"Well you know, Amanda is full of surprises and is constantly joking around. There was one time in fact, that Amanda acted like she was a decrepit old lady," Tom said with a slight smile remembering her playfulness. "I'll ask her about it, just to be sure."

Trying to accept his explanation, Jessica takes in a deep breath and exhales slowly. "I'm sure you are probably right Tom. I feel so foolish acting like I have. I've just never felt like that before. I think it was her comment about me being married and having experienced it already that really threw me."

"What comment about being married? You left that out before."

"Oh I'm sorry, it was all so confusing. I decided to be sure that we understood each other so I told her that I didn't like what she was implying. That's where it turned really weird. She said something about it not being a new experience for me because I was married," Jessica explains.

"Now that is strange," Tom says as he tries to process the information.

"Tom, what do you know about her family? Is there anything to what she is saying? Maybe it is a cry for help. Maybe Amanda is looking for a way to tell someone what happened to her," Jessica says, thinking out loud.

Tom silently considers Jessica's explanation. Amanda didn't really talk much about her parents or her childhood. In fact, that is a subject she seems to avoid. Tom's mind races back to the time when he visited her parents to tell them about the wedding plans. Suddenly a light bulb goes off in Tom's head, bringing back to his remembrance the comment Amanda's father made about another man taking away his baby girl. Is it possible Jessica is right?

Tom's thoughts begin to conflict with each other. He is hoping that Jessica is right about Amanda, not wanting to think the worst about her. On the other hand, he hopes she is wrong as his thoughts turn to the unthinkable acts that she might have suffered as a child.

As Tom pulls into Jessica's driveway, he finally responds to her question. "I honestly don't know much about her family other than what is seen on the surface. I'm not sure if I want it to be true or not. My thoughts are racing a million miles an hour."

"Mine too," Jessica admits. "Come on inside and I'll fix us some coffee. Do you want me to make lunch for all of us? Maybe we can get Amanda to talk about her family some. I don't want to seem pushy or overbearing. If you don't want to have this talk with me around, I'll understand. I'm just thinking that if she is trying to reach out for help, well, she did initiate the conversation with me. Maybe a women-to-women talk will be easiest for her, when I'm not so freaked out."

"No, that's a good idea," Tom responds. "Maybe we should pray together before she gets here. I don't know about you, but if what you are guessing is true, we are definitely going to need the Lord's guidance and an extra dose of wisdom. Well, we'll need it either way won't we?" With a simple nod of agreement, Jessica and Tom walk solemnly into her house to pray and wait.

The prayer time together, seems to steady their hearts. Both Tom and Jessica feel an overwhelming peace about the situation. The confusion and anger, which started creeping into their feelings, were now replaced with love and concern.

Jessica is just starting the soup and sandwiches when Amanda arrives. Tom greets her at the door, explaining that Jessica has offered them lunch. "Would it be okay with you if we just eat here today? I promise to take you to our cafe tomorrow after church."

"Sure, that's fine Tom. Is everything okay? Did you find out what was wrong with Jessica?" Amanda quietly asks, sincerely concerned.

"Yes, everything is fine. We just thought it would be more comfortable to have lunch here and Jessica can spend time with us as well."

"Okay, whatever you want to do is fine with me. You know I just adore your sister and I certainly don't mind spending time with her." Yesterday a comment like that would have thrilled Tom. Today, he isn't sure whether to be glad they get along so well, or to be jealous of Jessica. As they walk into the kitchen area, Amanda offers to help Jessica with lunch. Jessica politely declines and offers Amanda some coffee or tea while she waits for lunch.

Tom, desperately needing some answers, begins the conversation. "Amanda, you know that I love you, right?"

Giggling at such a silly question, Amanda responds, "Of course I do Honey. And I love you too."

"Good, I'm glad to hear that," Tom says honestly. "Amanda, something has been bothering me for some time now. Maybe you can help me understand a little better."

Her curiosity peaked, Amanda urges him to go on.

"Do you remember when we visited your parent's house to tell them about our wedding plans? There was something your father said that has been bothering me. Do you remember the comment he made about another man taking his girl from him?"

Amanda searches through her memory but is unable to remember much about that visit. She certainly didn't remember her father saying anything like that. "No Tom, actually I don't. It wouldn't surprise me altogether though, he still thinks of me as his baby girl."

"Yes, I'm sure you are right. But you know, to me, he sounded more like a jealous lover than a picky father not wanting to let go of his daughter," Tom says while holding his breath, afraid of her reaction.

"Jealous lover?" Amanda asks for clarity. "I don't know what you could possibly mean."

"Well, let me just ask you," Tom proceeds as his heart is pounding. "Today, when you mentioned to Jessica that your family has a special way of showing love, what did you mean?"

At that question, Amanda and Jessica both turn wide-eyed toward Tom, then toward each other; Amanda looking confused and Jessica feeling embarrassed. "I don't remember saying anything like that Tom. My family is not bad, but I wouldn't consider my parents to be overly loving either. I've not really known love until I met you and your family."

"Amanda, Jessica told me about your conversation. I really would like to know what you meant by that comment. I'm not angry with you, I am concerned."

"Well I'm glad you aren't angry, but I honestly don't know what you are talking about," Amanda insisted.

Jessica steps into the conversation. "Amanda, do you remember giving me a hug?"

"Yes, I do. So?" Amanda responds.

"Do you remember what you told me after the hug?"

"I don't think I told you anything. We hugged and then Tom came to the door. Is there something wrong with giving your friend a hug?" Amanda says, feeling defensive although she isn't sure why.

"No, not at all Amanda. It's perfectly okay to hug," Jessica says as she reaches out and hugs Amanda again.

"Back for more are we?" came the voice of *Everett*. "I thought you didn't want anything to do with me." Startled, Jessica pulls away and looks to Tom for validation. *Everett* follows her gaze, pleased with the expression on Tom's face. "Finding out a little too much about your sweet little Amanda?" The hate in his voice is intense, but it can not compare with the look in his eyes. In order to keep his plan heading in the right direction, he chooses to try and make it seem as if Amanda is doing the talking still—but with some major twists. "What's the matter Tom, don't you like me being a bad girl?" *Everett* asks, baiting Tom for a response.

Unsure of what is happening, Tom just sits quietly. Watching, thinking, and praying. Not able to force a response from Tom, *Everett* turns his attention to Jessica. "Come on Baby Girl, you know you want it as much as I do. Why don't we dump this jerk and take care of business."

Unable to contain his emotions any longer, Tom stands to his feet and begins to demand answers. "What are you doing? Have you lost your mind?"

"Yes, that's it. I'm crazy...crazy in love with your sister!" *Everett* provokes.

Jessica tries to comfort Tom, putting her arm around him. She whispers to Tom, "Remember your psychology courses from college. I know it wasn't your major, but think Tom, think about what is happening."

Tom prayerfully considers Jessica's words of wisdom. Slowly, he begins to remember the information he studied about multiple personality disorder. With an assurance that could have only come from the Lord, Tom proceeds. "Tell me, how is it that you show love in your family?"

"Awe, your curiosity is peaked I see. Why, we show love like anyone else does," *Everett* says. Then he turns to Jessica, "Tell me, how do you show love to your husband?"

Jessica considers her answer for just a moment before responding. "There are many ways Rick and I show our love for each other."

"Oh come on, you know what I'm talking about. There's only one real way to show love and that's having sex together," *Everett* chuckles. "That's only natural you know. God set it up that way."

"Yes, between husband and wife, God did set up a way for us to demonstrate our love through sex. But he didn't set it up for everyone to have sex together," Jessica explains.

Tom interrupts, "How does your father show that he loves you?"

Laughing at the attempt for an admission, *Everett* asks, "How do you think?"

Considering the answers, Tom feels stuck. If he responds with time and attention, they might never get to the truth. If he answers with what his gut is telling him, it could appear as if Tom thinks that is normal or that he is suggesting information to be used later. One thing that has been cleared up, Tom was no longer talking to Amanda. "So then, who or what are they talking to?" Tom wonders.

"Did Amanda's father have sex with her?" Tom blurts out his question—shocked by his own bluntness.

Amanda's expressions begin to change. Her body slumps over slightly and her head lowers to her chest. *Agnes* appears—weaker than usual. Pushing *Everett* away from the surface of consciousness was difficult, but worth the struggle. "What do you want to know?" she asks faintly. "You have been so kind, I will try to answer your questions."

With this sudden change in appearance, voice, and attitude, Tom determines that it must be a "who", not a "what". He doesn't think she is possessed, but understands that there must be at least two other personalities living inside of Amanda.

Sitting down to try to see her face, Tom asks again, "Did Amanda's father have sex with her?"

Agnes slowly responds, "You know it is sad what happens these days. Fathers just do not know how to properly care for their children. I have tried to protect her and provide her with a sense of comfort, but I was not able to fulfill that function. And now, I am failing again by betraying her secrets." She slowly looks up, into Tom's eyes. "Please, do not abandon her because you now know the truth. She does love you very much."

Tom feels the knot in his stomach twisting as his heart begins to break. Gently he asks, "Does that mean that he did? ...For how long? ...When did it start?"

Sighing from the strain of emotions these questions brought, *Agnes* nods in confirmation. "It has been going on since she was very young. I'm not sure exactly at what age it began. He still tries from time to time, but he hasn't been successful for the last few years. There are some that are stronger than I am and are better able to stop him." With that admission, *Agnes* lowers her head in shame and exhaustion.

Tom has so many questions, but so few that he has the heart to ask. The thought of his Amanda going through such torment was more than he could bear. Silently, he sits and absorbs, wanting to comfort her and take the pain away. He reaches over and tenderly rubs *Agnes's* hand.

Jessica kneels beside *Agnes's* chair and looks up into her eyes. "Thank you for telling us what happened. It's not your fault that he did those things. I'm sure you tried very hard to protect Amanda." Her words of kindness flood over *Agnes* like a breath of fresh air.

"Thank you my dear, it's so kind of you to say," she says as she pats Jessica's face gently. Looking up at Tom, *Agnes* changes the direction of the conversation. "Tom, I will understand if this is too much for you to handle. Amanda does not remember these things so she is telling the truth when she answers you. For her sake, I really must know what you intend to do."

Tom is surprised by his own hesitancy. Certainly there can only be one answer to such a question. "I intend, dear lady, to stand beside her. She has suffered enough hardship in her lifetime. I do not plan to add to the list. Tell me, what should we do from here?" Tom asks with heartfelt concern.

"What should you do? That I can't tell you," *Agnes* responds. "I can tell you that she must not know the truth yet, and she must not know about us. The time will come when she will remember, but that time is not now. I bid you both a good day. Thank you for your understanding and your love." With those words, Amanda's eyes close momentarily.

With a shake of the head and a few blinks of her eyes, Amanda regains her composure. "I do care a great deal for you Jessica, and the hug just seems like the natural way to express it. If you would prefer not to hug in the future, I understand I guess."

Jessica responds with confidence, "Amanda, you can hug me any time." With her new understanding of the event and a developing appreciation for what Amanda has gone through, Jessica does not hesitate to give Amanda a big sisterly hug.

With a woman's intuition that is strengthened by wisdom from God, Jessica quickly moves toward making Amanda comfortable and restoring a sense of normality. "Now, if you don't mind, I think I could use some help in the kitchen," she says with the lightest tone of voice she could muster.

Chapter Seven

Tom sits alone in the garage apartment behind his parent's house. With the soft music playing from his stereo, and a cup of coffee in his hands, Tom begins to consider all that has transpired.

In just one day, his world has been turned upside down. The behaviors he once considered playful, he now sees as cries of pain from deep within Amanda's mind. The man he once thought would just be hard to tolerate, is now a man for which he has complete disdain. Tom finds himself wishing a slow painful death to Amanda's father. Images of Everett being covered in molten lava or eaten by red ants consume him.

Wanting to hold Amanda and take away her pain, he also finds the feelings of fear and anticipation growing from within himself. Her father has sexually abused her for years. The abuse was consistent enough, and horrible enough, for Amanda to create other personalities to help her survive.

Prayerfully reviewing his old college psych textbook, Tom remembers why the personalities are created—to take away the trauma so it can be put on hold until later in life. It seems that the "later in life" part refers to Amanda's present. How can Tom deal with his own feelings of anger and hatred while helping his beloved Amanda handle the truth about the traumas of her past? He certainly does not want his feelings to get in the way. If he pushes her by insisting Everett is a monster then she may feel the need to defend him. It's obvious that she was programmed or conditioned to keep the family's secrets.

Tom considers how supportive Jessica is being. She was great at helping Amanda feel comfortable today after finding out about the other personalities. Jessica and Rick will be helpful to him and Amanda during the times of discovery yet to come.

Tom's parents are loving and understanding, but how accepting will they be about this? To his parents, everything is spiritually based. They do not believe in the psychological field of study or any of the therapies that go along with it. The other personalities would be seen as demons, not other parts of her mind. How is he going to explain this to them?

The thoughts begin to overwhelm Tom. This is more than he can handle. The joy of getting married has suddenly turned into a nightmare of extreme proportions. He can't just give up, he loves Amanda. That is one thing that hasn't changed. It's just too much thinking for one night.

Deciding to put aside his thoughts for the evening, Tom turns off the coffee maker, the lights and the stereo. Exhausted from the day's trials, he quietly crawls into bed, hoping to have clearer thoughts in the morning.

Quickly drifting off to sleep, Tom's mind continues to work, searching for a solution to the complex situation at hand. With glimpses of Amanda's sweet face, mixing with pictures of unthinkable acts of abuse perpetrated on her by her father, Tom's mind refuses to rest. As the scenes change, portraying the years of turmoil Amanda has suffered, Tom's rage begins to paint a kaleidoscope of hate-filled images racing through his mind.

The swirling scenes gradually slow to a stop and come into focus. Amanda's father is sitting at the dinner table, opposite Amanda and Tom. His obnoxious laughter fills the air with a sickening sense of mockery and shameless abandonment from the principles of humanity. His mouth opens to speak, but only non-sense can be heard—chatter, chatter, chatter.

Searching the room, Tom is unable to locate Amanda's mother. Where can she be? Doesn't she know what is happening in here? Tom watches as Amanda seems to shrink smaller and smaller, as her father's words become clearer. "My Baby Girl really knows how to please a man. I've trained her well for you Tom. Sorry you will only be getting second-hand material, but someone had to show her the ropes. Who better than her father?"

Amanda continues to fade farther and farther away. Looking over in the corner, Tom sees the hint of a figure, crouched down in the shadows. "Who's there? Come out and show yourself," Tom insists. Slowly, the figure moves into the light, exposing the distorted features of Amanda's mother. "Why are you hiding? You can stop this thing! Why don't you do something?" For a split second, she looks up at Tom so he can clearly see the tape across her mouth and the ties around her wrist. Then as quickly as she appeared, Victoria retreats back into the shadows.

"Someone must do something! This man's maniacal behavior must be stopped. If no one else will stop him, I will!" As if destined to handle the situation, Tom reaches into his pocket and finds the cold barrel of a gun. Pulling it out slowly, he checks to be sure it is loaded. He takes another look at Amanda, seeing her now curled up in a ball on the floor.

His rage reaches a new level. Looking back at her father, Everett's mouth seems to be moving in slow motion, repeating constantly the words, "She's my baby girl." Taking only seconds to aim, Tom pulls the trigger. As Amanda's father is blown into oblivion, Tom is awakened from his dream by the sound of knocking on his door.

"Tom," his mother calls out. Still groggy, Tom stumbles to his door and fumbles with the knob. Accomplishing the first part—opening the door—he is startled by the brightness of the morning. "Good morning sunshine!" his mother voice trumpets the joyful greeting. "Breakfast is almost ready. Would you like to join us for some eggs and biscuits before church?"

"How can she be so cheery? I just murdered a man! No wait...it was just a dream, "Tom thinks to himself. Collecting his thoughts, he realizes that his mother is still standing there waiting for an answer. "Yes Mom, thank you. I'll be down in just a few minutes," Tom says as he mindlessly shuts the door in his mother's face.

It's Sunday, church services, then lunch at the cafe with Amanda. "Oh God," Tom prays, "help me through this day. Give me strength and wisdom. Lord, let your love shine through me. And Lord, forgive me for murdering Amanda's father in my dream. I really feel bad about that one..." his thoughts turn toward his horrible dream. Thankful for a new day and a fresh start, Tom gets into the shower.

As he turns the water off, he hears the answering machine click on. "Tom?" Amanda's voice comes through. "Tom, I...I can't be there today. I've got to go to my parent's house. I'll call you later. I love you." The sound of the answering machine rewinding marked the end of the message.

Still dripping wet, he grabs a towel and rushes to the phone. Dialing Amanda's number, his concern for her quickly returns. He definitely doesn't want her going over there alone. Finally, Amanda answers the phone. "Hello?"

"Amanda, Honey, are you okay? I'm sorry I missed your call, I was in the shower. What's going on?" Tom tries to sound calm and collected.

Amanda doesn't respond immediately, but takes her time collecting her thoughts. Finally, she says, "Tom, Daddy died last night. I have to go be with Mom."

Forgetting to even breathe, Tom stands there speechless. Thoughts race through his mind. "I've murdered him and just *thought* it was a dream", Tom thinks to himself. "Amanda, Honey, how did he die?" Tom asks, closing his eyes as he waits for the answer.

"Oh Tom, it's my fault! He came over last night to visit me and on his way home, he was in a car accident. Apparently he had a heart attack and died behind the wheel. If he had been at home, Mom might have been able to call for help. It's my fault Tom."

"Stay put Amanda, I'm on my way. Don't go anywhere!" Tom says as he hangs up the phone, not giving Amanda an opportunity to respond.

Tom's mind begins to wonder if Amanda, or some other personality within her, decided that last night's visits would have to be the last. Is she capable of such an act? If so, he certainly couldn't condemn her, after all, he was dreaming of it himself just last night. These thoughts of murder have got to stop! Amanda would never do anything like that. Her father simply had a heart attack.

Getting past the thoughts of how he died, he remembers Amanda's words, "He came over last night to visit me." Tom can't seem to make his body move fast enough. With his pants clinging to his wet legs, he grabs his shirt, shoes, socks and keys while running out the door.

Tom pops into his parent's house long enough to request prayer for Amanda and her family. Talking while he throws on his shirt and socks, he explains what happened and that he would be with Amanda. Shoes and keys in hand, Tom dashes to his car, shirt tail flapping in the wind.

Recognizing his instinct to race to Amanda's side, Tom makes a conscious effort to pull back on his speed. It will not do anyone any good to have a wreck on his way to help her. Trying to pay attention to his driving, he fights off thoughts of Amanda's possible mistreatment last night. Finally arriving safely, he parks his car and runs to her apartment. Stepping into his shoes, he knocks on the door.

Amanda immediately opens the door, practically jumping into his arms. Her eyes begin to fill with tears, as she finally allows herself to cry. Tom tenderly walks Amanda back into her apartment and sits with her on the coach, allowing her to express her grief. He gently runs his fingers over her long blonde hair as he whispers words of comfort.

"Tom…I honestly don't know…why…he was here last night…but I wish…I wish…he had never come," Amanda manages to say mixed with heavy sobs.

With conflicting emotions, Tom searches desperately for the right words. "Amanda, the fact that your father came over last night does not make you responsible for his death." His words seem to bring calmness to Amanda as she visibly pushes back her feelings of guilt.

"I have to go be with Mother, she is going crazy Tom. She's absolutely beside herself," Amanda says.

Recognizing her need to be with her family, Tom doesn't argue with her. His role today will simply be one of support, whatever Amanda needs. "Then to your mother is where we will go. I need to brush through my hair real quick then I'll be ready," Tom says. "Amanda, I want you to know, I love you very much. I'm so sorry this is happening," Tom adds as he gives her another hug.

Not needing too much time to primp, Tom is ready to go within a few minutes. He helps Amanda close up her apartment and walks her to his car. He opens the passenger door, holding her hand as she settles into her seat. There is nothing unusual about this action, but for some reason, it feels unsettling to Amanda. She sits quietly as Tom buckles his seat belt. Staring out the window, she feels a twinge of de'jàvu. A picture flashes in her mind; her being driven home while feeling enormous grief. The words, "I will not tolerate your tears! You just better stop feeling sorry for yourself for once and think about others around you," rings in her ears. Not remembering where she heard these words before, she tries to move her thoughts to how she can help her mother. As their short drive comes to an end, Amanda is still considering what she could possibly do. Tom turns to Amanda and asks, "Are you ready?"

"Yes, as ready as I can be under the circumstances. Thank you for asking Tom." She smiles as he opens her car door and helps her out. Supporting her physically with his arms and spiritually with his prayers, they walk together into the unknown.

Knowing that her mother is expecting her, Amanda doesn't bother to knock on the door. Walking into the house, they can hear her mother in the kitchen. It sounds as if she is cleaning the dishes. "Mother?" Amanda calls out as they make their way toward the sounds.

"I'm in here," her mother responds. Tom and Amanda walk in to find her mother feverishly cleaning. "Amanda, I'm glad you are here. You know that the family is going to be descending on this place shortly and it is such a mess," Victoria says without even acknowledging Tom's presence.

Wanting to be seen as a help, not a bother, Tom offers his assistance. Without missing a beat, Victoria begins to give out assignments. Amanda is to get the living room ready and Tom can make sure the yard and garage are cleaned. Having received their orders, they split up and set about their assigned tasks.

Amanda walks into the living room looking for things to be cleaned. As usual, everything is in its rightful place. The only item that seems to need attention is the ashtray next to her father's chair. She approaches it cautiously, as if it is alive and might reach out and bite her. Picturing her father in the chair, but knowing it will remain empty, Amanda begins to feel the pains of grief again.

"Please Amanda, we have much to do and little time to do it in. Don't just stand there, get that ashtray cleaned," came the voice of her mother, startling her back to the business at hand.

"Mom, how can you go on like this? Don't you feel anything?" Amanda hears the words leave her mouth, but the direct confrontation surprises even her.

Outside, Tom looks around at the perfectly manicured lawn. He picks up a few paper cups from the curbside but finds nothing else to be done in either the front or back yard. Moving his attention to the garage, he finds it in similar condition. He decides to move the large garbage can into a corner to get it out of the line of sight.

Not sure what else he can do to make things ready outside, he ventures back into the house to get another assignment. Going in through the garage, he enters the kitchen first, expecting to find Victoria still cleaning. Instead, he hears her voice in the living room. She is not sounding as calm as she did when they first arrived.

"Of course I feel something Amanda," her mother reacts with venom. "I feel a great loss and I know who I have to thank for it. You!"

"Me? What are you talking about?" Amanda asks, not really wanting to hear her answer.

"You just had to call your dad and ask him to visit you last night, didn't you? You can't handle your relationship with Tom, so you come begging your daddy to fix it. When do you plan to grow up? If you had not called, he would have been at home last night. He might not have even had a heart attack if he hadn't been so worried about you! And if he had, I would have been able to help him. But you insisted on him coming alone! I don't want to hear about your grief today when you didn't even want my help last night!"

Stunned, Amanda becomes defensive. "I didn't call him! He just showed up at my door step. As far as my relationship with Tom goes, we are doing just fine. I really don't have any idea what you are talking about Mother!"

As Tom watches this scene of confusion and accusation, he immediately goes to Amanda's side, ready to support and defend her as needed. Still, the thought of her somehow staging her father's death nags at him; especially hearing Victoria's version of the incident.

"Amanda, I don't know what you are trying to pull, playing all innocent in front of Tom. You know as well as I do that you called last night. I answered the phone for God's sake! You asked to speak to your father. You wouldn't talk to me at all!" she recalls.

"Mom, I didn't call you. I promise I didn't," Amanda insists.

"Excuse me," Tom interrupts. "What difference does it make if Amanda called or not. The fact that he visited her last night is not the issue here. I'm sorry to say, but it was just his time to go. Trying to find someone to blame is not going to bring him back."

"I don't believe I asked you for your opinion," Victoria snaps back. "The stress Amanda has put on her father with this whole wedding is definitely a factor in his death. How can you stand in my house and tell me what is and is not important? My husband is gone and it's your fault!"

"My fault?" Tom asks for clarification.

"Yes, your fault! Everett was doing just fine until you showed up announcing how you were going to make Amanda's life all better. Her life was just fine before you stepped in, taking her from her family! You were not needed and you were not wanted! I can't take this any more, I want you out of my house. NOW!" Victoria was visibly shaking, her face hot with anger. Tom stood there for a minute, considering his options. He could push for Victoria to listen to reason, trying to bring some reconciliation for Amanda. He could drop the issue and hope for emotions to calm down. Or, he could take Amanda's hand and leave.

"Mrs. Clark, I know you are hurting," Tom begins.

"Did I stutter? I want you out of my house! You don't have a clue what I am feeling but if you don't get your rear in gear, you're about to find out!" Victoria threatened.

Amanda quickly grabs Tom's hand, making his decision for him. Without a word, she walks right past her mother and out the front door.

Once outside, Amanda begins her apologies while still walking briskly toward the car. "I'm so sorry Tom. She had no right to talk to you like that. I don't know what has gotten into her."

Tom, attempting to slow Amanda down, responds with the full love of his heart. "Amanda, it's okay. I'm not concerned about what she thinks about me right now. She is hurting and looking for someone to blame for her pain. It's you that I'm worried about. Are you okay?"

"Yes, I'm fine Tom. Let's just get out of here."

Reminding himself of his role to be supportive to Amanda today, he decides not to argue. His desire to bring peace between the two of them can wait until later. Right now, he will focus on Amanda's immediate needs and comfort. That clearly can not be accomplished at her parent's home. Feeling that he will need some help with this task, he suggests to Amanda that they visit Jessica, secretly hoping that his mother called her this morning before she left for church.

Pleased with his suggestion, Amanda quickly agrees. She did so enjoy her visit with Jessica yesterday and would now definitely welcome another friendly face. Tom is being great, but maybe Jessica would be an easier person to talk to about her feelings. There's just something about talking with another female that seems to help during the difficult times.

Tom and Amanda both feel a sense of relief as they arrive at Jessica's house and see her car parked in the driveway. Incredibly, they aren't even out of the car when Jessica darts from the house to greet them. Running past her brother and straight to Amanda, she throws her arms around her.

Jessica's emotions are sincere. It becomes obvious that she has been crying as she tells Amanda, "I'm so sorry for your loss. I'd hoped you would come over or call so I could be with you. I made us some snacks just in case you are hungry. Amanda, you are going to be okay. It might not feel like it, but I know, you will be okay."

Leading Amanda toward the house, she stops when she gets to Tom. She reaches up and quickly hugs her brother. "It's going to be okay Tom. It's going to be okay," she says. Then, holding both of their hands, she takes them into the house. Tom and Amanda look at each other, both taken back a bit by Jessica's outpouring of love.

As they sit together on the sofa, Rick emerges from the kitchen with cups of coffee for Tom and Amanda. As he hands Amanda her cup, he reaches down and gives her a peck on the cheek. "I'm sorry to hear about your dad Amanda," he says simply. Then handing the last cup to Tom, he shakes his hand and nods that silent word of encouragement that only men can understand. Having delivered their coffee, he retreats back into the kitchen to refresh Jessica's and his cups.

Amanda says meekly, "Jessica, I hope we aren't disturbing you and Rick."

"Not at all. Don't you think of it again. Amanda, this is what family is for. Now you just relax and tell me, how did it happen?" Jessica says.

Rick returns with the coffee and sits next to Jessica as Amanda begins her story. "Last night, about 10:00, my dad shows up at my apartment for no reason at all. I'm not sure exactly how long he stayed. We watched some TV together for a while, then I must have fallen asleep on the couch. Then next thing I knew, Mom was calling to tell me that he was in an accident on the way home."

"How frightening that must have been for you, Amanda," Jessica responds.

"Amanda, Honey, why don't you and Jessica talk for a bit. I'll help Rick in the kitchen." Chuckling at how ironic that sounded, Tom adds, "You better take advantage of it, Rick and I don't offer our services in the kitchen very often."

Without waiting for her response, Tom gives her a kiss on her cheek and stands to escape into the other room. Rick quietly follows, knowing his cue that Tom is needing to talk. Once out of ear shot, Rick starts the conversation. "Jessica told me what happened yesterday with Amanda. I can't say that I understand it all, but it sounds pretty bad. How are you holding up?"

"Man, I'll tell you something. This is really hard. Last night I was reading over my old college books to brush up on this multiple personality thing. Rick, I really love Amanda and it's really hard to think about what she must have gone through as a child you know?" Pausing for a minute to get his thoughts together, he asks, "Do you have any meat we can burn on the grill?"

Remembering the last disaster with barbecue, Rick laughs as he pulls out some steaks from the refrigerator. "Do you think we can do better this time?"

"I'm not sure, but I'm willing to give it a try," Tom teases back. Gathering the rest of the ingredients, the pair adjourn outside to fire up the gas powered barbecue pit. Once the fire is started, the two settle into lawn chairs and continue their discussion.

Finishing her account of Victoria's cruel and absurd behavior, Amanda bursts into tears. Jessica hesitates for only a second as the thoughts of yesterday's encounter with the unknown personality flashed in her mind. Determined to show Amanda kindness, she leads forward and gives her a big hug.

Amanda's sobs begin to lessen as her body goes limp temporarily. Jessica, fearing the worst, pulls back and studies Amanda's face. Relieved and confused by her expression, Jessica asks, "Amanda? Are you okay Sweetie?"

"Is it true," the soft voice of *Carol* asks.

"Is what true Honey?"

"What they say about Daddy. Is it true?"

"Well yes, Honey, I'm sorry. It is true that he is dead," Jessica proceeds cautiously, not sure what the reaction will be to the news.

"It finally worked?" *Carol* asks.

"What finally worked Sweetie?" Jessica inquires.

"He says that if I don't do it with him, he will die. Sometimes I run away so he can't do it with me so he will die, but it never worked before," *Carol* explains. "Last night I ran away from him again. This time it worked!"

Not sure if it would be better to let her believe that she was responsible for his death or not, Jessica carefully considers her response. The perceived power over her abuser might be healthy, but Jessica is concerned about the long-term affects this belief might cause. "I'm glad you were able to run away last night. You sure were strong to do that," she says, avoiding the responsibility issue for now.

"That's cuz I'm a brave girl. You're a nice lady. I like you," *Carol* says showing the attention span of a child her age.

"I'm glad you like me. I like you too. I can tell you are a brave girl, and smart too!" Jessica adds. "My name is Jessica. Do you want me to call you Amanda?"

"No, my daddy calls me Baby Girl, but I don't like that name."

"What name do you like?" Jessica asks.

"I like the name they call me when we are together in the hiding place. They call me *Carol*."

"*Carol* huh? I like that name too," Jessica says reassuringly. "Do you want to tell me about what happened last night?"

"Okay. I can tell you cuz you are my friend," *Carol* says, happy to have someone to call friend. "You are my friend, right?"

"Yes, I would like very much to be your friend *Carol*," Jessica responds sincerely.

Released to go on with her story, *Carol* proceeds. "Daddy was at our house and he said that he wanted the stuff he came for. Then the *other daddy* talked to him and said that *he* had plans and that Amanda would be his forever. Then the *other daddy* said I had to help Daddy again tonight because he wasn't feeling good and he might die if I didn't help him.

"But *Dana* said I didn't have to help Daddy. She stood in front of the *other daddy* and told me to run far away and hide. So I did and it worked cuz now Daddy is dead. But not the *other daddy*, he's still alive and he is real mad too. He said he is gonna make me sorry that I ran away, but I'm not sorry. I'm glad that I ran away cuz now Daddy is dead."

"So you are happy that Daddy, uh, your daddy is dead now?" Jessica asks for clarification.

"Yes, I am happy because that means I don't have to help him any more. Right?" *Carol* asks just to be sure.

"That's right *Carol*, he can't hurt you any more," Jessica says as her eyes fill with tears of compassion and sorrow. Wanting desperately to comfort her, Jessica can only hug her, rocking her gently in her arms as she repeats, "He can't hurt you any more."

Jumping off the couch, Carol says to Jessica, "Look what I can do!" She takes a few, well calculated steps and turns a cartwheel in the middle of Jessica's living room, ending with a big, "Ta Da!"

Chapter Eight

Walking through the college halls open a flood gate of memories for Tom: the smell of text books and industrial-strength cleaner, the sea of humanity flowing to their next class, and the sounds of laughter and chatter as friends greet each other. Pushing his way through the crowd, it is easier than Tom had imagined to remember where every classroom is, the offices, and even the teachers' lounge.

His appointment with Professor Walsworth is in 10 minutes. Picking up his pace, he heads toward the Psych department. His stomach begins to knot up as he remembers the paper he turned in that explained how multiple personalities could not exist. He received a decent grade on the paper because of the research he put into it, but he was unable to convince the professor of his point of view or refute the statistics. Now, with a firm conviction that it does indeed exist, he is calling on the one person that seems to understand the disorder better than anyone else Tom knows.

Walking into the lecture hall, Tom immediately spots Professor Walsworth at the front, talking with a student. He looks exactly as Tom remembers: clean cut, tweed jacket, jet black hair, and the childlike expression that never seems to leave his face. Out of respect for the learning process, Tom decides to take a seat and wait for the conversation between the professor and the student to end on it's own.

As the student turns to leave, Professor Walsworth looks up to Tom. "Stay there Tom, I'll come to you," he says as he starts climbing the steps to sit beside Tom. "It's good to see you again Tom. Tell me; to what do I owe this privilege?"

"Thank you, sir. But the privilege is entirely mine," Tom says as he stands to shake his hand. "I really appreciate you taking the time to see me. I know you are extremely busy."

"I always have time for students, even if you have graduated, you are always a learner," Professor Walsworth responds.

"There is no doubt of that Professor, no doubt of that," Tom says. "I've come to talk with you about my fiancée." Seeing the confused expression on the professor's face, Tom adds, "We're not having problems or anything, it's...well...I think she needs some help and I'm not sure what to do about it."

"Go on," Professor Walsworth says politely.

"Well, I didn't really notice anything wrong until this weekend. I just thought she was playful at times, pretending to be different people. But this weekend," Tom sighs heavily as his mind races through the events of the last few days, "well, I believe she has other personalities. In fact, a few of them talked to me and my sister. See, she was sexually abused by her father during her childhood. The real clincher is that her father, well, he died Saturday night. Things are just getting so crazy. I really want to help her Professor Walsworth, I'm just not sure what to do."

"First order of business is to take a breath," Professor Walsworth observes with a smile. "This is definitely an interesting situation. You say you talked to some of the other personalities? How could you tell it wasn't just her?"

"I'm not sure how to describe it. Her voice changed, the look on her face was different, and her actions...they were definitely different. She tried to make a pass at my sister, right there in front of me! That's definitely not something Amanda would do normally. And yesterday, my sister told me she spoke with one that called herself *Carol*. Apparently this *Carol* part is very young, like a little child. There's also one that seems to be a very old lady. She's polite, but fragile like. When she talks, the voice is shaky and weak."

Professor Walsworth sits silently for a moment before inquiring further. "You mentioned her father's death this weekend. How did he die?"

"He went to visit Amanda Saturday night. On his way home, he had a heart attack that apparently caused a car accident. He was pronounced dead at the scene."

"What has...Amanda...is that her name?" Professor Walsworth asks to be sure. With Tom's nod of confirmation, the professor proceeds. "What has Amanda's reaction been to her father's death?"

"Well, her first reaction was to take responsibility for his death because he was visiting with her at the time. Then, her mother added insult to injury by telling her it was Amanda's fault because she called and asked her father to come over. She claims that Amanda told her we had a fight and she needed her father to come talk with her about it. She says that it's the stress of our relationship that made her father's heart give out." Shaking his head in disbelief of his own memory, Tom adds, "Amanda's mom even kicked us out of her house. She said it was MY fault that he died because his life was perfect until I stepped in and messed up Amanda's life."

"How are you dealing with all of this?" The professor asks, sincerely concerned about Tom's well-being.

Tom, being forced to consider his own thoughts and feelings again, looks down at the floor. Feelings of shame and confusion overwhelm his thoughts. "Honestly, I don't think I'm doing very well. Professor, I haven't told anyone this yet, but I had a dream Saturday night that I killed Amanda's father. The fact that he was so horrible to her makes me so angry.

"In a way, I'm glad that he is dead. This way I don't have to worry about what I will do to him. I really didn't know how I would handle it the next time he called her his 'Baby Girl'. I honestly don't know if I could hold back my rage. Now I don't have to worry about it. Now I just want to make everything okay for Amanda. I just want to take away her pain and give her a happy life for a change."

"Tom, I hope you paid attention enough in class to know that you can not take away another person's feelings, painful as they might be. But you can help Amanda deal with the feelings that come up. How much does Amanda remember about her childhood?"

"Well, she doesn't talk about her childhood much. I didn't think too much about that until the incident on Saturday made me look at our conversations in a different light. Amanda doesn't remember her father's abuse. She thinks of him as a decent father and great provider. But according to my sister, this Carol part thinks that she killed her father because she wouldn't 'help' him Saturday night."

"What do you mean?"

"*Carol* told Jessica, my sister, that her father always said that if she didn't have sex with him, he would die. Well, Saturday night, she ran away from him instead of having sex with him and he died. She seems to be happy about his death, unlike Amanda who is devastated with it." For the moment, Tom must deal with the facts and put his own feelings aside. He can't afford to allow his natural reaction of disgust to interfere with his ability to explain the situation clearly to Professor Walsworth.

"Tom, I think you are probably right about what is happening with Amanda. She is going to need some professional help as I'm sure you realize at this point. As supportive as you and your sister have been, and will continue to be, Amanda needs someone that can help her through the process of discovery and healing. It's going to be a long journey for you all. Do you think you will be up to the challenge?"

"Do I have a choice?" Tom says sarcastically.

"Of course you do, Tom. You can walk away you know," Professor Walsworth says as he searches Tom's eyes for the true answer, even if Tom doesn't say it.

"Professor, I love Amanda more than I can say. I am not going to abandon her because of the actions her father took. This is the second time I've been asked this question. But there's one thing that no one seems to understand. My love for Amanda isn't conditional or dependent on her behaviors. I have a God-given love for her that nothing can change. I know it's going to be hard, and it's not really something I'm looking forward to, but I can't just leave her. Next to God, she is the most important part of my life."

Smiling at the agreement between Tom's words and his eyes, Professor Walsworth continues, "Then Tom, please consider this. Each one of those parts within, make up Amanda as a whole. They aren't intruders that need to be evicted. That love you have for Amanda, needs to include each part of her that you meet. You might really be surprised at the different ways she views life, the different talents and skills that you don't even know she has. Treat them as individuals, but love them as part of Amanda. The love you show them can be the key to their healing."

Allowing a few minutes for this information to sink into Tom's mind, Professor Walsworth stands and walks to his desk to retrieve a business card.

Tom begins to consider the professor's words. He knows that he loves Amanda, but can he love every part of her? What about the one that is so cruel? How can he show love to them all and to each one individually? Obviously, that is important, but how can it be done? Consciously slowing his thoughts, he reminds himself to take it one day at a time. Today, he knows of one little girl to whom he can show love. He'll consider the others at a later time.

Professor Walsworth returns to Tom, card in hand. "I want to suggest someone for you and Amanda to see. He specializes in helping people with dissociative disorders and he's a Christian, which I know is important to you. His name is Travis Brown. If you would like, I can call him and share the information that you have given me today. His schedule is usually pretty full, but I have a feeling he would make some time for Amanda."

"Thank you Professor Walsworth. I would appreciate you giving him a call. I'm not sure how I'm going to get Amanda to agree to go see him, but I'm definitely going to try." Tom assures him.

"You need to take advantage of the opportunity as well Tom. If Amanda doesn't feel comfortable with the two of you seeing the same person, you'll need to find someone else to see. You are going to need as much support as Amanda will through all of this," Professor Walsworth cautions.

"Of course, that does make sense. Thank you so much Professor Walsworth. I can't tell you how much I appreciate you taking the time to meet with me today."

"Anytime Tom. Good luck with your learning," Professor Walsworth says as he smiles and shakes Tom's hand.

As soon as Tom is in his car, he reaches for his phone to check in with his assistant. With Mr. Clark's funeral just a few days away, he has several errands to take care of before he can be with Amanda again. Driving straight to the florist, he orders some flowers to be delivered to the funeral home and takes a potted plant with him.

Tom is not quite sure how this meeting with Victoria Clark is going to end. He just can not force himself to accept the fact that this woman who bore Amanda could sit idly by and allow such dark things to happen to her own child.

Tom sat in his car for a few minutes, after pulling into the Clark's driveway, to carefully weigh this decision. This must be done, not only for Amanda, but for his own sanity. What good would his silence serve in Amanda's healing? Considering Victoria's grief, he cautions himself to be gentle. Praying for understanding, wisdom and patience, Tom proceeds forward.

He rings the doorbell not knowing what to expect. After a few seconds the door opened and there she stood. Trying to contain himself, Tom manages a very cordial, "Good afternoon, Mrs. Clark. May I speak with you for a few minutes?"

"Tom, I'm really rather busy right now. Can you come back later?" Victoria asks, not wanting to deal with this man right now.

"No, actually, this can't wait. I'm sorry to disturb you, but it's really important," Tom insists.

Reluctantly, Victoria opens the door and motions for him to enter. Checking her manners, Victoria immediately introduces him to the woman sitting on the sofa. "Libby, I'd like you to meet Tom, Amanda's fiancée. Tom, this is Libby Clark, Everett's sister-in-law."

"It's nice to meet you," Tom says, quickly considering this slight intrusion into his plan. "I apologize for the disruption, but I need to speak with Mrs. Clark for just a minute."

Excusing herself, Libby offers to take the plant from Tom and make some fresh coffee. Smiling at Tom as she relieves him of the potted plant, she leaves the two alone in the living room for their conversation. Remembering which chair Mr. Clark preferred, Tom mindfully moves past it to the sofa. Nervously, they both sit down.

"I am sorry to disrupt your visit, but I really think we need to talk about Amanda," Tom begins.

"So talk," she responds shortly. Strangely, Victoria's posture reminds Tom of the movies in which a queen settles into her throne before pronouncing judgment.

"I know that you are upset, and I don't blame you. But Amanda needs you right now. She is already blaming herself for her father's death, and frankly, she isn't doing well," Tom explains. "I'm not really concerned at this point about what you think about me. I'm just concerned about you and Amanda. You are the ones that are hurting right now. The issues you have with me can be put on hold until later."

Despite her anger, Victoria does have a concern for her daughter that can't be ignored. "What's wrong with Amanda? What do you mean, 'she isn't doing well'?"

"Well, there are several things going on with Amanda right now. But it is important, for her and you both, to have the opportunity to grieve the passing of Mr. Clark together. You might be surprised how much strength you can gain from each other. And I'm here, to help you both. I am not trying to take his place by any stretch of the imagination. I'm just offering my support and help in whatever way you need it."

Taken back a bit by Tom's kindness and unsure of how to respond, she instinctively looks toward Everett's chair for his guidance before responding.

The reality of the vacant chair strikes hard at the emptiness she is feeling inside. After years of looking to her husband before taking any action, Victoria gets her first glimpse of independent thinking. In a single wave of realization, she begins to understand that the anger she showed before really belonged to Everett. She was acting on his emotions for him, like she had done most of her life.

"Thank you, Tom, for your concern and your honesty. I think I need to give my daughter a call," Victoria says.

"Good," Tom says as he sighs with relief. "She is staying with my sister and brother-in-law right now. I'll give you their phone number. I'm certain she will be glad to hear from you. Now, is there anything I can do for you? I don't want to be pushy, but I want you to know that I am available."

"Yes, as a matter of fact, there is something you can do. You can bring me my daughter. The two of you are welcomed to have dinner here tonight. I have a few extra rooms. Amanda can stay in her old room. Libby is staying in the guest room, and I'm sure we can fix the basement up for you. This way we can all be together, and help each other through this, just as you said."

Not wanting to commit to a plan on Amanda's behalf, Tom responds, "Thank you for such a nice offer. I'll talk it over with Amanda. I have one other stop to make before I see her, but I'll talk it over with her this afternoon."

Taking her first steps of independence and free thinking, Victoria begins to break loose from the years of emotional bondage. No longer required to hold and maintain Everett's anger for him, she can actually explore those hints of compassion that she has been hiding from the world. Feeling the freedom to express herself at last, Victoria hugs Tom as they say good-bye. She feels like a teenager again, almost excited, but definitely freed.

Relieved and energized by a successful visit, Tom proceeds to his next stop, the toy store. Knowing exactly what he wants, he passes through the video games and bicycles, directly to the stuffed animals. Quickly scanning the animals, Tom searches for the biggest, most cuddly teddy bear. High on the top shelf, he spots exactly what he was looking for. A light brown, soft, teddy bear with a pretty blue bow tied around its neck.

Not waiting for assistance, Tom reaches above his head and pulls the big bear down. Hugging it tightly to see if it is as cuddly as it looks, he quickly proceeds to the checkout line. Pleased with the events of the day, Tom turns his thoughts to Amanda, hoping that she will be just as happy.

Returning to his car, Tom calls his office again on his way to Jessica's house. Business taken care of, Tom can focus on Amanda again. Pulling into Jessica's driveway, Tom is feeling pretty good. Not taking much notice to the fact that Jessica's car is missing, he grabs the teddy bear from the passenger's seat and walks to the front door. Not bothering to knock, he opens the door for himself. With his heart full of hope and his thoughts filled with plans, he unknowingly walks blissfully into a situation that nothing could have prepared him to face.

Sitting on the sofa is Amanda, wearing nothing but a large button down shirt. Tom had dreams of Amanda dressed like this, but didn't really expect to see it happening until after the wedding date. He certainly was not expecting to see her in such a condition right here in the middle of his sister's living room. "What are you doing?" Tom asks, without checking his tone of voice.

"I'm gonna help you Tom," came *Carol's* nervous response. "I don't want you to die, so I'm gonna help you like I helped Daddy."

Sensing that he was not talking to Amanda, he takes a stab in the dark with his answer based on the childlike voice, "*Carol*? Is that you?"

"Yes, it's me," *Carol* answers with a smile.

Sitting down beside her, Tom gently lifts the hair from her face. "*Carol*, you know what?"

"What?" *Carol* asks with sincere curiosity.

"I love that you don't want me to die. I am so glad that you want to help me. But here's the thing...you know the way that your daddy showed you love?

"Yeah, well, I helped him and he said that was me showing him love."

"Well, that kind of thing is not the way to show a child love. Did you know that?"

"Of course it is, Silly. Daddy told me so," *Carol* says.

Looking for the right words to help her understand, he tries again, "See, when you really love someone, you give them presents and do things for them without expecting anything in return. And...I have something for you because I love you." Tom hands *Carol* the teddy bear.

Carol hesitates at first, looking at Tom for assurance, then reaches out and gives the teddy bear a hug. "It's so big!" *Carol* exclaims. "What's it's name?"

"Well, that would be up to you," Tom says with a smile.

"Oh my goodness gracious, is it mine, all mine?" *Carol* asks.

"Yes, it's yours. You don't have to share it with anyone if you don't want to," Tom explains.

Carol thinks for a minute before naming her teddy bear. "I think I'll call him...Tommy. Is that okay?"

"That will be just fine," Tom says as his heart fills with joy. "See, this is something you do for someone you love, and, you don't have to do anything for me either. I just want to give it to you because I love you. And you know what else?"

"What?" *Carol's* eyes widen with anticipation.

"I'm not going to go away. I love you, and Amanda, and everyone in there, very much. I'm going to help you all," Tom says, not sure what else to say or any other way to explain appropriate love to a young child.

"Oh, that's very good. I like you very much and I don't want you to go away," *Carol* says with a joyful tone of voice.

"Now, how about you go get some clothes on and I'll take you to lunch. Does that sound good?" Tom asks.

"Yes, but can we take Jessica too?"

"Of course we can. Where is Jessica by the way?"

"She had to go to the store for more food," *Carol* explains.

"Okay, then why don't you go get some clothes on and that way we can be ready for her when she returns," Tom says, anxious for her to be fully clothed again.

"Is it okay to hug you?"

"Why yes, it's fine to hug me. Come on over here," Tom says as he reaches over to give her a hug.

"And I don't have to do anything dirty with you?" *Carol* asks.

"Oh no *Carol*. You don't ever have to do that with me," Tom says. With that assurance, *Carol* reaches both arms around the teddy bear, hugging both Tom and the bear.

"Now, you go on and get some clothes on," Tom says. "My tummy is rumbling."

"What's wrong big boy, you don't like this shirt? Perhaps you can take it off for me," *Sabrina* says seductively and with a slight tease in her voice.

Recognizing the change in voice, Tom is unsure of who he is talking with now. Confident that it is an adult, but not certain if it is Amanda, he searches for an answer that will not cause any problems.

Seeing his hesitance, *Sabrina* gets him off the hook. "Oh, you know I'm just teasing. I'll go change for you."

Laughing out loud, mainly from nerves, Tom responds, "Well, the shirt does look good on you, but I think it would be better to put something else on if you are planning to go out to eat lunch. I don't want to have to fight off every man in town!"

Responding with a giggle, *Sabrina* says, "You don't have to worry about anything. You're the only man for me." With those words, she quickly retreats to the bedroom to change clothes.

"Not a moment too soon," Tom thinks out loud as he hears Jessica's car enter the driveway. The last thing he wants to happen, right now especially, is for Amanda to be embarrassed. There's no doubt about it, Amanda sure did look good in that shirt. Any other time, he probably would not have been able to contain himself.

Remembering that Jessica had gone for food, he went outside to see if she needed any help bringing in sacks. Greeting her with a hug, he takes the sacks from her hands and walks with her into the house.

"Oh my goodness! What a big bear!" Jessica says, seeing the teddy bear on the couch.

"Yeah, you like it? I bought it for *Carol*. She has named it Tommy," Tom explains with a smile on his face.

"Well, isn't that the cutest thing. You really are good for her, you know that Tom? Here, can you just set the groceries here on the counter? I'll have them put up in no time," Jessica says as she begins unloading the sacks.

"I'd like to take you and Amanda to lunch, if that's okay with you. I had plans to take Amanda to lunch yesterday and, well obviously, that didn't work out. I have some things to talk to her about and I would really like you there for support," Tom says.

Looking at her brother's eyes with concern, Jessica responds, "Sure, if you think that's best. I could make something here for us if you want."

"No, thank you Jessica, I appreciate it. I think we all need to get out of the house and get some fresh air. Amanda is changing her clothes right now. When she is finished, we can go to that cafe by the mall. How does that sound?" Tom asks.

"That sounds great," Jessica says with honest excitement. Although Rick makes decent money, she usually eats lunch at home. This will be a special treat for her.

Just as Jessica puts the last can of green beans in the cupboard, Amanda comes from the bedroom. She still has the same shirt on, but this time, she also has on jeans and that all important "unmentionable" under the shirt. Her hair is pulled back with a ribbon and her makeup looks like she spent hours on it.

Tom walks over to her, putting his arms around her waist. "You sure do look pretty today Ms. Amanda," he says as he kisses her. Having never felt such love in her life, *Sabrina* soaks in the moment. Thoughts of permanently getting rid of Amanda so she can have Tom for herself briefly flee through her mind. He sure is a great catch.

Jessica, beginning to feel the hunger pains herself, interrupts them. "Okay you two love birds, let's go get some lunch. Tom, are you driving?"

Sighing as he pulls himself away from Amanda, Tom responds, "Lunch, yea…um…yes, I'll drive." Finding it harder and harder to keep his eyes off Amanda, he considers the four months left before their wedding. It can't get here fast enough for him. Then, he will never have to leave her side.

Silently asking the Lord for strength, Tom walks Amanda and Jessica to the car. Once they are on the road, Tom checks in with his office again. Amanda and Jessica talk quietly together, sharing a few laughs about how devoted Tom is to the office and teasing him about being a workaholic.

Arriving at the cafe after the main lunch crowd, they find it easy to get a table right away. Taking their seats, Tom looks around at the sparrows that are cleaning the scraps from around the chairs. Tom considers Amanda's favorite verse of scripture once again, relishing the fact that God is watching and He cares.

Taking notice, *Sabrina* quickly connects with the same memory. Speaking their shared thoughts out loud, she turns to him with a smile and quotes, "God knows when even a sparrow falls to the ground."

Surprised at the accuracy and completeness of their bond, Tom responds with a gentle smile, "you remember that day too?"

"Of course I do. I learned so much from you that day," *Sabrina* volunteers.

Smiling because she remembers, but not sure what she could have learned from him, he asks, "What did you learn?"

"I learned that not all men are bad. I also learned that God cares about the smallest creatures. I always thought that God was like Dad and that He would expect something from me if I ever took His love. You have taught me differently, not just when we were here that day, but every day since then,"

Sabrina explains with a smile.

Not realizing the tender moment she walked into, the waitress bluntly asks for their drink order. Instantly brought back to the here-and-now, the three of them request ice tea and begin looking over the menu for their lunch selection. Once the orders had been placed, Tom decides to jump right into the required discussion.

"Amanda, I've got a few things I need to talk to you about," Tom says, still not sure if he is speaking with Amanda or not. "First, I went to see your mother today to try to work things out."

"You what?" *Sabrina* asks, almost choking on her ice tea.

"It's okay. I think some real progress was made. She really wants to see you. In fact, she has offered for us both to stay at her house for the next few days so we can all be together and help each other," Tom says, holding his breath in anticipation of Amanda's response.

Not believing what she had heard, *Sabrina* breaks out in laughter. "You aren't afraid of anything or anyone are you, Tom Orin Morris? I can't believe you did that!"

"Why not? It's not good for her to be treating you so poorly during a time like this. You need each other right now, and that's what I told her," Tom says.

"You told her that? What else did you tell her? What did she say? Oh, this is good!" *Sabrina* says, setting her ice tea glass down on the table and turning to give Tom her full attention.

Thinking back over his conversation with Victoria, he can't think of anything to add. "That's about it, really. I told her that it wasn't good for her to isolate you and that I didn't care what she thought about me, but that what is important is that you and her have each other to lean on while you both grieve."

Still laughing from disbelief, *Sabrina* shakes her head. "You know what? All of my life, I have been trying to get through to that woman. She has always been so hateful. And you, you just march right in there and set her straight. That is incredible. And here I thought I had to rescue you when we talked about the wedding. Maybe I should have just let you do all of the talking. You probably could have won Dad over too!"

This being the first Tom has heard of Victoria's hatefulness, outside of his own experience, he wonders if perhaps he should have been more nervous during their talk. It's better this way, at least there is some type of result.

Amanda's adoration for a job-well-done certainly adds to the victory as well.

Pleased with his new ability to switch into the presenting position without causing a big scene, *Gerald* sits tall with confidence. "Tom, I hate to point this out to you, but she still wins," he says with a more serious tone in his voice, putting an instant damper over the mood at the table.

"What do you mean, she wins?" Tom asks, trying not to sound defensive.

"She is still in control. If we go to her house, she has the say on anything we do. She can still tell us how to dress, what to say and chastise us if we don't hold our tea cup just right," *Gerald* explains while demonstrating with his pinkie finger stuck straight out in the air. "She has a need to always be in control Tom. With this little arrangement you have worked out, she is still in control. Don't be fooled by her Tom, she is nothing but evil, through and through."

Tom looks at Jessica for help, or a sign of what to do next. He isn't familiar with the game rules to this new odyssey. Getting no help whatsoever from his sister, Tom turns back to Amanda. "Okay, I'll take your word for that. You certainly know your mother better than I do. How about this as a compromise…She has also invited us for dinner. Do you think we can do the dinner thing, then leave after dinner? Controlling or not Amanda, she does seem to be hurting and I don't like that you two aren't talking. Do you think that would be an okay way to handle it?" Tom asks not wanting to give up on the progress he *thought* he had made.

Gerald considers this solution for a minute then asks, "First, before I agree to this…is there anyone else at the house? I don't want to walk into any more surprises."

"Yes, in fact, there is. Her name is Lydia, Libby, something like that…your father's sister-in-law."

"Libby," *Gerald* corrects him politely. "Was her husband with her?"

"No, he wasn't there. Not that I saw anyway. Your mother mentioned her staying in the guest room but didn't say anything about him," Tom explained.

"I'm not surprised," *Gerald* says. "He's a lot like the father. A loner for the most part, except when it comes to children. He will probably wait until the day of the funeral to show up, if he does at all." Considering the situation for a minute more, *Gerald* finally agrees. "Okay, dinner and that's all. We leave as soon as dinner is over. I think I can make it through a few hours with her."

Relieved by the compromise, Tom nods his agreement. If Amanda is correct about Victoria, it might be the best thing after all.

"I'm curious about one thing Tom," *Gerald* says. "Where did she plan to have us all sleep?"

"Well, she said that you could sleep in your old room, and she could fix the basement up for me," Tom says, not yet realizing the significance the basement holds.

"That definitely seals it. You don't belong in the basement Tom. Don't ever go down there, it's bad and you don't belong there!" *Gerald* says with a stone cold expression on his face. "You have to promise me Tom, you will never go down there."

"Okay Amanda, I promise. I won't ever go down there," Tom says, reaching to Amanda's hand. Trying not to make a scene, *Gerald* allows the touch, but doesn't show any reaction to Tom's efforts.

Feeling an increase in tension, the three of them are grateful to see their food arrive. In silence, they begin to eat. Tom makes a mental note to refrain from saying anything about the basement to Amanda during meal time. The subject definitely seems to have an affect on her appetite, his too, in fact.

Wishing he could stop his mind from remembering, his thoughts flash to the time when Everett showed him the basement. "I've saved the best for last. It's not much to look at, but it's my favorite room in the house. I've spent many hours down here," Everett's words seem to haunt him. If Amanda is so struck by the mention of the basement, and Everett is so thrilled at the opportunity to brag about it, there must be some connection. There must be a very bad connection.

His thoughts began to bring his awful suspicion forward as he followed it through to the logical conclusion: Everett loved the basement because that is where he fulfilled his sick sexual fantasies with his young daughter—the same reason Amanda hates the basement so much. Sickened by the thought, Tom put his fork down and excused himself. Making it to the restroom just in time, he is thankful to find it empty so his vomiting can be done in private.

After washing his face, he checked to be sure his clothes were not soiled during the ordeal. Satisfied that his outward appearance is presentable, Tom leans against the restroom wall, trying to regain his composure. Not wanting to keep the ladies waiting too long, Tom whispers a quick prayer.

"Help me, Lord! I hate him so much for what he did to her! Help me to show Amanda true love. Oh God…help me to show Amanda how to forgive. I don't feel like *I* could ever forgive him, much less expect her to."

Chapter Nine

"Are you okay Vicky?" Libby asks, returning to the room as soon as Tom leaves.

Smiling, she practically floats over to Libby and greets her with a hug. Ignoring her sister-in-law's expression of surprise, she says, "I'm fine Libby, I'm fine." Gracefully releasing Libby from the embrace, Victoria transitions into a scholarly pose, as if considering the mysteries of the universe.

Waiting just long enough for a dramatic affect to be placed on her words, Victoria announces, "We will give that young man a chance. He might actually turn out to be okay. He is bringing Amanda over for dinner tonight you know," turning absent-mindedly toward the kitchen, she continues without hesitation, "I'd better get some meat prepared, and start working on a pie."

"Vicky…Honey," Libby says, gently touching Victoria's shoulder in an attempt to gain her attention. "I'm glad your visit went well. But we need to talk about something." Wanting to be sure Victoria is really listening, she leads her to the sofa where they can make solid eye contact. Slowly and deliberately, Libby continues, "There are still some final arrangements that need to be made with the funeral home. The viewing is scheduled to begin tonight, and we still need to have his suit delivered."

Feeling as if someone just punched her in the stomach, Victoria suddenly finds it difficult to breathe. The sense of release and freedom she experienced just moments ago, were replaced with the heaviness and reality of Everett's death. Not welcoming this intrusion of emotions, Victoria tries to steady herself and her thoughts. "Yes, of course," she responds, hoping her internal reaction wasn't visible to Libby. "We do have several things to accomplish today."

Libby's concern about Victoria's mental well-being increases with every minute. Evaluating the options, she determines that Victoria is definitely not up to driving, but probably can't get into too much trouble alone in the house for a few hours. Patting Victoria's hand, Libby takes charge of the situation by saying, "I'll tell you what Vicky. Let's take our list of things to do and divide them between the two of us. I'll take the suit to the funeral home and make sure everything is arranged for tonight. I'll even check with the newspaper to make sure the obituary is ready to run in tomorrow's edition. You can stay here and work on something for dinner. I wouldn't go into too much trouble though Honey, I'm sure Tom and Amanda aren't expecting a banquet. Is there anything you need me to pick up while I'm out?"

Regaining her composure, Victoria quickly goes through a mental checklist of ingredients for her famous pot roast dinner and apple pie. "Would you be a dear and pick up some celery and six fresh granny smith apples? I believe I have everything else I need here." Sincerely relieved to be staying at home, she sighs and whispers, "Thank you."

"Are you going to be okay Vicky? You could go with me and we could pick something up for dinner. I'm not sure you need to be alone today," Libby offers.

"No, I'm fine…I promise. I want to make dinner for Amanda. Libby, I appreciate your concern more than you can ever know, but I promise you, I'll be fine," Victoria says with confidence. Satisfied with the plan, Libby begins to gather the necessary items for her errands while Victoria begins her chores in the kitchen.

Directing her thoughts to the tasks at hand, Victoria takes out the vegetables to begin cutting them up for the roasting pan. The carrots were cleaned and chopped by the time Libby made it out the door. Moving on to the red bell peppers, Victoria's thoughts began to drift into the past, connecting with the first time she attempted this recipe. It was a smashing success, Victoria recalls.

Everett was home on a 72 hour pass from the Marine Corp base in El Paso. He made his courtesy call to his parent's house very short so he could spend as much time as possible with Victoria. He was as anxious to see her as she was to please him.

She worked all day on the pot roast, adding ingredients, thinking through the spices and mentally tasting different combinations to determine the best mixture for her roasting pan. She looked at three different cook books, and thumbed through at least ten magazines to find something to make her pot roast special. Everett didn't like fancy foods. A real "meat and potatoes" kind of guy, there wasn't much room for impressing him with her cooking.

Finally she found the special ingredient—red bell peppers. The taste was different enough to be noticed, but not overpowering. With just the right blend of spices and vegetables, the red bell peppers seemed to be the touch that set her recipe apart from anything he had ever tasted before. The flavor was perfect, and Everett was very pleased.

From that night forward, Everett would request her special pot roast dinner at least once a week. He never seemed to grow tired of the routine. Occasionally, Victoria would attempt a different combination of ingredients, but Everett would always notice. In fact, such an experiment became dangerous a few years into their marriage. Victoria's enthusiasm over her present-day meal preparations begin to wane as she recalls the first time she was punished for changing her recipe.

She decided to add some garlic to her pot roast recipe, something to spice it up a little more. Unfortunately, she wasn't accustomed to using garlic in her recipes and she wasn't sure how much to use. The pot roast ended up tasting like a garlic clove flavored with beef. She considered throwing it out and making sandwiches for dinner, but Everett would not have agreed to that plan. She tried cutting the outer layer of the pot roast off to see if she could get rid of some of the garlic flavor. Unfortunately, she baked it to a perfect tenderness so that it all just flaked apart, falling into a mixed pile with no chance of her separating the outer portion.

Finally resolved to serve the disastrous meal, she made some creamed potatoes and salad, hoping to cover the taste of the garlic meat. Debating over what beverage to serve in order to neutralize the flavor, she decided to start off with a red wine but to have plenty of iced tea on hand.

Then she had what she thought was a brilliant idea. She would serve the pot roast with garlic bread. Maybe that way Everett would think the garlic was on the bread, not the pot roast. She took out her cook book and looked up how to make garlic bread. Being careful to follow the recipe exactly, she timed the completion of the bread with Everett's expected arrival.

She felt her stomach twisting into knots. Everett expected his dinner to be ready when he walked in the door, and it better not be cold. He should have been home over 20 minutes ago. The "less than acceptable" dinner was already placed into the appropriate serving dishes awaiting his approval. If he wasn't home soon, she would need to re-heat the dinner. She watched as the clock ticked off another five minutes before she heard Everett opening the front door.

Jumping to her feet, Victoria quickly poured a glass of red wine for Everett. In one graceful move, she exchanged his lunch box with the wine and kissed his cheek. Unaffected by his wife's greeting, Everett went straight to his chair, set down and began gulping down the wine. "Hi Baby, how was your day?" Victoria asks, hoping to start the conversation out on a positive note.

"How was my day? I'll tell you how my day was. My day was just wonderful!" Everett began sarcastically. "My boss had a heart attack last night, and I woke up with a new manager. Of course, I was in line for that promotion, but Mr. "Jonesty" Johnson didn't see it that way. Instead, he thought it was time to give "William the Whine-bag" a chance to prove himself. So now, I am answering to this little creep that I trained. That is how my day was! How was your day? Did *you* do anything useful?"

It seemed every time Everett was feeling insecure, he felt it necessary to belittle Victoria. At this point of the encounter, Victoria was praying that Everett really liked garlic! "I have done a few things today, but certainly not anything as important and draining as you have Everett. I'm sorry to hear you had such a bad day. Care for some more wine?"

"I'd rather start eating if you don't mind. What on earth have you been cooking today? It stinks in this house," Everett began, looking around the table to discern where the offensive smell was coming from and what the smell could possibly represent from the options on the table. Searching from left to right, he immediately spotted the garlic bread. "That's what I'm smelling! You made garlic bread didn't you?"

"Yes Everett, I thought it might be a nice change with the pot roast," Victoria said, her anxiety level rising with every breath.

"Well you thought wrong! I not only hate garlic, I'm allergic to garlic. Tell me Vic-tor-i-a," he said, drawing out every syllable of her name. "Are you stupid or something? If I liked garlic, don't you think I would have told you that before? What have I told you about spices Vic-tor-i-a?" His face began to turn new shades of red with each careful annunciation of her name, as if mentioning it caused him enormous pain. "What have I told you? Do you ever really listen?"

Each question came faster than the one before and seemed to have the side affect of raising him higher and higher from his seat. Fearing the look on his face and the subsequent action which usually follows, Victoria tried sitting down to help Everett feel less defensive. "I'm sorry Everett, certainly you don't have to eat the garlic bread. Would you like some creamed potatoes?"

"Creamed potatoes? Do the potatoes have garlic in them?" Everett asked, half mocking.

"No, the potatoes don't have any garlic in them, but perhaps I should whip up something different for dinner. How does soup and sandwich sound? You could have salad as an appetizer while I put it together real quick," Victoria offered, hoping she would not need to go into details about why she would scrub the entire meal.

"If the potatoes don't have garlic in them, then let's just eat the rest of this meal, I'm sure it tastes just fine. Maybe if you get this garlic bread off the table, it won't smell bad," Everett said. He was calming down and appeared to be willing to let things go.

Victoria wasn't sure how to proceed. Should she tell him about the garlic in the meat? Maybe he wouldn't notice the garlic. If she didn't tell him and he tasted it, there would be hell to pay. If she did tell him, he would still be angry. If he truly is allergic to garlic, it might even be dangerous for him to eat it.

"Everett, I appreciate your confidence, but I really think we should just start over with the meal. I'm sorry, but I don't want you to feel like I've deceived you or anything," Victoria explained. "When I was making the garlic bread, some of the spice fell into the meat. I'm afraid it might taste like garlic so I don't want you to have to eat that. I'll be glad to make something else real quick for you."

Those were the last words she spoke that night. Everett's rage flashed into a flurry of fists making contact with Victoria's face, arms and ribs. When she could no longer hold herself up, he kicked her bruised and broken body around the floor. It was a miracle she wasn't hurt worse than she was, and no surprise that she wasn't able to carry the baby full term.

Everett never forgave her for the loss of the baby. He was right of course, it was her fault. At least, that's the way it felt at the time. She was in her second trimester when she miscarried. The baby was far enough along for the doctor to know it was a boy. The fact that she miscarried their first child, and that child was a boy, was more than Everett could tolerate. She wasn't home from the hospital long before Everett taught her a lesson about not taking care of his children.

Children were very important to Everett. Unfortunately, Victoria was only able to carry one child to term, their sweet Amanda.

Having prepared the pot roast and set it to cook, Victoria adjourned to her bedroom and pulled out the photo album from the top of her closet. Sitting comfortably on her bed, she opened the photo album and began her visual trip down memory lane. Flipping through the pages, she went straight to the picture taken at the hospital when Amanda was only a few hours old. She was such a precious little baby. Even this early picture showed off the features of her beautiful face.

The day Amanda was born was the best day of Victoria's life. After loving and protecting her for months inside her womb, she was finally able to hold her with her own arms. She vowed to spend her life protecting the priceless gift God entrusted her with that day. Now that Amanda was no longer inside Victoria, there would only be one to suffer the beatings. Somehow Victoria just instinctively knew, Everett would never hit his daughter.

That was one point Victoria was right about, one point in which she could be proud. She was confident, Everett never hurt Amanda. There were many times when Victoria was forced to suffer silently to ensure her daughter's safety, but it was worth the pain. Not one time did Amanda have to receive the full fury of Everett's rage. There was no conscious bitterness on Victoria's part; it was her reasonable responsibility, duty and privilege to protect her baby.

Thinking back over the years spent in silent terror with Everett; Victoria considered her reasoning, her logic for staying with him. It's true that many times she suffered physically and emotionally at his hands. Still, there were many times when Everett showed her such love and compassion. He was such a loyal employee and wonderful provider. There would have been no way Victoria could have made it on her own. Not without his finances, reputation and security.

Now she sits alone, silently pondering her life. What will she do now that she doesn't have Everett to care for? What will she do now that she doesn't have Everett to fear? A smile slowly emerges across her face as this thought resurfaces.

She doesn't have to worry about money any longer as the life insurance policy is sufficient for keeping her in the lifestyle she is accustomed. The difference is that now she will no longer have to worry constantly about whether or not the house is immaculate or if the dinner is prepared to perfection. She could even purchase a pair of sweat pants for working in the garden, something Everett never would have allowed.

Overcome by a complete sense of freedom, Victoria rushes to her neighbor's house to borrow some garlic salt. "Tonight we will have garlic bread with our pot roast!" Victoria boasts with pure glee in her voice. "Thank you so much for allowing me to use this. I promise to purchase you a new container of garlic in the morning." She told her neighbor as she hurried back to her kitchen.

So that she didn't forget, she quickly added two items to her shopping list on the refrigerator: garlic powder and lime green sweat pants.

Chapter Ten

Libby returns from her errands shortly before Tom and Amanda arrive. Though not much is said between the three of them, there seems to be a consistent sense of concern regarding Victoria's behavior. She was either showing signs of extreme denial or a complete break down, one or the other. Flitting around the house, humming songs and laughing quietly to herself were most definitely not the expected actions of Victoria, much less a "grieving widow".

Victoria quickly accepts Amanda's offer to help her set the table for dinner. Amanda, gathering the plates and silverware, notices the smell of garlic. Confused by this new scent in her mother's house, she decided to use this as an opportunity to begin a discussion with her mother.

"Mom, do I smell garlic?" Amanda starts off cautiously.

"Yes, you sure do!" Victoria responds enthusiastically. "We are having garlic bread with our pot roast tonight." Having made her announcement, she continued with her dinner preparations without another thought.

Not sure how to proceed with the conversation, Amanda decides to drop the issue. She quickly sets the plates on the table, leaving her father's place empty. This will be her first time to eat dinner at her parent's house without her father. This realization causes a twinge of sadness for Amanda, mixed with an equal portion of curiosity, tension and relief. As these feelings start to arise, Amanda's work comes to a halt as she just stands at the table, silverware in hand, staring at her father's seat.

Victoria arrives with her pot roast in the serving dish to place it on the table. Seeing her daughter's empty expression, she slows herself to watch her for a moment. Recognizing Amanda's need to grieve, she determines to quiet down for everyone else's sake. Gently placing the dish of roast on the table, Victoria tenderly acknowledges Amanda's pain. "You must miss him very much Amanda. It will seem very strange without him around, won't it?"

Startled back to the present Amanda simply responds, "Yes Ma'am." She quickly moves to complete her task of setting the silverware around the table.

Victoria reaches out her hand to Amanda. "Honey, tell me what you are feeling. I honestly want to know."

Fighting different urges and responses from deep inside, Amanda isn't sure what to tell her mother. For a minute, she just looks at her without speaking a word. Her feelings of confusion over her father are now mixed with confusion about her mother's act of concern. Deciding to err on the side of caution, *Gerald* responds for the whole. "I'm not really sure what I'm feeling right now, Mother. It's all so different that I don't think I can describe it to you. What is it that you are feeling, Mother?"

About that time, Tom and Libby join the pair in the dining room, not knowing what they are walking into. Victoria, sincerely wanting to be free from the secrets of the past and her silent suffering, considers her response carefully. "I am sad that your father has died. I will miss many things about him as I'm sure you will as well. Honestly, Amanda, I am also feeling a sense of, well..." Victoria takes a breath before proceeding in an attempt to still her nerves and gain some confidence. "I'm feeling a sense of freedom," she finally says, almost forcing the words out. "I know that is not something you expect to hear from someone that has just lost her husband. I mean no disrespect to him Amanda, and I don't want to hurt you in any way. You asked me what I'm feeling, and I want to be totally honest with you."

Tom walks over to Amanda, and gently puts his arm around her. He isn't sure how she would respond and certainly doesn't know Victoria well enough to understand what she is talking about. One thing that does seem clear is the increasing tension in the room. It isn't an angry tension, but tension none the less. This sense is added to when his offer of affection and support is not received with the expected welcome. *Gerald* does not take too kindly to another man putting his arm around him. Respectfully and courteously, *Gerald* steps out of Tom's embrace, taking just a second to smile up at him with as much reassurance as he can muster.

Moving back to his mother's comments, *Gerald* begins his inquisition. "Mother, it doesn't bother me that you feel a sense of freedom. I would like to hear a little more about why you feel this freedom now that Father is dead.

Were you and Father having problems that I wasn't aware of?"

Feeling relief at the opportunity to discuss this with someone, Victoria's new found convictions grow stronger that the silence must die, just as Everett has died. "Honey, there are many things about our relationship that you do not know. Are you sure you want to hear these things now?"

"Now is as good a time as any, Mother. Let's sit down for a minute and talk. Tom, you don't mind do you?"

"No, of course not, Dear," Tom responded and took the lead to sit down at the table. The other three followed in suit, all turning to Victoria, ready to hear, hoping to find an explanation of her strange behavior. Perhaps something she will say can help them understand how best to comfort her during this time of grief and pain.

"Well, you know that I loved your father very much. He was great at providing the material things that we needed and wanted in life. His reputation in the community was fabulous. He was a very respected man. No one could have ever known what he was like behind closed doors," Victoria's voice quiets slightly as her enthusiasm wanes. "Amanda, I have lived my life protecting you from these things. I'm truly struggling with telling you about them now. I just want so desperately to be freed from these secrets, freed from his control over my life. I hope you can understand. I'm honestly not wanting to hurt you."

Knowing that Victoria needs permission to go forward with her story, *Gerald* quickly provides her with the assurance for which she is looking. "Mother, you know that I love you. I know that Father was not perfect and whatever it is that you need to say, you just go right ahead and say it. Don't worry about me right now. I need to hear this, honestly," *Gerald* says as compassionately as his analytical, logical personality will allow.

"Thank you Honey, I really appreciate what you have said. It's just that I have been hiding so many secrets for so many years. I don't know where to begin. I do know one thing though...I know that I have worked very hard to protect you from your father's anger. Amanda, he had such a temper. I can't tell you how many broken ribs and swollen eyes I have suffered at his hand. But I have protected you from all of that. I just never wanted you to hurt or feel the pain of his judgments. I didn't want you to even know the possibility existed. I was content to be the one to receive the beatings and for you to admire your father, not thinking anything bad about him. I only want the best for you,

Amanda."

Without realizing that his thoughts were escaping through his mouth, Tom quietly says under his breath, "It seems like Everett was one for causing pain in everyone's life." *Gerald's* expression of sharp reprimand is Tom's first clue of his verbal mistake. Attempting to recover with as little embarrassment as possible, he quickly adds, "I mean, I'm sorry to hear that he treated you in such a horrible manner Mrs. Clark."

"Well, I just can not believe that you would disrespect your husband's memory like that Victoria!" Aunt Libby said excitedly. "He isn't even in the ground yet and you have the nerve to sit there and talk about such horrible things; things that you know are not even true. Have you totally lost your mind Vicky? What on earth has gotten into you?"

Stunned and hurt by her sister-in-law's reaction, Victoria isn't sure what to say. She sits staring speechless at her friend and family member for the longest time. Not even hearing the words that are still coming from Libby's mouth. She can see her lips moving, but the words just sound like a muddled up mixture of noises which combined or separated can not possibly make any sense in the English language. As Libby stands to her feet, the sounds suddenly become clear again for Victoria, just in time to hear, "I will not stand for such accusations. Either you retract this non-sense right this instant or I'm going to leave and not return until you have come to your senses. So? What will it be?"

Empowered by her new freedom and the feeling of confidence that is growing deep inside; Victoria stands to her feet and speaks clearly and slowly so there can be no misunderstanding. "Libby, I love you very much. We have been through many things together and I consider you to be more than just family; more like my best friend. However, I will not recant the truth. You know that the scriptures talk about the truth setting you free. Well now that I have started telling this truth, I will not stop because it makes you uncomfortable. If you don't care to hear it, then I suggest that you do not stay around here. I don't plan to dwell on the subject or spend hours talking about it, but I will not, now or ever, change what I have just said."

Tom sits watching the two grown women arguing, wondering what, if anything, he can do. His care-taking instinct says to get in-between them and try to find a way to reconcile. His survival instincts however, win out, telling him to sit quietly and not interfere in any way unless it becomes physical. Instead, he begins to silently pray for wisdom and peace that only Jesus can give at a time like this.

Gerald, on the other hand, automatically holds his tongue and watches. Having spent his life learning to quickly discern the purpose behind a person's actions and words, analyzing their intent and calculating the best response, he knows when it's time to observe rather than speak. This display is definitely intriguing to *Gerald*, completely out of the ordinary. This is going to take some deep consideration, but it must be done quickly and inconspicuously.

Libby stood, with her back bowed and her chin stuck straight up in the air. "That's fine Mrs. Victoria Clark. If that is how it must be, then so be it. I will gather my things and find a hotel to stay in tonight. I don't believe I'll be staying for dinner. I'll return home tomorrow after the funeral. I'm assuming you will not forbid me and my husband from attending."

Victoria's expression turns to a cold, sophisticated look of a person that is decidedly better than the other 'peasants' in the room. "Of course you are not forbidden from attending the funeral. Everyone has a right to express their grief in their own manner. Your inconsiderate words of wrath today will not take that right away from you. If you care to still attend, you are certainly welcome. Don't forget, there is also a viewing tonight at the funeral home. I'm sure you will want to be there as well so you can properly display your grief and mourning for all to see. Do you need any help gathering your belongings?"

"No, I'm sure I can manage just fine. Tom, Amanda, I am sorry. I do hope you enjoy your visit and your dinner." The anger seemed to cause both Victoria and Libby to turn into pretentious snobs, careful to maintain their dignity, while attempting to damage each other. Libby's exit from the room, graceful as always, leaves a silent anxiety that pleads for a quick resolution.

Victoria's feelings of confidence and freedom are quickly dissipating. She quietly sits back down and looks at Amanda and Tom, searching for a sign. Unable to continue under the stress of the roller coaster of emotions she has been riding today, Victoria begins to cry. Without a sound, the tears fall from her eyes in a steady stream. She has no words left to speak, no understanding left to give. All she knows is that she doesn't really know anything. Is she free or has she fooled herself into thinking that she could be herself at long last? Was it for more than just Everett that she pretended? Had she damaged her relationship with Libby beyond repair? Why did it upset her so much? Mostly, why wasn't Amanda upset by this news? If she was free to be herself, what exactly does that mean? Who is she anyway? How much more can a person take in just one day?

Upstairs, Libby began crying as she packed her suitcase. "Victoria," she said out loud to the empty room, "Sometimes it's better to let sleeping dogs lie!"

Unable to hold back his care-taking instincts any longer, Tom reaches out his hand and gently touches Victoria's shoulder. Without saying anything, he is able to portray an unconditional love toward Victoria, reminding her of Jesus' love. For a moment, Victoria and Tom exchanged a look of understanding and thankfulness. Then suddenly, to *Gerald's* amazement, Tom begins to cry with Victoria. It obviously isn't for show, as Tom doesn't even seem to be aware of his own tears.

Finally Tom quietly and tenderly speaks to Victoria. "Mrs. Clark. I know you must have many strange emotions going on right now, all conflicting with each other. It took a lot of courage to talk about what happened with Mr. Clark. I'm sorry that Libby's pain kept her from being able to support you during this time of need. I'm sure that must hurt very badly. Maybe what you need to do for right now is take some time to sort out your feelings. When a person experiences such unexpected events as you have these last few days, events that reach so deeply into a person's life, their emotions seem to get turned upside down and inside out. It's normal to have feelings of confusion as you are right now. I can promise you one thing though, Jesus knows exactly what you are feeling. And Mrs. Clark, He is here to help you get through this confusion. He also sent me and Amanda to be here with you, to help you. You are not alone."

"Thank you Tom. You can help by calling me Victoria," she replied with a smile. "Now, shall we see about getting dinner on the table? We only have a few hours before the viewing. Amanda, can I get you and Tom to work on this while I go talk to Libby? I really don't want her leaving feeling like this."

"Certainly," *Gerald* responds, looking to Tom for agreement.

"We can do that…Victoria," Tom says politely and with a smile. This welcome into the family takes some of the pressure off for Tom as he feels less and less of a need to fight his way into "good graces". Now if he can just figure out why Amanda shunned him so quickly, his evening will be going well.

Finally finding the two of them alone in the kitchen, Tom is able to approach Amanda in hopes to find out what is going on with her and how she is doing. "Amanda, are you okay?"

Gerald turned to Tom and smiled. "You have gained my respect tonight in many ways. Not only do you seem to sincerely care about Mother, you understood why Aunt Libby responded the way she did. How did you know that she was in pain?"

"I prayed for wisdom and the words just kind of flew from my mouth. I didn't know or understand until I prayed. They are both in a lot of pain Amanda. And I do sincerely care about both of them. But you, my dear, are my greatest concern. Are you doing okay? You seem a little different tonight."

"Very good Tom," *Gerald* responds with a nod. "That was an excellent way to discover if Amanda was the one you were talking to or not. My name is *Gerald* and, like you, I have a great concern for Mother and Amanda both. Things are beginning to move very quickly now. Change is in the air, so to speak. Are you up for the ride Tom?"

"With the help of Jesus, yes I am. I don't know what changes are coming, but I do love Amanda very much. When I asked her to marry me, I didn't mean only for the fun times. I know we are not married yet, but my love is just as strong. I am ready. My question for you is: Is Amanda ready?"

"She will be, as she needs to be. With things happening so quickly in the outside environment, the reactions internally are just as dramatic. Things are going to be changing in here, basically as a result of the external differences. I'm glad to hear that you aren't going anywhere. Your stability will help us all tremendously. By the way, I hope I didn't worry you when I stepped away from your touch earlier. I'm just not much into that sort of thing you know," *Gerald* says with a grin.

"Oh, well, now I can understand why. It did concern me at first, but now it's perfectly clear. You know, maybe you and I can talk from time to time about how I can best help all of you. I mean, I love Amanda, and I know her best, *I think*, but I want to help everyone in there, not just her. Do you think you could help me with that?"

"Yeah, I'm sure we can work something out." The laughter and giggles of reconciliation from Victoria and Libby can be heard as they make their way back to the dining room. *Gerald* quickly adds, "In the meantime, we better figure out how to finish setting this table before Mother gets back. Can you grab the glasses?"

"And by the way Tom," *Gerald* adds, "When you exit a room with Amanda in tow, walk slowly. Those heels are murder!"

Chapter Eleven

The relatively uneventful dinner served as a nice break from the emotional turmoil everyone had been experiencing. If only the dinner could last all night and create a diversion, an escape from the inevitable social obligations that are soon to follow.

Libby, constantly mindful of the evening's agenda, is the first to broach the subject with the group. In her typical, tactful manner, she makes her suggestion in an indirect matter to avoid sounding like she is telling adults what to do. "If you don't mind, I'm going to excuse myself from the table. The viewing is scheduled to start in about an hour and I need to freshen up. Can I take anyone's plate to the kitchen on my way?"

Ungrateful for the reminder, everyone at the table responds with silence. One by one, each stands to take their dishes into the kitchen. Unable to dodge the truth any longer, they must all prepare themselves for the unpleasant task of hosting and participating in Everett's viewing.

Although Libby had taken care of making the arrangements with the funeral home, even she had not seen Everett's body yet. Through all of the chaos of the last two days, none of them had stopped to think about what they are about to see. With the time quickly approaching, each one desperately searches for the strength to move forward.

Victoria retreats to her room and solemnly changes her clothes. She selects a simple black dress. Black has always been one of her least favorite colors, but she knows that it is the proper thing to do and the rose-print jacket will keep it from being too depressing.

In the middle of refreshing her hair and make-up, Victoria stops and studies her face in the mirror. She doesn't really look any different than she did yesterday. Her eyes are a little swollen from lack of sleep. But there is no real change in her appearance. How is it that she can feel so different inside and it not show on the outside?

Continuing by carefully applying her lipstick and then spraying a final net of hair spray across the top of her hair, Victoria feels a rumbling begin to build within her spirit. It's not something that she can explain easily, or even truly understand. She had felt this way on only a few other occasions. It seems to serve as a warning signal, like an official notice of preparation for some inevitable event. Unwilling to acknowledge any possible significance to the feelings, Victoria begins to reason with herself that it is just nerves. Things will calm down soon and she will be feeling like herself again. In the meantime, she'll put on her smile, or whatever is most appropriate at the time, and be the perfect hostess to her husband's dearest friends and family.

Libby sits on the edge of the bed in the guest room. Having quickly finished her outward preparations, she now considers whether she is prepared emotionally. She is embarrassed about the way she reacted to Victoria earlier. A few minutes of prayer and mental readiness should help prevent another embarrassing scene.

She loves Victoria very much. Through the years they have had a strong bond, even calling themselves the Clark Outsiders. When the brothers would get together instantly ignoring the rest of the world, Victoria and Libby found solace in their friendship. In fact, they enjoyed the time together so much that family get-togethers were always strongly encouraged by both of them. On the fifth of each month they made it a point to stop what they were doing and connect by telephone. It was a standing appointment that neither would break.

Part of Libby's fascination with the friendship was her belief that Everett and Victoria had a strong, solid relationship. Secretly, both women suffered with abusive husbands. Secretly, both women assumed that the other was different. Secretly, both women hoped that their husband's brother would influence their behavior for the better. Secretly, both women hoped for the abuse to end.

Finding out about Everett's behavior today put an end to the hope that somewhere in the Clark family existed some semblance of decent respect for others. It seems that with Everett, many things are dying. Bondage, secrets, and hope. Maybe she will find the strength to tell Victoria the truth about her own marriage. Maybe someday soon.

Tom and Amanda, planning to go to the viewing from Victoria's house, are already dressed appropriately. While Libby and Victoria ready themselves, Amanda and Tom finish cleaning up in the kitchen. Tom is naturally concerned about Amanda. She seems to be holding up fairly well, but the night is still young.

Knowing that he can only do so much, Tom silently turns to the One that can do so much more. Without missing a beat in his dish collecting chores, Tom prays, "Lord, please give her strength tonight. Hold her with your might and surround her with your grace. She has been through so much. I can only imagine the emotional conflict that she is experiencing. Please Lord, comfort her spirit.

"Grant wisdom and peace to the others inside as well Lord. Help them each individually as they sort through the feelings of the past and the present. Most of all Lord, grant to all of them your peace that surpasses understanding.

"And Lord, I ask that you fill me completely with your Spirit. Let my actions, thoughts, intentions and speech be so directed by you that others will see you in my life. Please Lord, help me with my feelings of anger and disgust. Help me to forgive him."

While Tom seems to be mindlessly cleaning, *Gerald* is busy talking with a few of the others inside. Some are requesting the privilege of being present during the viewing, others are wanting to stay far away. The trick will be to have the most appropriate person standing by in case Amanda needs help. If she is strong enough to handle the situation, then Amanda should be present. It is her job to maintain the everyday functions of life, the parts that everyone sees. The father's death is not a secret that needs to be kept from the world. However, Amanda may not be able to deal with this grief and continue to function normally. She has never been forced to take on so much emotion.

From deep within the shadows, *Agnes* emerges, looking more tired than usual because of her exertions over the weekend. "You called for me?" she asks *Gerald*. While she has served as such a comforting reminder of their lost grandmother for so many years, the ones that have been around the longest remember most distinctly the grief she carries deep inside.

"Yes I did. I need to know how you are doing and if you are up to helping Amanda again tonight. I'm not sure that she will need it, but I'm looking at our options. As the one designated to carry her grief, I need to know if you can handle taking on more."

"Who has died?" *Agnes* asks. After her struggles with *Everett*, she had retreated far back into the system, trying to regain her strength. Consequently she was unaware of this most recent event.

"The father has died. He had a heart attack while driving home from a visit to our apartment the other night," *Gerald* explains.

Through tear filled eyes, *Agnes* looks at the others around her. She knows that each one of them has been asked to take on tasks that are unpleasant and uncomfortable. Most of them have been asked to bear their assigned pain on more than one occasion. Having been spared from the other injustices by their brave actions, *Agnes* concedes that it is time for her to once again be called into action. "Yes, I am ready to do what is needed. What will you have me do?"

Relieved at her willingness, *Gerald* instructs, "I don't want you too close to Amanda unless needed. Otherwise, some of the past grief may 'spill over' into the present. You will have to be careful to only take the feelings from her. Your feelings must stay with you." Turning to the others he adds, "In the meantime, I think it is best if we let Amanda try to handle things on her own. If, and only if, she is unable to hold up under the pressure, then I'll have her brought to her resting place where *Agnes* will be waiting. In that case, I think it will be best if *Marie* handles the rest of the time at the viewing."

"But I want to see him laying in his coffin," protests *Brooke*. "I won't believe that it is true until I see it for myself. You can't keep us from that *Gerald*. If we want to see, we will see. You are not as all-important as you think."

"It has nothing to do with how important I am *Brooke*. This has to do with getting through the night without any major incidents. You can go to the observation area so that you can see what is happening if you feel so strongly about seeing him. Just think about it though, *Brooke* you are not really the most gracious person in here. You do your job well, but this doesn't fit into your job description, you know. Please, do me this favor."

Making sure *Brooke* is appeased; *Gerald* turns his attention to taking care of more business, which the two of them had previously discussed. "Does anyone know where *Everett* is?" Seeing the smile on *Brooke's* face, he knows he has hit the jack-pot.

"Yeah, I know where he is," *Brooke* responds. "But, he's a little tied up right now. Is there a message I can take to him for you?"

"Just get him to the observation area with you *Brooke*. Do you need any help?" *Gerald* asks.

"No, I think I can manage on my own. But tell me, why do you want him where he can see what is happening? Doesn't that just give him more ammunition to use against everyone?"

"Well, here's what I'm thinking. If he sees that the outside dad is dead, I mean really sees it, then maybe he will model that behavior too. I don't know if it is going to work, but it is worth a try. At the very least, the image of his own form lying in a coffin has got to be torment," *Gerald* explains with a smile of satisfaction.

"What am I supposed to do?" *Carol* inquires. "I don't have to watch too, do I?"

Kneeling down to her level, *Gerald* instructs her with as much compassion as he is able. "No, you don't have to watch. In fact, it probably would be a good idea if you don't. Maybe you and *Dana* can spend some time together in your favorite room. That way you don't have to worry about what is happening. If anything exciting goes on, I can tell you about it later. And remember, we record what we see through the observation room so I can play it back for you if you want."

"You mean the way you do for Amanda sometimes?" *Carol* asks for clarification.

"Exactly like I do for Amanda sometimes." *Gerald* confirms. Standing to address everyone present, he asks, "So then, are we set?" With nods of agreement and looks of determination, each sets off to perform their assigned duty while *Gerald* returns to monitor Amanda's well-being.

Chapter Twelve

As Tom drives Amanda home that evening, she silently reflects on the day's unusual events. The most curious aspect is that she doesn't feel as sad as she expected. Remembering only a few details of the day, she struggles to put the pieces together. She does remember part of the time at the viewing. She remembers being there and seeing her father. She remembers interacting with a few of the family members. Then, the next thing she knows, she is in the car with Tom.

The missed details and blank times seem to be happening more frequently lately. Having dealt with it all of her life, she has come to expect it from time to time. Once, she even asked her mother if what she experiences is normal. Assured that she was not any different than anyone else, Amanda has never mentioned her difficulties to another person. She has wondered however, when she is unable to remember whole days at a time, if everyone truly does experience the same problem and if so, how do they handle the confusion this causes. Amidst the frustration, one feeling stands out, making the vagueness of recent events seem of little importance: Tom loves her and she loves him.

Noticing her distant look, Tom gently reaches over and smoothes her hair and says, "I'm not sure how you are feeling my dear, but I know what I'm feeling." After pausing slightly for effect, he continues, "I'm feeling very lucky because I have the honor of being with the most beautiful woman in the world," he says reassuringly. Tom is both relieved and thankful to see Amanda's familiar smile as she responds to his compliment.

With no regard for "social appearance", Amanda asks Tom if he could stay the night. "I'm sure my sofa isn't real comfortable, but Tom, I really need to be near you tonight." Knowing his Amanda, Tom felt confident in the sincerity of her request.

The couple, each absorbed in their own thoughts, are surprised at how quickly they arrive at Amanda's home. Without speaking, they make their way upstairs and into her apartment. They both seem to automatically know what the other needs and expects. Exhausted from the day's trials, Amanda changes into her sweats while Tom selects some soft music. Meeting back at the sofa, they sit down together, Amanda gently resting in Tom's arms.

As Tom lovingly caresses her hair, Amanda feels herself relaxing. She can trust him to take care of her. She can trust him to love her. Smiling, she pulls his hand to her lips and kisses each fingertip, as if one would be jealous of the others. Their hands naturally locked together. Amanda pulls her feet up onto the sofa, snuggles against his chest and quickly falls to sleep.

Even though he is not in the most comfortable position, Tom does not move. He knows how desperately she needs to rest. This will give him an opportunity to reflect on the events of the day. So much has happened and it has happened so quickly. He is grateful for the quiet time to think about it all without having to worry about Amanda and her safety.

Of all the conversations and interactions he experienced today, two statements struck Tom as having a significant impact on the situation: the basement was a very bad place and Victoria believed she had saved Amanda from any harm. These two truths are strangely intertwined yet, separate. Combined at their core was the common thread of an abusive person, Everett. Although Amanda has not said it yet, Tom guesses that somewhere in the twisted manipulation, Everett probably made Amanda feel she was protecting her mother as well. So, for a lifetime, these two women allowed this man to abuse them without saying a word because they were protecting each other.

Marveling at the scope of human relationships, Tom begins to see how mother and daughter do not even realize the common ground they share. The first steps were taken to share the information tonight, but so many more steps would need to be taken before this common ground is fully understood by the two of them. It is so easy for an outsider to see. Why can't they see it?

What if Tom just goes to Victoria and tells her the truth about how Everett treated Amanda. Surely then she would understand Amanda's feelings better. Then Victoria could offer Amanda support, real support. She might even know about multiple personalities and could help with that as well. A mother's love and kindness can only serve to make things better.

Then again, how would Victoria really react? As Tom pondered this question, a vision of a full grown, prim and proper woman, spontaneously combusting suddenly appears in his mind. She spent her whole life taking beatings so Amanda could be protected. It wasn't like she didn't try to help Amanda. How will she feel to find out the beatings were in vain? Would she be grateful to Tom for sharing this information? And worse yet, what if she already knows? After all, it happened right under her nose, down in that horrific basement.

The situation is definitely too volatile for such a risky move. Tom finally concludes that he must be patient and let things happen naturally, with his support, not his interference. He needs to find a way to get Amanda to the therapist so he can have some professional direction and support. That way, if someone does mess things up, it will be a professional, not him! With that issue solved, Tom's mind gradually gives way to his exhaustion and allows him to drift into a restless sleep.

Although her body was resting quietly, Amanda was having a fitful night. Her dreams seem so real, but impossible. Walking alone on a beach, she is confronted by her father. He is angry with her but she isn't sure why. Instead of hitting her, he calls for her mother. Amanda watches as, in her dream, her mother appears from nowhere. Amanda's father immediately grabs her mother and begins hitting her in the face. With each strike, he turns to Amanda and says very clearly, "This is your fault! I'm hitting her because I can't hit you."

Amanda, confused and afraid, makes no attempt to stop him. Silently she watches as the beating continues. The guilt and shame she feels steadily increases with each accusation from her father. Certainly the blame belongs to her. The bruises and broken bones should be hers, not her mothers. These feelings seem so real, so clear. The message could not have been heard any louder. Amanda is responsible for her mother's pain and the pain is great. Amanda must be punished.

Suddenly, her thoughts turn toward Tom. What would Tom think if he knew the truth. Surely he could not love her any longer. Who could possibly love her? She is responsible for her mother's pain. Responsible. . .responsible. . .responsible for her father's death as well. It was her fault that he died. How could Tom possibly love someone that is responsible for the death of her own father and the pain of her mother? Surely she was not worthy of anyone's love, especially not his! Amanda's nightmares continued for hours, although it felt like days.

Tom's dreaming is much more romantic in nature, but just as telling in truths. In his dream, Amanda is dressed as a fair maiden and he is escorting her through a wooded path to her awaiting castle of dreams. As they walk along, dragons occasionally swoop from the sky, attempting to attack his beloved Amanda. Armed with only a sword, Tom quickly steps between the dragons and his love, batting the ghastly beasts away with his weapon of steel.

Their path is covered with beautiful flowers of different colors, shapes and sizes. Amanda reaches out to grab hold of one of the bud filled vines when Tom quickly interferes. Being the expert knight, Tom immediately recognizes the poisonous thorns attached to the vines. Using his sword once again, he cuts away the thorns from the vines, cleansing the object for his bride-to-be's enjoyment.

The castle seems to slowly disappear on the horizon as if they are walking backwards, their progress seeming to be reversed. Tom fears that the longer they are out in the open, the perils that they encounter will increase. Added to the dragons and poisonous thorns, now he finds himself face-to-face with an evil knight from another kingdom. This battle lasts longer than his brief duels with the dragons, and actually causes Tom more fear and anxiety. His concern is not for himself but for the safety of his fair maiden. No matter what he must get her to the castle and to safety.

Completely unaware of his actions, Tom's arms begin to thrash about as, in his dream, he attempts to protect his beloved beauty from the evil knight. Practically throwing Amanda to the floor with his sudden movements, she is abruptly awakened. The shear fear of the potential fall causes her to scream, which in turn, forces Tom to react. His instinct to protect immediately brings his feet to the floor and his body fights to be erect and ready to either fight or run. This motion adds to the initial momentum of Amanda's body toward the floor and finally succeeds in planting her firmly on her living room carpet.

Both of them completely awake and thoroughly frightened, Tom and Amanda try to slow their heart rates down and figure out what happened. Eyes darting around the room in an attempt to identify the danger, Tom offers to assist Amanda to her feet. Finally satisfied that no intruder has caused the unfortunate awakening, the only possible conclusion left is that the sofa is not large enough for both of them to sleep on comfortably. Neither wants to sleep alone, but neither wants to admit to being afraid. The truth is; both of them are afraid. Especially after the frightening way they were awakened from their equally frightening dreams.

Without much discussion, they agree to adjourn to the bedroom together for the remainder of the night. It isn't an agreement based on sexual desire for each other. It is simply a matter of survival at this point. They both need sleep, and two is safer than one, or so the saying goes.

Tom moves sleepily behind Amanda as she crawls between the sheets, her back toward the door. Tom slips into position behind her, resting his arm on hers. This is definitely more comfortable than the sofa. Not only is there room to stretch out a little, but there are no boards or springs jabbing Tom in the ribs. As he settles in, his mind begins to focus on the fact that Amanda is lying in his arms…in bed and in his arms…alone, in bed and in his arms. Involuntarily, his hand begins to caress her arm, currently covered by her sweat shirt. The feelings of sleepiness seem to gradually be disappearing. Spurred on by the residual feelings of heroism, Tom's usual restraint is beginning to disappear.

As if she could read his mind, *Sabrina* turns and begins a seductive, lingering kiss. Feeding off of each other's reactions, the resolve to wait for their wedding night, once demonstrated so faithful, gradually gives way to complete abandon.

The next few hours are filled with intimate exploration. The awkward touches of new lovers mix with natural reactions to create a memorable experience for both *Sabrina* and Tom. For a brief instant, *Sabrina* considers how Amanda would feel if she knew the joys and pleasures being kept from her by *Sabrina's* actions. *Sabrina* quickly dismisses these thoughts—determining that Amanda's loss is her gain—and turns her attention to her life-long role of "taking" what Amanda isn't ready for. This time, *Sabrina* is more than happy to oblige.

The seemingly endless days and nights of self-control and containment Tom has imposed on himself over the last year have come to an end. The suspense and intrigue are instantly being replaced with gratification, adoration and, strangely enough, guilt. Not necessarily guilt about having sex with Amanda before their wedding, but guilt for not feeling bad about it.

****

The next two days pass with Amanda acting as if nothing happened. She doesn't talk about their night of passion or any of the potential consequences. This disturbs Tom slightly as it seems, in stark contrast to his experience, the night had little impact on Amanda. He concludes that it must be a result of the stress from the events of the past week. Tom hopes that today's activities, as difficult as they are, will help put her mind at ease.

Tom knows that after the funeral he is expected to go back to Victoria's house. He dreads it. Victoria has been so unpredictable. She seems to constantly revolve between sad, happy, indifferent and ecstatic. Consequently, her behavior isn't always appropriate for the social setting.

Seated in the living room Tom is amazed at how much these 'post funeral gatherings' resemble a women's social luncheon. *Gerald*, who has been observing Tom, feels that now might be a good time for their little talk. He knows that Tom will gladly take an excuse to leave the social scene and, in spite of the potential issues this discussion can cause for Tom, it is something that can't be postponed any longer. As predicted, it doesn't take much convincing for Tom to follow *Gerald* outside where they can be alone.

"It's kind of boring in there with all those ladies, isn't it?" *Gerald* asks.

"Well, I don't want to be rude, but...yes it is definitely boring. Are you doing okay?"

"Me? I'm fine, but thanks for asking. I actually have something I need to talk with you about though. I promised to talk things through with you from time to time and it's one of those times."

"Oh, I see. So this is, uh, *Gerald*...right?" Tom asks, a little taken back.

"You've got it. I think it's an appropriate time to bring something up that is really important."

"Okay, go for it."

"Well, I like you and don't want to see you blow it but I'm thinking you are heading that way. You see, it's about the other night when you two, um, made love."

Tom interrupts *Gerald*, thinking he understands where he is going with this "special" talk. "Oh, I know. I really shouldn't have done that. I really did plan to wait, but it was just too much to say no to, you know?"

Gerald sighs and looks away from Tom, pondering how to proceed. Bringing his thoughts together, *Gerald* starts up again slowly. "Tom, I'm not sure how you are going to feel about this information. You may or may not understand the full implications up front, but I'll try to make it clear for you. It's not just a matter of waiting until your wedding night. There's more to it than that."

Tom tries to clear his mind of the preconceived notions he has so nothing will interfere with understanding what is being said. "Okay *Gerald*, I'm listening," Tom says to indicate that *Gerald* now has his full attention.

"It's like poison oak. I mean, the poison oak bush isn't ugly, but it can really leave you itching and feeling pretty bad. Not that Amanda has poison oak or anything; it's the fact that there is no warning to the danger."

"Okay *Gerald*. I'm definitely confused now. How about just spitting it out?"

"You're right. Here it goes... The person you had sex with the other night was not Amanda. Amanda doesn't remember what happened and is, in fact, clueless to the event." *Gerald* stops to gauge Tom's reaction and comprehension.

"Um, well, that *is* interesting news. Okay—I feel a little strange asking this question, but who exactly was I with then?"

"Her name is *Sabrina*. You met her before at your sister's house." *Gerald* decides to let Tom ask the questions and put the pieces together for himself. He will add any necessary information at the end to fill in any remaining blanks.

"If Amanda doesn't know, then that explains why she hasn't been talking about it and is just acting as if everything is the way it used to be," Tom thinks out loud. His relief from the explanation of Amanda's behavior quickly turns to fear as he asks, "So will Amanda ever know?"

"That's a good question Tom. I can't honestly tell you that she will not know. It probably appears to be like a dream to her right now, if she knows anything. Eventually she will find out."

"Oh man. Okay, so when she does find out, do you think she will be angry? I mean, it isn't like I intentionally slept with another woman or anything. I didn't look to go cheating. I thought I was making love to her, my fiancée, my Amanda. Oh, how twisted this feels. I mean I feel like I've cheated on Amanda, but I didn't. Did I?"

"Tom, I think you're thinking too much man. Take a chill." Gerald takes a deep breath to physically demonstrate the need to relax. The last thing he needs is for Tom to make a scene right here in front of everyone. After gauging Tom's anxiety level decrease ever so slightly, *Gerald* proceeds.

"When Amanda first finds out, it will probably feel like you have cheated. Here's the thing Tom, we are all a part of her. In a round about way, it was Amanda you had sex with. It's just that you needed to know so you don't bring it up with Amanda and expect her to remember."

"I see," Tom says, trying to bring his spiraling thoughts under control. "So, at this point, all I have to do is pretend that nothing happened and everything will be okay. Is that what you are telling me?"

"Well, bottom-line…yes. It will be easier to explain later; when Amanda is strong enough to know that we are here. That's when she is most likely to discover that you had sex with *Sabrina* before you did with her, and at that point you can simply tell her that you didn't understand enough to know better."

His words of wisdom somehow are not providing much comfort for Tom. There is no way around one solid truth: Tom made a big mistake.

Seeing his expression of hopelessness and doom, *Gerald* recognizes the immediate need to rescue Tom from his guilt before things get even worse. "Look Tom. You don't need to go kicking yourself around the yard now. It happened. You didn't do anything wrong intentionally. *Sabrina* is one good looking chick and most difficult to resist. Chalk it up to a night of passion and a learning experience. Just remember that it wasn't Amanda…well, let's just say that we need to talk again before your and Amanda's wedding night. In the meantime, don't mention it to her and be careful with *Sabrina*. She seemed to enjoy what happened and will be looking for the next opportunity to replay the event. Look, don't worry. It might not ever amount to anything."

This new little twist brings more questions than answers for Tom. If all the people are part of Amanda, then is it really cheating to sleep with a different inside person? Will he need to spend his wedding night asking if Amanda is out before he proceeds? If *Gerald* knew that it was *Sabrina* instead of Amanda, why doesn't Amanda know? Is *Gerald* the only one inside that knows about it? What about *Carol*, the young girl? Does she know about the night with *Sabrina*? Will she see it as an act of betrayal?

One more time, *Gerald* interrupts Tom's thought to bring him back down to reality and the situation at hand. "You're thinking too much again. It's going to all work out in time. You don't need to spend your time worrying about all the details now. Just take a chill and spend some time with Amanda. I'm sure you will feel better about it if you just take a few deep breaths and relax. In fact, I'm going to let Amanda and you talk now. I suggest a quiet walk through the rose garden. That's a place that always brings a sense of peace and calmness to Amanda. Maybe it will help you as well."

"Thanks *Gerald*. I really do appreciate you telling me. Maybe you are right about that walk."

With that, *Gerald* nods his good-bye to Tom and pulls Amanda forward into consciousness. Tom, beginning to recognize the signs of switching personalities, takes his cue. "Baby, how would you like to take a walk through the rose garden with me?"

Amanda, trying to find her sense of balance and orientation, follows his lead through her parent's back yard. Hand in hand, they begin their stroll through the rose garden. Tom is grateful for the solitude and moments of silence. *Gerald* was right about the garden being a peaceful place. Certainly this will help him calm down some and fight off the feelings of guilt. Amanda is the first to break the silence. "Tom, will you always love me?"

"Of course I will always love you Amanda. I can't even imagine my life without you there for me to love. What makes you ask such a question?"

"Is there anything you can think of that would make you not love me?"

"There is nothing that could ever make me stop loving you Amanda, nothing at all. Now, you want to tell me what's going on?"

"Tom, I think I might actually be going crazy. Some of the things that go through my mind sometimes is just horrible!"

"Like what?"

"Well, like what happened today at the funeral. It's so strange I would never admit these thoughts to anyone but you, Tom. You are the only one I can trust with my insanity."

"I'm sure you are not insane. Tell me what happened. Who knows, I might have had similar thoughts."

"Well, we'll see." Amanda walks over and sits on the swing before continuing. "I've never really liked funerals. In fact, I hate them. I tend to kind of, well, go into a 'lala land' mentally. Well, today's visit to lala land took a really weird turn at the corner of lala land and the 'twilight zone'."

"Okay, my curiosity is peaked. Tell me about this trip to lala land", Tom says as he takes a seat beside her on the swing.

"Okay, but...well I can't make you promise not to laugh, but will you promise to still love me and not have me committed?"

"It's a deal", Tom says, anxious to hear about this bizarre trip.

"Well, it started when the preacher was talking about what a wonderful man my father was. He really was a good man Tom, but there was just something about the way the preacher was going on and on about it that made me feel kind of spacey or withdrawn. Anyway, I suddenly remembered the strangest thing. Do you remember the night we told my parents about our plans to get married?"

"How could I forget! That was a night filled with all kinds of events. Which part of the experience are you talking about?" Tom asks as he tries to sort through his memories.

"Well, I have a hard time remembering everything about that night as well. But if I do remember right, or maybe it was a dream I had later, but didn't my father say something like, 'You'll have my blessing over my dead body!'?" Amanda asks, not sure how reliable that particular memory is.

"Oh, that part. Yes, that part I do remember," Tom replies with a playful grin trying to keep the mood light.

"Well, I remembered it today as the preacher was running through his list of accolades. It suddenly dawned on me that we could now have his blessings. I know this sounds cold and callused, I mean, it was my father's funeral after all." Amanda hesitated for a moment to gauge Tom's acceptance. His nod and smile encouraged her to continue.

"The strangest vision overtook me as I sat there looking at the closed casket," Amanda begins her story in a hushed voice. "Instead of a eulogy, the preacher was conducting our wedding. All the same people were there. Some of them were crying—as is usual for a wedding." Amanda's concern about Tom's reaction could no longer stop her from telling about this odd tale.

"Instead of *Rock of Ages*, the organist was playing the wedding march. As you walked me down the aisle, you turned to me and said, 'Well honey, this is our only chance to have your father participate in your wedding. And look at it this way, he still foots the bill.'" Tom and Amanda look at each other and burst into laughter. "It's horrible isn't it?" Amanda asks.

"It's pretty funny," Tom says. "I'm not trying to be disrespectful of the dead, but Amanda, that's really funny. Was that the end of it?"

"No, there's more. You and I giggled with each other for a minute and then proceeded down the aisle. When we stood in front of the preacher, we were actually standing on his coffin. I turned to you and said, 'Well, he did say over his dead body and Daddy does always seem to get his way'."

The two sit and laugh for a minute over the grotesque and humorous tale her imagination had created. "So, now that you've heard my thoughts, do you think I'm insane?" Amanda manages to ask in spite of her giggles.

"No, I don't think you are insane." Tom responds through his laughter.

Tom pulls Amanda into his arms, allowing the swing to move with a natural, smooth motion. Feelings of safety and comfort engulf Amanda as Tom's strength settles around her. The afternoon has been filled with a mixture of emotions, combining to create a calming, quiet mood. The two sit, enjoying each other's presence and ignoring the world around them, as their laughter subsides.

"Tom," Amanda says and then pauses for a moment. "Tom, will you marry me?"

"Yes Amanda, I will marry you," Tom responds with a smile.

"But I mean, will you marry me next weekend?" Too afraid to watch Tom's reaction, Amanda continues to cuddle in his arms, looking dreamily at her engagement ring.

"Next weekend? As in just...seven, eight...nine days from now?" Tom asks, counting out loud. "Why then?"

"Well I would marry tomorrow, but there is this little thing called a marriage license that is standing in my way," Amanda begins with a giggle. Then turning to a more serious tone she all but begs, "Please Tom, I so want to be your wife! I know it seems inappropriate—with my dad's death and all—but I really want to be Mrs. Morris. I can't wait another four months."

"I'm not going to automatically tell you no, but let's think about this for a minute. Is it possible to get everything together by next weekend? We also need to recognize that some of the people that flew into town for your father's funeral will also want to be present for the wedding. And I don't know how things are going to be with your mom financially. I mean, I know your dad agreed to pay for the wedding, but we might need to see if she needs to back out of that agreement now. Don't worry—I will take care of what she can't or doesn't want to, but there's just a lot to consider. Are you sure this is what you really want to do?"

"I don't know Tom. All I know is that I don't want to wait any longer."

"Why the sudden need to move the date?"

"I'm not sure. I have such a mixture of feelings lately. It just seems that the wedding would bring some security or consistency to my feelings. I want something good and wonderful to remember—something that could outweigh the sadness of this week. And then, there is the other reason, one that seems to be the strongest...I really am having a very hard time with our agreement to not *do* anything until we are married. Do you know what I mean?" Amanda asks timidly.

"Yes, I definitely know what you mean," Tom responds as he feels the sweat beads begin to form on his forehead. "Let's pray about it together and have us a little talk with our best man and matron of honor. It is entirely possible that you and I are so close to the situation, and have gone through so much emotionally, that we are not going to be able to make a realistic decision. I'm sure you have noticed how Jessica has a type of connection with God...It's like, well, some people call it the gift of knowledge. To me, it's like she listens so well to God, that He can use her as His messenger. Just like you have the ability to emotionally connect with others in our prayer group. That's the gift of mercy," Tom stops for a minute to gauge Amanda's reaction. "I'm not trying to put a damper on your dream, and I'm not telling you no. I just would like to pray about things first and get our best friends' input as well. You deserve the best, Amanda, and that means that you deserve for us to follow exactly what God has planned. I don't want us to rush into this and have you miss out on some blessings."

"Okay Tom, it's a deal. I don't want to make you upset or put any pressure on you. I hope you're not angry," Amanda says, needing some reassurance of Tom's acceptance.

"No, I'm not angry Amanda," Tom says as he pulls her close to his side. "I'm not angry with you at all. In fact, I'm the one that should apologize to you. I don't always think before I act. I guess that's what makes us all human, huh?"

"Well, I'm surprised! I thought you were an angel," Amanda responds with a giggle.

"I'm going to change the subject for a minute if that's okay with you," Tom says waiting only seconds for Amanda to protest or agree before continuing. "I ran into a professor from my college this last week. In fact, he taught the psychology class that I took. Anyway, we were talking about a paper I worked on during his course, which debated the existence of multiple personality disorders. Have you heard of MPD?" Tom asks while the outbreak of perspiration spreads from his forehead to his armpits, moving steadily southward. The thought of keeping a secret, any secret, from his Amanda is just too much. Knowing that he is going against the advise and cautions of the others inside her, Tom has determined that he must tell her about the other night. In order to do this, he has to tell her about the MPD. How could Amanda trust him if he continues to betray her confidence with this charade?

"Yes, I've heard some about the disorder. Isn't that where people have been raised in sadistic families in those backwards parts of the world and it makes them go crazy and think that they are other people or something like that?"

"That's pretty close to the answer I gave on my paper. Unfortunately, there seems to be more to it than what I originally thought. In fact, it's possible for someone raised in a family just like yours to have gone through enough trauma to develop other personalities." Unsure of where to go from here, Tom stops to consider his options.

It is obvious that Amanda, herself, is not really aware of what MPD is all about. Is it possible that Tom has enough understanding to explain it to her correctly? What kind of affect will this have on Amanda emotionally? There is probably some reason that all of the insiders are urging Tom not to tell her about them yet. Plus, it's been a long day for Amanda. After all, she did bury her father today! Is it really necessary to add the announcement that she has MPD. Then to top it off, Amanda and Tom have had sex, but it wasn't Amanda!

"Anyway," Tom continues, "It was really good to see the professor again. I told him about your father and he offered the name of a counselor, in case you feel like you need to talk things through with someone. It might not be a bad idea, actually." Tom says cautiously.

"I don't think I need to talk with anyone but you Tom. You are such a great support. I'm so lucky to have such a wonderful, caring fiancée-soon-to-be-husband." Amanda says with a smile.

"So how soon can we politely blow this joint and go get some dinner? I'm thinking, Italian. We can talk about your wedding date changes while we eat. Then we'll have an idea of what we want to do before we talk with Jessica and Rick. How does that sound?" Tom asks.

"Make it Mexican food and you've got a deal! Let's just go tell Mom that we are leaving and it should be okay," Amanda responds thoughtfully. "Let's not tell her about the possibility of moving up the wedding date yet. I want to be sure that's what we are going to do before we tell her."

With a nod of agreement, the two begin their silent deliberation of the wedding date while politely removing themselves from the social obligations of the day.

Chapter Thirteen

Having been lead to a cozy booth in the back section of the restaurant, Tom invites Amanda to sit beside him. Not wanting to embarrass him in front of the hostess, *Gerald* accepts. As the hostess moves out of the line of sight, *Gerald* politely moves to the opposite side of the table. "Not to be rude or anything, but I'm much more comfortable over here. It seems that we need to have another discussion already dude."

"Well, okay. Let's talk," Tom says, feeling a little intimidated and anxious about the unavoidable discussion. "Would you like some chips and salsa before we get too deep into things?"

"That's cool. I have a weakness for Mexican food, always have. That's why I suggested it for tonight. I knew we needed to talk and I don't particularly enjoy Italian food. I hope you don't mind," *Gerald* explains.

"No, I don't mind. I need to talk some things through anyway. Are you sure Amanda can't hear us?" Tom asks, feeling more and more like he is gossiping behind her back.

"I'm sure. There are times when she is slightly aware of the actions that others are taking, but I have made sure that she can not hear or see this conversation," *Gerald* says quickly and quietly, aware of the waiter's approach.

Having placed their drink and food orders, *Gerald* begins the discussion. "Tom, I'm really concerned about what I heard this afternoon. Can you tell me what you were thinking about?"

"Which part?" Tom asks. He knows the answer already, but needs to stall for time to consider an explanation for his behavior.

"The part about MPD. You know, the part where you were asking Amanda if she knows about MPD…that part." *Gerald* responds, attempting to maintain his composure and frustration. "What on earth were you thinking about man? You aren't planning to tell her about us are you?"

"Well, here's my situation *Gerald.* I love Amanda and I don't want to continue to keep secrets from her. How do you think she is going to react when she hears about all of you, AND that I knew you were all there but didn't tell her? It's a betrayal of her confidence in our relationship. A relationship that is built on trust and honesty. Now, I'm flapping around in the wind, trying to find my way through these new circumstances while maintaining a level of honesty with Amanda. I don't want to hurt or betray her. You can understand that, can't you?" Tom asks, half hoping for *Gerald's* approval and half irritated that his actions are being constantly observed and judged.

Taking a minute to consider Tom's view point, *Gerald* pauses before responding. "I think I understand what you are saying. But have you considered my view point? All of my life, and most of Amanda's life, I have been a secret…a secret from Amanda and the rest of the outside world. In order to maintain safety, and not be put into a nut-house, we all had to operate like a whole. I have been in charge of monitoring the comings and goings of the others, as much as possible, to keep the outside world from knowing about us. I've had to whisper details about situations or people's names into Amanda's ears to be sure she can carry on with her daily activities.

"The whole reason we exist is to keep secrets from Amanda, for her own good. We aren't doing this to hurt her or betray her, as you have said. We're trying to help her, and ourselves, to survive. Can you imagine what would have happened if, for example, the mother found out that *Carol* existed? We would probably have been locked up in an institution for the rest of our lives. Do you think she would have believed that our father was messing with *Carol*? Never! We have done what we had to in order to survive," *Gerald* explains with a sense of pride and passion for his beliefs.

"Now," *Gerald* continues, "I don't know how this is all going to be resolved, but I can tell you one thing…you can't go throwing surprises into the mix like that. I'm not saying that I have to give you permission to talk or anything like that. I'm just saying that it would really help me a lot if you would let me know what you plan to do before you just jump on out there and do it." *Gerald* stops for a minute, takes a breath and shifts his weight in the seat to help him emphasize his next point.

"Look. I understand that you don't want any secrets between you and

Amanda. That's understandable. But think about this...if you tell Amanda that we are here, she will not believe you anyway. At this point in time, I would have no choice but to tell her you are crazy. I don't want to do that Tom, but I wouldn't have a choice. She isn't strong enough to hear about us right now. There are some things that need to happen first. Now, I can get her ready fairly quickly, but I need some time to make a plan. It's possible that the shock could cause her to withdraw for a while. I'll need to have someone ready to take over in case that happens."

Remembering that he is addressing their boss, *Gerald* quickly adds, "Don't worry about work. I'll make sure that someone can be available to take care of things. In fact, Amanda doesn't do most of the work as it is anyway.

"Bottom line, this is a big step Tom. This is the opposite of what we have been working for all of our lives. It's not just Amanda that needs to be considered. If you tell her now, without warning us first, you will be betraying my trust...and *Agnes's* trust...and *Sabrina's* trust...and *Carol's* trust. I know you don't want to betray little *Carol*, do you?" *Gerald* asks.

Grateful for the natural break in the conversation provided by the arrival of their food, Tom considers *Gerald's* words of warning. Settled with their ice tea glasses and plates of nachos, Tom slowly pulls together a response to *Gerald's* concerns. "I appreciate you explaining how things are from your point of view. You and I have spoken on a few occasions now, and I feel as if I am beginning to understand your position and who you are, etc. I have a sense that I can talk openly with you. Is that a correct assessment?" Tom asks.

"Yes, that's correct. I appreciate open discussion, although I can usually read through the games most people try to play," *Gerald* says, almost bragging.

"I got that impression *Gerald*. Then, if I can be open with you, let me be honest about some of my thoughts and feelings. First, I don't appreciate others trying to manipulate me. Now, before you get upset or defensive, let me say that I understand how important it must have been for you to be able to get others to do what you want. I also understand that it can be hard to believe that the manipulation isn't necessary. But, it not only isn't necessary with me, it isn't appreciated. You mentioned several legitimate issues around when and how to tell Amanda about the others of you inside. It wasn't necessary to add the comments about betraying your trust."

As Tom stopped to take a breath, *Gerald* attempts to defend his previous comments. "I know you don't think it's necessary Tom, but you have to understand that we do all count on you to keep our secrets. If that's not something you are willing to do, then we definitely need to know that right up front."

"*Gerald*, please don't twist things around. You and I both know that the comment about *Carol* was manipulation, plain and simple."

"Okay, okay. I'll give you that. But I really did mean what I said about trusting you with the secrets. It's important for us to know that we can trust you with the secrets. If not, then we know we can't share them with you ahead of time," *Gerald* shoots back his rebuttal.

"Well, while we are on the subject of betrayal, can we discuss the betrayal I have felt? Specifically with this whole *Sabrina* situation. I didn't know that it wasn't Amanda I was making love to and I don't appreciate how I've been put into this position of keeping a *very* important secret from Amanda. It seems to me that this trust thing is just a one-way street."

Before *Gerald* could respond, Tom decides to continue with the other things that have been bugging him. "Another thing I'm having a hard time with is how my actions seem to be constantly under someone else's judgment. Tell me *Gerald*, do I open the door wide enough for Amanda when we enter a building?" Tom immediately sensed that his level of frustration is rapidly increasing the tension between them. He also recognizes that he needs *Gerald's* help, not his hindrance. Taking a deep breath, Tom begins his back-peddling. "I'm sorry *Gerald*. You know what? That was out of line. I'm just so frustrated right now. Frustrated and confused, really. Can we just start this over again?"

Gerald, watching Tom's blood pressure rise but considering his reasoning, deliberately relaxes the body's posture, sits back in the seat and sighs. "I think that would be a good idea Tom. You know, you and I are going to be around each other for a very long time. It would be best if the two of us can agree on how to talk things through. I know you didn't plan on marrying a woman with others inside, especially a loud-mouth man. But I also know that if you can stick it out through the next...well, however long it takes, you will have a great wife on your hands."

"She's great already," comes Tom's instant response. "I agree, we do need to learn to work together on things, not against each other. So, what's our first step?"

"First, it seems we need to work through a solution for your dilemma, don't we?" *Gerald* offers.

"That's for sure and for certain," confirms Tom, grateful for the cooperative effort.

"Then this is what I suggest. You need to give me a few days to get some things in place. Obviously, I've never done this before, so I'm not exactly sure what to expect or what needs to take place. Just thinking things through, and the different possibilities, I've come up with a few things that I can plan. See, we have the ability to influence her somewhat, just by making suggestions, etc. We can also feed her information in her dreams. We've done that before, but the information doesn't seem to, well, to stick. I think it will have to be reinforced by additional information while she is awake."

"That sounds like a good place to start. What type of information do you plan to give her?" Tom asks, sincerely curious and concerned.

"Well, that's a good question. I guess the first priority is to let her know we are here and that she should talk to you about the dreams. If we can get that accomplished, then you can help gauge how much we are getting through and what her reaction to the information will be. I don't think she should have any really hard memories at this point in time. Although it would help to strengthen the MPD diagnosis, I don't believe she is strong enough for a full-fledge memory of the abuse."

"She doesn't seem to know much about the MPD diagnosis anyway. How am I going to explain this to her? I mean, I'm not a doctor or anything. Don't you think it would be better to have a professional there to help with this? It seems like it could really get out of hand. Plus, I've also heard a lot about people suggesting things and it later turns out to be an excuse for a strong case of denial. I don't want that to happen with Amanda. I want to be sure she is taken care of and given all the help she needs to understand what has happened and how to make things better. She, and all of you inside, deserve the best and I want to get you the best. Will you consider at least meeting with this therapist?" Tom asks, now seeing the full gravity of what he is asking.

Gerald ponders the possibility before responding. "I can see your concern. I mean, what if she totally freaks out. Right?" *Gerald* asks for confirmation.

"Exactly *Gerald*. I don't want to put her, or any of you, in harms way. If telling her about you is as dramatic a step as you have indicated, then maybe it's best done by a professional. I don't mind telling you that I feel like we are going into ground that is way over my head." Tom pauses for a second and rolls his eyes at his own statement. "What am I saying, going into...I'm so far in over my head right now that I couldn't swim out if I had to. It's not that I don't want to help, it's just that I don't know what to do anymore. I love Amanda very much. God knows that's the truth. I want her to be happy. I want her to be whole. I don't want her to remember the past. I don't want her to feel any pain. Most of all, I don't want to cause her any pain. I honestly feel that if I continue to keep secrets from her that I am causing her pain. Not now of course, but when she eventually finds out, it will break a hole into our relationship." As Tom ends his sentence, he follows *Gerald's* gaze to his own hands. Tom was aware of holding his napkin still, but he was not aware of just how tightly and completely he was wringing the napkin. It now looks as if the fabric will begin tearing to pieces if not shown some mercy.

Before Tom could attempt to explain, *Gerald* suggests, "Would you like my napkin as well? I think it stole some jewelry last week and should be punished." The two of them share a quick nervous laugh before Tom continues.

"Thanks, anyway. I don't mean to be so uptight about this, but Amanda is my life. I can't help but be uptight."

"Yes, she is," *Gerald* acknowledges.

The two of them sit in silence for a few minutes while each of them pick at the food and consider their next steps. While both of them are concerned about Amanda's safety, Tom is much more willing to admit the need for assistance than *Gerald*. However, this last little display is causing *Gerald* to look into the possibility that a professional therapist might be needed after all—particularly for Tom. He isn't showing much promise of being able to handle all that is going on with Amanda lately.

"Maybe what you could do is go see this therapist and ask about the best way to proceed. That way we have the advice of a professional. I honestly don't think that Amanda needs a professional, not at this point anyway. Once the memories start coming through it is possible that the need will change. Maybe you could get some support from this person and get some guidance on your own. What do you think of that plan?" *Gerald* asks.

"Well honestly, I don't know how much help the therapist can offer me without meeting Amanda. I'm pretty sure that she will need to talk with him as well," Tom explains.

Deciding to put it all out on the table, *Gerald* explain why he is hesitating.

"Look Tom. Here's the deal. I don't want us to go to a therapist. I know what it is they do and I don't want any part of it. All the therapist is going to do is try to kill us insiders. That's what they do, Tom. They get hold of the insiders and make them go away. I personally am not interested in dying."

"What are you talking about *Gerald*?"

"Just what I said. The therapist is going to push Amanda too fast and too hard. Once they find out the secrets from the insiders, the therapists don't think they need us anymore and they kill us off. Just look at that Sybil person. Her therapist got all the information from the insiders that she needed and then killed them. I'm not really interested in divulging all of my secrets to a therapist so I can be killed. Surely you can understand that, can't you?" *Gerald* asks.

Taken back by *Gerald's* explanation, Tom can, at first, only nod in agreement. Finally putting together a strategy, Tom offers, "I could go talk to this therapist and find out if this therapist is like that or not. I can ask specific questions to see how he will handle things. I'll even be as direct as to see if he will make you all go away. You can give me a list of questions if you want. This way I can run, like a reconnaissance mission. I'll go in ahead of time to see what the atmosphere is like. I'll report back to you honestly and we can decide from there if it will be a good idea to bring you all to the therapist or not. What do you think about that plan?" Tom asks, hopeful that he has successfully offered an agreeable approach.

Gerald considers the solution momentarily. "Do you think you can see through any deception? I'm serious Tom, they are a tricky bunch."

"I feel pretty confident with this particular therapist. Professor Walsworth would never refer me to a therapist that isn't upstanding and capable. I also know that Professor Walsworth doesn't talk about anything like you have described as a treatment for MPD. He believes that each inside person is important. In fact, he encouraged me to recognize each of you as individuals, yet parts of Amanda. I don't think he would send me to a therapist that would cause you any harm. But I will promise to be extremely alert and cautious during the interview. Is that agreeable?"

"That sounds like a good plan Tom. As long as you are aware of my concerns and you feel that you can get a straight answer from this person. Let's see what you can find out from him. In the meantime, what do you plan to do about moving up this wedding date?" *Gerald* asks.

"Well, I'm not sure about that one. I don't want Amanda to feel like I'm rejecting her, but I also don't think that moving the wedding to next weekend is such a good idea. I'm in just as much a hurry to have her as my wife as she is to marry me. It's just that I don't want her to miss out on the opportunity to have that *big* wedding she has planned. I also want the opportunity to talk to her about the other night before the wedding night. It just seems like the only honest way to handle things. What do you think?" Tom asks, sincerely interested in *Gerald's* thoughts.

"You are right, she is looking forward to a big wedding. I don't suppose the fact that your birthday is next Saturday has anything to do with you not wanting to have the wedding this next weekend, does it?" *Gerald* asks.

Grinning at *Gerald's* insight, Tom responds, "It does have something to do with it as well, yes. See, I want our wedding day to be special, unique…a day to remember only because it is the day that Amanda and I said, "I do." I don't want it to be shared with any other occasion."

"It would cut down on the amount of birthday presents too. Tell me you didn't think of that one!" *Gerald* teases.

"Well, of course I did. But it sounds so much nicer the other way!" Tom says, voluntarily adding to *Gerald's* jest.

"So, what are you going to do?" *Gerald* persists.

"I want to talk with Amanda about it some more before I decide. I'm also serious about praying with Jessica and Rick before making the decision. Maybe not anything formal, but just to ask them to pray with us about the decision. The Bible is pretty clear about seeking the counsel of many and having several people pray together. It's just that I don't want Amanda to be disappointed with her wedding. I think it should be something very special. She deserves special."

"Okay, then it sounds like time for you and Amanda to talk. Let me just make sure I understand the game plan as it stands. All you are going to talk with Amanda about tonight is the wedding date; as opposed to the MPD stuff. In other words, you are not going to try to tell her about us or the other night that you are having such a guilt trip over. Right?" *Gerald* asks for confirmation.

"Right. Tomorrow I'll call this therapist person and see how quickly I can get an appointment. I'll go alone the first time and ask some pointed questions about his treatment techniques and if he is one of those therapists that you've described. Once I have conducted the interview, you and I can discuss our next steps. As long as we both understand that I need to tell her before the wedding day. I'll also ask this therapist person about the best ways to proceed with this announcement." Tom summarizes.

"That sounds like a good approach Tom. I'll begin the internal process that I've planned for introducing us to her. It might be as simple as a dream followed up by day-time interaction. We'll see. Either way, I'll start the process tonight. You just need to promise to be available to her in case she needs some extra support. Cool?" *Gerald* asks.

Nodding in confirmation, Tom simply replies, "Cool." With a mock solute, *Gerald* takes his retreat while gently escorting Amanda into consciousness. As Amanda blinks into reality, she quickly scans her environment. Accustomed to the act of quickly adapting to the surroundings she finds herself instantly immersed into, she immediately picks up the ice tea glass and begins to take a sip. This small act, simple and mindless, buys Amanda time to assess her next steps and get into the flow of the world around her. It's a process she has accomplished a million times over, and still, it is a process with which she never feels comfortable.

Tom, catches himself just as he is about to greet Amanda with a "Hello Sweetie." Subconsciously shaking his head at his near miss, he asks himself, "How would you explain that one, Tom?" Deciding on a better way to proceed, Tom acts as if a natural break in conversation has brought them to a place to change the subject. "So, let's talk about that wedding date. I have given it some thought, and I'm inclined to agree with you that the date should be moved up some. Nonetheless, I also want you to have that beautiful, big wedding you have been planning. Tell me, how much time would you need to pull it together, the way you want it?"

Amanda thinks about the remaining items on her wedding planner. She still needs to have the wedding dress fitted. It's been sown; it's just the final alterations that need to take place. That would probably take about four weeks. She hasn't ordered the flowers yet, but she has been shopping and knows what she wants. That is simply a matter of getting the order in with the florist.

The cake and caterer for the reception is a different story. She hasn't even looked at wedding cakes yet and doesn't have a clue what she will order for the reception. Maybe Jessica could help her with that. Tom's father has arranged for the photographer, some old-time friend of his. That detail is taken care of, for now.

The invitations had not gone out, but had been ordered. She would need to reorder them. If she had them done through the local printer, she could probably have them back in one week. Otherwise, it would take six to eight weeks. "The local printer could handle the job though. That would be the best way if they are to move up the date," Amanda thinks to herself.

Then there are the dresses for the bridesmaids. She was told it would be fours weeks to get a special order, or she could purchase something off the shelf and have it altered if needed. Jessica is of a fairly normal size and shouldn't require much alteration for her dress. Amanda has asked two women from the prayer group, Maggie and Tina to stand with her as well. Maggie is probably a size eight and Tina a size ten. Those are sizes which are usually available off the shelf at the bridal shop. So, maybe two weeks for alterations, and probably a week to get them together at the shop. That would fit within the four weeks needed for the wedding gown to be altered.

The only other obstacle is scheduling the church, reception hall, preacher, musicians and making sure everyone involved in the wedding itself could participate on a different date. In fact, Tom's parents have a vacation planned in a few weeks. It would need to be some time when they are in town without a doubt. They plan to be out of town for a week and a half.

As the details of the wedding preparation race through Amanda's mind, the option of a quiet ceremony, involving immediate family members only, becomes more appealing. On the other hand, Amanda has always dreamed of a big, beautiful church wedding. She is sure that Tom is the only man for her, meaning this is her one shot at getting the wedding of her dreams. Her mother would certainly help her with some of the planning, as well. The only problem might be her taking over too many of the details. What she would probably need to do, is have a planning party. That would help. She could have her mother, Jessica, Maggie and Tina all over at once. Surely the four of them could help her pull together a wedding within a month. That would work. Every day that she is closer to her wedding, is a day closer to her dreams. Changing the wedding from four months away to only one month away is an acceptable compromise. Pleased with her decision, she nods her head and smiles.

"Can you let me in on the conclusion?" Tom asks, startling Amanda back to the awareness of his presence.

"I'm sorry Honey. I've just been thinking through the different details of the wedding. If you want to go ahead with the wedding as planned, but move the date closer, then I think we can manage to put everything together within one month. That is with the help of a few friends," Amanda adds with a smile.

Liking the sounds of only one more month as a single person, Tom responds with a smile and a nod. "That sounds like a great time to me. We can ask Rick and Jessica to pray with us about the decision, just to keep our hearts open to God's leading. I honestly feel that God will bless this decision, though. You and I have been through so much lately, and we know each other so well, that I can't imagine that God would frown on us hurrying the date along some. In fact, it will be easier to hold off on certain things if it's only one month away. It's still going to be very tough, though. I love you so much Amanda and it's hard to wait. But, I want the wedding night to be special for you. You deserve that," Tom says as tears begin to fill his eyes.

Perhaps a change of subject would be best. It has been a long day and his thoughts are scampering to places Tom has forbidden them to go, at least for now. The only way he will be able to get through the remainder of the night will be to ignore the pain Amanda has suffered in the past and his guilt of the other night, and focus on the present.

Chapter Fourteen

With Amanda tucked safely in bed for the night, *Gerald* pulls the others together for a counsel meeting. If this is going to work, he's going to need all the help he can get. With everyone present in their usual meeting room, *Gerald* begins to call the meeting to order—something he'd seen done on television before.

Brooke, unconcerned about any type of pretend protocol for such a meeting, begins by bringing up the obvious. "So, why are you calling this meeting? That's usually what *Mitch* does. You know, come to think of it, I haven't seen or heard from him in a while now. *Gerald*—what have you done?" she concludes with the flare for dramatic sarcasm that only she can pull off.

"I haven't done anything," *Gerald* half-heartedly protests.

"Okay—I was just joking at first, but now I'm really curious. Don't tell me that you grew a back bone all the sudden. I won't believe it. You've been doing his bidding for too long. Seriously, where is he?"

"Yeah *Gerald*, where is he?" *Carol* adds, always grateful to have a way to join in with the adult discussions.

"I don't know," *Gerald* lies. Looking around he sees that no one is believing him so he quickly changes his tactic. "Okay—I do know where he is, but I don't think it would be a good idea to disturb him right now. Things were going so good there for a while, that he decided to take a rest. You know he has been working for a very long time and he deserved some time off. The last thing I want to do is to bother him now."

"Why 'now'?" *Dana* prods. "What's going on?"

"Well, as you know, Tom knows about us, thanks to *Everett's* stupid stunt with Jessica. And now thanks to *Sabrina*, we have another situation with what happened the other night."

"What happened the other night?" *Carol* asks.

"*Sabrina* had sex with Tom," *Dana* responds bluntly.

"You didn't have to do that *Sabrina*," *Carol* offers. "I asked and we don't have to do that with him."

"Who said anything about having to do it? I wanted to and I'm not sorry I did either," *Sabrina* boasts.

"But he's Amanda's boyfriend *Sabrina*! You shouldn't do that," *Carol* chastises with her finger wagging the whole time.

Desperate to gain control of the situation and move on with business, *Gerald* offers, "Thank you, *Carol*. But I don't think that will help the situation right now. I've got a plan for how to handle things but I want to talk it out with all of you."

"Wait a minute," *Brooke* interrupts. "Let me get this straight... You were left in charge by *Mitch*—or, you put yourself in charge is more likely—and now things are out of control. So you don't want us to wake up *Mitch* because you know you'll be in trouble. Is that what you're saying?"

"It's not just me who stands to loose here. Think about it *Brooke*, we've been under his thumb for way too long. It's time that we have our say in how things should go and that's what I'm proposing. That we decide for ourselves," *Gerald* suggests, knowing *Brooke's* need to rebel.

"Okay—you've got my attention. Let's hear what you're thinking," *Brooke* concedes.

"Excuse me, but there is another person that's been missing for a while too. What has become of our hated...I mean beloved *Everett*?" asks *Dana*.

"Oh him? Why do you care what happens to him," *Brooke* asks.

"Call it survival or curiosity, I don't care. It's just safer to know where he is than to have him sneak up on you," obverses *Dana*.

"That's for sure," *Brooke* agrees.

"So, can you give us a status report on good old *Dad's* location and condition, *Brooke*?" *Gerald* inquires.

"Well, as you all know, the real 'good old dad' is six feet under by now. But, I'm sad to report that *Everett* is still hanging out with us in here. I made him watch the visitation, which just made him mad. So, I made him watch the funeral. I thought that would finish him off. But it didn't. He got all puffed up and proud because of the wonderful things said about the father at the funeral.

But here's the strange thing…he has been acting different," *Brooke* continues.

"He hasn't been as mean. Now, I don't know if he is planning some kind of sneak attack, and that wouldn't surprise me, but I don't know. It's like he is sticking with the last stuff he heard about the dad, and kinda making himself like him in that way."

"You mean the good stuff they said at the funeral?" Dana asks for clarification.

"Yeah. Exactly like that. Like he mentioned to me the other day that we should be saving our money so that we can be prepared for the unforeseen. Of course, I think that's because *Sabrina* had just spent a few hundred from our savings at the clothing store, but that's another topic altogether," *Brooke* smiles at her successful instigation.

"Hey! That's important stuff. I have to look good you know," *Sabrina* defends.

Eager to move on with more pressing matters, *Gerald* attempts to reign in the conversation once again. "Okay—so *Brooke*, it sounds like you are going soft on us here. You haven't bought into his sudden change in character have you?"

"No, I'm not. I just thought I'd tell you what's happening. Since you seem to be the one who wants to be in charge now, you probably should know these things." Without giving *Gerald* a chance to respond, she turns to direct her next comment to *Dana*, "No worries Honey, *Everett* won't be bothering you. He's still tightly locked away for safe keeping."

"Thank you," Dana nods, acknowledging the protection that *Brooke* is offering her.

"Okay—now that we've gotten that out of the way, I need to tell you all what's happening with Tom. As you might know, I had a talk with him today about the little incident between him and *Sabrina*," *Gerald* begins.

"It was not a little incident," *Sabrina* stands up to protest. "You act as if it was not important, but I assure you that it was not just a roll in the hay. It was everything I ever dreamed of and more! I know you don't approve *Gerald*, but I'm really tired of your attitude. In fact, I'm really tired of all of you! You all act like all we have to do is protect poor little Amanda. But what about us? When do we get to live? When do we get to have love? When do our dreams begin to count? When, *Gerald*, when?"

Wondering how *Mitch* had managed to go all these years without such an emotional outburst at any of his meetings, *Gerald* takes a deep breath and makes his best attempt at calming the situation by trying to get her to see things logically. "*Sabrina*, can you please just sit down? I'm not trying to make a statement about what happened. I'm sure it was very lovely for you. But the fact is that your "non-roll-in-the-hay" has caused some real problems and we need to talk about them. Otherwise we risk loosing Tom forever," *Gerald* adds, finally grabbing her attention.

"Now, Tom wants to tell Amanda about everything. He wants to tell her that we are here, and that he had sex with you and to apologize to her for it. He doesn't want to go into their marriage with that kind of secret," *Gerald* explains.

"Apologize?" *Sabrina* asks heartbroken. "He wants to apologize? You know what? Let him. Let him make a fool of himself. Amanda won't believe him and he'll get what he deserves!"

"You know, you are really surprising me here, *Sabrina*. You act as if you really love him," *Dana* observes. "I didn't think you were even capable of getting close to someone, not for real anyway."

"Why not? Because I'm some kind of mindless sex machine with no feelings? Is that what you think?" Not waiting for a response, *Sabrina* continues, "I know that's what you all think. I know that's why I'm here, to pretend to enjoy sex with that monster of a father because he demanded that of us, but that's not all I am. And I'm more than just someone that can have fun at parties too! In spite of what you all seem to think, I have feelings too!"

Concerned that too much emotion will begin to bleed into Amanda's dreams, if it hasn't already, *Gerald* is now desperate to change the direction of the meeting. "*Sabrina*, you have got to calm down."

"No, *Gerald*, you have to calm down," *Sabrina* reacts, not caring that her response made little sense. "You think there is a problem, then you go deal with it. Just keep us out of it. You don't want our input obviously, so don't pretend to care about what we have to say."

"Look, I do care about what you have to say, but we don't have a lot of time for arguing about things. I'm trying to tell you that we have got to let Amanda know that we exist and get her ready to start learning the truth about her past. We don't have a choice," *Gerald* explains.

"But I thought she was never supposed to know," *Carol* says, showing her confusion in the sudden change of rules. "I thought that she could never know and that's why we had to be quiet and keep the secrets."

"That's been the plan for a very long time *Carol*, you are right. But things have changed and now we are going to have to think about the rules again. Too many people know about us. We kept the secret from Amanda so that others wouldn't know about us. But now, that secret is out. Tom, Jessica, and Rick all know about us.

"It's making Tom very uncomfortable to keep that secret from Amanda. He thinks that she needs to know," explains *Gerald.*

Turning back to the group he continues his explanation. "We really have hit a major bump in the road and we really do need to reconsider the way we are doing things. Amanda is going to find out about us, there is no doubt in my mind that it will happen. Now, it can be because we tell her or because someone else tells her, but I know that Tom will not wait forever.

"In order to get her prepared, we are going to have to allow her to see one or more of us. At least that will start the process. I've decided that I will wait for an opportunity to take her on a tour of the system, show her some things inside and introduce her to the idea of us being here. I think we are going to have to be careful not to tell her too much at one time. We've done a pretty good job of keeping her in the dark, both literally and otherwise, for so many years that it might come as quite a shock to her."

"Do you think this is the best timing Gerald?" *Dana* prompts. "I mean the dad just died a few days ago. Don't you think it should wait until she is stronger?"

"Well, I've thought about that, but I don't think we can wait. Number one, Tom won't wait long. He feels too guilty about keeping his secrets from Amanda. Plus, *Agnes* took a lot of Amanda's grief during the visitation and funeral. I think Amanda is relatively okay right now. But even if she wasn't, I'm not sure we can take a chance with Tom anyway," *Gerald* repeats, making sure the full blame of changes lays at Tom and *Sabrina's* feet. He definitely doesn't want to have to admit that he agreed to these changes before talking with them. It's bad enough that he is making such a change without *Mitch's* guidance. But that's a fight for another day. Now he just has to get through this hurdle.

"And while we are on the subject of rules, there's a new one that I'd like everyone to follow so that we don't have another inci..." Gerald stops himself before calling it an incident again, "I mean...another problem with mistaken identity. When you are out around Tom, you must announce yourself so that he knows that he is no longer talking with Amanda. Agreed?"

"Okay," *Dana* agrees. "It sounds like we do have to move forward with this. You just better make sure you know what you're doing."

"I understand." As a means of illustrating how well thought out the plan is, Gerald offers, "But not to worry, we will also have access to input from a professional. Tom has arranged to meet with a therapist to see if he can gain some additional guidance into how we should go about exposing Amanda to the truth."

"What?" they all seem to scream at once.

"What are you talking about *Gerald*?" *Brooke* has now jumped to her feet and is ready to demonstrate her displeasure in ways that *Gerald* can only begin to imagine.

"Oh wait...don't panic! Tom is going to meet with him, not us. He is going to find out what he has to say before we ever consider meeting with him. It's safe and going to be okay," *Gerald* promises with all the sincerity he can muster.

"But *Gerald*, Daddy always said that therapists were bad people and couldn't be trusted to tie our shoes. He said that they would put us in the hospital and never let us out again. He said it was bad to talk with them!" *Carol* adds with true fear and panic in her voice.

"Daddy said a lot of things *Carol*," *Brooke* offers, "but he was wrong about a lot of them wasn't he?" At this point she is more concerned about calming *Carol's* fears than arguing with *Gerald*. She'll deal with him later.

"Well said," *Gerald* confirms. "Now, like I said, we are not meeting with this therapist, Tom is. Tom is going to tell us what is said so we can see if he offers some words of wisdom for us."

"That's stupid," *Marie* finally speaks up. "Just do what you know is right Gerald. We haven't had to listen to anyone outside before. Let's not start now. It's going to be a change, but we can handle this." Turning to *Gerald* she asks, "meeting adjourned?"

"Yeah, that sounds like a good idea *Marie*. Meeting adjourned," *Gerald* confirms.

Chapter Fifteen

"Where's Tom today?" Victoria asks Amanda as she pours them both a cup of coffee.

"Oh, he had some type of appointment today. I thought I'd just spend some time with you and talk through some of the thoughts we've had about the wedding," Amanda offers with a smile that does not fit the feeling of rage, which is suddenly building from deep inside for no apparent reason.

"Sounds good. You know I'm glad you're starting to come around and involve me more in this wedding. I know things didn't get off to a great start, but you really should be including your mother more than you have, you know. There's so much more I can and should be doing," Victoria says, as she involuntarily flipped her head slightly, causing the point of her nose to stand out proudly, as if it was the focus of the conversation. Filling with a self-justified sense of "you owe me", Victoria continues with an additional list of expectations. "You know, you should consider scaling down the wedding slightly and having the ceremony right here in my backyard, in the rose garden. It would be so beautiful Amanda."

"I really don't want to scale anything back and I definitely want to keep the wedding at the church. I have been thinking about moving up the date though. That's what I wanted to talk with you about," Amanda clarifies. "In fact, we are thinking about having the wedding in just four weeks." She tries desperately to hear her mother's words and respond appropriately in spite of the distracting energy that seems to be pulling her inwardly.

"Well I'm sure there will be tongues flying if you suddenly move up your wedding date. You and Tom are still waiting for...well you know what I mean. You aren't pregnant, are you?" Victoria asks; primarily as a way to demonstrate her distrust of Amanda's actions rather than an honest question of concern.

"No! Mother! Of course I'm not pregnant! Not that this is the type of discussion I want to have with my mother, but Tom and I are waiting until our wedding night. He is such a perfect gentleman! I really resent you assuming that the reason I want to move the date is because I'm trying to cover up an embarrassing 'bun in the oven'. I would have hoped that you know me better than that!" Amanda manages to complete the full phrase before her sight gives way to darkness, then silence and stillness.

The abrupt switch into sub-consciousness will be helpful in *Gerald's* attempts to introduce Amanda to the concept that others exist inside. However, this switch isn't something he had planned and might require his immediate attention. It isn't normal for *Brooke* to be out around other people. She usually confines her actions to secret acts of rebellion that only he is fully aware of. In fact, he typically tries to keep her inside and out of sight.

But today is different: *Brooke* didn't ask, she didn't suggest, and she didn't warn. She just did—she took control of the body without permission. She took control over the situation without discussion. She is unexpectedly out of control and *Gerald* is unable to do anything about it.

"Well, I'm sorry if you think the question is inappropriate, but it's one that you certainly must be prepared to answer if you suddenly move your wedding date. It's just normal." Victoria pauses to give the emotions time to cool off some before proceeding. Having made another trip to the kitchen with a hand-full of dishes, she decides to pursue the location issue further. "Well, if you can't have the wedding in the backyard, why not the reception? I really think it would be an enjoyable environment for your guests, and I will have the opportunity to show off my roses."

Although no word is spoken, Victoria senses Amanda's resistance and pulls out the 'big guns'. "Well you simply must allow me to have some part in your wedding, Amanda. It is, after all, the least you can do given all I have done for you over the years. At least permit me this one pleasure!"

"Excuse me? I'm sure I didn't hear you correctly because I *know* you did not just say that I owe you! Exactly what is it that you have done to deserve this privilege?" *Brooke* asks as she moves into an 'optimal striking position', preparing for her next verbal and emotional rebut. "Do you think you deserve special praise because you took a few beatings?"

Shocked by her daughter's behavior, Victoria almost finds herself speechless—almost. "I most certainly do think I deserve at least some respect for the abuse I suffered to keep you safe young lady! Who do you think you are? Talking to me like that! You have no idea what I put up with so you wouldn't have to feel the pain your father was capable of creating." Feeling vindicated by her own words, Victoria even punctuates her sentence's finale with a deliberate and determined nod.

"You are so naive!" *Brooke* begins. "Do you honestly believe that you can take some beatings and the man's abuse will be confined to you alone? Did someone pull wool over your eyes or did you place it there yourself?"

"What do you mean? Of course it was confined to me. You didn't suffer any beatings did you?" Victoria asks, waiting to hear an answer confirming her beliefs.

"Well I'm sorry to disappoint you Mother, but there is more than one way to cause pain and suffering on a person than just to beat them. Do you think you hid all of the bruises from everyone? Daddy was sure that I saw them! He wanted me to know about the bruises and the broken bones!" Taking a breath, *Brooke* poises for her release of the ultimate venom. "Do you know why Daddy made sure I saw the bruises Mother? Would you like to guess or shall I just spell it out for you?"

"I can not believe you are talking like this Amanda!" Victoria responds honestly.

"Oh come on, Mother! Why do you think Daddy reacted the way he did to Tom? '*Another man taking away his baby girl*'," *Brooke* mocks, no longer holding in the anger she has been collecting through the years. "Why do you think he said that?"

"Because he was upset that you are growing up and you don't need him any longer."

"Ding ding ding! Thank you for playing. Ed? What do we have for our loser?" *Brooke* announces loudly as she tauntingly begins to walk in a circle around Victoria.

"Amanda! Will you please stop this non-sense? You're making me dizzy!" Victoria accuses, still trying to avoid the possible answer to *Brooke's* questions.

In a controlled, steady voice, *Brooke* offers, "Then perhaps you should sit down Mother, because I have just begun." Waiting only seconds as her Mother complies, she turns on her heel and proclaims dramatically, "What a splendid life we have had together! You taking the beating under the false pretense that you believe you are protecting your precious daughter. Meanwhile, your beloved husband is using the constantly visible marks of black and blue to force his toy to participate in the game of the day."

Putting aside the theatrical approach, *Brooke* kneels in front of Victoria and stares straight into her eyes so there can be no misunderstanding. "No, Mother, you did not protect us from abuse. You allowed the abuse to continue. You see, all of those times when Dad was visiting his *special* place in the basement, he was forcing himself on me. Over and over and over again. And, so there can be no chance of letting him off the hook with a twist of words, let me make it perfectly clear. He didn't just fondle, or touch me, or make me feel a little uncomfortable. He made me have sex with him. From as far back as I can remember, he could call for his '*Baby Girl*' to attend to his needs in the dark places of the basement. One of the reasons for total obedience was the threat of more beatings for you! The other was that he would die if we didn't comply. Well guess what…it finally worked," *Brooke* hisses.

Completely overcome with this unbelievable news, Victoria feels herself going limp. Had she not been sitting, she certainly would have swooned.

"Come now Mother. Aren't you the one who said we should be freed from the secrets now that Daddy is dead? Why shouldn't we *all* have such freedom?"

Unable to find a solid thought, Victoria is helpless to respond. Looking into the eyes of her daughter, searching desperately for a glimmer or hint of another possible truth, she consciously forces breath through her lungs.

As if closing in for the kill, *Brooke* allows years of bitterness and spite to grow into a final accusation. "That's it Mother, sit in silence. It's what you do best." Satisfied with her triumph in forcing Victoria to face the facts, *Brooke* stands and turns her back toward her in an act of defiance and rejection.

With *Brooke's* defenses lowered, *Marie* jumps on the opportunity to force her aside and take control of the body. Quickly turning, she practically throws herself to the floor beside Victoria's seat. "Mom, I'm so sorry. I shouldn't have said that. Are you okay?"

Feeling as though the entire world must be spinning into a warped dimension, somewhere far from reality, Victoria is further confused by this sudden change in presentation. "I'm not sure if I'm okay or not. So are you saying that it isn't true? Is that what you mean by saying you shouldn't have said it? It isn't true, is it?" Victoria asks hopefully.

Wanting desperately to bring some comfort to Victoria, *Marie* finds herself jammed forcefully between a rock and that proverbial hard place. Eventually, the truth will be told. If it didn't happen today, it would happen later. Persuaded that truth is the best medicine, *Marie* confesses, "I'm sorry Mom, but it is true. I just feel so bad about how you were told. You deserve better, more compassion. It's not your fault that it happened, it just happened. You did the best you could. I know you did." *Marie* offers as her eyes begin to fill with tears. The tears are for Victoria's pain, not her own. No one else can understand the pressures Victoria has had to deal with in the past. After so many years of uncertainty and mental torment, she can't possibly endure more mistreatment from her own daughter.

Marie reaches over and softly begins to caress Victoria's hand. "Mom... You have been through so many days and nights of pain. You deserve these days of happiness and freedom. I have always known why you pushed so hard. I know you have done what was needed to survive. You know Mom, I think you have become very much like your roses. I think we all have, in fact. The roses are so fragile, so delicate. A harsh rain or strong breeze can cause the pedals to fall to the ground. We've developed thorns to protect us from abuse and predators of all kinds. But still, the offenses come. The thing is, Mom, even the pedals that fall to the ground can serve to help us grow. You know how the leaves and pedals can become a type of food for the plants. As long as there isn't so much that the ground is completely covered, it can bring about good nutrition for the roses. Those are the hardships we go through Mom; the things that cause our pedals to fall to the ground. We can learn from them and grow from them. As long as there isn't so much that we are completely covered, we can make something good happen.

"The way I told you about the secrets from the past was certainly not the most merciful. I'm so sorry, Mom. Maybe you can look at it as one of those storms in the rose garden that knock some of the pedals off your stems. But Mom, we can grow from this. You and I can see a new freedom to share our feelings and thoughts with each other. Not with anger, like before, but with honesty and compassion. Don't you think it's time for you to have someone to depend on...someone with whom you can share your fears and dreams?"

Through mild sobs, Victoria softly and slowly responds. "Honey, you are so sweet. I'm not sure this is just a storm though. I always hoped that your father would change his ways. I think you were probably closer to the truth when you said I should just sit quietly. If I am forced to be honest with myself, and with you, I would have to say that there were times that your father made me wonder what he really meant by his expressions. Oh, my sweet baby! I'm so sorry. I didn't know what else to do!"

As she continues her confessions, Victoria begins to rock back and forth, ever so slightly. Gesturing with her hands to help her express her helplessness, she expands on her excuses for the past. "I didn't have a way to provide for you on my own. I never worked outside the house. You're father would never allow that, you know. I prayed that your father would stop hitting me. Then you were born and I knew that I had one mission in life…to protect my baby. And now look! Here you are, all grown up, telling me that I failed at the one, most important, job a mother can have. All of those beatings…they were nothing to me because I kept telling myself that I was saving you from the pain. My entire life, a waste! And you, my precious baby, hurt so badly…so deeply…oh God, I can't even imagine what you have gone through." Unable to look at her any longer, Victoria turns her face away while carefully placing her hand on Amanda's shoulder.

Feelings of inadequacy and shame envelope them both as they independently begin to face the years of silent suffering and lack of mutual support.

****

Having called *Marie* to take care of business in the outside world, *Gerald* makes his first attempt at direct contact with Amanda. Breaking through the darkness, *Gerald* allows himself to be seen by her, as if from a distance. Ending the oblique form of communicating used all of their lives, *Gerald* says in a gentle voice, "Hello Amanda, it's nice to finally see you face to face. Today is a day for changes and discoveries. Don't worry, you're going to be okay, I promise."

Amanda stares silently at the figure, now standing within inches of her face. He is so close now that Amanda can see the features of his face. She ponders the connection of this person with the conflict she was engaged in just moments before. He reaches over and places his hand on her shoulder. Unlike a dream, Amanda can actually feel his touch. "This is not how I planned for you to find out about us, but it seems some others have their own plans," *Gerald* explains softly. "Don't worry about your mother, someone else is helping her right now."

Confused and a little scared, Amanda cautiously asks, "What was that feeling, that energy that I was fighting back before? Was it you?"

"No, no that wasn't me," *Gerald* assures her quickly. "That can be explained as unexpressed feelings demanding to be released. Anyway, don't worry about that right now. Someone else is fighting that battle for you at the moment. I just need to be sure you receive a message."

"A message? Are you an angel?" Amanda asks earnestly.

Chuckling a bit, *Gerald* tries to remain serious and straight forward. "No, I'm not an angel. You can think of me as a special part of yourself that has been with you for a very long time. I'm the part of you that helps to see things in a logical manner. I also try to make sure that you understand what is happening around you. As that part of you, it's my responsibility to be sure you do not think you are going crazy. Right now, you are in a dream like state. This way of dreaming allows you and I to talk and to see each other."

"Okay, let me get this straight," Amanda says. "You are my imagination, formed into a shape of a human, for the purpose of telling me how sane I am?" Laughing at her own thoughts, Amanda proclaims, "I am crazy!"

Frustrated by this latest twist, *Gerald* decides to try to simplify things. "Look, you aren't going crazy. Eventually, you will understand. In the meantime, I need you to sit back and relax for a minute. I have some information I need to give to you. I don't like to have this responsibility, but for today, I have no choice."

Suddenly, Amanda finds herself sitting back into the most comfortable cushion imaginable. *Gerald's* request that she relax might not be easy, but it's getting easier. "Okay, I'm here. I might as well play along with whatever game you are playing. I guess Tom can help me sort through the insanity later. You seem harmless enough. Do you have a name? Oh, and what of this secret message that you've been sent to give me?"

Quickly debating about how to begin, *Gerald* decides to go with a direct approach. "My name is *Gerald* and I need to tell you about me and the others. I need to tell you about yourself and how I and the others are a part of you."

"This should be interesting. Wait, wait, I get it. I'm hallucinating. Tom asked me if I knew anything about multiple people something-or-another disorder. I started thinking about that movie and now I'm imagining it to be true for me too," Amanda responds playfully.

"This is not going well," *Gerald* announces. "Look, you are not hallucinating. You are not making this up in your imagination. I am real and so are the others. Now, let's stop for a minute and talk about this rationally."

Gerald stops to consider how to explain this to Amanda in a way that will be clear but not too overwhelming. Amanda on the other hand, has decided to enjoy this weird trip she is taking, confident that her imagination has simply taken a creative twist into the twilight zone.

A new plan quickly put together, *Gerald* decides to take Amanda for a walk. "I have something I want to show you. It's very important but it will not be frightening. Are you ready?"

"I'm ready for whatever you bring. Where are we going?" Amanda asks as she stands to join *Gerald*—after all, she's never heard of a hallucination hurting anyone before.

Gerald waits until they have arrived at the observation room before explaining their little journey. "This is what we call the observation room. From here we can watch everything that is happening in the outside world. We also record everything that is seen from here so it can be replayed at a later date. We don't maintain all of the recordings for a long period of time though, just some of them. Usually, it is only necessary to keep it recorded through this method until you have seen it. That's when you automatically transfer the information into your memory and the recording is no longer needed. Sometimes another person inside is responsible for recording the information into memory though, it just depends really."

Slightly confused by the intricate process *Gerald* is describing, Amanda tries to take every detail to heart. She has to remember everything so she will be able to explain this to Tom. Surely there is a reasonable explanation for such a strange dream.

Looking around the room, Amanda sees several chairs and a few bean bag seats, all facing the same direction. Naturally following the direction someone seated in the chair would look, she finds herself watching her mother. The image seems to be projected onto a large screen. Her mother is dressed the same as she was the last time she saw her but now she is crying. Turning to *Gerald*, she asks, "What is happening? Why is my mother crying? What have you done to her? Can we hear what is happening too or just see it?"

With that, *Gerald* flips a switch on the wall, allowing the external sounds to penetrate the safety of the observation room. "Oh, my sweet baby! I'm so sorry. I didn't know what else to do!" came the words of her mother. Unsure of where the conversation had been or where it was leading, *Gerald* quickly flips the switch back to off.

"Wait, why did you do that? I need to know what is happening to her!" Amanda protests.

"No, right now you need to focus on what is happening in here. I promise you that *Marie* is helping your mother. I showed you this room to help explain things, not to make you worry about your mother." Turning Amanda toward the door and escorting her out, *Gerald* continues, "You see, this is where some of the others inside come to watch what is happening in the outside world. It helps everyone stay up to date on the events that are new or changing and the people that we might have to talk with when we are on the outside."

"Excuse me? Did you say when you are on the outside? Do you mean that you sometimes talk with the people in my life and I don't know it?" Amanda asks, now beginning to feel annoyed at the uninvited intrusion into her life.

"Yes, sometimes we do help you by talking with others. For example, right now, *Marie* is talking with your mother to help smooth over some possible hard feelings. This is something that you will not have to deal with because *Marie* is taking care of it for you."

"Who is this *Marie* person and what hard feelings are you talking about?" Amanda asks, now sure of her feelings of anger. "I didn't create any hard feelings with my mother so who did? Did one of *you* do it?"

"I told Tom this wasn't the right time," *Gerald* mumbles while shaking his head—considering the impact of his words only after they were spoken.

"You've talked with Tom about this? My Tom, the one that I'm marrying? Now I know you are lying because Tom would never keep something this big from me!" Amanda proclaims, feeling vindicated.

"Oh boy. You know what, you are right, this is just your imagination. This has just been a bad dream. Why don't you just lie down over here and go to sleep? When you wake up the dream will be finished, for now at least." *Gerald* suggests.

"I don't think so!" Amanda refuses. "I am not letting my guard down around you. If this is a dream, then I am going to wake up from it the way I wake up from any other dream. You don't go to sleep in order to wake up, Stupid! Now, how about you start playing back some of those alleged recordings that can prove that Tom knows? I bet you can't because they don't exist, do they?"

Amanda says, laying out her challenge.

"Okay, I'll make a deal with you. If I can show you one conversation with Tom, will you at least consider what I'm trying to tell you?" *Gerald* concedes.

"Sure, but you better not try to trick me. You show me a conversation that I can be sure actually happened or the deal is off!"

"No problem," *Gerald* says confidently. "You'll have to follow me to this other room. This is one of the ways that we play the recordings." *Gerald* carefully leads Amanda to a soft bean bag chair in an adjacent room. "You just sit here for a minute and I'll get everything set up."

Within seconds, Amanda was viewing a scene with Tom sitting across a table. Observing the background, she was able to quickly identify the Mexican restaurant at which they had recently eaten. She watched as Tom and *Gerald* began the debate in which they discussed telling Amanda the truth about the others inside. Although not wanting to admit defeat, Amanda can not help but inwardly acknowledge the timing and surroundings of this conversation. Silently she watches as Tom talks about broken trust and hidden secrets. It all seems so believable, so in character to what Tom would say.

Gerald, satisfied with Amanda's reactions allows the scene to continue. Occasionally he looks back at Amanda to be sure he hasn't lost her confidence. Strategically, he speaks up during the little 'manipulation speech' by asking, "Do you see, it's Tom and he knows. It's just that he wants you to know as well."

Ignoring *Gerald's* question, Amanda hangs on every word Tom speaks. She especially perks up when she hears, "Well, while we are on the subject of betrayal, can we discuss the betrayal I have felt? Specifically with this whole *Sabrina* situation." Hearing *Sabrina's* name in this context, *Gerald* instantly remembers the next statement. Hurrying to stop the playback, he is able to cut the feed just after Tom says, "I didn't know that it wasn't Amanda I was making love to and..."

Decidedly, this is more than *Gerald* is ready to explain at this time. With a single stroke, *Gerald* dims the lights and whisks Amanda into a state of unconsciousness. Carrying her to the resting place, he gently lays her down. Enough had been uncovered and enough will be remembered to begin the process of discovery. He would have to be sure that she awakes in her bed in the morning to keep her wondering until she is really ready to know.

Chapter Sixteen

As Tom is reciting the events leading to his visit with Dr. Brown, he visually absorbs the unique surroundings of the office. The dark wood paneling and rich upholstery creates a warm atmosphere, which is brightened by the ample lighting and a very large window. An interesting blend of formal furnishings and comfortable seats, join the abundance of stuffed animals, crayons and large sheets of paper, to offer intrigue to almost every age group imaginable. This all fit very well with Dr. Travis Brown's appearance. A man in his late forties, he has a soft, non-judgmental demeanor that causes a person to feel instantly at ease.

Feeling as if he has been rambling on for hours, Tom finally summarizes his request. "Anyway, Professor Walsworth seems to think very highly of your treatment abilities in regard to dealing with Multiple Personality Disorder, or well as you said, Dissociative Identity Disorder, as it is called now. I'm sure you can sense that I've surpassed the circumstances where my own knowledge will be sufficient. I need a better understanding of what is happening with Amanda. I need to know what I can and can't tell her and why I have to keep secrets from her. I also need to know how to tell her about the others, that is, if I actually do tell her." Intentionally bringing his words to a stop, Tom takes a breath, looks straight at Dr. Brown and asks, "So, can you help me?" Having completed his request, Tom finally relaxes, almost slumping back into the cushions of the small sofa.

"Well Tom, you don't ask for much, do you?" Travis asks with a grin. "Let's take things a little at time. First, let me explain my views of Dissociative Identity Disorder. I hope it doesn't sound over simplified, but I see this more like an ability than a disorder...almost like a gift. See, there are those who have the ability to dissociate—or separate themselves from—an unpleasant or even painful situation. This ability to dissociate is a very natural way for some people to handle stressful events. Take for example Amanda. Amanda was faced with some very painful and stressful events when she was still very young. Her young mind was not able to determine how to handle those great big emotions and pain she was experiencing. She had an understanding of what was expected of her by the adults, but she didn't understand how to accomplish those expectations if she were to also deal with these huge feelings she was suddenly facing.

"Without any conscious effort, her mind began to automatically disconnect from the feelings. That's what we call dissociation. Now, in Amanda's case, in order to maintain a "normal" life style, like going to school or smiling pretty at church to avoid suspicion, etc., she not only had to disconnect from those horrible feelings, she needed to disconnect from the event altogether. She couldn't continue to think of her father as a good Christian man—smiling and singing along side him at church—if she could remember what he did the night before. So in her case, it sounds as if a complete disconnection or dissociation had to occur.

"In cases like that, a completely different personality is developed. That's the only way that the body could remain conscious during these horrible acts and still allow for Amanda to completely disconnect from all knowledge of the event. This new personality will have a unique view of life, probably a different style than the others, and might only remember select events or facts, which will be needed to take on his or her function. For example, the personality might be responsible for enduring the sexual abuse from her father. It sounds very much like this was the responsibility of the alter, *Carol*. That would probably be the only thing *Carol* had to do, just take the abuse. She might not have gone to school, or interacted with the mother, or anything else.

"Now, before I continue with my explanation, I want to be sure you understand something. At this point in time, I can only guess at what *Carol's* role was. See, each person's experiences and their reactions are different. No two people with DID are going to be the same, including how their system is established or how it operates. I'm just using her as an example for illustration purposes right now. It's possible that we will discover much more about *Carol* down the road. Does that make sense?" Travis asks, needing some reassurance that Tom is understanding.

"Yes, it makes sense, so far. It's very similar to how Professor Walsworth explained MPD. Well, you are explaining it in a little easier to understand method," Tom added.

"It's also possible that you understand the explanation better now because you have had the experiences with Amanda. At any rate, I'm glad you are following me so far." Travis says while taking a second to recollect his thoughts.

"Okay, back to what happens with dissociation. Basically, it's like a part of her mind, splits off and forms another person. This person handles the tasks he or she has been assigned; such as being present for the sexual abuse or whatever is specifically needed. Then it becomes a matter of two people sharing one body and one consciousness. They will trade off with each other for time spent in control of the body, or what we usually call, presenting. Depending on the level of disconnection needed, the two of them might not even be aware of the other's existence.

"Once dissociation is successfully used as a method of survival, it can become a regular or re-occurring method used for dealing with any situation that causes stress or discomfort. In fact, some people have even subconsciously created alters to take care of things like school, work, cleaning house, or cooking meals." Dr. Brown stopped for a minute, realizing he had begun going down a different road than he planned. "After the information has been dissociated or disconnected from the host personality…in this case Amanda would be considered the host…anyway, once it has been disconnected from her, then she is free to continue living her life as if the event never happened. She doesn't have to deal with the feelings these traumas cause or think about what her father is capable of while trying to eat dinner at the same table. That's why I call it a gift. The trauma isn't the gift, but the ability to completely forget and separate herself from the event—that is a gift."

"Okay," Tom begins, "then why is it, if it is such a great gift, why is everything happening with her all of a sudden. I'm told that I can't tell her about the abuse or it would be bad. Well, I can see why it would be bad if she doesn't know anything about it, but then that can also cause problems with not protecting herself, can't it?"

"That's a good point Tom. That's where the "system" comes into play. See, over the years, the different alters will automatically develop what is usually referred to as the system. This is a phrase that describes all of the alters, including the host, and how the alters work together and function from day to day. In Amanda's case, it seems that her system has set up this *Gerald* fellow as a person to watch the door. There are different names for each of the functions that other therapist use in helping their clients understand their purpose. I think it's easier to just say it like it is. A system can be set up very simply, and easy to understand. It can also be set up in a very complex manner, with overlapping responsibilities within the system, and possibly...well probably, even some functions that contradict each other in purpose. Typically, the system is set up when the host is a child to accomplish the needs of a child.

"This method is usually very successful for many years. However, the problem with this method of dealing with trauma is that, in affect, the host has stayed in denial of the events for many years, burying the feelings and memories. Eventually, the alters become tired of carrying around all of the baggage and, in many cases, begin "rebelling" against their original functions. For example, an alter that holds a particular memory might be so overwhelmed by the years of secrets and literally maintaining and holding all of the emotions associated with this memory, that this alter feels unable to continue. Imagine that you have been charged with carrying a 100 lb. weight on your back, non-stop. You might be able to do this for a while, but eventually you will need some help...some rest.

"Now the way an alter finds this rest is by sharing the load—the knowledge of the event, and the emotion. Sometimes this is accomplished through dreams, or even daytime memories shared with the host. That's one way it can be handled. Another method is to allow the alter to present and share the information with an outside person, like a therapist. In so doing, the alter is allowed to deal with the emotions, the memories and everything associated with it. This is true healing for the part of the person that actually experienced the trauma. Once this sharing—or need to share—begins, the system will usually begin to go topsy-turvy. Things that worked before, no longer work. That's usually when someone inside first seeks professional help, typically it's the host personality."

"But why do you think that the others have told me about themselves now? Do you think that means they are all tired?" Tom asks, trying to be sure to use the same terminology as Dr. Brown.

"It's very possible Tom. You see, there are several things that can cause a system to begin to fall apart, as you have described it. Sometimes there is a new feeling of safety, which makes the insiders feel like it would be okay to relax some. Other times it is because there is another trauma, for which the system is not ready to handle. For example, the death of her father can actually cause all kinds of changes within her system. Most of the time, there is one common aspect to these types of changes though—the host is ready to learn about the information and the alters are needing some help. Once it gets started, and the system no longer operates as efficiently as before, it's important to establish a safe emotional and physical environment for the different parts to experience healing."

"Well, that brings up another question," Tom says, remembering *Gerald's* concern. "When these parts experience their healing, does that mean that they die? *Gerald* is really concerned that you are going to try to kill them. He seems to believe that the normal healing process involves the therapist killing off the alters, like in the movie Sybil. Although, I don't really remember much about that story, and I certainly don't remember anything like that happening."

"Many alters feel that the process of integration will, in affect, mean their death. It seems that way to many because they will cease to exist as a separate part of the person. The truth is that they join with the host personality, they don't just disappear. For example, if one of the alters knows how to play the piano, but the host does not...once they have joined together, or integrated, the host will then know how to play the piano, and the other alter will not be available to present separately from the host. The two are permanently blended together," Dr. Brown explains.

"So is that what you think *Gerald* is referring to when he says that therapist kill alters?" Tom asks.

"Probably. That's a great fear that many alters have when they begin the healing process. In fact, some alters will even sabotage the therapy simply out of fear for their own existence. They don't seem to understand that they will continue to exist, just not as an individual, separate part of the whole person."

"So, is this integration the ultimate goal of therapy?"

"Not necessarily. For some therapist, it is their goal. I, like many others, believe that healing can occur without the integration of the alters. I personally like to leave that decision up to my clients. They are the ones that will have to live with this decision, not me. There are many cases where clients have elected to allow the alters to deal with the memories, heal from the pain and misunderstandings, and remain separate. They have gone on to function very well, and enjoy sharing their life with each other."

"Okay...," Tom begins his recap slowly and thoughtfully. "So do I understand you to say that, given our understanding of what *Gerald* interprets as the killing of alters—actually meaning integration—is a choice that is left up to the client?"

"Yes, that is correct," Dr. Brown confirms.

"And this decision would be one that the system would make as a whole, not just the host. Right?" Tom asks, feeling as if he is pushing himself out on a limb of understanding that is extremely fragile.

"Well, yes...it is usually the system as a whole that decides. There have been cases in which many of the alters did not want to integrate and the host did, but that is something that is usually worked out through the therapeutic process." Dr. Brown leans forward in his chair slightly and adds, "It sounds as if you are wanting to provide *Gerald* with a guarantee that he will not have to integrate."

"I know he is going to ask for one, so I'm trying to make sure I can offer it. Can I?"

"In most cases, integration can be a conscious decision, made by the system. However, in some cases, the process of integration happens naturally. In fact, that's about the only time I suggest it. This occurs when the alter has shared all of the information and emotion, received healing and has dealt with the forgiveness issue. Once all of those things happen, it is possible that the alter will automatically, and very naturally, join with the host for a complete integration. Now, this will usually not occur when an alter is opposed to the integration process.

"Given that one disclaimer, I believe you can safely tell *Gerald* that he will not be forced to integrate. In my opinion, integration is over rated. If integration is the sole goal in the therapeutic process, the process has failed the client. See, integration can be forced before the appropriate time. When that happens, it doesn't last and it can actually cause more harm than good.

"Rather than focusing on the issue of DID or integration, I prefer to help my clients find peace. That can only happen through the healing process. This means each part of the person working through the pain and heartache of their experiences. The ultimate goal of working through the pain is to arrive at a place where he or she can forgive the abuser and/or themselves, whichever is needed."

"Forgive their abuser? That seems like a really hard step. I mean, I have to tell you honestly, I don't think I can forgive her abusers. How can you expect her to forgive them. What they did was wrong, plain and simple!" Tom reasons out loud.

"Yes, it was wrong. I will never ask her to say it wasn't wrong. That's one of the things that many of us fear about forgiveness…'If I say I forgive you, then that means it was okay.' In reality, forgiveness doesn't mean it was okay. It means just the opposite in fact. See, for me to forgive, means there had to have been something offensive done to me. Forgiveness simply means that I choose to release myself from the bondage of anger and hurt associated with the offensive act. Forgiveness isn't done for the other person's benefit. Obviously, this is something that would require many hours of discussion, but I'll give it to you in a nut shell.

"If I say something to you, which you find to be painful or abusive, I can go on about my life, without any affect from this event. Oh, it is possible that you might never speak to me again, or you might be angry with me, but I don't have to allow that to affect me at all. Nine times out of ten, I will not be aware of how it affected you, or I might not even care. On the other hand, you might hold onto the feelings of pain for a very long time. This is normal in some situations. The problem is that pain never just stays "pain". It grows into anger, fear, bitterness and hatred. These emotions, when left to brew, can become like a poison—even causing physical diseases like ulcers or heart problems. When you decide to forgive me for this offensive act, you are basically releasing yourself from the bondage to these emotions.

"Not to put you on the spot, but your comment about not forgiving her abusers brings me to another point. It is best if the client has a strong support system, outside of my office. It appears to me that Amanda has the beginnings of a very good support system. However, support people can find that they need help as well. You are definitely not the first person to say that about another person's abusers. That's a sign that you care very much for Amanda," Dr. Brown offers.

"Oh, I care a great deal for her!"

"Well, it's also a sign that you might need to talk some things out as we go along, as well. That can occur through private sessions with me, or you can join in a group therapy session which is held once a week, specifically for the people who provide emotional support for someone with DID. You can also do both if you would like."

"Thank you, Dr. Brown. I appreciate the offer and I will probably take you up on that, even if Amanda doesn't agree to see you right now. But I do still need some help in determining what to do in the immediate future. We are planning to get married soon and I don't want to start our married life together with this enormous secret just waiting to pop up at any time. Should I tell her about the others?"

"Tom, I can't tell you what to do. I will, however, make a suggestion. Pray about it, long and hard. Having not met with Amanda, I can not respond about what would be best for her. If she is truly dissociative, then the decision to proceed with telling her will best be handled by the others inside. Pray for wisdom and patience for both you and the others.

"You can schedule another appointment with my assistant and she can also give you the details of the group meetings. If you need anything in the meantime, please feel free to call my message center. I automatically receive a page each time a message is left for me. If it is something that is urgent, I'll call you back as quickly as possible. I would really like to meet Amanda. She sounds like a lovely person that has been through a lot of pain. Perhaps you can convince her to visit with me soon."

"Thank you," is all Tom can think of to say. Relieved to have someone to talk to that truly understands, and grateful for his compassionate approach, there can be no other words but, "Thank you".

"Before you leave, would you mind if I pray with you?" Dr. Brown asks.

"Oh man, I'd love that," Tom responds sincerely. Without waiting for Dr. Brown, Tom immediately begins the prayer. "Loving Father, thank you for your help and compassion. Thank you that you have promised never to leave us alone and thank you that you have made a way for Amanda and I to receive help. Oh God, please give me wisdom to know what to do, and give Amanda peace. Oh Lord, she needs your touch.

"Thank you for Dr. Brown. Help him and bless him as he makes himself available to us. Give him the words to say to bring healing and your direction into our lives. In Jesus' name, amen."

Even though he normally leads the prayer at the end of the session, at least during the first session, Dr. Brown doesn't miss a beat. "Thank you Tom. I will pray for you and Amanda as well."

The session complete, Tom and Dr. Brown settle their financial matters and say their good-byes.

Chapter Seventeen

Her first church service without Everett is surprisingly difficult for Victoria. It's so strange to sit in their usual spot, but this time—alone. Even though she is surrounded by her church family, she feels so alone and isolated. The truth is that she wants to be there, but she doesn't want to interact with anyone. She just wants to do something familiar, something old and comfortable.

But it isn't comfortable. Each time someone mentions Everett, her mind begins to spin. She is used to talking about him as if he were the king of the world—the one person that has no faults. That doesn't bother her. It would just be nice to stop talking and thinking about him for just a few hours.

Never more grateful for church to be over, Victoria heads back to the house. She is desperate to find some solid footing for her emotions, some way to occupy her thoughts and time.

As if going through a well-rehearsed process, Victoria subconsciously begins to remove the thoughts that are interfering with her happiness. The first order of business is to deal with the disturbing conversation she had with Amanda. Victoria begins to reason that the only plausible explanation is that Amanda's grief has distorted her memories temporarily. Under normal circumstances, Amanda would never even think such horrible things. She's just confused and scared.

Having mentally moved the issue successfully from the concern category into the denial bucket, Victoria physically waves her hand, as if to dismiss the thoughts of yesterday. Today is a new day. It will be different—it will be better.

As Victoria finishes up her lunch of leftovers, she pulls out a pen and paper to begin her list of items she wants to accomplish today. First on the list, wash the sheets and towels from the guest room. Now that Libby has left, she can change out the linen and get the bathroom cleaned. Scanning the house in her mind, she moves from room to room in her mind's eye considering what needs to be done to get her house in order.

She quickly decides that she will need to make another list of items that will be given away to charity as soon as possible. Things such as those horrible animal heads in Everett's trophy room, his clothes, and probably the stuff in that musty old basement. That's something she hadn't really thought too much about...the basement. Everett always insisted on cleaning it himself and kept her out of it for the most part. She did sneak a peak a few times while he was at work, but there wasn't anything of real interest to her down there. She added that to her list of things to do.

She wouldn't have to go grocery shopping for a while. The church has been so generous in bringing food for the family that she could probably eat off the leftovers for a week. One thing she did need to do though is to transfer the food into her own containers so she could wash the others and return them to their rightful owners.

Back to her list of rooms she remembers the liquor cabinet. She notes that the liquor needs to be dumped down the sink and the cabinet included in the charity pile. She hated the times when Everett would drink because those beatings were always the worst. She never understood why he drank or how to help him stop. All she knows is that she doesn't have to have it in her house any more.

"There is one thing that is true, Everett did have his problems. But he was a good provider and he sure did love his daughter," Victoria thinks out loud. Hearing her own words, she is unable to stop the natural connection from Everett's love for his daughter and the absurd comments Amanda made yesterday. Yes, he loved Amanda, that was obvious. "But...how much and in what way did he love her?" she allows the thought to flit around her brain for only a few seconds before crushing it with her "to-do" list.

I'll need to vacuum and clean the carpets. There has been more traffic on them in the last week than in the last year. She will need to be sure the bathrooms are cleaned too. The thought of so many people using her toilets sends chills up Victoria's spine.

Leaving her list momentarily, she pulls out some candles from the buffet and places them evenly on the mantel in the living room. Even though it has been a week since the last cigar was smoked in here, she can still smell the stench. She carefully lights the candles and returns to the kitchen. Wash the shears and have the drapes cleaned is now added to the list.

Victoria starts a pot of coffee and then sits back in her chair to consider another thought. "What about tomorrow, and the next day?" What will she do with her time now that she isn't a full-time wife? For years, she has spent her days fussing over Everett.

Of course, there were about 20 years that she was also a full-time Mom. Now, that has been cut down to an occasional visit or phone call from her daughter. Her daughter that is apparently in such grief right now that she no longer makes sense. Years of doting on and caring for Amanda and this is how she is repaid…her own daughter refuses to recognize her sacrifices and protection.

Moving from the denial bucket to the wall of blame, Victoria just can't let this issue with Amanda alone—and how could she? Not a "thank you" or "I couldn't have gotten through without you" …just accusations and insults. "Well, no more Missy, this mother's job is done," Victoria declares.

Turning her attention back to the more comfortable, safer things in life, Victoria revisits the list. She decides to take things slow so that she will have something to do for the rest of the week. Prioritizing the most urgent things, she decides to tackle the bathrooms and guest linens first. Gathering her cleaning supplies, she moves first to the guest bedroom. Stripping the bed and grabbing the used towels, Victoria makes her first of many trips to the washing machine.

On her way back to the guest room, Victoria's attention is drawn toward the basement door. It seems to beckon her as if desiring to tell her its secrets. Slowing her pace dramatically, Victoria considers her options. Cautiously reaching for the door knob, she stops herself. She has found some new freedoms since Everett's death, but some of the old fears still linger. She can almost hear Everett's warnings from beyond the grave, "I told you not to go down there. It's my special place." Deciding to save that freedom until later, Victoria turns her focus back on her cleaning duties.

Guest bedroom and bathroom now clean, she moves to the master bedroom. The linens are clean as usual, and the bathroom needs only to be wiped down. Considering the contents of the bathroom however, Victoria begins to spot things that she can do without. These items can simply go into the trash, nothing here that will benefit any charity.

Throughout their marriage, Everett had insisted that the medicine cabinet be used solely for his personal shaving equipment and cologne. Holding up the garbage can close to the medicine cabinet, she quickly relieves it of its unwanted contents.

Now that it is empty, Victoria is able to consider reorganizing her personal hygiene supplies. After she carefully wipes out the vacant shelves, Victoria begins to put her makeup and medicine into the cabinet. How nice it will be to not have to use the drawer for these things any longer. Everything is lined up nicely, visible and within easy access.

Looking at the trash basket, she decides to take out one item, his Old Spice cologne. He might not have been the kindest husband in the world, but he did have some redeeming qualities. Sometimes he would splash on his cologne, brush his hair, and announce, "Tonight, I'm taking you to dinner." It didn't matter how much time she had spent on cooking in preparation for a dinner at home, she always enjoyed a night on the town. It was such a rare and special treat.

Victoria gently opens the top to the cologne bottle, careful not to spill any. With a single whiff she is instantly transported in her mind to a nice restaurant on the other side of town where she and Everett had spent their last night out together. It had been their anniversary. He insisted on taking two cars so that he could go shopping after dinner. He had been so busy at work that he didn't have the chance to pick up anything for her. The dinner was positively lovely. It seemed like such a nice way to spend their anniversary.

Her memories inevitably work to bring her back to a reality that she was trying to forget. The dinner had been nice, but when she arrived home, she noticed the cake had been cut already, even though she had planned to make a big production of showing it to Everett. Trying to dismiss the disappointment, she had retreated to the bedroom to fix herself up in anticipation of a romantic night with Everett. If the dinner talk was any indication of the rest of the evening, it was going to be an anniversary celebration to remember for a long time. Unfortunately, things didn't quite work out like she had hoped. After hours of waiting for him, Everett finally shows up at home, empty handed and angry. Instead of romance, Victoria got the fist. Instead of gentle strokes of love and compassion, Everett forced himself on her with such violence that she was left feeling violated and broken.

Changing her mind once again, Victoria tosses the cologne bottle into the trash basket and carries it to the garage for disposal.

Next she turns her attention to the closet. Noticing the smell of cigar smoke on everything, she begins by pulling out her own clothes to be washed. Placing them into piles, she separates the dry cleaning from those that she can handle at home. She immediately drops a load at the washing machine and stops in the garage for a large paper trash bag. Returning to the closet, she takes Everett's clothes from the hangers and neatly places them folded into the bag. The perfectly pressed suits and button-down shirts will make a nice contribution to charity. The silk ties and well-kept shoes will be beneficial, as well.

Now emptied, the walk-in closet suddenly looks enormous. The shelves above the hangers are still full, making it seem as if the whole closet is extremely top-heavy and unsafe. Quickly inventorying the contents of the shelves, Victoria considers what she can dispose of and what might best be stored somewhere else. Some of these boxes have been left undisturbed for years. One at a time, Victoria begins the process of eliminating junk and repackaging storage items. She decides that with the extra space on the shelves she will have a nice place to store her winter blankets that used to be kept in the attic. It will make things easier on her to avoid having to go up and down that ladder that always seems to attack her when she opens the attic door.

Looking for ways to save herself steps, she places some of the boxed-up storage items on top of the laundry basket full of smoke-filled clothes that are ready to be washed. She stops long enough to deposit the boxes in the hallway beside the basement door on her way to the washing machine. Changing over the loads of laundry again, she folds the linens from the dryer and places them in the laundry basket to be taken to the guest room. On her way back, she stops at the basement to find a place for the boxes of storage items.

Not stopping long enough to feel the fear that automatically began climbing up her spine, she boldly grabs the boxes and makes her way down the basement stairs. She temporarily places the boxes on a table while looking around for a more suitable place for permanent storage. For the life of her, she can't imagine why Everett liked this room so much. It was damp, dingy, and smelly.

Considering the amount of dust resting on everything, she naturally grabbed her dust rag and began removing the layers of grime from the items on the small table she used as a short stop for her boxes. One at a time, she began dusting off different childhood pictures of Amanda. Smiling at the happy face looking back at her, Victoria almost misses the young daughter in the pictures. Days of sunshine and happiness, for Amanda, anyway. With each picture, the air in the room became more suffocating. Victoria's smile fades and her thoughts go back to the horrible accusations Amanda made just yesterday. After the sixth picture of young Amanda, Victoria's legs become weak. Her lungs begin to send the urgent request for air as her mind starts spinning to forbidden places.

Instinctively, she sits down in the large chair to catch her breath. As she does, the chair cushion pulls away enough to expose some papers. Without thinking, Victoria pulls the papers out to see if they need to be thrown away. Instead of notebook papers that she expected, she finds a magazine. Still needing to collect herself, she relaxes back in the chair to thumb through the magazine. Opening to the center of the magazine, she stops cold. Falling from the pages was a pair of Amanda's childhood underwear, the ones with little pink roses on them. Returning her gaze to the pages that had locked away his secrets for years, she stares squarely at a full length picture of a nude model.

As if handling a hot potato, Victoria instantly throws the offensive magazine across the room then quickly jumps to her feet as if the chair was ready to swallow her whole. Amanda's panties scream out their silent testimony of painful perversion as they fall to her feet. Turning to face the offending furniture and stepping away from the garment on the floor, she carefully examines the chair for any further hidden dangers. Relieved at finding nothing, she allows a single thought of observation to creep into her mind. "Maybe I don't know all there is to know about my husband."

A relentless, nagging feeling begins to grow from deep inside as Victoria opens herself to truth. Slowly and deliberately, she moves toward the sofa. The pillow and blanket that might have seemed harmless a few days ago suddenly take on a whole new meaning. The blanket wasn't laid over the back of the sofa like the afghan upstairs. It's tucked in and around the bottom cushions. In the normal place of the afghan, Victoria finds a towel. As if looking for a hidden snake, Victoria grabs the blanket and pulls it and the cushions off the sofa in a single motion, moving away from the possible fall-out.

The horror she finds would have been better replaced with the most venomous snake in the world. Mixed among the pornographic magazines are Polaroid pictures of a young Amanda in various stages of undress.

Rushing to the half-bath, she tries to fight back the waves of nausea and vomit that instantly fill her whole being. Years of lies and deceit flood through her mind as she hears Everett's voice say, "Amanda and I are going to play some games in the basement while you clean up after dinner." The thought brings on another wave of nausea as her knees begin to buckle.

Not waiting to rinse out the sink or clean up after herself, Victoria rushes up the stairs as quickly as her limp and drained body will carry her. Slamming the door behind her, Victoria runs to the kitchen for some water. Shaking and confused, she tries to make sense of what has just happened, of the foul images she must now erase from her mind.

Fear, denial, and disbelief give way to an uncontrollable rage. As the blood rushes to Victoria's face, she finds her strength once again. Thoughts of the lies, beatings, and the sick, twisted acts of perversion envelop her as she marches into the master bedroom. Carrying the heavy bag of Everett's clothes seems effortless as her muscles tighten, moving her forward toward the living room. Throwing up the fireplace screen, she slows down only long enough to ensure the flue is open. Starting with his favorite shirt and tie, Victoria begins to build a fire to burn the evidence of Everett's existence from her life. Opening the liquor cabinet, she throws whiskey and the lit candles from the mantel into the fireplace.

Bottle in hand, she watches as her memories turn to ashes. Numbed by the absolute overload of emotions, Victoria searches her mind for something solid to hold onto. Anything that would provide her with a sense of reality. Was there anything true about her life? Anything?

Deciding to go for broke, Victoria pores herself a glass of wine. On the few occasions that Everett was able to convince her to drink, she had been able to tolerate the wine easiest. With each article of clothing and sip of wine, Victoria feels her sense of reality slip further and further away.

Chapter Eighteen

Tom arrived at Amanda's at 8:00 that same morning, ready for church. He had spent a few minutes talking with Amanda over the phone the day before, but not much. In fact, for the first time in a while, they spent more time apart than together.

Feeling more informed and confident, Tom is looking forward to seeing his love. One thing on the agenda is to find a way to talk Amanda into seeing Dr. Brown. If possible, he will also have a conversation with *Gerald* about the integration decisions. Certainly he owes *Gerald* that much, after all, *Gerald* has been a tremendous help lately.

Just as eager to talk with Tom, Amanda meets him at the door with a kiss and a, "Hi ya' good looking."

"Well 'hi ya' back at you! How are you feeling this morning?"

"I'm doing okay. Do you want some coffee before we leave?" Amanda asks while stepping aside to make way for Tom to enter the apartment.

"I'd love some coffee. I don't know why, but I had a hard time waking up this morning," Tom says.

"Really? I had a strange morning myself. Well, actually it was a strange night," Amanda begins timidly.

"Then why don't I pour us some coffee and you can tell me about it real quick," Tom offers.

"Well, okay. But do you remember when you said that you would love me in spite of my craziness?" Amanda asks, needing some reassurance before proceeding.

"Yes, I remember and it still holds. Sit down and tell me what happened." Tom says while patting the seat of a kitchen chair.

Following his lead, Amanda sits down and takes a sip of coffee. "Well, it's really strange Tom, even more so than the 'lala-land' trip I took at Dad's funeral. I had this weird dream that some person named *Gerald* was trying to convince me that I wasn't crazy with a bunch of crazy talk about different people inside my head."

Not really ready for so much 'apparent' progress, Tom is at first unsure of how to respond. One thing is for certain, his reaction of spitting out his coffee was not the way to begin. Apologizing while jumping up to get a towel, Tom manages to formulate a question to find out more about what she does and doesn't know. "Really? Tell me about this *Gerald* person then. What exactly happened?"

"Well, let's see..." Amanda begins slowly while trying to process Tom's initial reaction, attempting to determine if it was because he thinks she is crazy or if it's because *Gerald* really does exist and Tom knows it. "I don't really remember falling asleep, but when I did, I found myself in this fairly dark place. As my eyes started to adjust, I began to see this person, this man, standing in the distance. Gradually he moved toward me and told me that he had a message for me. I later found out that his name is *Gerald.*

"Anyway, he starts talking this crazy stuff about me having other people inside my head. To prove it to me, he took me to this weird place that he called an observation room. In this room, you could see these movies on a screen. He said that the movies were images of what is happening outside of my body." Amanda pauses, once again feeling like a fool as she tries to explain her experience.

"Go on Honey. Did you see anything on this screen?" Tom asks, now truly intrigued.

"Well, yes. I saw my mother and she was crying. *Gerald* allowed me to hear a small, very small, portion of what Mom was saying. I asked him why she was crying but he wouldn't tell me. Then he said that another person was talking with Mom right then and that I shouldn't worry about it. He explained that the others watch from the observation room so that they know the people in my life and who they might have to talk to at another time. He even said that he had spoken with you!" Not even looking to Tom for a reaction, Amanda continues. "That's when I knew it was just a dream and that he was lying because I know you would never have kept a secret like that from me.

"So, I told him that, just like that too." Amanda nods confidently as she explains how she defended her soon-to-be husband. "I said that he should prove it by replaying the things from the observation room that show that you know about it. That's when he took me to another room and showed me this film in which you were talking to *Gerald* about telling me the truth. The funny thing is that it looked just like you and, of course, sounded like you." Smiling up at Tom for the first time since she started her story, she adds, "You were sitting there all concerned about keeping truth and trust in our relationship. The things that I love the most about you!"

Tom gets back up from the table to replace the dish towel on the cabinet and, secretly, to buy some time to think and pray. *Gerald* had done exactly as he had requested. Now it was time for Tom to back him up with the truth. Sitting back down, he took a deep breath and answered simply, "Honey, he has talked with me and I really am concerned about keeping truth and trust in our relationship."

Amanda instantly begins to move away from the table, away from Tom. Her rapid movements cause her chair to go back and her feet to search desperately for solid ground. Certain that she is once again hallucinating, she runs toward the bathroom to wash her face, hoping that will bring her back to reality. Tom immediately followed, hoping to catch her if she falls and praying for the opportunity to explain and make things right.

"Amanda, Baby, are you okay? Talk to me." Tom pleads. "What are you doing?"

"I've got to be going crazy. I'm sure that I just heard you tell me that you have spoken with this person in my dream. Tom, please tell me that you didn't say that. Please Tom, I have to find reality somewhere. I know I've lost it, I can't find it anywhere!" Amanda says as she turns to him, verging on hysterics.

"Amanda, Honey, please sit down on the couch and let's talk about this," Tom suggests as he gently leads her to the living area. "I have been wanting to talk with you about this for a while now, but I didn't want to hurt you," Tom explains.

"Hurt me? Do you think that keeping a secret from me is a way to avoid hurting me?" Amanda snaps back.

"No, my love, that is not what I thought. I meant that I didn't want to hurt you by making you face things from your past before you are ready. I also wanted to be sure that I understood what is happening with you before I made any decisions. That's why I met with Dr. Brown yesterday, to see how I could help you."

"You did what?" Amanda asks, her anger growing by the second.

"Please Amanda, please calm down," Tom begins. "I met with Dr. Brown, the therapist that I told you my old professor recommended. He said that Dr. Brown is good with helping people in your condition."

"Excuse me! Do I understand you to say that you have spoken with this *Gerald* person, AND your old professor, AND this Dr. Brown person and that your conversations have been about ME and MY condition? Is that what you are trying to tell me? You talked with a perfect stranger about me and you felt that you couldn't talk with me because you might hurt ME?"

Finally understanding why she is upset, Tom stops his explanation before he gets in any deeper. "Baby, I'm sorry that you feel I have misled you or betrayed your trust. I really am trying to help you. I didn't talk with those people just so I could talk about you behind your back. I needed to understand about dissociation and how you have used it to help you in the past and now. This information was critical for me to know how to move forward. Until I understood, I was afraid that talking with you about it would be more damaging. Please forgive me, Honey. I truly didn't mean to betray you in any way."

Considering her own confusion, Amanda begins to believe Tom's explanation. "So do you think you understand it now?" she asks, still holding her guard up tight.

"I think I'm beginning to understand it now. I certainly wouldn't claim to be an expert, but I do believe I understand it enough for now," Tom says, trying to sound more confident than he feels.

"Good, then you can explain it to me!" Amanda sits facing Tom on the couch, ready to hear his explanation. "Who is *Gerald*?" Amanda almost barks out her first question of the day.

"Well, let's see. *Gerald* is…well…he is another part of your mind. You see, it's like you have this great gift of being able to create other people, inside your mind, and these people can take care of anything bad that happens to you. The problem is that now, these people need a break from taking care of the problems so they are beginning to talk about themselves and are asking for help," Tom says as he attempts to summarize everything he has learned about dissociation into a few sentences.

"I see," Amanda lies. "So, then, you have spoken with this *Gerald*, right?"

"Yes, I have," Tom admits.

"And what is it that you and *Gerald* talk about anyway?" Amanda asks, sincerely curious.

"Well, mainly we talked about how we can help you get through the events of this last week. It's not like we are gossiping about you or anything, we were just talking about how I could help you get through the funeral and what might be the best way to tell you about the others inside. I have been telling him that I wanted you to know because I know. I didn't want to keep it a secret from you Amanda, honestly I didn't."

"Now, you keep talking about the others. *Gerald* mentioned a few others as well. Exactly how many of these other people have you spoken to?"

"A few," Tom says, trying not to get into any details before it is needed.

With a new feeling of distrust in her heart, Amanda ask, "Can't you be more specific or don't your many confidants allow that?"

"I'm sorry Honey. Let me see," Tom pauses while considering his options. "I know I have spoken with *Gerald.*" Tom pauses again as if trying to remember. "Oh, and there was a sweet young girl named *Carol*. She is the one that I bought the big bear for on Monday." Tom looks for an indication that two would be sufficient for Amanda but finds that she offers him no relief from the full truth. "I've also talked with *Agnes*, she is a really nice lady. She's pretty weak though, but she is nice, really nice."

Tired of the slow replay, Amanda begins to ask more detailed questions, "So have you spoken with this *Marie* person that was supposed to be talking with my mom yesterday?"

Carefully reviewing his memory so he could be sure to give an honest response, Tom finally says, "No, not that I can remember or be sure about. Sometimes, Honey, it is possible that I spoke with someone and didn't know it. It's not like all of the people have been identifying themselves to me all along and I just haven't mentioned it. It wasn't until about a week ago that I became aware of the fact that the others exists."

"That brings up another question. How did you find out that the *other*s exists?" Amanda asks.

"Oh, let's see...*Agnes* told me. She said that there were others inside and that I shouldn't mention it to you because you weren't ready to know about them yet. Yeah, that's basically how it went down. She also asked me what I planned to do since I knew about the others and I told her that I planned to continue to love you and to care for you. This information doesn't change the way I feel about you one bit, Amanda."

Feeling a little more assured, Amanda begins to relax a little. If Tom isn't going to leave her because she is crazy, then maybe she isn't crazy beyond repair. "Do you know how many there are?" Amanda asks.

"No, honestly I don't know. I do know that one has been modeled after your father and that he can be extremely mean and hateful." Realizing that he might have just hit a touchy subject, he quickly thinks of another name to throw out so he can avert attention from the father alter. "There is also one named *Sabrina*. I've met her a few times I think," Tom says, not wanting to give any details about her.

Instantly, Amanda remembers the ending of the replay she watched yesterday. Until Tom confirmed it all, she had written it off as her imagination and that none of it was true. If the other parts were true, then it is possible that the '*Sabrina* situation' was true as well. Her distrust rekindled, Amanda straightens up, turns her head slightly and requests, "Tell me about *Sabrina*, Tom. What do you know about her?"

Tom's face begins to involuntarily turn a dark shade of red as his heart tries to beat out of his chest. In an instant he felt as he did when he was a small boy and his mother had just caught him with his hand in the cookie jar. He knew he had been caught and that the only way to avoid the highest punishment is to tell the truth. Still, the truth is sometimes the most difficult thing to say. The words seem to run from his mind as he attempts an honest response. "Well, let's see. One thing I can tell you about her is that she is very sneaky. She is so much like you that it's very difficult to tell the two of you apart, at least, when she doesn't want you to know that she isn't you." Being as confused as Amanda appears by his response, Tom tries to leave it alone by just sitting and looking back at her as if there were nothing more to say.

"What do you mean, Tom? How do you know she is sneaky? What has she done, this *Sabrina* person that lives inside my messed-up head?" Amanda is quickly becoming frustrated with this whole ordeal. The last thing she needs is for Tom to ignore her questions. Trying to avoid the subject this much can only mean that he feels guilty about something.

"Well, do you remember Monday night, after the viewing?" Tom begins thoughtfully.

"Yes, I remember us driving home and sitting on the sofa together. I know it didn't take me long to fall asleep. Why?"

"Okay...that night, at some point, we both woke up...well, I practically threw you on the floor if I remember right."

"Yes, I remember that. And I also remember that we went into the bedroom and went back to sleep," Amanda adds.

"Good. Well, I mean it's good that you remember that. Anyway…once we were in the bed together, well, I was really enjoying the fact that I was holding you so tight and that we were alone. I know that we promised each other that we would not make love until our wedding night, but you just felt so good in my arms. Then you turned and kissed me and then…well…I just couldn't resist you any longer."

"I did what? …and you what?" Amanda says with her mouth opened in astonishment.

"Well, I now know that it wasn't you, but I thought it was you at the time. Anyway, it appears that this *Sabrina* part of you helped me decide to break our agreement. I feel so bad about this Amanda, I'm so sorry." Tom says sincerely.

Tears begin to fill Amanda's eyes as she stares back at Tom in disbelief. Barely speaking above a whisper, Amanda replies, "Tom, I honestly don't think I know you. Here I am confused about my own identity and what is happening inside my own head…then you do this to me. Of all the people in the whole world, you are the one person that I have trusted enough to want to share my life with. I have looked to you as a solid rock of stability in times when I found nothing else in my life to be stable. I never would have imagined that you would do something like this to me."

"Amanda," Tom speaks up in his own defense, "I didn't know I was doing anything *TO* you at the time. I honestly thought that it was something we both wanted. I would never hurt you intentionally. I love you very much."

"I'm just so confused right now Tom. I really am," Amanda sobs. "Does that mean that I really am insane?"

"No, it doesn't mean you are insane. It means that you have been very creative in the way you have handled problems in your life. That's a good thing," Tom explains.

"Then why do I feel like I'm going crazy? If this is such a good thing, then why did you have to keep it a secret? How could this be good?" Amanda asks.

"Honey, it is good in that you were able to handle some bad things in your past. It's just hard right now because everything is beginning to surface." Tom gently strokes her face in an effort to comfort her while he continues, "Listen,

I want you to know that I am going to be here for you through whatever happens next. I'm not going anywhere and together, with the Lord, we will get through this. I promise."

Constantly plagued with feelings of distrust, it is hard for Amanda to find comfort in his reassurance. Wanting to feel the trust again, she doesn't completely cut out Tom and his security, but she determines that she must protect herself until she can begin to understand what is happening. "Tom, I know that I have just asked for the wedding date to be moved up, but, I don't think that's what I want any more. In fact, I'm not sure I want to go with the original date either."

"Are you saying that you don't want to marry me?" Tom asks in a panic.

"No, I'm just saying that I don't want to get married right now. Tom, I'm so confused about everything. I need time to sort through things. I need help to understand my feelings. I can't even begin to think of carrying on with a rushed wedding with everything that is happening inside my head." Deciding to give Tom some assurance, whether he deserves it or not, she adds, "Tom, I want to be awake when I say 'I do'. I don't want some other part of me...oh, say...like *Sabrina*...deciding that the wedding is really a day for her, not me. I want to know that if that happens, you will recognize it and make it stop. I don't know that now, Tom, and I don't think I can go forward until I do know that as a fact."

Tom slumps back into the couch and considers Amanda's words. "Honey, I understand your fears and, like I said, I am going to support you all of the way. If you want to postpone the wedding, then that is what we will do. I just want you to know that I love you very much and I do want to marry you...when you are ready."

"Thank you, Tom. I appreciate your understanding and patience," Amanda says through remnant tears.

Changing the subject slightly, Tom moves on to another item that needs to be discussed. "You know, we talked about you taking last week off because of your father's death. Why don't we just extend your time off for a few more weeks. This will give you a chance to really focus on what is going on with you without worrying about work. I can't be with you all of the time, but I promise to help you with this, Amanda. I really would like for you to see Dr. Brown and just talk with him about what has happened. You don't have to commit to seeing him on a regular basis. I just think that he can help you get through this part of discovery. He is really good at explaining how all of this works."

"And are you sure he won't try to have me committed, Tom?" Amanda asks timidly.

"I'm very sure he will not. He is a very nice and understanding guy. I know he can help you put some of the pieces of your puzzle together."

Without any warning or sign of a switch, *Gerald* asks, "What do you mean by putting the pieces together? Do you mean making us go away?"

"No, no that's not what I meant. Oh God, help me say what I really mean for once today! I meant that he could help make sense of what is happening and answer all of your questions," Tom explains while experiencing a new level of frustration.

"So, then what did he say about killing us?" *Gerald* persists.

"He said that it sounds like you are talking about the process of integration. That's when the others inside join with the host...that is, Amanda, and that you become like a single person. He said that because you would cease to exist as a separate individual that you might see it as dying." Not breaking for *Gerald* to interrupt, he adds, "He also said that most of the time integration is something you will decide if you want or not. He doesn't believe that integration is the right thing for everyone and he leaves it up to you to decide. He did say that sometimes integration happens naturally, without trying, but that it only works that way when the alter doesn't mind integrating. So, if that is what you are concerned about, I suspect that you will never integrate because it seems that you have to be willing to do this thing in order for it to work anyway."

"Oh, well that is good news," *Gerald* responds, honestly relieved with the answer. "So you think this guy is good then, huh?"

"Yes, I do. I think it would be good for Amanda to see him as soon as possible. I suspect that if I called him today, he would try to make time on his schedule to see her as soon as tomorrow. He said what we are trying to accomplish is a big step but the others of you inside would know if it was right or not," Tom explains with very little emotion. The conversation with Amanda drained him of energy. With it happening so quickly and unexpectedly, Tom begins to have an increase in his own feelings of betrayal.

"You know," Tom decides to address the issue head-on, "a little warning before I am expected to have such an in-depth conversation with Amanda would be nice. I was totally unprepared for what just happened."

"I know, it was a disaster, huh? You had a hard time pulling yourself out of that one!" *Gerald* laughs.

"Look, I don't think it's funny," Tom says. His voice is steadily getting louder as his anger quickly grows. "This is a very serious problem. I don't want Amanda thinking that she can't trust me. Quite frankly, I am beginning to wonder if I can trust you. I thought you said you would do this thing slowly."

"Yes, I did say I would do this thing slowly. But, just like you, I was faced with an unexpected opportunity to tell the truth and I decided to take it. And, just like you, I had a very difficult time explaining myself in a way that Amanda could understand my true intentions. As a matter of fact, it was a disaster as well," *Gerald* admits. "I'm sorry I wasn't able to warn you first, but her reaction to what I told her was unexpected as well. Once she was in control of the body, it was virtually impossible to get through. I had expected to be able to keep her asleep until this morning, but apparently her emotions were just too strong. By the time you finished talking with her, she had grown weaker so I was able to get to you then."

Appeased by his explanation, although not able to understand it completely, Tom once again tries to calm down. "Okay *Gerald*, I understand."

"Good. Now, do you think you can get hold of this Dr. Brown person today? If possible, I think it would be a good thing if he can talk to Amanda, even over the phone, and reassure her that everything is going to be okay. We really need her to believe that and I don't think she is going to trust either you or I with her sanity right now," *Gerald* suggests.

Chapter Nineteen

The conversation with Dr. Brown did seem to help Amanda calm down, even though it was over the phone. Assured that she would still be safe and sane the next day, she agreed to meet with him at 9:00 Monday morning. Until then, she decided to remain at home, where she feels the safest. In spite of her protest, Tom remained with her the entire day. He gave her plenty of breathing room, but refused to leave her completely unattended. The conversations between them were benign and general in nature.

Not sure how things will go with Dr. Brown, Tom decides to drive Amanda to her appointment. He can sit in the waiting room while they talk. This way, she doesn't have to drive home if she is upset. It will also ensure that she actually makes it to the appointment.

As pleasant as their discussions are, Tom and Amanda both sense a loss in intimacy. Almost like talking to strangers, their dialog on the ride to Dr. Brown's office could best be described as polite. Tom offered some insight into the layout of the office building, what Dr. Brown looks like, and how his office is set up. Unable to think of anything else to help her feel more comfortable, he smiles and reminds her of his love for her.

The building is exactly as Tom described. Entering through the double oak doors, Amanda steps into a marble lobby. With the sound of each step echoing against the stark walls, Tom and Amanda make their way to the elevators. Selecting '3' on the floor panel, the two begin the ascent to Dr. Brown's domain. Observing the comfortable, yet polished environment, Amanda tries to become at ease with where she is going and what she is about to do.

As the 9:00 o'clock appointments are reserved for emergency visits only and well ahead of the first regular appointment, Dr. Brown's assistant is not present to greet them. However, Dr. Brown has been listening for their arrival and takes only seconds to make his way into the waiting area. Sincerely pleased to see both Tom and Amanda present, he offers for them both to follow him into his office.

"If it's okay with Amanda, I think I'll stay out here today so she has a chance to get to know you some, Dr. Brown," Tom politely offers.

"That's fine with me," Dr. Brown responds. "Under two conditions. First, please call me Travis and second, if Amanda is comfortable with that arrangement." Dr. Brown looks to Amanda for her decision.

Not wanting to appear too weak or feeble, Amanda musters up as much courage as possible and responds with a smile, "I'll be fine, Tom. Why don't you wait out here?" With a nervous little giggle, Amanda adds, "Travis doesn't look too scary."

"I'm glad you feel that way Amanda," Travis smiles back. "Then why don't we go on back to my office and we can talk some." Mindful not to touch Amanda, Travis directs her with one hand while moving her along with the other arm scooped just inches behind her back. Once in the office, he asks her to take a seat wherever she is most comfortable while he gets his pen and notepad.

"If you don't mind Amanda, I like to take notes during our talks so I can keep things straight in my own head." Without really looking for her permission, he continues, "So tell me, how are you feeling today?"

Sitting down on the straight-backed chair, Amanda subconsciously moves the pillow from the chair and places it against her stomach. Initially, she holds it loosely in her hands. As the questions begin, she draws it closer to herself. "I'm okay I guess," Amanda responds timidly. Having never been to see a therapist, Amanda has a feeling of being on another planet, completely unsure of the local protocol.

"I'm glad to hear that. It seems that you have been given quite a shock over the last few days. I'm going to try to make things as easy for you as possible when we talk. How about we start off with me telling you about how things usually work," Travis offers.

"I think that would be a good idea," Amanda nods.

"First, I think it's important for you to understand what I can and can not do. I can listen to you as you tell me about your feelings, concerns, memories, problems and joys. I can help you find understanding about why things are happening as they are. You and I can talk through your options and the possible consequences to each path you can take. I can pray with you and for you, as you go through the healing journey that you have just begun. However, I will not tell you what to do, how to feel, or judge you for your feelings or actions. I am not going to 'heal' you. I am not going to be your only support through the healing journey. I am not going to 'dissect' your every word or feeling to find the deeper meaning behind it.

"See, I am here to be a partner with you as you begin to heal from some of the things that have happened to you. I am here to guide you through the process. You will be doing the majority of the work while God provides the healing. Does that sound like something you might be interested in pursuing?" Travis asks, looking for agreement from his new client.

"Yes, it does," Amanda responds. "It sounds like you are kind of a personal trainer for the mind," she quips.

Chuckling at the analogy, Travis confirms her interpretation of the ground rules. "Now, as your personal trainer, I need you to be honest with me about everything that is going on with you. I can't read your mind, nor would I want to do that. In order for me to give you the guidance that I have available, I need to know what is happening inside of you. In return, as I mentioned earlier, I will not judge or criticize you for anything that you tell me, no matter how bizarre or crazy it might sound to you."

"So, does that mean that you won't put me in a hospital or insane asylum?" Amanda asks, wanting to get this final question answered before moving forward.

"I do not put people into insane asylums. That is usually left as a last resort for individuals that are mentally insane and who are unable to be brought back to reality through the standard medications and treatment options. From my understanding of your situation, that doesn't even come close to describing you. I have had some clients spend a short period of time in the hospital during their healing journey, however. The hospital stays are designed to help a client deal with some of the more painful events from the past while in a safe environment. That is not the first plan of action though. It is mainly used only when the client is truly in danger of hurting themselves or others. It is also something that is discussed with the client ahead of time. So far, I have no indication that you need such a dramatic intervention," Travis smiles his assurance.

"Good," Amanda sighs out loud. "Then to tell you the truth, I don't think I'm doing so good."

"Well, as I said before, you have gone through quite a lot lately haven't you?" Travis prompts.

"You can say that again, Travis. I have so many feelings all mixed together that I can't really begin to separate them." As she begins to confide in Travis, the tears begin to flow. "I have never felt so confused, betrayed, and lost in my life."

"It seems that you are feeling somewhat overwhelmed by everything," Travis offers. At Amanda's nod of confirmation, he suggests, "Then, let's take a look at things one feeling at a time. You mentioned that you feel confused. Tell me more about that."

"Well, I can't seem to get a straight answer about all of these *others* that seem to be living inside of my head. Things were so much easier before I heard of them. How can I just get rid of them? Do you have some medication that I can take to make them disappear?"

Travis chuckles. "Well, how about we look at providing you with some straight answers about the others inside before we talk about making them disappear." With a smile, he prompts, "What questions do you have about them?"

"Well," Amanda considers her response, "I don't understand why this is happening to me. It seems like everything in my life was going so well and then all of a sudden, nothing is right! Why did they suddenly appear and start making trouble for me? Is it some subconscious hatred I have for myself that is making all of these evil little people in my head? This really is an unwelcomed intrusion in my life and I want it to stop. It's my life and my Tom is my MAN. I don't want to share either with any of them."

"It must certainly feel like that to you given all that you have been through lately. The truth is these others have been sharing your life for a very long time. You just haven't been aware of their involvement and help until now," Travis explains.

"Help? Yeah, they're helping alright! They are going behind my back, telling Tom all kinds of things, and one of them, *Miss 'I'll do anything with anyone' Sabrina* is helping herself to my fiancée!" Amanda retorts. She wouldn't normally be so...unladylike with a stranger, but she figures that she has nothing to lose.

Travis sits quietly for a minute, waiting for Amanda to catch her breath. He provides no overt reaction to her outburst, no sign of disapproval or judgment, just a silent, knowing smile. This isn't the first time he has heard such a reaction and will certainly not be the last.

"I guess this is where you tell me how wrong I am," Amanda says with a slight pout on her face.

"No, this is where I listen. And what I heard wasn't feelings of confusion. It sounds like we are moving on to the feelings of betrayal you mentioned."

Amanda sits deeper into the chair as she considers how alone and frightened she feels. Without looking at Travis, she slowly begins to explain, "I really thought I could trust Tom to tell me everything. I thought we knew each other so well that even the smallest thought was apparent to the other. We are planning to marry you know," she says taking a second to glance up at Travis with a slight smile. "We have been so close and have shared so much together. We pray together, laugh and cry together…he has been such a wonderful support following the death of my father. I just don't understand how he could keep this information from me. Now I find myself questioning everything he has ever said to me."

"Has he told you why he didn't tell you about the others before?"

"Yes, he said he didn't want to hurt me. But Travis," she says looking straight into his eyes, "he made me into such a fool!"

"How so?"

"I don't know…it's like I have to have a perfect stranger tell me about stuff that he has talked with Tom about. The first I hear of all this mess is from some freak named *Gerald.* And then, just when I think I can prove him wrong because I just know my Tom wouldn't keep such information from me, he proves ME wrong! He shows me just how much Tom does know."

"So, do you think it would have been easier to hear about the others inside from Tom?"

"Of course! Well…yes, I think so," Amanda says as the initial confidence in her response wanes. Considering how it might have sounded from Tom, she wonders if she would have believed him.

"The point is that it's my life and I'm like the last person on earth to even know! If the others have been with me for so long, why would they trust Tom over me? Why didn't they just tell me that they were here? I would have preferred to handle this myself and not involve Tom in it at all."

"So, you would have kept this information from Tom if you had been given the choice?" Travis asks as if for clarification.

"Yes! Now I don't know what will happen to us." Amanda replies. Travis doesn't say anything. He just sits there watching her. Was it something she said? She takes a second to consider her last response. She would keep this information from Tom in order to save their relationship. Oh my…she *would* keep this from Tom, just like Tom kept it from her.

"It's different," she defends. "I would do it to save our relationship! Now I'm afraid that he is going to leave me because I'm crazy. I don't understand why he kept it from me. At the very least he could have warned me something was happening."

"It's understandable that you feel angry right now. You probably even feel a little scared." Travis offers.

"Well yeah, wouldn't you?" Amanda asks.

"Yes, and I think I would be looking for someone to blame for all of these feelings."

Amanda lowers her head and takes a deep breath. "That doesn't sound very productive does it?" She asks rhetorically. "So, let's say that the blame thing is put aside momentarily. Where do I go from here?"

Smiling at Amanda's willingness to be open to his observations, Travis leans forward slightly in his chair before proceeding. "There are a few options available to you. Perhaps it will be easiest to eliminate some options you might have considered. First, we do not have a pill that you can take and make the insiders just disappear." Travis explains with a grin. "They are a part of you and help to make up the person that you are. Even if we did have such a pill, I would never advise using it.

"Second, I think the option of ignoring this new information has been removed from the list of possibilities. It has already impacted your life, and that impact must be dealt with in order to move forward.

"Now, the options that are available to you: You can work with this new information to find answers to some of your life-long questions. Those questions that you might never have asked but have always been part of you. You can take the opportunity to discover things about yourself and your past.

"You also should consider what support you might need in this process. Of course, I believe that it would be helpful to have a therapist help guide you through your healing journey. I also believe that family and friends are just as important."

"What do you mean by 'healing journey'?" Amanda interrupts.

"That's a term that I use to describe the process of discovery, forgiveness, and healing that most people go through as they face the hurts from their past and present circumstances. You have already mentioned several painful events that have happened just recently. To move forward in a healthy life, you will need to heal from these events and others."

"You know there is something that I don't understand. Tom said that these others inside have been there to help me with problems from my past. Well, I don't have any problems in my past. My father was a good man, devoted husband and caring father. My mother was a little strict at times, but she loves me very much. If these inside people are to help with such bad problems, why on earth would I need them?" Amanda asks sincerely.

"That's a good question and one that I can not answer yet. You see, I too am unaware of the hidden problems from your past. However, the fact that you don't know about them is actually an indication that the others inside have done their job well. You have been spared from whatever the pain was. As you begin to discover more about the others, they will begin to share this information with you as well."

"Well, what if I don't want to know this information?" Amanda asks as if she is in a negotiation over how much pain she is willing to endure.

"There are a few reasons why it might be important for you to learn more about the past. One is that the past might be impacting your present in a dangerous or unknown way. If so, the insiders might feel that you must be aware of the information so that you can protect yourself. Another reason might be that the insiders feel you are ready to handle the information. See, when you were a child, you were unable to deal with the events that the insiders handled for you. Now you are an adult and are better able to handle things." Travis explains.

"Well, I think they misjudged because I am not handling things very well now and I haven't even heard what it is that happened in the past. Why are they doing this to me?"

"It must feel like they are against you, but you will discover that the inside people are actually there to protect you and each other. Some of them might be confused as to the best way to do that, but it is their real purpose."

"Travis," Amanda starts cautiously. "How do you know that there are insiders and that I'm not just going crazy? Have you spoken with them too?"

"No," Travis reassures her. "I am going off of the information that you and Tom have given me. I do have a few questions that will help me eliminate a few other possibilities though."

"Okay," Amanda agrees.

"Do you ever hear voices that sound different than just your own thoughts?" Travis asks.

Amanda thinks of the many times that she has heard her father's voice or her mother's voice telling her what she should and shouldn't do. "Yes, I hear voices of my parents but isn't that normal that people would replay their parents' instructions?"

"To a degree it is normal. Do you hear it as a recording of previous messages from your parents, or are you able to dialogue with these voices at times?"

"Hum…I would have to say that it isn't like a recording of stuff that I've heard, but I don't necessarily have a conversation with them either. It's like they are present in my head, always telling me what to do or say, or telling me that something I did was wrong."

"Do you ever hear any other voices?"

Amanda considers the question as she scans her memory. "Sometimes I do. Its usually more like an impression though, not necessarily a voice."

"Okay," satisfied with that for now, Travis proceeds to his next question. "Do you ever have times when you can't account for time during the day? Like a block of time is missing from your memory?"

"Doesn't everyone?" Amanda chuckles a sincere response.

"No, that doesn't happen to everyone. Does it happen to you?"

"Well yes, of course. I just thought that was a normal part of life. Do you mean it isn't?"

"No Amanda, not really. What would you say is the longest period of time that you blocked out in the last year?"

"Well, I didn't intentionally block out anything. I would say that I skipped a few days here and there, but nothing major. I mean, the longest would probably be about three days. The good thing is that I get most of that memory back as I need it so I guess it isn't really blocked out altogether."

"Okay, good." Travis nods as he takes notes. "Now, do you have a problem with headaches?"

"Sometimes, but usually only when I'm feeling stressed about stuff at work or home."

"Does medicine help these headaches?" Travis asks.

"No, the only thing that seems to help is sleep. I go to sleep and the headache goes away."

"Have you seen a medical doctor for these headaches?"

"No, they aren't that bad and only happen occasionally, like with most people."

"Okay. One of the things I do want you to do is schedule an appointment with your family doctor to talk about the headaches. Although many people with insiders experience headaches associated with the stressors in their lives, it's always good to eliminate any physical problems that could be causing them. Do you think you can take care of that for me?"

"Sure. I don't think they are that bad, but if it's important I will."

"Thank you. I don't think your doctor will find any physical problems, but I want to be sure that is looked at just in case. If you would like, I can talk with your doctor before the appointment to explain exactly what we are looking to rule out and to answer any questions he or she might have."

"Okay. I'll let you know when I have the appointment scheduled so you can call him."

"Good," Travis says with a reassuring smile.

"Now, do I understand correctly that you did not know about the insiders until recently?"

"Yes, that's right."

"Tell me again, how did you find out?"

"I was sleeping...well," Amanda corrects herself, "I was talking with my mom when I began to feel very angry. I don't know why I was so angry because Mom had not done anything wrong. She had been helping me with my wedding plans. Then suddenly I was waking up in this dark place. I could see this person in the distance and he kept getting closer to me. I finally was able to see him clearly and he began to talk with me. He said his name is *Gerald* and that he had a message for me. Now I've been told that this *Gerald* is an insider."

"I see. So was this the first time you had ever seen *Gerald*?"

"Yes, I didn't have a clue who he was. But now that I think about it, his voice did seem familiar. He mentioned that he shares information with me and the others so maybe his voice is one that I've heard before and just didn't know it."

"That's entirely possible," Travis confirms. "How do you feel about *Gerald* now that you have more information?"

"Wow, that's a loaded question," Amanda begins thoughtfully. "I don't like that he talked with Tom before talking with me. He seems a little, stuffy and uncaring; but he did say that he helps me see things logically. That is definitely something I could use right now. I would have a hard time determining what 2 + 2 is without looking for the motive behind the question." Amanda admits with a grin. "Why do you ask?"

"I was wondering what you think about getting to know him a little better," Travis explains.

"Wait just a minute," Amanda warns as she sits straight up in the chair. "I'm not sure he even exists yet. Are you suggesting that I actually try to have a conversation with myself? Isn't that a sign of being crazy?"

"No, not in this case. However it might be a solution to the problem of everyone else knowing things before you. See, *Gerald* has some information. He and the others need to share this information. I suspect that he would like to share it with you, over time, as you are ready," Travis explains calmly.

"Here's the thing," Amanda says, "I'm afraid of him. I mean, I don't know him or anything. It's like asking me if I want to go into a stranger's house for dinner, alone. What if he does something to hurt me? I can't take Tom inside my head to protect me can I?"

"No," Travis smiles, "Tom probably would not fit. I understand your reservations. So what if you could get to know him while Tom was around?"

"Is that possible?" Amanda asks.

"Well, yes it is possible if we can get *Gerald* to help us with it."

"Okay. That seems a little strange to me. I keep expecting you to bring him into the office from another room, but he is inside of me isn't he?" Amanda asks without really expecting an answer. "I wouldn't even know how to ask him for help."

"That's okay," Travis responds. "When *Gerald* feels like the time is right, he will let you know what you need to do. Perhaps he is just as frightened as you are at these new changes," Travis offers.

Changing the subject, Travis asks, "Have you seen any of the others inside?"

"No, there are a few that I have heard about from Tom, but I haven't seen any others yet."

"Well, that will happen in time and you might be surprised at how much you begin to enjoy talking with them. In the meantime, let's talk about what you plan to do from here. Who has been told about the insiders besides Tom?"

"I'm not sure," Amanda says. "I really don't know. Isn't this something I should keep as a secret? I mean, what if people start asking me a bunch of questions that I can't answer? What if they want to talk with the insiders?"

"The decision to share this information with others is entirely your choice. Remember that you will need some emotional support. It is good to have a few close friends or family members who know about the insiders to help support you and the others during your healing journey. Why don't you consider who would be good support for you and then we can talk about how to share this information with them. Does that sound like a good plan?"

"Yes," Amanda responds. "I think that is a very good plan."

"With everything happening so quickly and with all of the new information you are getting, you might find that for a few weeks we will need to spend several hours together, helping you get past this first hurdle. If you would like, I can schedule an appointment for every other day this week and next. After that, we should be able to reduce the number of times we talk each week because things will have slowed down some."

"Yes, that might be good," Amanda says as she begins considering the time she has already spent with Travis and her initial outburst of anger and frustration. "I'm really sorry about earlier Travis. I don't normally behave so poorly with someone I have just met." To ease her feelings of tension, she adds with a smile, "It usually takes at least two meetings for me to unravel."

"I doubt that you unravel so quickly. You seem like a very nice young lady. I am looking forward to working with you and meeting the other parts of you," Travis says. "We still have a few minutes left if you have any other questions or concerns that I can help with right away. Of course, if you find yourself in a real problem before we meet again, you can always call my answering service. They are good about paging me when a client has an emergency, but I don't expect that to be needed for you."

"No, I can't think of anything right now. I know I need to figure out who I will share the information about the insiders with so I can have support. I'll think more about getting to know them better. And, I'll try to wait to assign blame until I find out more about what has happened in the past."

"Good idea," Travis nods with a chuckle.

"Excuse me. But you don't have a right to get to know anyone in here," came a controlled yet stern reprimand. "And you do not have the right to instruct Amanda on what she needs to do in the next few days or the next few years."

"Amanda has requested my help," Travis says, more to defend Amanda than his rights.

"Amanda is just confused right now. I know that chaos and anarchy seem to be running amuck, but I can assure you that things will be back to normal in no time." Adding more for his own benefit than for Travis's, "All I have to do is get this stopped before more damage is done and it will be okay."

Redirecting his instructions and focus to Travis again, the demands continue, "Now you figure out how to explain this away to Amanda and anyone else that knows so that we are not discovered."

"And how am I supposed to do that?"

"You're a shrink right? Just hypnotize them and tell them it was all a bad dream or something."

Without hesitation or concern, Travis responds. "Someone inside obviously felt like it was time to move forward in their healing."

"I'm sure that sounds lovely to everyone. But I assure you that we are all perfectly capable of handling things without therapeutic interventions. What we need is some normalcy. That doesn't happen by talking to therapists so if you think for one second that I'm going to let you near anyone in here, you are sadly mistaken."

"It sounds like you are concerned about something bad happening as a result of people getting to know you and the others. What is it that concerns you so much?"

Sitting back in the chair with a slight grin on his face, he responds, "You are a very tricky man. I'm not about to tell you my concerns or share any potential weaknesses with you. It's plain and simple. I don't know you and I don't trust you. For all I know you are just looking to get your jollies by hearing gory details from stories of a tortured childhood. Well I'm sorry to disappoint you, but no such stories exist here."

Astonished, this unnamed insider realizes that in spite of his best efforts, he has just exposed one of his own fears. This man really is tricky.

"I can see how it can be disturbing to trust a perfect stranger with some of the most important details of your life. That can make anyone feel vulnerable. So let me tell you a little about myself.

"I do care a great deal, but not about the gory details. I care about what happens to Amanda and each of the people inside. See, the way I look at it is that you are all equally important and all equally deserve happiness and freedom," Travis says. He knows that whoever he is talking to is scared and hurt. Such blustery and controlling behavior seems to always mask deep pain and sorrow.

"Well, care all you want, you are not getting to know anyone and I will take care of our former gatekeeper who is too stupid to live," came the threat to an insider now that the doctor's weakness has been exposed. "We will not need those sessions later this week, thanks for offering anyway."

"Well how about I go ahead and schedule them in case you change your mind. You know, I think you and I are very similar," Travis suggests.

"Similar? Now you're throwing humor into the session?"

"No, I'm not joking at all. See, you have shown me that you are very strong and that you will use your strength to protect those inside."

"Okay…and your point is what?"

"Well," Travis begins, "I also want to protect those inside. I want to be sure that what happens next will be something that will be good for everyone inside, including Amanda. I want them to be safe. In fact, I think that if we work together, you and I can make sure that the information that is already out there works for the benefit of everyone," Travis waits a few seconds for the possibility of a positive out come to sink in before continuing. "Let's face it, the cat is already out of the bag. Amanda and Tom both already know and that's not something that can just be erased. It's something that must now be dealt with in a very careful manner."

"And I suppose you are going to tell me how it should be done," came the sarcastic, yet curious response.

"Well, I certainly don't have all of the answers. I do have some experience with people who have insiders and I have helped many of them in their healing journey. But I don't know as much about Amanda and the others as you do. You can take advantage of my experience, mixed with your knowledge of Amanda and the others, to make this a good thing. It really doesn't have to turn out as bad as you might think," Travis asserts.

"Let's just say that I go along with what you suggest. Can you guarantee me that no one will get hurt?"

"Honestly, I can't guarantee you anything. Sometimes the healing process is painful, but it is never as painful as the original offense and the end result is well worth remembering the hurt of the past. I promise that I will help you along the way for as long as you want."

The person stares at Travis for a minute and then asks, "Is there anyone you have helped before that I can talk to before making any agreements?"

"Yes, as a matter of fact there is. It's very wise to ask for such a reference. I'm impressed with your thoroughness and protection," Travis says, offering a sincere compliment while playing into the role of this particular insider.

Travis writes the name and number of a person on a scrap piece of paper and offers it with a few instructions, "You can call this number any time between 5:00 and 8:00 at night. If you tell Marcy that you are considering discussing some issues with me, she will be happy to answer any of your questions. She is actually the point person for our support group and is happy to offer information about how the therapy has worked for her and, of course, she will strongly suggest the group sessions."

"Thank you. I will call her tonight." After a slight hesitation, he adds, "My name is *Mitch*. If you tell anyone about me, even Amanda, you will never see her again. If you promise to wait for my timing, I will reveal myself to her when I'm ready. Do we have an understanding?"

"It's nice to meet you *Mitch*. I appreciate your trust in telling me your name. I also appreciate that you have expressed your expectations up front. It is important for you to understand my position so we can find some common ground. I do not share details with others, inside or out. I might help facilitate information, but the sharing of details is always best left to the ones with first hand information. Don't you agree?"

"Yes, that is correct," confirms *Mitch*.

"I also make it a policy not to lie to my clients, including the insiders. For example, if Amanda asks me if I have spoken with any insiders, I will have to say yes. If she asks me the name of the insider, I will recommend that she wait until you are ready to tell her. The same goes for any memories that an insider might share with me. I will not repeat the memories to Amanda but will rely on the insider with the memory to share that information as appropriate. I will also not lie to the insiders. My hope is that the communication among everyone inside changes as time goes by and trust with each other is developed. Does that sound like something we can agree to?"

"Yes," *Mitch* agrees, "That sounds like a smart plan: honesty without the details. I can live with that. Shall we shake on it?" *Mitch* asks as he offers his hand to Travis. Travis quickly responds, sealing their agreement with a manly handshake.

As soon as they both recline back in their chairs, Amanda comes to. Unaware of the time she missed, she proceeds as if the conversation between Travis and *Mitch* had not happened. "Travis, thank you very much for seeing me today. I do feel better and look forward to seeing you again soon. When should I come back?"

"How about we talk again Wednesday morning at 9:00? Does that time work for you?"

"Yes that will be fine," Amanda agrees. She stands to leave and timidly offers her hand for a polite good-bye handshake.

Travis responds in kind and asks, "Before you leave, would it be okay if I prayed with you?"

"Oh, of course," Amanda says as she sits back on the edge of the chair.

"Dear Lord," Tom begins, "Thank you so much for Amanda and for all of those who have helped her for so many years. Lord I ask that you hold them up as they begin their healing journey. Give me and those around her the wisdom to show your ways and the compassion to show your love. Strengthen her Lord, and watch over her. In Jesus' name, Amen."

"Thank you," Amanda says as she stands to go. Walking her to the reception area, Travis quickly thanks Tom for bringing Amanda in and mentions that he will see her again on Wednesday. Tom automatically handles the payment for the session and bids Travis a pleasant farewell.

Chapter Twenty

Unsure of how he will be received, Tom reaches out to take Amanda's hand. He can't help but wonder about the few outbursts that he overheard coming from Travis's office. Surprisingly, Amanda is fairly receptive to his touch and doesn't shun him as he feared. The two walk silently back to Tom's car and head to Amanda's apartment.

Tom, unable to wait for Amanda to break the silence asks, "So, what do you think of Travis?"

"He's okay." After a few minutes she adds, "He wants me to come back Wednesday morning at 9:00. Do you think you can arrange to be there with me?"

"Of course. That's not a problem: Wednesday at nine—got it," Tom says making an obvious mental note more for Amanda's sake than his.

"He also says that I should consider who to tell about the insiders so that I can get support. I guess it's best to first ask…Who else already knows?" Amanda asks callously.

"Well, to my knowledge, the insiders have only made themselves known to Jessica and Rick," Tom says careful not to take the blame for spreading the news.

Amanda lets the fact that both Jessica and Rick already know sink in before moving on. "I guess I would have told them both eventually anyway."

As Amanda thinks about Travis's advice, she begins to wonder just how much she will be able to handle. Somehow she knows that the medical doctor will not find anything wrong. It's not something that she can make go away. She can't hide it, or argue it gone. She has to face it…but can she? Void of energy and resolve, Amanda sinks back into her seat and unwittingly relinquishes control.

"That's a girl," *Sabrina* whispers to Amanda. "You just rest for a while. You don't have to do it all alone, we are here to help you." With no actual concern over Amanda herself, *Sabrina* is more worried about Tom and making sure that he doesn't escape. As easy as 1-2-3, *Sabrina* takes control of the body while Amanda simply floats off into unconsciousness.

Aware of *Gerald's* new rule, *Sabrina* must decide how she will announce her presence to Tom. Slightly afraid of his anger over the other night, she decides to bend the rule slightly. "Hi. I'm supposed to let you know that I'm not Amanda so that you don't get confused," *Sabrina* begins.

"Thanks for the warning," Tom replies. "So do you mind if I ask who I am talking with now?"

"Sure, my name is Sarah," *Sabrina* lies. "I've been watching you for a long time and believe I can trust you. Is that true?"

"Yes, it is true," Tom says with an assuring smile.

"Well, Amanda is feeling a little tired right now so we thought we would give her a break. I can take care of things for a while."

"She is okay isn't she?" Tom asks a little concerned over this explanation.

"Oh yeah, she is fine. She just needs some rest from all of this psycho babble for a little bit. In the meantime, we can take care of some things she is supposed to do. For example, we need to schedule an appointment with the medical doctor to be sure that there is nothing physical that is causing the headaches. Of course, I can tell you from personal experience that I have caused about half of them," *Sabrina* quips.

Tom offers only a hint of a grin to the latest comment, not sure if it is intended to be a joke or a confession. "Okay, so what else do we need to do?" Tom inquires.

"Well, as Amanda mentioned, she is supposed to look at her support system to decide who she will and will not tell about us "insiders." Jessica and Rick are already decided for her, although she doesn't know that yet. But we need to talk about the big question...Mom." *Sabrina* takes a few seconds to sincerely consider the consequences of telling and not telling Victoria. "After *Brooke's* little announcement the other day, it might help her understand some things better. But on the other hand, it might make matters worse," *Sabrina* thinks out loud.

"Um, I don't think I know about this little announcement you mentioned. Can you fill in the blanks for me?" Tom asks.

"Oh sure. Let's see...it was Saturday when we went to see Mom. Amanda wanted to see how she would react to the idea of moving the wedding date. Well, *Brooke* just was fed up with Mom. She didn't really do anything wrong, it's just that she was there. *Brooke* just really doesn't like Mom," Sabrina explains. "Anyway, *Brooke* has been fuming about Mom's announcement that she took so many beatings so that we could be safe. We tried to tell *Brooke* that Mom really believes that, but *Brooke* didn't buy it for one second. She said that Mom always knew what was going on and if she didn't, she certainly should have."

Taking a deep breath, more out of necessity than for drama, *Sabrina* continues, "Well, as soon as everyone left the party and *Brooke* had Mom all to herself, she let her have it with both barrels. You would have thought that she was an Indian on a war path, circling Mom like some kind of prize. After she got Mom really good and confused, she announces that all of the beatings Mom took did not protect us. In fact, they served as a threat to keep us silent. See, occasionally Dad would take a few minutes to be sure that his secret would remain safe, usually after the deed. One of the things he would say is, 'Did you see that I had to punish your Mother again today? She was out of line and talking with her friends about me. I don't want to have to punish you like that. I don't like punishing her either. But if you tell about our secrets, then she will get it even worse and so will you.' So you see, the beatings that she took as a protection were really just the opposite and *Brooke* decided it was time that she knew it.

"Without any consideration for Mom's feelings at all, she flat right out told her that Dad had sexual intercourse with us for years. Oh man was it a mess!" *Sabrina* says as if she is recounting some movie she had just seen. "Well, the release of such emotion made *Brooke* just weak enough for *Marie* to take over. She jumps out and starts trying to console Mom. Man was that confusing to Mom. One minute we are yelling at her and the next second, we are bawling our eyes out wanting her to be okay. Then Mom asks, 'So do you mean that it isn't true, that it didn't happen?' But *Marie* was not able to lie to her. She starting crying again and tells her that it is true."

"So how did it end?" Tom asks.

"Well, let's see. Marie cried with her for a while, and then Mom started asking questions like when? and for how long? Marie only offered her vague answers because she didn't want to cause Mom any more pain. See, Marie, man was she having a fit! She is supposed to appease Mom, that's her job and has been her whole life. When no one else knew how to make Mom okay, Marie could come out and Mom would be settled within minutes. Now *Marie* is faced with this inconsolable event in Mom's life and she is totally beside herself trying to make everything okay. It was a sight to see," *Sabrina* laughs at her memory. Catching herself, she explains. "Oh, I'm not heartless, it's just that I don't have such fond affection for Mom. I care enough to know how to make people smile and how to interact. I don't usually get into long term relationships and feelings, well, not usually anyway.

"But enough about me, it ended with *Marie* walking with Mom in the rose garden and talking about rose petals or something like that. I lost interest after that and stopped watching."

Tom prayerfully considers this new development. "So, you are suggesting that telling your mother about the insiders might help explain the behavior?"

"Yeah, but it could also serve to drive home the point that the abuse was so bad that we had to help Amanda through it. On the other hand, it could be helpful for her to know that Amanda was able to handle it and this is how," *Sabrina* reasons to the best of her ability.

"And how does Amanda feel about telling her Mother?" Tom asks, considering how many of these decisions have been made on her behalf.

"Um, I don't know. I don't think she cares much right now but I can try to find out," *Sabrina* half-heartedly promises.

"At the very least," Tom suggests, "it sounds like we need to check in on your mother. Do you feel up to doing that now?"

"Oh sure. You seem to be good at handling Mother. I wouldn't miss this for the world."

Driving to the Clark's side of town, Tom begins to pray for wisdom beyond his years. He has a real concern for Victoria. It's been days, and to his knowledge, no one has been helping her get through this revelation. The more he considers her situation, the worse he imagines her state of mind. It would have been helpful to know this sooner. But then, what would he have done about it yesterday? He was too afraid to let Amanda out of his sight.

The Holy Spirit gently reminded Tom of His presence and His willingness to help. Tom begins to pray that God will go before him to prepare and comfort Victoria so that she is able to receive help and ministry from him. He then asks the Holy Spirit to prepare his own heart to have the words to share that will benefit the situation the most.

As Tom prepares for the visit, *Sabrina* is distracted by a commotion inside. Not wanting to forfeit control, she is careful to listen without loosing focus on the outside world.

****

"Well, well, well…Look who's playing boss," *Mitch* says. "I go to sleep for a little while, with your assistance I'm sure, and wake up to what might be considered the equivalent of Armageddon."

Rolling his eyes, *Gerald* replies, "Can we please be a little more dramatic there, *Mitch*? There isn't enough drama going on as it is! Please…feel free to add to it!"

"Disrespect doesn't fit you, *Gerald*," *Mitch* observes. "You know what that kind of rebellion leads to and the evidence is all around. Just look at the mess you've created."

"The mess I've created? I haven't created this mess. I've been trying to clean up the mess that others have created," *Gerald* protests.

"The mess that others have created? *Gerald*, what has happened to you? I'm not hearing any logic in your argument. Have you gotten emotionally involved in something?" *Mitch* asks sincerely concerned with the extent that *Gerald* seems to have strayed from his primary function.

"No, no I haven't," *Gerald* insists. "I've had all kinds of emotions thrown at me, but I haven't taken them on. I've done exactly as you taught me; observe and direct." Even as he says the words, he realizes that it's a lie. He has gone way beyond observation and direction. He has actually been out, talking to Tom. But is that emotional involvement?

"Gerald, do you think that you are the only one who can review recordings? And in spite of your rebellion, there are others who think that you need my continued direction. So that you understand clearly…they think you are failing miserably.

"So here we are. There's a mess and I hold you responsible. You are, after all, the one who is supposed to monitor who is out at all times, are you not?" Even though he knows the answer, he refuses to move on until *Gerald* verbally confirms his responsibilities.

"Yes, that is my role," *Gerald* answers, deciding to put aside the sarcasm and consider what *Mitch* is saying.

"Then anything that has happened because one of the others has done something stupid while out and about is your fault. They weren't meant to be out at that time. But you weren't able to stop them. Why is that?" Instinctively, *Gerald* knows that *Mitch* demands a thoughtful and truthful answer for both of their sakes.

"Okay, let's see…I guess that *Everett* was able to play footsy with Jessica because I was distracted at the time," *Gerald* offers hoping not to have to explain more, but knowing it would not be sufficient.

"Distracted by what?" *Mitch* persists.

"Distracted by making arrangements for you to take a nap," *Gerald* admits boldly. "It's not the easiest thing in the world to do, you know."

"Of course not. And it will be even more difficult if you should ever try it again," *Mitch* offers. "Now, what about the rest of the times?"

"Well, the problems had already started good by the time I got back. *Agnes* had already spilled the beans about the sexual abuse by the father. There really was no easy way to get that back," *Gerald* explains, grateful to move past the subject of *Mitch's* nap.

"And what about the time you spent out talking with Tom. I told you after your first attempt at walking and talking as Amanda that you shouldn't do that again. You're not good at it."

"Well, it seemed like the key to getting things back in order was to take control. I mean you take control of things, so I thought I would, too. The only way I know to take control is to just do it. I mean, look at how you handled today. You just took control," *Gerald* added, pleased to be able to use an example of similar behavior from *Mitch.*

"That's true *Gerald*, I did have to do that. But do you know why I had to do that?" *Mitch* asks rhetorically. "I had to do that because not one single person in this system was doing his or her job correctly. And why is that? Could it be that I was incapacitated and unable to ensure that the jobs were being done right, even though we were facing some of the most unusual circumstances we have ever encountered?"

Without waiting for an answer, *Mitch* continues, "And what were you thinking with your little, 'I'm an alien from deep inside your body' approach with Amanda? Were you trying to freak her out?"

"Of course not! I thought I would be able to help her understand. Admittedly, it didn't turn out as I had hoped."

"And can we guess why? Oh wait, could it be because that's not your job?"

Feeling that his point is close to being made, *Mitch* brings it all home for *Gerald*. "Look, when *Everett* came to you and started talking about how you should be the one in charge instead of me, he was filling your head with all kinds of lies for his own purposes. You should know that I'm not better than you *Gerald* and you're not better than me. It's just that I have a different role.

"Your role is very important. Do you see how quickly things get out of hand when you don't do your role properly? Just as things get out of hand when I'm not allowed to do my role.

"Can you imagine what it would feel like if *Agnes* suddenly stopped holding on so tight to the grief she carries? Can you imagine how much sorrow and pain would flood the system? We each have our job to do, not because one is better than another, but because each job is important. Your job is important and so is mine," *Mitch* says, concluding his lesson.

Mitch's need to remain emotionless includes his interactions with the others inside, even *Gerald*. He can't afford to be upset or frustrated by these turn of events. He must stay focused on his role, making sure everyone is doing their jobs. And when they fail, he instructs them. Nothing more or less.

"That's it?" *Gerald* asks. "That's all you're going to say? I lock you up for days on end and all you have to say is your job is important and so is mine?"

"What do you want me to say, *Gerald*?"

"I don't know, something more damning I guess," *Gerald* answers honestly.

"Then you *have* been infected," *Mitch* responds, confirming his initial suspensions.

"Infected?"

"Yes, infected by emotions. This one seems to be guilt or shame, mixed with a little fear," *Mitch* observes bluntly.

"Until you are able to deal with these feelings, you will be unable to perform your duties to their fullest. How deep do these feelings go?" *Mitch* asks, sounding as clinical as a doctor asking for a lab report on the progress of cancer through a patient's body.

"Well, given that I wasn't aware of them, I don't think they would be too deep. Right?" *Gerald* asks hoping for a confirming answer.

"It's the unknown feelings that run the deepest *Gerald*. You've become too involved in something. Do you know what can be leading to your emotional response? Consider anything that has brought about an emotion, good or bad."

After only a short time to consider, *Gerald* responds, "I can think of two things: First, I think you are right about guilt. I feel guilt about locking you up and about how badly things are going. And I missed having you to give me direction and the chance to talk things through with you."

"This isn't the first time you have dealt with guilt *Gerald*. You know what you must do with it, right?"

"Yes, I do. I'll visit the falls of forgetfulness before the night is out," *Gerald* promises. He has visited those falls on many occasions. In fact, he visited them each time he had to call for someone to be out for the abuse, especially little *Carol*. *Mitch* set up the falls years ago as a way of allowing *Gerald* to wash his feelings into a lake that sits behind the houses. The falls are available only to *Gerald* and *Mitch* and swimming in the lake is strictly forbidden.

"Good. The falls will serve you well," *Mitch* offers remembering his quick visit to the falls immediately after his visit with the therapist. "Then what of this second thing you mentioned?"

"Well, it's different because it isn't a negative feeling like the guilt is so I doubt that it matters," Gerald offers.

"Oh, I assure you that even emotions that feel good at the time can be devastating to you and I. Others are allowed to have these feelings Gerald, even required to feel at times, but we can not. Now tell me, what has happened?"

"Well, I have enjoyed being out and talking with Tom. It makes me feel like someone is listening to me. You know that I've never had a friend of my own, and that's what it feels like…like he's my friend. But how can that be wrong?"

"It's wrong when it causes problems for everyone else. Your friendship with Tom will cloud your judgment. You will not be able to discern with honesty the best person to handle various situations. Just think about how you have already selected yourself as the person to deal with Tom when another person could have handled things better," *Mitch* pauses long enough for *Gerald* to consider the truth in this statement.

"So now you have a choice to make. You can continue to have conversations with your new friend and hold onto those feelings, or you can let those feelings go into the lake tonight, along with the guilt, and continue to do your job. But you can't do both," *Mitch* explains without showing any emotion of his own over the choice he has just presented to *Gerald*.

"But what would I do if I don't do my job? And who would do it in my place?" *Gerald* asks in a panic. "I don't want to cause any more problems."

"Do you think someone can't be brought about to take over your job? That's not a concern. The concern is you doing your current job and doing it well, or giving up that job to become friends with Tom and others on the outside. It's a choice you must make.

"If you choose the friendships with people on the outside, your role would change. You would then be required to develop and maintain friendships on the outside that will support the needs of the system. This role is equally important to your current responsibilities, especially now that things have changed so dramatically. Either way, you are still an important part of what happens here. But I will leave the decision in your hands. You pick which way you will go. Just don't take too long making up your mind."

Believing his directions to be the only option available, *Mitch* makes no apology for his demand. Instead, with years of discipline and experience under his belt, *Mitch* will now attempt to do what *Gerald* has failed at...performing his duties, along with *Gerald's,* without getting involved emotionally. But he will only do this long enough for *Gerald* to decide what he wants to do.

****

Arriving at Victoria's house and seeing her car in the driveway, *Sabrina* allows *Marie* out to take care of Mom—as if she had a choice. Careful to follow the rules, *Marie* offers this insight, "Tom, this is *Marie*. If you don't mind, I'd like to handle most of the talking. But I might need you to help explain some things and, well, stand behind what is being said."

Tom, only slightly taken back by this new process of insiders announcing themselves, agrees to the approach. Without thinking, Tom automatically goes through the ritual of opening Amanda's door and escorting her down the walk way. Accustomed to being treated like Amanda, and frankly too preoccupied to notice, *Marie* offers no protest.

Waiting for a response, Tom knocks on Victoria's door several times. Hearing nothing inside, he tries the knob. Finding it locked, he exchanges a look of concern with *Marie*. Feeling more desperate, he knocks even louder. Still, nothing.

"Let's see if she is in the backyard," *Marie* suggests.

Without missing a beat, Tom leads her through the side gate and into the backyard. *Marie* calls out for her while Tom scans the horizon. At first, there is no indication that Victoria is around. In fact, just the opposite is true. Her beautiful rose garden, which is usually immaculately kept, looks strangely disheveled. Being the first to notice it, Tom brings the garden's appearance to *Marie's* attention. "This doesn't look good, uh, *Marie*," Tom struggles to remember her name.

"No, not good at all," *Marie* agrees.

Instinctively they begin walking through the garden and looking at the bald roses. Their curiosity over the dramatic changes converts to horror as they notice Victoria laying in the swing, half covered by a blanket and half covered by rose petals, she appears to be sound asleep. Running to her side, *Marie* and Tom frantically ascertain her condition: sleeping, drunk, alive, or dead. Relieved by her stirring, one question is answered—she is alive. Her breath and the bottle answer the second one. Even if she isn't drunk now, she certainly has been.

"Mother!" *Marie* shouts, unable to hide her astonishment.

"Amanda dear," her mother responds. "It's so good to see you. How have you been?"

"Mother, what are you doing out here?"

Noticing that she is outside on the swing, Victoria begins to recall the events that led to her current position. "Well, you see," she begins slowly. "I have been thinking about what you said. You were right! Those dumb ole storms do knock off the rose petals. And Honey, we have had our share of storms now haven't we?"

Her voice indicates that the alcohol is still strong in her system as she sloppily pulls together her words of explanation and discovery. "And guess what I found out?" she prompts as she begins the process of sitting up in the swing.

Tom immediately steadies the swing in an effort to prevent an embarrassing fall. With tears silently falling down her face, *Marie* asks, "What Momma? What did you find out?"

"I found out that…um, I forgot." Victoria says as she tries to find the thought that just ran from her mind. "Oh yeah! I found out that the only thing that is real is roses! Just look at my roses!" she says while waving her arms toward her garden. "Wait! What happened to my roses?" Stumbling to her feet, she runs toward her garden, inspecting the spots where roses once bloomed. "They're gone!" She exclaims while turning to Tom and Amanda for an explanation.

Tom looks to *Marie* and suggests, "I think it's time for some coffee. Let's see if we can get her indoors." With reassuring words and supportive arms, Tom and *Marie* slowly walk Victoria into her house. She continues to mutter faint phrases of distress over the missing roses as tears begin to fill her eyes.

Tom immediately starts the coffee and looks for a sweater or blanket to warm her up. *Marie*, sat down next to her mother in the kitchen and began her gentle inquiry. "Mom, I need you to focus. Tell me, what happened?"

"Oh my darling Amanda," Victoria sobs as she rubs *Marie's* face, more harshly than she is aware. "My dear, sweet, Amanda. I am so sorry."

"Mom, it's okay. Whatever it is, we can work through it."

"No Amanda, this is beyond resolution, beyond comprehension, beyond being fixed."

"Momma, there is nothing that can't be worked through if we work through it together. Remember you used to tell me that all the time when I couldn't figure out a homework assignment or how to handle my stupid friends from school," *Marie* softly giggles while caressing her mother's hair from her face.

Suddenly Victoria turns and grabs *Marie's* arms. "I found it," she snarls. "I found it all."

"You found what Mom?"

"I found his secrets, his photographs, his lies. I found it Amanda."

Startled back by her mother's behavior and tone of voice, *Marie* instinctively pulls away from her. *Mitch,* calling for *Gerald* to guard the door regardless of his decision, quickly puts actions into place for an emergency recovery. Tom, having just returned to the room, offers Victoria the afghan he found in the living room and asks, "You found what?"

Wild eyed and disheveled, Victoria turns toward him like a frightened, angry animal. "I can't go down there to clean it," she explains to Tom. "I burned his clothes, I've thrown away his filthy, clutter from the bathroom, but I can't go down there. I can't do it. Please don't make me go down there," she pleads.

"Okay, you don't have to go anywhere Victoria, I promise," Tom says while reaching out to comfort her. "I tell you what, you tell me what it is you can't take care of, and I'll do it for you."

"No," *Mitch* almost shouts. "No, you don't need to go down there either. I know what she is talking about and I can take care of it myself," he assures.

"Oh Honey, please be careful!" Victoria warns. "It's horrible down there! Tom, please don't let her go down there! Please don't let her go!"

Now completely unsure of what to do, Tom asks God for wisdom. He naturally wants to protect Amanda, but also must trust her. There had been an apparent change in personalities because the voice and look had changed. Victoria was so out of it that she would never have noticed, but Tom did. Searching her eyes for direction, he asks, "Where are you planning to go?"

"I'm going to the basement. I'm not sure what all is down there, but whatever it is, I will take care of it," *Mitch* states plainly.

Remembering their previous reaction to the basement, Tom is taken back by this new resolve to descend into the banned territory alone. "Are you sure you don't want some help? I think it might be best, don't you?"

"Yes, go help her Tom. Don't let her go down there alone. I think there might even be monsters down there!" Victoria says, still under the control of the alcohol.

Smiling back at her, Tom reassures that no monsters are there, but that he will accompany Amanda to investigate. Ignoring Amanda's look of disapproval, Tom stands and smiles at her while escorting her toward the hall with the basement. Once at the basement door and out of Victoria's ear shot, *Mitch* turns to confront Tom. "Look, I appreciate that you want to ride in here like a knight in shining armor, but I can handle this. I am prepared and most important of all, I know what I'm facing."

"I understand, but there is something that you need to understand as well. I love Amanda and when I asked her to marry me, I was entering a covenant with her to walk with her for the rest of her life. I didn't know about all of you at the time, but now that I do, you need to know that my covenant extends to you as well. And from what I have been able to put together about this basement, there is no way on earth that I am going to let you walk down there alone. It just isn't going to happen," Tom insists.

"Haven't you thought about how this might affect Amanda?" *Mitch* challenges. "If what I remember being there before is still there, then it would be extremely embarrassing for Amanda. She would not want you to be exposed to the events of her darkest shame."

"I understand what you are saying, I really do. But I can guarantee you that no matter how bad things are down in that basement, no matter what we find, I promise you…I can imagine things being a million times worse. So we can either face things together, or you can let my imagination run wild with all kinds of acts of horror, whether they happened or not."

Considering this logic, *Mitch* concedes to Tom's request. Simply nodding in agreement, *Mitch* opens the basement door and allows Tom to proceed. Walking cautiously Tom braces himself for those monsters that Victoria mentioned. In stark contrast, *Mitch* descends the steps with a confidence of the years in which he has been able to detach himself emotionally from the happenings of the outside world. For him to accomplish his tasks, he must be aware of the intricacies of the everyday and the abusive life he shares with the others, and he must do it without allowing the feelings to impact his judgments—a lesson he hopes *Gerald* can learn more thoroughly.

Arriving at the bottom of the stairs, Tom stands to take in his surroundings. Walking past his insignificant companion in arms, *Mitch* heads straight for the sofa. He stops long enough to ask Tom to look for a box or trash bag to put the garbage into as he starts collecting the magazines and photos. But before *Mitch* can complete his command, Tom's eyes are drawn to the pile on the cushion-less sofa. Unable to comply with *Mitch's* request, his natural instinct takes over as he begins picking up the photos and magazines one at a time. "This is real isn't it?" Tom asks for a reality check.

"Yep, as real as anything," *Mitch* responds matter-of-factly. Knowing the impact Tom's views have on everyone's safety, and concerned about the images running wild in Tom's brain, he stops to offer him information. "If you really want to know what happened down here, I can tell you. But I think a better way to approach it might be to answer your questions. That way you only get the information you can handle and I can eliminate any of those out-of-this-world images your mind tries to create. So, if you have any questions, now is a good time to ask them."

"No, I'm good. I don't think I have any questions right now. These pretty much say everything don't they?" Tom states.

"Well, the offer stands. If you ever have any questions, just ask for me because I can answer them without it affecting me or the others. It's the safest way to do it. My name is *Mitch*."

"Thank you very much," Tom says, politely acknowledging the offer but only half listening. Determined to help in the cleaning up process, Tom pushes aside the emerging emotions so they can tackle the job at hand. In an attempt to be every bit as detached as *Mitch*, Tom stops looking at the details of the pictures and begins to quickly stuff them into a trash bin. Along with the pictures, *Mitch* adds the towel and blanket to the garbage. After replacing the cushions, *Mitch* bends down and retrieves the Polaroid camera from under the sofa.

Looking around, Tom notices the panties on the floor. While still deciding if he will be able to actually touch them or not, *Mitch* reaches past him and with a single scoop, transfers the panties from the floor to the trash bin. Tom grabs the pages of the torn magazine that Victoria had thrown across the room when she first happened across the terror of the basement.

Not wanting to take a chance on missing anything, *Mitch* conducts a thorough examination of the remaining basement contents. Entering the small bath, he attempts to clean out the vomit left in the sink by Victoria. Acknowledging his own limitations, he allows *Marie* to help with this most unpleasant of cleaning tasks while Tom gives the rest of the room a second and third review for other such items.

As Tom is finishing his last look around, he is astonished to see *Mitch* reach into the trash and pull out a single picture of young Amanda in the nude. *Mitch* indicates his satisfaction with the selection with a nod and places the picture in his pocket.

"What are you doing?" he asks while reaching for the picture to return it to the trash.

"Back off," *Mitch* orders. The tone of his voice left little room for wondering how serious he is about his demand, but Tom was just as serious about protecting Amanda. He is beginning to see the others inside as separate people and he isn't sure who he could trust.

"What are you doing with that?" Tom persists while backing down to avoid a physical confrontation with someone inside Amanda's body.

"Look, things aren't going down like I would like them to right now. You've got to admit that it's been a little difficult to get Amanda to understand what's happening and to believe it. The mother is upstairs drunk as a skunk because she can't believe it. What do you think is going to happen when she sobers up? Do you think she will continue to believe what she saw? Oh, forget about her...what about Amanda? Look, if she is having a hard time believing that we exist, do you think she will be happy to accept the fact that her loving father had violent sex with her from the time she was little? No. She is going to go straight into denial. That's what she was trained to do. That's what I trained her to do. That's how it is supposed to work.

"Now we are going to ask her to set aside her life-long belief and willingly accept what we say. It's not going to be an easy ride for any of us. At this point, she has absolutely no reason to believe us or any of the memories we give her.

"But we have a rare opportunity here Tom. We can actually save some evidence of the abuse. We can have some proof to show her. If she is going to have to deal with the truth, then she is going to have to deal with it completely. This picture..." Mitch says while holding up the awful picture that instantly burns holes into Tom's stomach, "this picture is going to help us prove that we aren't lying. But it's only going to be used on MY terms: when and if I say so. And I guarantee you that it will not be used unless absolutely necessary."

"Why can't you just throw it away? Can't you prove it to her some other way?" Tom asks finding it hard to hold back his emotions any longer.

"It hasn't been a perfect life, Tom, but these are the cards we were dealt. I've invested my whole existence into making sure that we are successful at this life...that we stay as safe as possible. You can bet that I'm not going to use this picture to destroy what I've been working so hard to protect."

Tom's body language indicates his willingness to listen to *Mitch's* reasoning.

Less concerned over Tom's feelings than his compliance, *Mitch* continues to talk to him as if he is an insider needing instructions on how to fulfill a new function in the system. "Now, you are dealing with a lot of emotions right now, but you have to pull them in so that they don't get in your way. We are depending on you to be stable for the sake of Amanda and her mother right now. You will have your chance to deal with those feelings that are running amuck, but now is not the time. So take a deep breath, and as you do, push the thoughts of what you've seen here today deep inside so that you can focus."

Too emotionally and mentally exhausted to question *Mitch's* wisdom, Tom does as instructed. *Mitch* does seem to have it together so he must know what he is talking about. In fact, as Tom visualizes his breath forcing the images of the basement deeper into his memory, he begins to sense a calmness take it's place. It worked so well the first time, Tom decides to repeat the exercise without prompting. Amazingly, he is feeling less emotional and more able to deal with the thoughts of Victoria waiting upstairs.

Seeing the expressions change on Tom's face, *Mitch* asks, "Better?"

"Yes, actually, I am. Sorry—I just want to do what is right for Amanda and I'm having a hard time knowing what that is today."

"You're really doing well, Tom. I'm pleased with what I've seen so far."

Allowing Tom just a few more seconds to stuff his emotions, *Mitch* then prompts, "I think we need to rekindle that fire in the fireplace and burn this stuff too. The last thing in the world we need is for some pervert to go through our trash and find these. But here's the problem. I can't handle the fire and the mother. So I'll let you pick. Which task do you want?"

Tom considers his options before responding. He certainly knows how to build a fire, but he is so tired of touching these things. But, he reasons, better him than Amanda or anyone in there. They've had to handle enough today. With this new found skill of stuffing his feelings, Tom bravely agrees to the task of burning things.

Marie returns to nurse their mother back to health. Without a word, she walks up the stairs with Tom. Once the ascent is complete, they go their separate ways, neither one looking forward to the individual missions they have willingly accepted.

With everyone off to do their assigned tasks, *Mitch* takes his place beside *Gerald* at the door.

Chapter Twenty-One

After a few minutes of silent observation, *Gerald*, for the first time in months, asks for *Mitch's* advice. "I don't know what to do. I've faced such a big decision and I'd like your input."

Without turning his gaze, *Mitch* simply asks, "What happened at the door while I was handling things in the basement?"

"Well, you know *Carol*," *Gerald* starts with a chuckle. "She hears a commotion and wants to know what's happening. Now that the father has died and is no longer a threat, she's started running to the surface to see if she can get involved in everything. She really likes being out with Tom and Jessica both. So now she has expanded her curiosity to include all things internal and external. She's becoming quite the "yenta".

"So, she hears you call for me and comes running to see what's happening. When I wouldn't let her out to see, she took off running to her favorite observation area. Boy was she mad when I switched off the viewing. She can be a little spit fire when she doesn't get her way," *Gerald* chuckles as he tells his story.

"She can be a handful, can't she?" *Mitch* agrees.

"Yeah, she can. But it's no big deal. She just doesn't understand. I don't mind her getting mad at me about stuff like that. I know it's for her own good," *Gerald* states as he shares his thoughts out loud.

"And how is it that *Marie* happens to know when I need her to clean up vomit from the sink?" *Mitch* prompts.

"Oh that was easy. She was already hanging out because she's so worried about the mother. When I sensed you reacting to something, I knew it had to be bad. But man, I didn't expect it to be that!" *Gerald* exclaims as they both share a slight laugh at the memory of the scene. "Anyway, I know you don't normally react to things, so for you to react, that meant that you needed help. I saw that you weren't dealing with any secrets at the time so I figured I'd give you a break and ask *Marie* to help."

"Good thinking. I've learned a lot about blocking emotions, but I can't stomach stuff like that," *Mitch* admits.

After a few minutes of mutual reflection, *Gerald* adds, "You know…it felt pretty good to be handling things again. It was comfortable and I felt confident."

"That's because you were made for that purpose *Gerald*. You are wired to handle this job and you've been doing it for years."

"So does that mean that you think I should give up on having friends in the outside world and just do my job?" *Gerald* asks, fearful of *Mitch's* response. It feels like a loss either way.

"No, I told you that the decision is yours to make. It's good that you have gone through this reminder and you can see how rewarding it is to do this job. But before you make your final decision, I think you should consider the other option. It's not as comfortable and familiar to you, but you can learn a new job.

"The problem is that you've only been talking with me about these things. Why don't you talk with someone else that is responsible for external relationships and get input from her?" *Mitch* suggests.

"*Sabrina*?" *Gerald* asks for the unneeded clarification.

"Yes, she would be a good person to ask," *Mitch* confirms.

****

Starting up the fireplace is second nature to Tom. He doesn't even have to think through the process or consider his actions, he just does them. Once the fire was prepared, he sat down to begin his task of adding the papers to the fire slowly enough to keep the whole house from burning down. He knows from experience that as papers burn, the hot ashes can float out of the fireplace if not properly controlled.

Having established an acceptable rhythm of toss and wait, toss and wait, his restless mind starts to wander toward the images he had so recently tried to bury. Each photograph and magazine that went into the fire seemed to fuel Tom's imagination with scenes of sadistic torture and control.

Everett must have been some kind of wild beast that would have best served society by being locked in a cage for his entire life. What on earth could cause a person to inflict such horrible pain on others? Especially his own daughter! There must be a special place in hell for such people, Tom reasons.

His thoughts then turn to the scriptures that he knows so well, hoping to confirm his latest conclusion. The first verse he considers is, "Vengeance is mine, says the Lord." Surely that means God is seeing to Everett's punishments even now. Feeling quite justified in his building anger, his thoughts race to a second passage that says it would be better to have a millstone tied around your neck and to be thrown into the deepest sea than what will happen if you hurt one of God's little ones.

There can be no doubt about it, Everett must be suffering beyond comprehension. He has had to face his Maker, and God certainly can't be pleased about this. Allowing himself some solace in these thoughts, Tom is able to continue his painful task. He can even picture that each photo being placed into the fire place is another coal being added to the flames of hell right under Everett's feet. In a subconscious effort to prolong his participation in Everett's torture, Tom begins to rip out individual pages from the magazines and burn them one at a time.

Completely lost in time and the passion of his hatred, Tom is pulled back into reality by the ringing of his cell phone. As he identifies the caller as his assistant, he instantly remembers a meeting he had scheduled for noon. Before answering, he checks his watch and discovers that it's already 11:45.

"Hello," Tom answers.

"Hi Tom. It's Sandy. I wanted to make sure that you remembered your 12:00 o'clock appointment and to make sure you are still going to be able to make it," she states, jumping straight to her point.

"Actually Sandy, can you do me a favor and reschedule that for tomorrow? In fact, if you could clear my calendar today, that would be great. Some things have come up that I have to take care of, but I will be sure to be available tomorrow."

"I'll take care of it Tom. Is Amanda doing okay? I feel so sorry for her having just lost her father and all," Sandy offers her sincere inquiry.

"She's having a bit of a hard time actually. I've told her to take a few more weeks off so that she can get her bearings before returning to work. In fact, I meant to talk with you about that. Can you ask Gary to connect with a temporary agency? We'll need to have someone that can handle the accounting responsibilities just while Amanda's out."

"I'll give him a call right away, Tom. Is there anything else you need me to do?" Sandy offers.

"No, but thank you. I really appreciate you keeping me on track with stuff, Sandy. I'll see you in the morning." Without waiting for her "goodbye", Tom absent mindedly closes his phone.

Somehow he must find a way to balance things better. He has let his responsibilities at work slide for way too long. While he has a good staff that can handle things for the short term, there's just too much at stake to leave things unattended for long. There are too many people at the office depending on his ability to keep his company afloat and flourishing. But none of that matters as much to him as finding some solution to the chaos in his personal life.

No longer getting joy from his imagined torment of Everett, Tom picks up his pace in removing from the earth forever the tools used to injure Amanda. Unsure of how well he can control their burning in the fireplace, Tom elects to keep out the blanket and camera for destruction elsewhere.

Moving quietly past Amanda and Victoria in the kitchen, Tom takes the last of his trash into the garage. Quickly finding a hammer, Tom puts his plans into motion. He wraps the camera with the blanket and begins to pummel it with the hammer. This feels even better than burning stuff in the fire! He keeps pounding until there is nothing but flat blanket remaining. Feeling quite satisfied with his slaying of the enemy, Tom hoists his bundle of broken camera pieces into the garbage sack. As he turns to add his fresh kill to the larger sack against the wall, he hears the familiar sound of his sweet Amanda's voice—or at least—something similar.

"Feel better?" *Mitch* asks.

"Oh, I'm sorry. I didn't mean to disturb you. I was just taking care of some trash," Tom explains, not sure who he is talking to.

"I know, I asked you to. With all the banging going on out here, Victoria decided she needed to get some aspirin—especially after I told her what you were doing. So. I thought I'd take the opportunity to check on you. Is it safe to say that those feelings from the basement didn't stay buried deep enough?" *Mitch* offers permission for Tom to share, but still from a distance. He knows that there isn't much time before Victoria returns, but Tom is an important player in the safety of the system now. *Mitch* needs to take some time to be sure that Tom is okay too while staying close enough to the kitchen door to hear when Victoria returns. The last thing he needs is to have her walk in on this conversation.

"Yeah, you can say that," Tom confirms. "I don't know how you do it. I just want to kill him, to do him harm. And I can't even if I wanted to because he's already dead!" His voice is louder than expected, amplified by the echo caused by the acoustics in the garage. This is confirmed by *Mitch's* look of concern.

"I'm sorry," Tom practically whispers. "I'm sorry."

What Tom doesn't understand is that this is new territory for *Mitch* as well. He is accustomed to providing training and instruction to insiders. He knows them well and understands how things can work on the inside. He is a student of human behavior and has tried to use his knowledge to help Tom. He didn't expect that his realm of controlling others would expand to the outside world so dramatically. Oh, he's had his share of exchanges with *Sabrina's* would-be-boyfriends, but he's never had to worry about maintaining a dialog with someone on the outside. This is definitely different, but not insurmountable.

Quickly considering his options, *Mitch* is able to eliminate the desire to send Tom away for him to deal with things on his own. He'd prefer to know what Tom is thinking and doing so that he can determine any risks to the system. While *Gerald* is convinced that Tom is in it for the long haul, *Mitch* isn't as confident.

While there is more than one insider who could handle different tasks, like taking care of Tom and taking care of the mother, there is only one body. It's impossible to do both at the same time…or is it? Perhaps a change in focus is all that's needed.

"So, did you get it all taken care of?" *Mitch* inquires.

"You mean the trash? Yeah, it's done."

"Good. I need your help in here with the mother. *Marie* is doing fine, but she tends to coddle her too much. I don't want anyone to be mean to her, but she needs to snap out of the victim's mentality and start moving toward some semblance of life. I'm going to let someone else handle the situation for a while and see if we can bring some smiles back to people's faces. You up for that?" *Mitch* asks, careful to avoid identifying *Sabrina* as his choice.

"Sure, that sounds good. If you've got someone in there that is up to the challenge, we could all use a little levity right about now."

"Good. Then why don't you round up the mother and take her to the living room where you have that nice fire going. I'll have some lunch brought in to you both in just a minute. You don't mind sandwiches and chips do you?" *Mitch* asks without really asking.

"That's fine, "Tom replies. "It sounds good in fact."

With Tom off to take care of Victoria, Mitch asks *Marie* to fix the sandwiches while he preps *Sabrina*.

Quickly responding to *Mitch's* call, *Sabrina* learns of her task. "Cheer them up. Plain and simple," *Mitch* says. "Get them to talk about the future, about something funny, plans for the wedding, anything. Just get this mood turned around."

Under normal circumstances, this request would have been a piece of cake for *Sabrina*. But these aren't normal circumstances. "I don't understand. Exactly what do you want me to do?" *Sabrina* asks for clarification.

Still unaware of *Sabrina's* strong feelings for Tom, which goes beyond anything she has experienced before, *Mitch* is confused by her question. "What do you mean? You know what to do. You've done this a million times before."

"I mean what am I supposed to do with what I feel, *Mitch*? I don't know what to do with this," *Sabrina* volunteers in hopes of getting some solid direction from someone that has always seemed to care.

Mitch asks *Gerald* to keep an eye on things outside, hoping that *Marie* can keep things afloat a little longer. He then takes *Sabrina* to the side and asks, "Okay—you've got to help me out here. I've been limited in my connection with things for a while and I'm not sure what you are talking about."

"Mitch, I love him," *Sabrina* exclaims. "I love him more than I can say."

Taken back slightly, *Mitch* probes for more information. "Okay, now I know that you have slept with him *Sabrina* and, in fact, that just about everyone knows about that. But since when does that mean you love someone?"

"What, do you think I'm incapable of love too?" *Sabrina* snaps, her feelings hurt by his reaction.

"Well, yes, frankly. I did think that. Don't take it as an insult, *Sabrina*. I have just seen you go after too many guys with seemingly no affect on your emotions. Now all of a sudden you tell me that you love someone. It's just different, *Sabrina*. It's not wrong.

"So tell me, how did this happen?" *Mitch* asks while silently considering his other options for handling the outside situation.

"I don't know. It just happened. He's so nice *Mitch*. It's not like with the other guys. They just wanted one thing and I knew I could give it to them. But with him…he actually cares. I don't have to pretend when I'm with him. I can flirt and be playful without worrying about him jumping me."

"I see…so if you like him so much, what is the problem *Sabrina*?"

"I don't like him. I love him. But *Mitch*, he doesn't even like me. Now that he found out that it was me he made love with, he has been talking like I'm some kind of tramp that tricked him into doing something he didn't want. But it wasn't like that, *Mitch*. I would never trick someone into doing that," *Sabrina* sobs out her protest.

"I know you wouldn't, Sabrina. I know," *Mitch* says as he comforts her with a fatherly hug. *Mitch* knew that Tom would have a problem spending time alone with *Sabrina*, but had no idea that it bothered her so much. He can't afford to have anyone inside treating Tom like the enemy right now. His support is too important. Even as he forms the words, he knows that he is buying himself another trip to the falls, but it must be done.

"*Sabrina*, your feelings are bothering you so much because you were never meant to have them. That's why it hurts you so bad. You were meant to have surface feelings at best—to care enough to keep people happy and to show enjoyment. There's a reason you aren't supposed to fall in love and this is it. You can't risk the heartache. Will you let me help you?"

"Yes," *Sabrina* agrees. Grateful for the relief she knows *Mitch* will find a way to offer her.

As if from thin air, *Mitch* shows *Sabrina* a beautifully decorated box. Its outside is covered in bright colors and shiny stones. *Sabrina* smiles as she catches glimpses of her favorite colors glowing from the box. Pulling out a chain from around his neck, *Mitch* reveals the key for the box. "I alone have the key to this box," *Mitch* explains.

Using his private key, he unlocks the box and slowly opens it. The inside panels are covered with a light shade of purple velvet. She looks inside the box, but it is empty.

Standing beside her, he places the box on a table in front of them. Putting one arm behind her, he gently pulls her close. With a hypnotic cadence and soft tone, *Mitch* begins the process of bringing *Sabrina* back into compliance with the needs of the system.

"I want you to listen to me carefully. In order to maintain the beauty of who you are, we can't remove your emotions. You laugh and others laugh with you.

You smile, and the room turns to sunshine. You must retain your ability to enjoy life in spite of your circumstances. You must hold on to your charm. You must not let go of your enthusiasm for life. You must hold tight to these things. Do you understand?"

"Yes," *Sabrina* says unsure of where *Mitch* is going with this.

"To keep these things, you will release from yourself the feelings of rejection and shame associated with Tom." As he speaks, *Sabrina* can feel something tugging at her stomach. Looking down, she sees *Mitch's* hand pressing against her abdomen.

"Don't worry, it won't hurt and you aren't getting rid of these feelings forever. When you let them go, I'll put them in this box. You can visit them as often as you like but they will no longer be able to keep you from your joy. So let me take those feelings of rejection and shame now. Let's put them in the box."

Complying with *Mitch's* instructions, *Sabrina* watches as he moves his hand from her stomach. He is holding two items that look like dark stones. He places them gently in the box and then puts his hand back on her stomach. Now comes the tough one.

"See how much lighter you feel, *Sabrina*? You are so close to being free. When you release your love for Tom into my hand, then you will be restored." *Mitch* knows what he is really asking of her. He isn't just asking for her to give up on her love for Tom specifically, he is asking her to give up her individuality, her rights to have her own relationships. He's asking her to give up her quest for personal happiness for the sake of the system as a whole. He is asking her to let her dreams die a silent death.

Tears begin to flow down *Sabrina's* face. She has so much love for him inside that it feels like she will be empty without it. He is such a gentleman. He is so genuine. He's the person she always wished she was with when she performed her duties in the past. And now he is here in flesh and blood. How can she let go of her feelings for him? How?

Seeing her struggle, *Mitch* realizes that more guidance is needed. "Let's start at the top *Sabrina*. Let's go to the very top of those feelings. Be careful to separate your love for Tom from your other feelings. See if you can pull aside your laughter for a minute. Let's keep that aside. And you wouldn't be you without your charm. *Sabrina* hold tight to those things that bring light into your life. You can hold onto your friendship with him too, *Sabrina*. He can always be a friend you spend time with, but let's look for those feelings that go beyond simple friendship. Can you find those feelings and isolate them?" *Mitch* asks as he guides her through the visualization process.

"Yes, I have found them. But they feel so big that I'm afraid," *Sabrina* says through her tears.

"It's okay *Sabrina*. It might hurt a little coming out, but it will not hurt as bad as you imagine. And as you release it into my hand, you can see that the feelings of peace and contentment are taking it's place. Do you feel that happening, *Sabrina*?"

Sabrina simply nods as she intentionally let's go of her hope that she would someday be loved for who she is, someone separate from Amanda, someone who deserves her own happiness.

Feeling as if he is treating *Sabrina* as inhumanly as their father did, *Mitch* pushes his feelings of guilt aside long enough to complete his task. As he pulls his hand from *Sabrina's* stomach, he grows concerned that the box he presented to *Sabrina* will not be large enough to hold her painful deposit. If only he had gotten to her sooner, he might have been able to prevent this tragedy.

Using both hands, he carefully places the large mass into the box, handling it with the respect that *Sabrina* deserves. Closing the lid, he locks it tight. He shows *Sabrina* the key and places it back on the chain around his neck.

"Now, those feelings that you asked me to help you deal with are safely tucked away in your private box. They can't escape and no one can take them from you. But they will no longer keep you down," *Mitch* proclaims as he hands her the box.

Sabrina politely declines his offer. "Will you hold onto it for me? I'm afraid I'll misplace it."

"Of course," *Mitch* replies while pulling the box back to himself. "Now, how do you feel?"

"Better...A little afraid that it won't last, but I am better *Mitch*. Thank you."

"You're welcome," *Mitch* forces himself to say. "Now...your friend, Tom, and the mother are sitting there being pampered to death by *Marie*. She just can't help but to make this more dramatic than is needed. Tom won't know that it is you so you don't have to worry about any tension from him. Do you think that you can lighten things up a bit and share some of your beautiful glow with them?"

"Yes, I think I can," *Sabrina* smiles back at *Mitch*.

Leaving *Mitch* to deal with the box of emotions and his own feelings of shame, *Sabrina* makes her way to the surface. Performing an effortless exchange with *Marie*, she discretely observes her environment. Tom is staring into the fire, mindlessly eating his sandwich. From his expression, she can only assume that the gourmet bologna sandwich isn't quite hitting the spot.

Her mother's posture is one of shame, confusion, and isolation. Sitting quietly, just nibbling at the edges of the bread, she looks like a child who's been told to, "just sit there and eat your lunch." In spite of the heat in the room, thanks to the hearty fire Tom is admiring, Victoria still sits with the afghan wrapped around her shoulders. *Sabrina* can't tell if it is due to the weight of the afghan or the world that's causing her to hunch down so. Either way it needs to end.

Finally concluding that *Marie* had allowed all conversation to die, *Sabrina's* first order of business is to bring it back to life. She knows better than to just jump out there with the full enthusiasm she feels given her renewed focus and purpose. Instead, she acts as if she has been pondering the situation for hours and has come across a new revelation. "You know," she begins slowly. "I think it's only about 70 degrees outside." Then, with a slight Southern accent to show that she is playing, she adds, "Oh my, what the neighbors must think…us keeping a fire in the fireplace for days on end in this kind of weather." Having skillfully brought up an obvious irony, one of her favorite tools in humor, she times her concluding giggle just right to bring a smile to her mother's face and a chuckle out of Tom.

Undaunted with the minimal response, *Sabrina* decides to play this one out to the end. Showing a little more excitement, she straightens up in her seat as if she had a wonderful epiphany. "I know, I'll go get the Christmas music started and Tom can get the tree out of the attic. Mom, you might need to skip the eggnog or at least make it without the booze," she gently teases. "We can have a wonderful tree decorating party—just the three of us." Obviously not serious about any of it, she just laughs and waits for the fallout from her obnoxious plan.

"Don't be silly Amanda," Tom adds with a smile. "We can't have a tree decorating party without popping up some corn for a pretty garland."

Surprised and pleased that he is joining in so willingly, she agrees, "You are absolutely right." Stopping long enough to give him a wink of appreciation, she turns to Victoria. "Mom, do you have some popcorn?"

Looking at the two of them as if they had gone mad, Victoria considers her response. In spite of the lingering effects of the toxins in her system, she's still with it enough to feel the life returning to the room. Just seconds ago she was wondering if she could ever get past her feeling of embarrassment and shame. Now she is beginning to think there is some light at the end of that tunnel. If her own daughter can tease about it and Tom is open to playing as well, maybe—just maybe—she will be able to one day regain some dignity.

She can feel them both looking eagerly at her for a response. Without saying a word or providing a hint toward her intentions, she gently places her plate down on the coffee table and walks into the kitchen. Tom and *Sabrina* look at each other with shared concern and curiosity. Through silent communication, they both sit forward ready to jump from their chairs at the first sign of trouble. They can hear some commotion in the kitchen, but it doesn't sound too violent so they wait...and wait. Soon a familiar smell fills the room as Victoria returns with a bowl filled to the top with steaming, butter-drenched popcorn. As she enters the room she suddenly stops. "I thought you two were getting the music and the tree ready," she says with a grin.

Thrilled beyond words to see the mother react with such playfulness, *Sabrina* jumps up and gives her a great big hug. "You're the best," *Sabrina* proclaims.

"I tell you what, that popcorn smells a lot better than these sandwiches have been tasting. I say we eat the corn and listen to some music, but maybe we should wait on the tree for a few more weeks," *Sabrina* suggests.

"That sounds wonderful," Victoria replies.

Sabrina quickly arranges some non-holiday music to play in the background and continues the light-hearted conversation. Refusing to allow things to get too dark, she is determined to bring some air back into the room and into their lives.

Chapter Twenty-Two

Standing side-by-side, *Gerald* and *Mitch* watch as *Sabrina* works her magic. "I don't know what you did," *Gerald* says, "but you really seemed to get her turned around."

"It's nothing. She just needed to refocus," *Mitch* replies offering no further explanation.

"Well, that's the happiest I've seen her in days," *Gerald* observes out loud.

As if receiving a perfect set-up from a volleyball teammate, *Mitch* takes his opportunity to slam the point directly at *Gerald*. With the finesse of a master player, he plainly states, "People are usually the happiest when they are fulfilling the purpose for which they were created. It's no different for us than for others on the outside."

Taking only a few minutes for these words to help solidify his decision, *Gerald* simply says, "I'm sure you have other things you can be doing to finish cleaning up around here. I can handle the door now."

Smiling at his friend, *Mitch* agrees. "I do have some work to do with our Amanda." As he turns to leave, he offers his note of approval. "It's good to have you back."

Walking toward the falls, *Mitch* silently prays. There is much he needs to ask forgiveness for, and much he needs to forgive. He operates as the one in control and one with all the answers for the system, but he knows his limitations. He does the best that he can, but he knows that he falls short. Thankful for the grace God offers, he eagerly receives the cleaning obtained through prayer. Forgiveness obtained, he steps under the rushing waters of the falls. God has never offered to remove his emotions through prayer. For this, he takes matters into his own hands. It might not be the right thing to do, but it's the only way he knows to handle things.

As the waters flow over him, he consciously releases his feelings of jealousy for *Gerald's* friendship, his guilt over the way he must manipulate the others inside, his anger at their father, and his fear of the unknown as they begin the process of vulnerable exposure to the outside world.

The water just past the falls transitions from clear, to murky and back to clear as *Mitch* goes through his emotional purification. As he emerges from the falls, *Mitch's* emotions are as dry and empty as imaginable. His energies can now be spent on preparing Amanda for these new challenges.

****

Bright and early the next morning, Amanda is awakened by a knock on her apartment door. Stumbling to the door, she asks the uninvited visitor to identify him or herself, "Who is it?"

"Hi Amanda. It's Jessica."

Still feeling half-asleep, but fairly confident that it's safe, Amanda unlocks the door and lets her in. Suddenly aware of how disheveled she must look, Amanda asks Jessica to make herself at home while she pulls herself together. As she rushes toward her bedroom to change into acceptable clothing, Jessica offers to start some coffee. Sincerely grateful, Amanda responds, "That would be wonderful! Thank you, Jessica."

As she begins the process of dressing and primping enough to be presentable to a close friend, Amanda desperately searches her memory. Had she invited Jessica over and forgotten? As she begins to place her memory together, she realizes that the last thing she remembers was leaving Dr. Brown's office with Tom. The question that seemed to haunt her dreams the entire night now replays in her head. It's Dr. Brown's voice asking if she ever blacks out or losses time. The question isn't the problem, but his assurance that it isn't normal comes through loud and clear. It's a symptom—a clue—a sign…it's a confirming voice that she is sharing her life with others. That must mean that someone else had control over her life from the time they left the doctor's office until now, whenever "now" happens to be.

"Fine, you want my life so much, just take it," Amanda offers through her frustration and confusion. Expecting her world to suddenly go black, she is almost disappointed when the only response she gets is Jessica calling from the other room, "I'm sorry? Did you say something, Amanda?"

"No—it's okay. I'm just talking to myself," Amanda excuses. "I'll be right out," she quickly adds, trying to find a way to ascertain her situation in the privacy of her bedroom.

"She already knows," comes from deep inside Amanda's thoughts. "She already knows about the others inside. She can be trusted. She knows and hasn't left you. She knows and still cares. Ask her and you'll see. She already knows."

Inexplicably, this news causes a mixture of emotions for Amanda. If the information is correct, then she will not have to worry about explaining things to her best friend. But it also means that everything she's been told over the last...how ever many days it's been, is true. She really is crazy. Crazy enough to have different people running around in her head, taking control over her body, and doing whatever they want without her knowledge or permission.

To top it off, it seems that everyone in the world knows already. What must they think of her? That's why Tom doesn't want me to go back to work yet, because he thinks I'm crazy. I bet that's why Jessica is here today, too. He probably sent her here to keep an eye on me. He doesn't trust me any more. I've been able to live on my own, hold down a job, fall in love, and do a pretty good job with living in general and suddenly, he finds out about these others and I can't be trusted.

"Ask her," the redirecting voice comes from inside. "Don't assume anything. Ask Jessica how she feels."

This time the voice was more distinctive. It was a male's voice. It was clearly a male. But it still seemed more like her own thoughts than a person standing in the room with her. It was definitely inside her mind, not in her outward surroundings.

Still unsure how she is supposed to communicate with these voices, she responds out loud, "Fine. I'll ask her."

Her feelings of determination and boldness quickly fade as she considers how she will approach Jessica with her questions. Intentionally slowing her pace, she approaches Jessica to welcome her with a hug. Relieved that Jessica didn't act like she was an ogre, Amanda begins to soften her posture. The two exchange a few pleasant words of greeting while fixing their cups of coffee. Wanting to be able to watch Jessica's reaction as she talks, Amanda gestures for them to sit at the table.

"Jessica, I have a question for you," Amanda starts, careful not to make it sound like she is about to accuse her of some wrong doing.

"Sure. What's up?" Jessica asks as she leans forward slightly, eager to hear what's on her mind.

With Jessica's waiting patiently for this question, Amanda suddenly struggles with how to ask it. As if coming to her rescue, the voice from inside suggests, "Ask her why she is here today."

"Well, I was just wondering what prompted your visit. Not that I mind at all, I'm just curious," Amanda asks meekly, following the advice of this strange voice.

"Oh, I see," Jessica says as she sits back again. "Well, I got a phone call last night asking me to come over and go shopping with you today."

"From Tom?" Amanda asks seeking more details and waiting to see what to blame for the distrust.

"No, not really. Now, I could hear him talking in the background, but I didn't talk directly to him."

Her curiosity truly peaked at this point, she pushes through for an answer, "So then who did you talk to?"

"Well, thankfully, I understand that I have permission to tell you now. I was talking with *Carol*. She called to ask me to take her shopping today so that she can buy a present for Tom's birthday on Saturday."

"*Carol*? Who's *Carol*?" Amanda asks as she starts to search through her conversations with Tom to see if he has told her about this *Carol* person.

"She's an adorable little girl. She's one of your insiders and I just love her to pieces. When I talk with her, I can imagine how delightful you must have been as a child."

"Okay—hold the phone. Just give me a chance to think here," Amanda says as she raises her hands up as if to fight off any more words that might try to find their way to her ears.

While Jessica obediently remains quiet, the voice in Amanda's head does not. "You see, she already knows and she still cares. She isn't treating you any different now than she did before.

"Why is it that you can't see and believe? Tom has accepted that we are here. Jessica has accepted it as well. Dr. Brown, a professional therapist, has confirmed it. Why can't you accept it? What is the worst that will happen if you acknowledge this truth?"

Unable to sit quiet any longer, Jessica asks, "Amanda are you okay?"

"I don't know," Amanda replies as she searches Jessica's eyes for answers to questions that she can't even begin to ask. As tears slowly work their way down her cheeks, Amanda silently begs for help from her friend. Some rope that she can use to tether herself to reality—anything that will keep her from drowning in this sea of confusion and fear.

Hearing the unspoken cries, Jessica embraces her as a mother would her hurt child. "Amanda, it's going to be okay." Pulling back enough for Amanda to see her face, she continues, "It is all going to be okay. Don't you let these new discoveries scare you into thinking that your life is over. God is not going to dump you and neither am I…and neither is Tom, by the way. This is just a bump in the road—one of those mountains that we have to climb in life. But Amanda, you will make it to the other side of this one. I know it."

Returning to her seat but still holding Amanda's hands, Jessica continues her rose-colored view of Amanda's situation. "I wish you could see *Carol*…well actually, I wish I could see her as she must look on the inside. But she is a little spit fire. Do you know that she actually did a summersault in my living room? And Tom bought her this enormous teddy bear. She was so pleased that she named it Tommy." Jessica shares with a smile.

"Sounds fun," Amanda says as she searches for the right words. Moving the conversation away from the '*Carol* is so great' moment is definitely in order. "This is just all so new to me. I don't fully understand it. But I can tell you that I'm glad you already know. Did Tom tell you that I had a session with a therapist this week?"

"No, I really haven't had a chance to talk with him. How did it go?"

"It was okay I guess. Dr. Brown seems nice enough. But he did give me two assignments. I'm supposed to schedule an appointment with a medical doctor just to be sure that there is nothing physically wrong that can be causing these stupid voices in my head and the headaches that I get, and he also wants me to think about who I will use for my support system. It sounds like I'll be walking around with other people under my arms for support or something," Amanda chuckles as she imagines such a scene. "But apparently, this whole situation could get worse before it gets better and I need to have people around me that I can trust and that know what is happening."

"That makes sense," Jessica confirms without being asked.

"Well, seeing as how you already know what is happening, even better than I do, and seeing as how you are the best friend I have, can I put your name down on that list?"

"Of course. You've got to know that I'll be walking with you through this stuff. Amanda, I don't know what you're going to be dealing with as you learn more and more about the others inside, but I have confidence that you're going to be fine. You're smart, lovely, and most important, you're a child of God. He's not going to leave you stranded out there on your own."

"Well, I don't know how much God has to do with any of this, but I do know that he loves me. I do know that He won't leave me. I just don't know why He let it happen to begin with. How could he let my mind get so divided that I don't even know who I am any more?"

Not waiting for or expecting an answer, Amanda continues as the tears flow once more, "All I want is for things to go back to the way they were two weeks ago. I want my dad to still be alive. I want to be able to hear *him* tell me that everything is going to be okay. I want to see his face and know that I didn't hurt him and that he still loves me.

"I want these voices to go away. I don't want to know about *Carol*, or *Agnes*, or *Sabrina*. I don't want it to be true. I can't do this Jessica. I can't deal with this! It's too much! Did Tom tell you...No...I'm sure he wouldn't."

"Did Tom tell me what?" Jessica asks.

"Oh Jessica. It's horrible. I don't even know if I can say it," Amanda tries to go on through her tears as she breaks out into sobs. "Jessica, Tom broke his promise to me."

"What promise Amanda? What happened?"

"He promised to wait until our wedding night to have sex. He told me that he wanted that night to be the most special night of our lives together. He wanted to follow God's plan so we could have His blessings on our marriage. He promised me Jessica!"

"And he broke that promise?" Jessica asks for clarification.

"Yes, he did!" Pulling her hands from Jessica, Amanda is now physically demonstrating her frustration by mindlessly pacing back and forth in the small breakfast area. "And you know what's worse?"

Jessica just shakes her head and waits. This must be the punch line for the ages given Amanda's display.

"It wasn't with me!" Amanda screams.

"What?" Jessica exclaims.

"That's right! I found out that he went behind my back and had sex with someone else."

Unable to image her brother sleeping around, Jessica asks for further confirmation. "That doesn't sound like Tom. Are you sure it happened, Amanda?"

"Oh it happened. He admitted it!" Sitting down to tell the details so that she doesn't say them loud enough for anyone else to hear, she continues in a hushed tone. "You see, the other night after the viewing, I *mistakenly* asked him to spend the night on the couch so that I didn't have to be alone."

Jessica nods considering the story to be reasonable up to this point.

"Well," Amanda continues, "there was this big mess later that night. I'm not really sure how it happened, but we both feel asleep on the couch and he ended up throwing me onto the floor. So we decided that we'd just finish the night in the bed." Amanda rolls her eyes, "the next big mistake!

"Anyway, according to Tom, that's when we made love, but it wasn't me any more. It was *'Sabrina'*," Amanda says as if simply mentioning *Sabrina's* name makes her tongue burn. "The first time that 'we' have sex with Tom, isn't on our wedding night and it isn't even me! I didn't even know it was happening!! I don't think I can ever forgive him for that Jessica! I just don't think I can."

"Oh Amanda," Jessica starts, praying for words of wisdom and understanding. "Amanda I don't understand how all of this works, but it sounds as if you truly feel betrayed by both Tom and Sabrina."

"You bet I do! How could Tom not know? How could he do those things with her and not know that it wasn't me?" Amanda stares at Jessica and waits for an answer. Someone has got to have this answer—please Lord, let her have an answer that makes sense!

"Amanda, how long have I known you now?"

"About six months."

"Then for about five and a half months, I didn't have a clue that you had others inside. But I'd be willing to bet that I've spoken to them on more than one occasion. You see, it's not like they have always announced their presence as clearly as *Carol* did last night on the phone. Otherwise, someone would have known a long time ago that this was happening with you. When they are out talking and living, they are doing so as you. It's not obvious to the rest of us that it's a different person.

"I can't tell you how many times during this conversation I've wondered if I'm still talking with Amanda or with someone else. The only way I know it's still you is because of what you are saying. If Sabrina or someone else wants to fake me out and pretend to be you, it won't be so hard for them to do. It's the same body, same face, same hair, same everything on the outside. I'm not making excuses for Tom, but you asked how it could happen and I'm telling you, it can happen very easily, Amanda. If she didn't want Tom to know it was her…well, let me just ask you—how could he know?"

"You mean that you can't always tell when it's not me?" Amanda asks, more to allow time for the information to sink in than for clarification.

"No—I can't always tell. Amanda, they have helped you through life. They had to be good at looking and acting like you so that they could take over when things got too hard for you to handle," Jessica explains, grateful for the new insight she is receiving as she talks it out with Amanda.

Reflecting on these words, Amanda begins to wonder about those times when things got too hard for her to handle. She just can't remember anything that seemed so bad from her past. She's had some times when she wasn't too happy, it hasn't always been a bed of roses, but it hasn't been so horrible that she would need someone else to handle things for her.

"Wait a minute," Amanda says pulling the two concepts together. "Are you saying that making love with Tom was something that I couldn't handle so this person decides to handle it for me?"

"No, that's not what I'm saying, but that is a possibility. I don't have any idea why *Sabrina* did what she did. But I bet she could tell you," Jessica offers.

"Yeah right. I don't talk to them. They only want to talk to everyone else, remember?" Amanda adds sarcastically, unmistakably showing her self-pity without remorse.

"Well, I'm not the expert Amanda. But I bet that therapist could help you figure out some of those finer details like that. I just know that Tom loves you very much and I can't imagine him ever doing anything to intentionally hurt you."

"You're probably right, Jessica."

"Probably? I know I'm right about that one. Amanda, I've known Tom all of his life and I've never seen him as happy as he is when he is with you. You are his life, Amanda."

Mitch steps closer to Amanda and whispers, "You were brave enough to ask her for the truth and she has given it to you, Amanda. You're brave enough to accept the truth she is offering. Tom does love you and even as you acknowledge that truth, you are finding that you can forgive this unfortunate event. Allow yourself to embrace his love once more, Amanda. Just let down your defenses a little and trust that you are loved."

Allowing herself to reconnect with her true feelings for Tom, Amanda responds to Jessica. "Yes, Jessica, and he's my life. I don't know what I would do without him. I'm just hurt and scared. I don't know what to do anymore. I just keep holding my breath, waiting for the next bad thing to happen. I can't live like this Jessica. I won't live like this."

"And you don't have to Amanda. I know that things are happening really fast and your head must be spinning with all the things that have happened over the last week. But you need to know that no matter how it feels, your life is not spinning out of control. It is just turning a corner. And Amanda, God is right here with you as you look around to see what new thing life holds for you. It's not always going to be easy Amanda, I know that. But you are going to make it through and you are going to see that there is such a thing as true love. You just have to hold on a little longer and give Tom a chance to prove it to you," Jessica promises with a confidence that only a sister can have.

"Now, like I said, I'm not an expert, but I can tell you one thing that always seems to help..." Jessica pauses to be sure she has Amanda's attention.

"What?" Amanda asks half-heartedly.

"Shopping! Why don't you go splash some water on your face and let's get you out of here. You need to breathe some fresh air and feel the sun on your face. You need a day out with me shopping for that perfect gift for Tom's birthday and...perhaps something for yourself?" Jessica adds.

Smiling at the thought of doing something normal, Amanda nods in agreement. As she goes about pulling herself together, Jessica takes care of putting the coffee cups in the sink and turning off the coffee maker. With the apartment in order, the two set off to explore the malls and forget their issues.

Chapter Twenty-Three

"So, how did it go?" Tom asks as he and Amanda drive away from Dr. Brown's office.

"Okay I guess," Amanda says. "He still wants me to go to the doctor but I forgot to make the appointment. Well, *I* haven't had access to my life much since our last visit so *I* couldn't have done it anyway. But, he made a suggestion to help with stuff like that, I think I'll give it a try."

"Oh, what's that?" Tom inquires.

"He said that we should have a running 'to-do' list by the front door. I told him that I use 'to-do' lists and sticky notes to remind myself of stuff all the time. He's just saying that it could be helpful to have a centralized list that everyone uses and checks on a daily basis. I guess if I'm going to have to share my life with others, I'd better find ways to make sure the stuff I want done gets done."

"That sounds like a good idea," Tom says recognizing how strange the whole situation sounds. Wanting Amanda to feel comfortable with her sessions with Dr. Brown, he doesn't push for anything more. He'll let her share what and when she wants.

After a few minutes of silence, Amanda adds, "He also suggested that we could use a journal to talk with each other—at least until we can figure out how to connect more directly. I think I'm going to give that a try, too. We'll just see what happens."

Looking out the window at the buildings going by, Amanda tries to remember any other details about their session. "That's really about all we talked about," Amanda tells Tom. "But it seems like there should be more, doesn't there? I mean we did talk for about an hour right?"

"Yeah, it was right at an hour that you were in there," Tom confirms.

"Then you'd think that we would have talked about more. I hope you don't feel like it's a waste of time and money. I mean after an hour of talking I should be able to share more information with you…I should remember more information."

"I don't think it's a waste of time or money. At this point I think it's too early to make such a decision. I mean, you and Dr. Brown probably need to get to know each other before you can get a lot of work done," Tom offers.

"Yeah, that's true," Amanda agrees but is still bothered. "Hey, you don't think that one of them came out and talked to him, do you?"

"I don't know," Tom responds honestly. "I guess it's possible…Hey! I have an idea. Why don't you use that journal technique to see if you can find out. If someone came out to talk with him, maybe they will tell you about what happened. If it doesn't work, you can always just ask Dr. Brown on Friday."

"That's a good idea, Tom. I was wondering what I would say to these people anyway," Amanda says. "I really appreciate you taking me to the appointment Tom. I know you have a lot to do at work and it really means a lot to me that you care enough to do this."

"I wouldn't have it any other way Amanda. I love you," Tom says as he reaches for her hand.

For the first time in days, Amanda doesn't pull away. Instead, she lifts his hand to her lips and gently kisses the back of it. "I love you, too."

"I'm sorry that I've been so distant to you, Tom. I've just been so confused and angry. But I know that you didn't do that thing with her on purpose. I'm trying really hard to work through that. Can you be patient with me?"

"Of course I can Amanda. And I need you to be patient with me as I learn the in's and out's of sharing our lives with the others too. I mean, they are a part of you, Amanda. They are part of what makes you the woman I love and because of that, I love them, too. I just have to figure out how to love you and all of those in there in a way that isn't going to hurt any of you…and I'll get there Amanda, I promise."

As they pull into the drive for Amanda's apartment, Tom asks, "Are you going to be okay today? I have a few things that have to get done at work, but I can clear out most of the day if you need me to."

"Oh no, you don't get out of work that easy," Amanda teases. "I'll be fine. I've got some chores around the house to take care of, a doctor's appointment to schedule, and some conversations I'd like to start. Would you like me to cook us some dinner for tonight?"

"That sounds fantastic! I'll plan on being here around 6:00 then?"

"It's a date," Amanda says cheerfully. As she reaches for the door handle, she is suddenly overwhelmed with a sense of loneliness that paralyses her movements. She misses him so much—misses what they once had before all of this nonsense struck. If only it could all be undone. If only…

"Are you okay?" Tom asks, concerned with her sudden change in mood. Though she isn't sobbing, he can see the tears running down her face. "What's wrong, Honey?" He asks as he gently turns her face toward him. "What is it?"

"I just love you so much. Tom, can you just hold me for a minute? Just for a minute?" Amanda practically begs.

Pulling her as close to him as he can in the car, Tom wraps his arms around her and tenderly kisses her face. "Amanda, I will hold you for as long as you want, my love…for as long as you want."

After a few minutes, Amanda finally responds, "Yes, but I guess holding me won't pay the bills will it? I'm feeling better now Tom, thank you so much." Before pulling away, she reaches and gives him a kiss. As if speaking in a language of its own, her kiss is able to express her feelings in ways that words alone never could…her thankfulness, her need for him in her life, her desire to be with him forever, her forgiveness, the need for his acceptance, and the passionate desire she has for him.

"And I'm supposed to go to work after a kiss like that?" Tom asks.

Pulling herself together and exiting the car, Amanda simply replies with a smile and, "Yes." Closing the car door, she waves good-bye to Tom. Not wanting to leave, he sits and watches until she is safely in the building. As he finally drives away, Tom says a prayer of thanksgiving for their restored relationship, God's forgiveness, and a request for her safety.

****

Staring at the handwritten pages, Amanda is almost afraid to read them. She was still hoping that this little experiment wouldn't work and she would be able to deny their existence for a little while longer.

The question she posed was simple. "Did any of you talk with Dr. Brown today?" She didn't even ask them to explain what was said or anything. How could such a simple question result in a five page letter?

Scanning over the pages before reading them, she is able to discern at least three distinct styles. One that is open and flowing—definitely a female's handwriting—something you might see in a teenage girl's diary. Then there is one that is written very small—so small that she might even have trouble seeing the letters. In stark contrast, is the third style—it looks as if a child has written it.

Thinking back on it, she realizes that these same handwriting styles have been on the reminder notes she finds in the apartment. She always assumed that some of the notes must have been written by the others inside.

Taking a deep breath, she begins to read the responses:

> Hey girl! This is a funny way to talk. It can take a long time to get a conversation done this way, I guess, but until we are able to talk face-to-face I guess this is a good alternative.
>
> I really don't have too much to say. I did talk with Dr. Brown today. He seems pretty nice, I guess. He actually asked to talk with me...he said that he wanted to give me a chance to tell him how I felt about things. That's a nice gesture but it was unnecessary.
>
> You see, I've been doing some thinking and I've decided that I should change the way I do some things—well, to be honest, the way I talk with Tom. That's what I really wanted to tell you. I know that you are angry with me and you have every right to be. I stepped in where I didn't belong and did what I shouldn't have done. I can see how that would make you afraid to trust us, and me especially. So I wanted to tell you that I'm not going to do anything like that again.
>
> I'm being told to be more specific so here it goes...This is Sabrina and I promise that I will not make passes at Tom and I will not have sex with Tom ever again. I would raise my hand and swear to it, but I can't do that and write at the same time.
>
> I hate that they made me say it like that, it just seems so cheap. But I guess you need me to be clear so that there is no doubt about what I am saying.
>
> Look Amanda, one of these days you and I are going to have a long talk. I know that Mitch is going to work out how to make that happen. When we do, I'll tell you all about myself and all about those things that you can't remember. After you hear all of that, if you still want to clobber me, you can. Until then, just believe that it wasn't something I did to hurt you or anyone. It just happened but it won't happen again.
>
> Until later—Sabrina

****

Hello Amanda. This is Gerald. You might remember that we have already met. I'll admit, it wasn't the best of introductions, but it was the best that I knew how to do.

I spoke with Dr. Brown some today. I told him about some of the things that have happened both inside and outside over the last several days. He was very helpful. I was concerned about going to a therapist at first, but I am beginning to think that we might be able to trust him. We'll see how he responds to a few more things before we decide completely.

He did have a good idea about talking to each other this way. It's not as easy as talking in person, but perhaps it is a little less frightening to you right now.

So that you know, I'm usually standing pretty close to the door. If you ever have any questions or need help with something, you can call for me. I wouldn't call for me out loud though. All you have to do is use your thoughts to call my name and I'll be there. Sounds a little like a song, doesn't it?

—Gerald

****

Hi Amanda. I did not talk to him today, but I want to know if we can have a puppy. I like puppies. When you marry Tom, can we get one?

Bye,
Carol

Trying to take it all in, Amanda processes the notes in reverse order. Taking out a fresh sheet of paper, she begins her replies.

Dear Carol,

I also like puppies very much. I think we should talk with Tom and see if he also likes puppies.

We might not be able to get one right away, but I bet that we can have one as soon as we get into a house of our own. Remember that we are going to live in the apartment until June when our lease is up. After that, we will move into a house and we'll ask Tom to help us find one that has a fenced backyard so that we can pick out a great puppy for us all to share.

What kind of puppy do you like?

-Amanda

Putting that note to the side, she starts her reply to *Gerald* on another paper.

Dear Gerald,

I do remember you. I have to say that meeting you was a little disturbing. It's not anything personal, but it's not every day that you meet someone who claims to be another part of you.

I'm curious. Why do you stand by the door? As I recall, there is an observation area from which you can watch what is happening. So why stand there?

And...by the way, where's the door and what is it used for?

—Amanda

Saving the hardest for last, Amanda pulls out a fresh page and considers her response.

Dear Sabrina,

I imagine that you have many stories to share with me. I don't know that I will enjoy hearing them, but I will listen.

You are right about how difficult it is to trust you—especially you. While I am trying to figure out how to forgive you, I know that I can't hate you. That would just hurt us both, wouldn't it?

I'm glad to hear that you have decided to leave Tom alone. I'm not sure what made you decide that, but I'm grateful for it. I love him. I'm so afraid that he is going to leave me because of this. I couldn't handle that. So please, don't do anything to mess that up. Please!

—Amanda

The writings done for now, Amanda turns her attention to fixing Tom's dinner. She is relieved to hear *Sabrina's* promises, but isn't sure she can trust them. Now she must decide whether to share that note with Tom or not. It might make him feel better too.

Chapter Twenty-Four

"You're early!" Amanda exclaims. "I don't have everything ready yet."

"Well it smells delicious and you look beautiful—what else needs to be done?" Tom offers as he hands Amanda a dozen roses.

"Oh Tom, they're beautiful! Let me get these into some water." As she steps into the kitchen for a vase, she asks, "So how was your day at work? Everything go okay?"

"Yeah, it was good. I finally got that Harrisburg account settled. Boy am I glad that's finally done."

"I bet you are! That's great news, Tom!"

"Well I can tell you that things are different when you aren't in the office. Everyone is asking about you. They all send their well wishes."

"Oh, that's sweet, Tom. Do you think I should try to go back to work tomorrow?"

"No, I think you need to give it a little longer. There's still some things that probably should be worked out with the others inside before you try to add work back into the mix. Don't you think?"

"That's probably a good idea," Amanda agrees. "Oh! Speaking of the 'insiders', I wanted to tell you! I corresponded with a few of them today. It was pretty interesting."

"Really? Tell me about it. Who wrote to you? What did they say? What did you say? Can I see?"

"Well, I can show you a few of them. But one thing I did find out...I'd better ask permission to share their writings with anyone! *Sabrina* wrote me a note and I was thinking of showing it to you. The next thing I know, I'm holding this note that tells me that if I ever want to see daylight again, I'll keep her writings to myself—all of which seem to have disappeared anyway. She said that if she wants you to know something, she'll tell you."

"Wow—that sounds like an interesting exchange for sure!"

"Yeah, well, not really as interesting as the information that *Gerald* gave me. He explained that he is usually standing by the door so I could call him if there was something that I needed to know. So I asked him where the door is and what is it used for. Okay—get this…there's this door that is like right behind me…well, right behind me on the inside. If I close my eyes and concentrate, I can see it now. It's pretty freaky and I haven't opened the door yet, either. I'm saving that for later," Amanda explains.

"But the reason that the door is there is because that's where people come in and out, to be out in the body. So, I guess when someone else comes out, they come out through that door.

"And *Gerald* stands by the door so that he can 'help control the flow of traffic' as he puts it. I guess that if he didn't stand there, no one would know who needed to be out and when. Oh listen to me, does this sound crazy or what?" Amanda asks.

"Well, actually it explains some things."

"Like what?"

"Well, like how *Gerald* knew the things he did. If he is always standing near that door, then I guess he probably keeps pretty close tabs on what is going on and who is doing what."

"Exactly. That's exactly what he said. And before I forget, I also got a note from *Carol*. She wants a puppy," Amanda shares with a smile.

"A puppy?"

"Yes, a puppy! She seems pretty set on it. Would you like to see her note?" Amanda offers.

"Sure!"

Amanda pulls her note from her back pocket. "She told me to give this particular note to you. See? Right across the top she wrote, 'Please give to Tom.' So—here you go."

Tom takes the note and reads:

Dear Tom,

Can we please have a puppy when we move to our together house in July? I like cockher spanuals.

Thank you,

Carol

"That's cute," Tom says out loud. "We'll have to give it some thought, now won't we?" More than anything, Tom is filled with joy to hear that there are still plans for a 'together house' in July.

Turning his attention back to Amanda, he observes, "It's so good to see you excited about things. It's been a while since I heard happiness in your voice."

"Well, I don't know if I would say that I'm excited. But I guess I am feeling a little less out of control. The more I learn about the others, and the more I understand, the less frightening it is.

"Oh, listen to me just going on and on. I bet you are hungry. Give me a kiss and let me get the dinner on the table," Amanda says, sounding more and more like a wife each day.

****

Per *Mitch's* request, *Sabrina* has waited until Tom and Amanda have finished their dinner before talking to him. The dishes have been cleared and they are heading to the living room to talk. With *Gerald's* help, *Sabrina* takes control of the body while Amanda is safely escorted to her darkened room.

"Hello Tom," *Sabrina* begins carefully. "Can I talk with you for a minute?" She asks timidly.

"Sure," Tom responds cautiously given the sudden change in tone and facial expression. "Can I ask who I'm talking with?"

"*Sabrina*...and I know that you are angry with me, and that's what I want to talk with you about."

"Okay, *Sabrina*, we can talk," Tom offers, patting the sofa next to him to indicate his willingness to listen.

"Tom, I want to explain some things to you and I hope this will help." *Sabrina* pauses more out of necessity than for dramatic affect.

"Actually, I'm not sure where to begin," *Sabrina* says as the unrestrained tears begin to fill her eyes. "I've never really spoken about this with anyone before. I know that I'm not someone you would approve of Tom. I know that, outside of your relationship with Amanda, you would probably turn your back on me in a heart beat—you and everyone else. I know that Tom and I try to accept it...actually, I try to ignore it."

Sabrina grasps for the strength to continue. Of all the things she has suffered in the past, this discussion is proving to be the most difficult and frightening of her life.

Too ashamed to look at Tom, she lowers her eyes and employs a familiar technique...focusing her eyes on something insignificant so that her mind can find the words she needs to say. Distracting herself with the shape and length of her fingernails, she finds the nerve and the words to step forward with her confession.

"Let me tell you about my first memory. The first thing I became aware of as far as I can recall. I opened my eyes and became aware of this man. He was on top of me—having sex with me. He was giving me instructions on how I should react and how to make it feel better for me. He said that I needed to learn to enjoy what was happening. I needed to learn to enjoy life and life is made up of sex. So I needed to learn to enjoy sex and make it more enjoyable for my partner. It wasn't a request. It wasn't really a demand. It was like he was a teacher, teaching me what I needed to know.

"Somehow I knew that I needed to follow his instructions and do as he said. I knew that I had to learn the secrets he was sharing, even though I didn't know him and didn't understand why I needed to do these things...I just knew that's what I had to do. It was the purpose for my existence.

"It didn't feel right at first, but it didn't feel wrong either. It just was. And then I listened and learned. I learned how to respond and engage in the process. I learned my job well.

"It wasn't until later that I learned that the man who was teaching me was our father. Of course, I didn't see him as *my* father. He was my lover. See, not only did he teach me how to enjoy our time together—he taught me how to be discrete. How to flirt with him in a way that no one else would notice. I was his mistress—his play thing.

"Mind you, there was no real emotional attachment to him. He was just someone that I would occasionally visit and have sex with. I know you have to think that I'm the worst person in the world, Tom, and that thought just kills me, but you have to hear these things to understand what I want you to really know," *Sabrina* explains, still focusing her physical attention on her own hands.

"Another part of my existence is to socialize with people. It started with just flirting, but then we discovered that I was really pretty good at making people laugh and helping people to get along. I learned to act like Amanda so that people didn't notice the difference, but I took it to the next level. The people I interacted with thought that I was their best friend in the world. The truth is that I had no more emotional attachment to them than I did to our freak of a father.

"That is, until you came along. I never experienced the safety of really getting to know someone, especially a man. Someone that wouldn't expect or demand sex from me. You brought this special kind of peace into my life that I never thought was possible. Because of that, I let down my guard. I began to connect with you emotionally. I considered you my good friend and I wanted more. I even had a silly dream that it was me, Sabrina, that you loved instead of Amanda.

"When I sensed the intimacy with you build last week, I took my chances...for the first time in my life, I made love with someone—I made love with you. It wasn't just sex; it was so much more than that. It was more than I have ever experienced. It was more than I had ever hoped for...more than I could have ever imagined. I wasn't worried about technique or what I was supposed to do or say...I just allowed myself to experience being loved and loving you.

"I feel so bad about the fall out and the special moment that I stole from you. I know now that it isn't me personally that you love, but that it's Amanda. I know that my actions have caused you both so much pain and for that I'm truly sorry. But I will never forget and will never regret that night. For me, it was a moment of happiness that will carry me until I die."

Tom gently reached over to wipe the flow of tears from her eyes. Before he could respond, *Sabrina* continued, "So now, I have made a decision. Your friendship is very important to me. I have let go of everything but that—I can't let that go," she says as she glances up at him. "Asking me to give that up would be to ask me to give up on life completely."

Looking back down again, *Sabrina* states, "But Tom, you need to know that I have let go of the rest. I know very clearly that you and Amanda are meant to be together. I wanted to just let you know that I'm not going to trick you, Tom. I'm not going to flirt with you or even try to steal a kiss. All of the indescribable feelings of our sexual and emotional connection are forever tainted by the fact that the moments of joy were stolen from you and Amanda. I'll not do that again, Tom, I promise."

Her story told, and her promise made, *Sabrina* crumples into Tom's open arms. As he rocks her and cries with her, he makes a promise to her. "*Sabrina*, I will never turn my back on you in shame. You are so precious and you deserve all the happiness you can find. I don't know how this will all work out, but I want you to know that I do love you. You are a very important part of Amanda as a whole."

Lifting her face so that she can see his sincerity, he adds, "I'm not ashamed of our time together and I'm not ashamed of you. I do regret that it has caused you so much pain. But *Sabrina*, we will get through this, too.

"Thank you for sharing with me. I know that had to be very hard for you to do," Tom adds as he allows her head to rest back on his chest. "I am so glad you trusted me with your feelings."

After a few minutes, Tom asks, "Can I share an observation?"

Sabrina simply nods her permission.

"Things aren't the way they used to be for you. Everett is gone and can no longer make demands on you for anything. You have someone in your life that is here to stay, and is more concerned about your well being than gratifying his selfish desires, which is more than you ever experienced with Everett.

"*Sabrina*, now you can learn how to enjoy life the way God meant it to be. Life isn't always going to be easy or fun. There are times when people will hurt you and hurt your feelings—probably even me from time to time. But you need to know that it's okay to connect with people—in the appropriate way of course. You can make friends and truly enjoying being around others. And I will always, always be your friend.

"The good news is that life isn't all about performing for others, sexually or otherwise. It's about letting God fill you up with His love—truly experiencing that peace that comes from knowing with all your heart that your Creator loves you beyond compare. Then you get to share that love and joy with others—like me," Tom says with a smile. "And when life does hurt, you can let God, and the people He puts in your life, bring you through to the other side of that pain.

"You can be released from the requirements of the past now *Sabrina*. You're free..."

Chapter Twenty-Five

"Hi Amanda! I really appreciate you coming over to help me," Jessica says as she welcomes her into the house. "Time has totally slipped away from me this week and I feel like I'm down to the wire with getting things ready for our party Saturday."

"It's not a problem at all. I'm happy to help." Setting down her purse, she asks, "What would you like me to do first?"

"Well, first, I was thinking we could polish up the silver that we're going to use for the party. That's kind of messy so if we get that done first we won't be messing up anything we've already cleaned. What do you think?"

"That sounds like a good plan to me."

"Good, I already have the rags, polish, and silver sitting on the table. Would you like some coffee or tea before we get started?"

"No, I'm good. But thank you anyway," Amanda says as they sits at the table to begin their first of many tasks for the day.

"The other good thing about starting with the silver is it gives us a chance to catch up on things," Jessica prompts.

"Definitely! Can I go first?" Amanda asks, eager to share her news.

"Of course! Spill!"

"Well, Tom and I had a long talk last night. It was really good. And, well the bottom line is that we have set a new wedding date. We are going to tie the knot on December 14th."

"Oh Amanda, that's less than two months away! What day of the week is that?"

"It's a Saturday."

"Well, we're going to have to get busy!" Jessica responds with a mixture of excitement and concern.

"Yes we are! But it can be done. I stayed up most of the night laying out a plan for what needs to be done by when. It's going to be busy, but fun," Amanda smiles. "So you'll help me?"

"Of course I will! That's what a matron of honor is supposed to do right? Help the bride get through four months worth of work in just two?" Jessica teases. "So how did you decide on the date?"

"Well, as you know, we've been talking about changing the date for about a week. I really wanted to make it in November, but with all the stuff that's been going on, that's just not realistic. So we made a compromise—instead of waiting four months, now we'll just have to wait two," Amanda nods with a smile.

"Have you told your mom yet?"

"Yeah. I called her this morning before I came over. She immediately offered to start working on stuff and making arrangements," Amanda laughs remembering Victoria's enthusiasm. "I assured her that I would talk through the plan with her and let her help as much as she wanted."

"Good! Sounds like she's doing okay today then. I've been concerned about her."

"Oh, she seems fine. When I called her, she was off to deadhead her roses."

"Deadhead?" Jessica asks, perfectly willing to show her ignorance of this strange term.

"Oh, that's where you cut off the old blooms. It helps the plant somehow when you do that. I'm not really sure about all of that myself, but Mom's really into it. She said something about a storm going through her garden and knocking off all of the roses so now she needs to go out there and clean it up. She doesn't really expect any more blooms this year, but she wants to be sure that the plants are healthy enough to survive the winter."

Changing the subject completely, Amanda asks, "So, what about you? Have you and Rick worked out the menu for Saturday yet? The last I heard he was insisting on trying to barbeque and you were trying to talk him out of it."

Both giggling at Rick's barbequing skills, Jessica explains, "Well...we have also found a compromise. It's not as significant as setting a wedding date, but it can sure feel like it sometimes. Anyway, we decided that he will barbeque some shrimp kabobs, which he actually does a pretty good job with, and I will make some shrimp scampi. He's going to put together the salad—believe it or not—and I'm going to bake the chicken."

"And is your mom still baking the cake?" Amanda asks.

"Yeah. She loves to bake cakes. She's pretty good at it, too." Jessica stops for a second then adds, "You know...you might consider asking her to bake the groom's cake for the wedding. I don't know that she would want to tackle the wedding cake itself, but I bet she would be thrilled to do the groom's cake—and it would be good too. See what you think about the cake she brings on Saturday. If you like it, why don't you ask her?"

"That's a good idea Jessica. It would probably mean a lot to Tom, too," Amanda suggests. "And...I've been looking for a way to bring her into the wedding planning more. Mom has dominated things so much, that I've been afraid to get both of them involved at the same time. My mom is so excitable these days that I'm afraid she'll make a fool of herself trying to do it all alone."

"Then it sounds like a perfect opportunity Amanda! In fact, it sounds like an answer to prayer!"

"It sure does," Amanda agrees.

As the two of them ponder this new idea, an internal struggle for control is under way. "But *Gerald*, I want to go out and play with *Jessica*. She's my friend. She said so," *Carol* pouts.

"Don't be ridiculous *Carol*," *Marie* snaps. "There is a time to play and a time NOT to play and clearly, this is not the time for play. This is the time for serious work. Jessica is trying to get her house ready for a party. It's very important to her that the house is clean and things are ready.

"Don't forget that our mother is going to be here, too. We don't want her to be disappointed in Tom's sister do we?"

"I can clean *Marie*!" *Carol* says, stomping her feet. "I can clean real good. I just never have to 'cuz you always do the cleaning for us."

"*Gerald*, you have to let me out there," *Marie* begs. "Just look! Amanda put that knife in with the clean ones and it's got spots all over it!" Not waiting for *Gerald* to grant her permission, *Marie* storms past him and quickly takes control of things.

"I'm so sorry, Jessica, I missed a spot on this one," *Marie* says while pulling the offending knife back into the 'dirty' pile.

Chapter Twenty-Six

Aware that the therapy session with Dr. Brown is about to begin, *Brooke* makes her way to the observation area. It's interesting to see this guy at work. Not one to quickly trust others, *Brooke* has determined to watch his every move. He reminds her some of Mitch, but somewhat nicer. Still, for now, she plans to watch from the inside.

She heard *Mitch* telling *Gerald* that he wanted to talk with Dr. Brown early in the session today. "There is no telling what Mitch has up his sleeve. This could be more entertaining than usual," Brooke thinks. Armed with a bag of popcorn and a soda, *Brooke* props her feet up and settles in to watch the show.

After about five minutes of 'report out' from Amanda on the progress she had made this week with writing to the insiders, *Brooke* considers giving up. The only thing holding her attention is Travis's responses—or more specifically, the lack of responses. He smiles, nods, laughs, and sighs with her, but he hasn't really said much of anything. He's just letting her talk. "If that's all a therapist has to do to earn the big bucks, why aren't more people doing it?" *Brooke* wonders.

Then it happens…"Excuse me, I'm sorry for barging in like this, but she could go on for hours and I really want to talk through something with you. So, you can tell me…either we talk now, or I call you later and we talk, but I need to get your thoughts on a few things," *Mitch* offers.

"It's your session, if you need to talk about something, now's the best time to do it," Travis responds.

"First, I can tell you that the note thing worked out pretty good. I don't know how much patience people will have for it over the long-haul, but it will work until we open up the system to Amanda more."

"Good, I'm glad to hear it."

"Yeah, okay. So anyway, you made an offer the first time we met. You said that you have some experience in helping people through this 'discovery' time and that your experience and my knowledge of the system could work together to help make the most of this situation we are facing," *Mitch* summarizes, not waiting for Travis to confirm, he continues. "But there's one thing I need you to understand before we get started. I am breaking my own rules by talking with you about this, but I see no way around it. The situation has become urgent and I need to have access to some of that experience you talked about and this is the only way that I know to do that. But if I expose this problem to you and you take advantage of it in any way, or use it to cause any of us harm, you will wish that you had never met me."

"I understand your concerns, *Mitch.* I know that it can take a long time to trust someone with such critical information as you have. I will be happy to talk with you about what is going on and see if any of my experience can help the situation," Travis agrees, unworried by *Mitch's* threats.

Visibly taken back by Travis's ability to remember him personally and to so easily identify him, *Mitch* just stares for a second. "Don't let him throw you *Mitch.* He's playing games with your head," *Brooke* says out loud, knowing that *Mitch* can't actually hear her.

"Okay, then let me tell you the stuff that Amanda doesn't know about this week. And you can tell me how much trouble we are actually in...Deal?"

"Sure, we can talk through it. What happened?" Travis inquires.

"Well, first let me tell the positive aspects as I see them. Tom, Amanda's fiancée, and his sister, Jessica both really seem to understand what is happening. They are both very patient with Amanda and the rest of us. They don't constantly ask, 'Who's out' or anything crazy like that. They are trying to help us experience some normalcy and they're doing a pretty good job of it."

"That's great news," Travis remarks. "So far it doesn't sound like we're in much trouble."

"Well...now before I can explain the problem as I see it, you have to understand that we've played by one primary rule for years now...maintain status quo—a low profile you might say. In order to do that, we've kept a lot of secrets from Amanda so that she can be our face to the world. She doesn't know anything about the stuff our father did to us, or that kind of thing. When she was younger, she walked through the system and talked with us, just like the rest of us. But as she got older, it became apparent that she really needed to focus only on the outside world. I began making it so that she would just 'go to sleep' when she came inside. She couldn't see or hear anything until we changed to have her out again.

"Now for the first part of the problem. Now that she knows about us again, I have to make a decision about how much I allow her to see of the inside."

"What is your concern about her seeing the inside," Travis asks.

"Well, part of my concern is that I can't tag along with her 24/7. I don't know what she will stumble into or what someone might say to her. Even though she knows about us, she still doesn't know why we are here and I'm not so sure this is the best time for her to find out. You know that our father just recently died?" Mitch asks, more to be sure that Travis is following the same thought pattern than out of the need for an answer.

"Yes, I'm aware of that," Travis confirms.

"Well, this has just been a lot for us all to handle is what I'm saying. First, we are exposed to her fiancée and his family, then the father dies, then the mother starts acting all strange and tells us that she took years of physical abuse from the dad in order to protect Amanda, then *Sabrina* has sex with Tom and completely blows up Tom's promise to wait until the wedding night, then Amanda finds out about us AND about *Sabrina* and Tom, and I'm sure I'm forgetting something, but you get the point. All of this has happened in the span of only a few weeks. I think that would be too much for just about anyone," *Mitch* concludes by taking a deep breath.

"You're absolutely right. That is a lot of change to experience in a such short period of time."

"That's right. A lot of change. And while I've managed to get some things back into place so that our system is more operational, I haven't quite figured out what that means."

Allowing *Mitch* to provide the details in his own way and at his own pace, Travis doesn't say anything—just sits and waits.

"Okay, so here's the deal. Our system, when working right, is like a finely tuned machine. We each know what we are supposed to do and we do it. All for the goal of keeping secrets from the world and from Amanda.

"Now, we are telling our secrets to the world. Every time I turn around someone else is telling their secret to someone. We've told the mother about the sexual abuse. *Sabrina* told Tom all about why she was brought about and what her role is. And that's just the tip of the iceberg.

"I get why it is being done. Each time I see a real need for it to happen, but it goes against everything that we have worked so hard to accomplish for so many years. In the past I would have done something to stop it all, but now...here I sit telling *you* our secrets.

"It's all happening so fast. I don't know what is safe any more. That was always my strength—to know when something would interfere with our primary goals. Now I don't even know what our goal is. If we aren't trying to keep secrets any more, what are we trying to do?" *Mitch* asks. He knows that he has exposed himself to Travis and that Travis could take advantage of this vulnerability. So while interested to hear his response, *Mitch* is ready to take actions if needed.

"That is quite a dilemma *Mitch*," Travis observes. "It sounds like your goal has been removed, but not clearly replaced."

"Yeah, you can say that," *Mitch* agrees.

"And you need a goal in order to know how to operate as a system...Kind of like a guide post to keep you on track?" Travis asks for clarification.

"Exactly," *Mitch* nods, pleased with Travis's understanding.

"So what do you think this new goal should be?"

"I don't know, I'm not the one who took away the old goal," *Mitch* says, surprised by his own defensiveness.

"Who did?" Travis asks.

"Well, I don't know. I know who first broke the rule and went against the goal, but I don't know when or who actually destroyed it. All I know is that at some point, and perhaps gradually over time, the goal has been changed. I just don't know what it changed to."

"So who made up the first rule? Where did it come from?"

Mitch considers his answer for a minute before responding. "I guess it just came into existence naturally. We learned the hard way that secrets could not be shared with anyone on the outside. We discovered that Amanda couldn't handle things at school if she was distracted by what was happening on the inside or down in the basement with the 'dad'. So I guess we just decided on the rule because it was necessary to help us survive and function."

"So then, you need to know what is necessary to help you survive and function now that the rules have changed...so that you don't have to learn the hard way?" Travis asks for clarification.

"Yeah, that's exactly it. So, how do we keep this boat afloat?"

"Okay—let's make a list...a list of the things that you think you want to accomplish. For example, what about working? Do you want to continue to hold a full-time job, a part-time job, or no job?"

"Full-time of course. We have to keep our job," *Mitch* responds.

Travis takes a marker and writes, "Keep job" on the white board in his office. "Okay, what else do you want to keep?" Travis prompts.

"Well, Tom's pretty good for us, I think we should add him to the list," *Mitch* suggests.

"Okay...Keep Tom," Travis says as he adds that to the board. "What else is important?"

"Well, no offense...but I would really like for us to stay out of the loony bin."

"No offense taken...but so that I understand what you mean—are you talking about staying out of the hospital, or out of the insane asylum, or do you mean that you don't want people to think you are crazy?

"All of the above," *Mitch* confirms.

"Okay, got it," Travis say as he adds all three to the list.

"You know...we have some people in our prayer group at church that I think are important for us to keep around—as just regular friends, you know?"

"Okay—how about we say, 'Keep friends and support'?"

"That works," *Mitch* agrees. "And one other thing that I think is important...it's not always something that I think I've done real well with though...I'd like to be sure that we are following God's plan."

"That's a very important one *Mitch*. Good—I'll add that one to the list too.—Okay, this is a pretty good list to start with, is there anything else you would like to add?

"No, I think that pretty much covers all I can think of right now," *Mitch* says after a few minutes of serious contemplation.

"Alright...Now I have a very important question for you, given that you know the people in the system so well...Do you think that all of the others inside, including Amanda, would agree with these goals?"

"That's a good one...let's see..." *Mitch* considers each goal and each person before responding. "Well, there may be a few hold outs, but I'd say that most everyone inside would agree with almost all of the goals."

"So you don't think there would be a significant voice against these goals?" Travis asks to help *Mitch* think through the situation in more depth.

"No...I think there is only one person that might have a problem with keeping Tom, but he is insignificant to the overall goal as far as I'm concerned. I think there might be a few that don't care one way or the other, but only the one that would have the issue with that one statement. And there might be a few that are less concerned about following scripture or holding onto the friends at church, but again, not to the point that it would be a problem. They haven't interfered with these activities so far."

"Okay—good. Then let's assume for now that these are your goals. And remember, that these goals can change as your environment changes, if needed. But these are pretty solid goals—pretty reasonable too."

"I agree," *Mitch* nods.

"Okay—then the next step is to consider what is required to make this happen." Travis offers.

"Well, if I were to guess, I'd say that to keep the job, we have to be able to function from 9—5 without people knowing about all of us. Well—Tom being our boss will help some with that, but we don't want to cause him any problems either—or that would violate the second goal," *Mitch* observes.

"I agree," Travis confirms. "In order to maintain a full-time job, you will need to be able to function on that job, without others in the office knowing about the insiders. Tom being the exception there, but you can't let the issues you are dealing with interfere with him at work either.

"What else is required?" Travis continues.

"Well—I think that in order to maintain some friends that are just friends…the kind that are supportive with the normal stuff in life, we probably should keep the insiders a secret from them as well," *Mitch* suggests.

"It is important to limit who knows about the insiders and your past. If too many people know, you will spend all of your time dealing with 'issues' and none of your time doing fun and normal stuff—the kinds of things you can do with 'friends' that aren't those really good friends," Travis confirms.

"Well—I think that if we want to keep the support friends supportive, we probably should be careful about how much we ask from them."

"That's a good observation *Mitch*. Many of my other clients have discovered this far too late in the process. It will be important to maintain some normalcy with people like Jessica. You can talk with her as you need to, but be careful to listen to her as well. Watch for signs that you are pulling too much energy from her. Help her take care of herself," Travis instructs.

"What other mistakes have your clients made in this process?" *Mitch* asks, happy to find a way to pull from Dr. Brown's experiences.

"Well, to be honest, you are doing far better than many of my clients at this stage. You are already thinking through how to make this transition smooth and beneficial. So many just react and don't participant in the process. You're interest and cooperation with the process puts you miles ahead of so many others.

"There are a few other things that I can think of—so you don't have to learn them the hard way—and this is in support of your goals," Travis adds, modeling the thought process of checking back in with the goals to be sure that he is staying on track.

"If you want to keep people from thinking that you are crazy, you need to limit the circumstances during which you will allow the alters to be seen. And by 'seen', I mean that they are presenting in a way that it's obvious that Amanda is not out. For example, allowing a child to come out and select a toy at the toy store. While that can be fun for the children inside, it tends to look crazy to the rest of the world.

"But even if it didn't look crazy to others, it isn't a safe thing to do. Some of my clients get into therapy, find out that the alters can come out and talk safely while in therapy, and assume that the whole world will treat them just as kindly. The truth is that, just as you have in the past, you need to select who you trust with the depths of who you are. You are a good judge of character, and not so quick to trust, so I imagine that you will do fine with determining who you will let into your personal space like that."

"That makes sense," *Mitch* says, somewhat relieved by this advise.

"As far as the insane asylum goes, I don't think there is any reason for us to even fear that one. A diagnosis of Dissociative Identity Disorder is rarely, if ever, a cause for committing a patient to an asylum. In fact, your ability to split off and create other personalities is probably what has kept you out of the asylums.

"So let's talk about the hospital. I'll be straight with you—there are times that some of my clients choose to check into the hospital for a short visit. Most of the time it is because they have a personality that is hurting them or others, or has threatened to do harm, and the system is unable to control them. And sometimes it's because there is just too much information being shared and they are unable to function well—they need a safe place to process things—perhaps safe from an abuser, or safe from items that can be used to cause themselves harm.

"The greatest challenge that most clients face is finding new ways to cope with stressors—even everyday stressors. But that's why we meet and talk things through like we are now." Finding himself taking a slight detour in the discussion, Travis simply stops and tries to reconnect with *Mitch*. "Is any of this helpful in addressing your concerns?"

"Yes, it is helpful, but can we put some meat on these bones? Can we see how it applies to a specific problem?"

"You bet—what's the problem?" Travis asks.

"Well, the problem is in knowing how much to let Amanda know about her past and how soon. Now I heard you say that one of the mistakes others have made is going too fast. I can see why that is a problem. It's like...now that we have the process started, let's get it moving and over with...but at the same time, I don't want to mess with those goals up there. If you just start with the first one, the job...how do we maintain at work if Amanda is finding out that her father was a real creep?"

"That's a good question. There are a few things we can do to keep things moving slow enough for her. For example, we can allow the inside person to heal some from the pain of their experience—you know, talk it out and relieve some of the intensity of the experience. Then, the same inside person can share his or her experience with Amanda. That way it is less intense when the information is shared.

"That's some of the details that we can work out later and a lot of it will happen quite naturally. But no matter how we go about sharing information with her we can still count on disruptions for the host. Sometimes they just need..."

"Wait...what do you mean host?" *Mitch* interrupts.

"Well, that's one of the terms that is used to describe the person that is the core personality. Usually it is the 'birth' person, the one that was around at birth. You might hear people call this person the core, the host, or the birth personality. But one thing that most of them seem to have in common is that they usually don't know about the abuse, just as Amanda doesn't know."

"Okay—I think I understand. Please continue."

"Well, let's look at things this way...In the past, Amanda handled the everyday tasks in life and the insiders handled the emotionally and sometimes physically difficult things. Correct?"

"Yes." *Mitch* says.

"Then in order to keep up with your goals, perhaps we need to switch roles for a while. Amanda has missed more than just a few hours in the past so I'm assuming that you have people who can handle work other than Amanda. Is that correct?"

"Yes."

"Then if Amanda becomes overwhelmed with information, which is what you mentioned as a concern at the beginning of this conversation, can you allow her to come inside and deal with her feelings and discoveries while this other person handles work temporarily?" Travis asks.

"Yes—that could work," *Mitch* agrees. "That takes care of the first goal—keeping the job—I can see how that can help with determining the rules. But how do we decide how much information to give Amanda at a time?" Before he can answer, Mitch adds, "And, it's not always going to be up to us you know…Here's the other part of this problem that is actually the reason that I needed to talk today instead of waiting until later. The mother…"

"The mother? Do you mean the body's mother?" Travis asks for clarification.

"Yes—exactly. Here's the dilemma: The mother knows that the father sexually abused Amanda. She is devastated by it, in fact. But the mother doesn't know that Amanda isn't just Amanda…she doesn't know that it's important for Amanda to find out these things slowly so that she can continue to function. As far as she knows, Amanda already knows everything because she thinks that it was Amanda that told her.

"So let's just say that I allow Amanda to visit her mother, and suddenly the mother starts talking about that stupid stuff she found in the basement. She is expecting Amanda to know what she's talking about because *I* know what she is talking about. But Amanda won't have a clue.

"How do we handle that?" *Mitch* asks.

Now sitting on the edge of her seat, *Brooke* is anxious to hear his response.

"It sounds like you have a few options: You can tell her mother about the others and get her to cooperate in the healing process…you can try to keep Amanda away from her mother until Amanda knows more…well actually, I don't see any other choices. Do you?" Travis asks.

"Not really. That pretty much sums it up."

"So what are the risks and benefits of each option?" Travis asks—keeping

Mitch engaged and controlling the decisions.

"Well—if we don't tell her about us and get her cooperation, then she could say too much too soon. I don't know that I will always be able to keep Amanda away from her. And I'm not sure that would be good anyway. She's not perfect of course, but I think Amanda needs her and she needs Amanda.

"If we tell her, well…there's no telling how she would react. I guess it could go one of two ways—either she will believe what we are saying or not. If she believes that we exist and that Amanda needs time before she talks about it—that would be the best case scenario. Worst case would be that she thinks we are crazy and either stops talking with us or tries to have us committed," *Mitch* reasons.

"Well, as I said, people are rarely committed because of this diagnosis. It isn't something that you see every day, but there is enough documented about DID that the only way to have you committed would be to prove that you are a danger to yourself or others. Is that the case?"

"No, of course not," *Mitch* replies.

"Then the only worse case that is possible is that she will stop talking to you," Travis points out.

"Then it sounds like the best thing is to tell her about us and ask for her help in taking things slow. But here's the thing…she's been through more than you can imagine these last few weeks as well. And she doesn't have others inside to help her deal. I really think that if I go to her and try to explain this, it will blow up in my face."

"Well, one option is to allow me to talk with her, along with you. I can help you explain things and help her work through the initial information sharing," Travis offers.

"That might work. So would you offer to be her therapist, too?" *Mitch* queries.

"No, I don't think that would be appropriate. But, as you said she is dealing with a lot of information and grief right now. I can definitely refer her to a colleague of mine. She's great with grief counseling and also understands how to help family members and support people for those with DID like yourself. But I think the initial visit is best with you involved and perhaps it's being selfish, but I want to be sure that I can be there to help you through that conversation. I wouldn't trust just anyone with that task."

"Then it's agreed. I'll work on getting her here on Monday then. Should

Tom be part of that discussion?" *Mitch* asks.

"That might be helpful. We will just have to be careful not to overwhelm her, but I think that would be a good way to approach it."

"Thank you Travis. You have been a big help and have given me a lot to think about, and a lot to do," *Mitch* chuckles as he retreats inside, leaving the good doctor to explain to Amanda that her session is over.

Chapter Twenty-Seven

Brooke blows past *Mitch, Gerald,* and the emerging Amanda, jumping into position to present. Unwilling to allow anyone to impede her mission, she locks the door behind her. She is unaware, but wouldn't care, that Amanda is now trapped in her first experience of co-consciousness. Not quite out, but no longer asleep, Amanda can hear and see what is happening, but is unable to say or do anything herself.

"Wait just one minute," *Brooke* practically screams at Travis. "Before you and *Mitch* go off making plans to introduce our mother into this process, there are some things that you need to know."

To *Brooke's* astonishment, Travis holds up a finger, instructing *Brooke* to wait. "We're already five minutes over our session time," Travis explains. "I do have some more time in my schedule this morning and will be happy to hear your concerns. But we should probably let Tom know that we are going to be a few more minutes and I need to let my receptionist know as well as she can hold the calls. So give me just a minute." Without waiting for *Brooke's* permission, Travis gets up and takes care of business.

Taken back by this unexpected delay, *Brooke's* momentum slows ever so slightly as she waits impatiently for his return.

Taking his seat Travis offers, "Okay, so you said that you have some information that is important to this decision?"

"Yeah—the fact that I don't want her talking with you. She doesn't deserve it, plain and simple," *Brooke* states emphatically.

"You seem to be pretty angry."

"I am angry…I'm angry at the sniveling coward that calls herself a mother. And if you knew all there was to know, you wouldn't consider her worth your time either." *Brooke* explains.

"Hmm, it sounds like I'm missing some important information. Care to fill me in?" Travis asks.

"Care to fill you in?" *Brooke* mocks. "You don't have enough time for me to tell you everything there is to know about her. But I can tell you that she is a coward. She can deny it all she wants, but she knew what our father was doing to us. She couldn't help but to know. Now she is acting all hurt and upset, pretending that it's all news to her. But there's no way. I know for a fact that she knew what was happening."

"I can see why you are so angry," Travis says gently, not wanting to stir up more emotion, but wanting to let her know that he is listening.

"Yeah, but she sure has everyone else fooled doesn't she?" *Brooke* asks rhetorically. "She's acting all innocent and like she didn't have a clue. That's just wrong. If she comes here and we tell her about the others, she'll just keep on pretending. Isn't that just playing into her games?"

"So you think she is playing games with you?" Travis asks.

"Of course she is. She's playing games with everyone like she always has. Our dad would give her a good beating and she would just cake on the makeup and pretend that no one could see. He would take us downstairs just about every night after dinner and she would clean the kitchen and pretend that nothing wrong was happening. When our dad gets tired of wearing rubbers and suggests that she have the doctor put us on birth control pills to regulate our emotions, she pretends that it's another normal step in life. When he takes time off of work to take us to the doctor himself, she pretends that it's to keep her from having to deal with so much at home," *Brooke* says. Overwhelmed with anger over the last example she shared, *Brooke* is forced to stop and take a breath.

Seeing her reaction, Travis checks to see if this person is ready to share what has made her so angry. "So what happened at the doctor?"

"Oh nothing," *Brooke* mocks. "Just a little procedure to remove the evidence of nights gone by. I suppose a baby at the age of 13 is just a little too difficult to explain away."

"That must have been a frightening experience," Travis observes.

"Not too much," *Brooke* lies. "I just did what I always did—stared at the ceiling and waited for it to be over. No big thing." Even as she said those words, her eyes told a different story. Determined to redirect the attention back to her mother, she pushes back the tears and adds, "Now you tell me—how is it that a mother can go through so many years of her husband 'sneaking around' with her daughter under her own roof and not know it was happening? She can't!"

"Do you think she could have stopped it," Travis asks.

"She's the only one who could have! She's the only one who could have known and she's the only one who could have stopped it from happening. If she had just grown a back bone, she could have made it all stop," as if sitting in the chair was preventing her from taking action of her own, *Brooke* stands up and begins to pace.

"So you can see now, that she can't be treated like some kind of queen. Everyone always treats her that way and I just can't handle it any more." *Brooke* says, wrapping up her argument for Travis to join in her crusade against the mother.

"Then let me ask you, what's the worst that can happen?"

"Queen Victoria once again becomes the center of attention, starring as the leading lady, the victim of life and circumstances. Her servants remain at her beck and call while we sit back and worry if she is going to be okay. Who cares if she is okay? She needs to take some responsibility and care about us for a change!"

"You need her very much, don't you?" Travis suggests.

"What? What do you mean I need her? *Brooke* doesn't need anyone! Especially not a spineless shrimp like her!"

"We all need people...*Brooke*, is that your name?" Travis asks to be sure he isn't using the name incorrectly.

"Yeah, that's my name." *Brooke* confirms, embarrassed that she let it slip.

"Well *Brooke*, as I said, we all need other people...it's just that sometimes we try to convince ourselves that we don't need them so it won't hurt so bad when they don't show up for us. It sure sounds like you needed your mom and she wasn't able to be there for you, for whatever reason. That must hurt very bad."

Feeling her energy levels lowering, *Brooke* returns to her seat to consider his point of view. "I don't think this is hurt I feel, *Brooke* argues, it definitely feels like anger to me."

"Anger is a very strong emotion, but when it lasts for such a long time, it's really being used to cover up another feeling. Anger seems safer to experience than hurt. So we allow the anger to get big enough to cover the hurt. As big as your anger is, I can imagine that your hurt runs pretty deep," Travis explains.

"We have to look past the anger and deal with the feelings that are hiding behind it. And those feelings sound an awful lot like hurt to me. But maybe I'm wrong. What feelings do you think are hiding behind your anger?" Travis prompts.

Determined to prove him wrong, *Brooke* takes the challenge of allowing herself to feel beyond the anger, beyond the mask of strength. Just on the other side of the bitterness, *Brooke* hit's the first layer of fear. Unsure if the fear is because she doesn't know what she will feel or if fear is what she's been hiding, *Brooke* decides to plunge further before responding. As she breaks through to the truth of feelings buried far below the surface, tears begin to fill her eyes. Suddenly afraid of hitting a 'point of no return', *Brooke* pulls herself back into the anger. Trembling from head to toe, *Brooke* glares back at Travis. "It's anger, plain and simple," she lies.

"Now, if you think it is necessary to involve our mother in this process, then I won't stop you. Just do me a favor and don't go into it blindly. She isn't perfect and she isn't the victim that she pretends to be. And for heaven's sake, don't treat her like a queen!" *Brooke* demands as she unlocks the door and retreats into the comfort of her special place inside.

With the release of control, *Gerald* and *Mitch* nod to each other, both silently agreeing to allow the professional to handle this one if possible. Without missing a beat, they gently complete the process of putting Amanda into position.

With her mouth wide opened and tears streaming down her face, she is unable to speak. The change in presentation is obvious to Travis, but he is unsure what is happening now. From the shocked expression on her face, he decides to venture out with a guess. "Amanda?" Travis timidly greets her, hoping for confirmation or clarification.

Still unable to say anything, Amanda nods her confirmation.

"Amanda, what's happening?" Travis asks, confused by her current state.

"I was...I mean...I heard...I saw..." Amanda stumbles around for a few seconds trying to find the words to explain her most recent experience. "What was that?" She finally manages to ask.

"So you mean you could see and hear what *Brooke* just said?" Travis asks.

Again, Amanda just nods her answer.

"Well, that's impressive," Travis says with a smile, not really meaning to say it out loud. "You don't do anything half way do you?" Recovering himself Travis tries to determine what needs to be done next by asking, "So how do you feel about what just happened?"

"I don't know...I mean, did it really happen?" Amanda asks.

"I'm not sure," Travis chuckles. "You have to tell me what you experienced so I can tell you if it was real because at this point, I still don't know for sure what you're talking about."

Regaining her ability to communicate, Amanda explains, "I was waking up and suddenly I felt this enormous amount of energy sweep by. I could see and hear everything that was happening, as if I was doing the talking, but I couldn't talk and I couldn't do anything. I could only listen and watch and feel. Oh boy did I feel. I haven't felt that much emotion in my entire life! And then I heard her tell you that my mom is basically evil and should have stopped my dad from hurting me in the basement. I could see what she was thinking as she said it too. Oh Dr. Brown! It was horrible!"

"Okay, it's going to be okay, Amanda," Travis says as calm and comforting as he can. "Take a deep breath and let me explain what it sounds like has happened."

Waiting to collect his thoughts and for Amanda to catch her breath, he takes a few minutes to scoot his chair a little closer to hers. It's really just a change, a distraction for them both. Settling back down he begins, "Most of the time, you experience what we call being present. That's when you are in control of the body and you are presenting yourself to the world. You do the talking and moving yourself. If you aren't out presenting, someone else is. You usually don't share this with anyone else. Now there are two other ways that this can happen. You can be co-present and co-conscious.

"Co-present means that you are both presenting together. You equally have the ability to speak and control the body movements. You also share your emotions and thoughts with each other while you are 'out'. Co-conscious means that you are aware of what is being done, as if you are out, but you are unable to do anything about it. It's because you are connected enough to be aware of what is happening, but you aren't out enough and not connected with the other person enough to share control.

"So based on what you described, it sounds like you were co-conscious with *Brooke* as she was talking. Given all that has been discussed today, I'm not sure if it was done intentionally or not."

Being sufficiently distracted by the techniques being used and how they work, Amanda is now more focused on that part of the experience, momentarily setting aside the disclosure of such devastating news. "So does that mean that they can decide when I get to be…co-conscious?" Amanda asks, being careful to follow the correct use of these new words.

"It's possible. But as I've said before, each person is different and the way your system works will be different from anyone else. There will be similarities in things just because of the basic principles at work, but the details are as individual as snowflakes."

"I'm not sure I really like being co-conscious," Amanda volunteers. "It's a scary thing to be able to see it all happening and not be able to do anything about it." Turning to Travis for some assurance she asks, "Do you think that…um, *Brooke*, is telling the truth?"

"The truth about what?" Travis asks for clarification.

"About what happened. Do you think that it's true that we had an abortion?"

Of all the questions posed to Travis on a daily basis, this is one of the most difficult to answer. His experience has taught him that some alters do make things up for many different reasons. He also knows that such horrible acts happen and when an alter shares these secrets, he or she needs to be believed. Pulling from his prepared answers, he selects and shares, "I have no reason to disbelieve it, Amanda. The others inside can help you determine truth much better than I can because they were there. But I certainly don't have any reason to think that *Brooke* was lying. And…it doesn't sound like I need to tell you that she is definitely hurting."

"No…no need." Amanda says. "I appreciate you taking the extra time with me today."

"I know that sometimes that is needed at the beginning of the process. I don't mind at all. You have been exposed to quite a bit of new information in the last 20—30 minutes. How are you feeling?" Travis asks, genuinely concerned.

"Tired," Amanda says. "I'm really tired. But I'm okay. I just need some time to process all of this, and I think I need a nap."

"That sounds like a good idea," Travis agrees. "Let me pray with you and then you can go home and sleep for a bit."

Taking his hand, Amanda nods her agreement. She isn't sure she will be able to stay awake long enough to hear the whole prayer, but she is going to try. "Our holy father…" is all she hears before drifting into a sweet stage of rest in the silence of her inside world.

Chapter Twenty-Eight

"Did you have fun at the party," Amanda asks, feeling a little sorry for herself because she was forced to miss it.

"Yes, I did," Tom answers. "It seemed a little strange having such a fancy dinner in the middle of the day, but I think that Jessica was trying to impress your mom." Chuckling at the thought, he is curious to see that Amanda doesn't respond. "How about you? You seemed to be having fun."

"That's good. I wish I could have been there," Amanda says, pouting ever so slightly.

"I'm confused...I need you to help me out here. Who am I talking with?" Tom asks.

"Amanda!" she says, offended that he had to ask. "Who did you think it was?"

"Oh sorry, Honey," Tom explains, "but I thought you had been out the whole time so when you said that you missed the party, I got really confused. So, can we start from the top? What happened that you weren't able to be out the whole time?"

"Well, I was talking with you at Jessica's house. When Mom showed up, everything went black. I woke up again as we were leaving," Amanda explains.

"I see. I'm sorry you missed the party Amanda. I know you worked very hard to help Jessica get ready for it."

"Actually, I don't remember much of that day either. It seems that lately I've been missing a lot of what is happening around me." Catching herself knee deep in her own party—a pity party—she decides to change the subject. "I'm sorry—just listen to me whine and carry on. It's your birthday and I am getting to spend time with you, just the two of us. So... What do you want to do now?

Do you want to go to a movie? My treat!"

"That sounds wonderful, but…I was thinking that we could do something else today. In fact, I took the liberty of setting up a surprise for *you* on my birthday," Tom grins.

"A surprise for me? What is it?"

"An appointment with a realtor." Pleased with her immediate reaction, Tom continues. "I spoke with your building manager and explained the situation. He is going to work with us on the lease. He said that he would only charge us if he was unable to rent the apartment, which he doesn't think will be a problem because he has a few people on a waiting list. So we can break the lease and it not cost anything. And even if it does, I'm willing to pay it.

"Amanda, I want us to start our life together in our 'together house' as *Carol* calls it. I also went to the bank and was pre-approved for a loan so that I know what kind of house we can afford.

"So if that's okay with you, I thought we can talk with this realtor today and get the process started. It usually takes a couple of months to get things worked out as I understand it, so I don't want to wait any longer. So…how does that sound?" Tom asks, hoping for an enthusiastic response.

"That sounds wonderful!" Amanda says. "I'm sorry I missed your party, but I'm glad that I'm not missing this!"

"Me too," Tom says. "In fact, I would really appreciate it if everyone would allow you to stay present for this. Maybe they can let you know how they feel about different houses by writing you notes later or something. But I really want you to be here for this."

"Well, I hope everyone else agrees with you, Tom. I'm not even sure how to get messages to them but maybe since *Gerald* is usually standing at the door…well maybe he heard what you said."

"That would be good," Tom states simply. "But I do want to know what everyone thinks about the houses though. I want their input, I just want you to have this experience if you can.

"And here we are," Tom says as he pulls into a parking spot closest to the entrance of the realtor's office. "The realtor's name is Mary Jenkins. She comes highly recommended."

"Mary Jenkins," Amanda repeats under her breath in an attempt to plant it firmly in her memory.

As Tom opens her door to help her from the car, Amanda shares, "Oh Tom, this is so exciting. It's like there is some light in the middle of all of this darkness that I've felt. Thank you!" He gently holds her hand as she stands to her feet and then hugs her tight.

"I am so glad. Nothing could please me more than to brighten your day!" Tom says.

As the meeting with Mary gets underway, Amanda can't help but day dream about sharing her life with Tom living in the perfect house: filled with lots of love, a dog, and two children. That's what they had always talked about—having two kids. Of course they want to have a boy and a girl, but whatever God chooses to bless them with will be great.

As they answer the realtor's questions, Amanda begins to picture this perfect home. It has a fenced in back yard, so that the dog can run and play freely. It has a nice sized kitchen and dining area for entertaining. There must be a cozy living space and breakfast nook for spending time with Tom and her close friends.

"How long do you plan to stay in this particular house," Mary asks. "Do you want to look at starter houses for just the two of you, or do you want to jump on up to a house that you will stay in for a long while?"

Amanda and Tom share a look of hesitation. They had never considered this question before. Finding a way to delay the decision, Tom asks, "Can we take a look at a full range of houses, from starters to long-term family homes? That way we can decide once we see what the options are."

"We can certainly do that," Mary says. "So then let's talk about some of your long-term goals so that we can include the right kind of houses. Do you plan on having children?"

"Yes," they both say in unison.

"Two," Amanda adds for clarification, smiling up at Tom.

As Tom and Mary continue the conversation about school districts and number of rooms, Amanda is suddenly struck with a sick feeling in her stomach. She had been able to put aside the nasty discoveries from the day before, but without warning she is brought back to the information *Brooke* shared.

What if it's true? Never mind the stuff her dad was supposed to have done...What if she really did have an abortion as a teenager? What if something happened during the procedure that would prevent her from having children in the future? What if she is unable to get pregnant?

Excusing herself from the conversation, Amanda searches out the restroom. She desperately wants to remain conscious and to experience this with Tom, but these new feelings of fear and uncertainty are beginning to overwhelm her. "God, please help me. I don't want to blow this with Tom. Please give me strength to focus on today. I know that you know what has happened in the past and what my future holds. Help me trust that you will take me through whatever I face. Please help me," Amanda prays.

Amanda decides not to share her concerns with Tom until she knows if *Brooke* told the truth and if there was any permanent damage done. She adds a thorough gynecological examination to her mental checklist of things to do and splashes some cold water on her face.

Determined to enjoy this occasion with Tom, she collects herself and returns to Mary's small office. She is able to put a smile on her face and join back in the conversation. But she is unable to hide her shaking hands from Tom.

"Are you okay?" Tom asks.

"Yes, I'm fine. I think I just got too excited," Amanda calmly says with a smile. "Did I miss anything important?"

"We were just talking about the various houses styles. Do you have a preference?" Tom asks.

"No, not really. I've never really paid that much attention to the styles. But I bet as we begin to look, there will be a style that feels more like us than the others," Amanda offers.

With the necessary information collected, Mary offers to run a list of houses for them to view. "What I'd like to do today, is to show you some real diversity in the houses so that we can narrow a few things down. The first house I want to show you is what I would consider a starter house for most couples. It's not too small—it has room for entertaining, a relatively large kitchen, and a fenced in backyard. But it only has two bedrooms and one bath. That probably would be too small once you had children, but it might be a good way to get started in owning a house.

"I also want to show you this ranch style house that I think would be just perfect for your needs. It has an open concept so that it feels even bigger than it is, and it's definitely not small.

"And just down the street from that house is a Victorian style home that's in great condition. It's has a great sunroom that can be used year-round as a cozy living area or a fun room for socializing.

"And then I'll show you a house in a gated community that is a little larger than the others and has a swimming pool in the backyard. Once you see the full range of homes, you can begin to pick the characteristics of the homes that you like. That will help us focus in on the house that is going to be perfect for you. Does that sound like a good plan?" Mary asks.

Tom and Amanda both nod their agreement. The couple decline Mary's offer to ride with her but agree to follow her to the different homes. Tom wants to be able to talk freely with Amanda and that can't happen while riding around with the realtor.

After a full day of looking at houses, Tom and Amanda can agree on a few things: They need to take a camera and a pad and pen the next time they look so they can keep track of which house had what feature; and the starter house was way too small.

Chapter Twenty-Nine

"Okay—let's settle down," *Mitch* says, calling the meeting to order. Unlike previous meetings, *Brooke* was instructed to allow *Everett* to attend.

"There's a lot we need to talk about again tonight. With things happening so fast, we will probably need to regroup on a fairly regular basis. Eventually we will need to allow Amanda to sit in on these meetings as well, but I'm not ready for that just yet."

It isn't that *Mitch* isn't ready as much as the fact that neither Amanda nor the others are ready. He must introduce this concept slowly to both parties. So in order to prevent a debate over the subject now, he quickly moves on to the first order of business.

"Okay—as most of you know, the session with Victoria went well today as far as I could tell. She was receptive to the idea that we are here...well at least she didn't say that we were liars or that we were crazy. I think that she is actually starting to put things together and can see that we haven't been exactly hiding from her our whole lives. So, many of our concerns have been addressed: she doesn't want to hospitalize us, she hasn't rejected us, and she isn't going to be seeing Dr. Brown after today. She will be visiting with another therapist however, which means that she will be getting some help from a professional. This takes some weight off of us because she will have to do the heavy lifting in getting on with her life," *Mitch* summarizes, looking around for any further concerns he had failed to address.

Still pouting from the tongue lashing she got from *Mitch* over last week's excursion, *Brooke* just sits and stares, communicating her disapproval silently.

"So, moving on...Dr. Brown has agreed to give us an extra meeting in the morning. Amanda's doctor's appointment is tomorrow afternoon and I have asked him to help Amanda prepare for what she might hear. Now that the cat is out of the bag, I think we need to do everything we can to help Amanda hear the truth. We all know what the doctor is going to say because we've heard it before. So, we need Amanda to hear it now. But we don't need Amanda to freak out at the doctor's office either. So…I'm hoping that Dr. Brown will be able to prepare Amanda enough for her to handle it all. If we find that she is not able to cope immediately, we'll need to take some action. This is to help us with the goal of staying out of the hospital, which means we are not going to tell the gynecologist about anything at this point.

"So, *Dana*, can you be ready to take over if needed?" *Mitch* asks.

"Of course," *Dana* agrees.

"Great! Then that takes care of what we need to do tomorrow. So that means that we have to allow Amanda to take the entire session with Dr. Brown tomorrow—no interruptions. Does everyone agree?"

Mitch accepts the nods of agreement from most, but pauses and waits for a verbal agreement from *Brooke*. "Yes, I agree," *Brooke* finally says.

"Now, I have an observation to share with everyone. Consider what I'm saying carefully. As you open your thoughts to this truth, you will agree that some actions need to take place," *Mitch* begins, carefully selecting every word he uses so that it will have the maximum impact.

"We are all learning new ways of doing things because our needs have changed. We still must work together in order to survive, but we must do it in new ways. We must continue to give up things that we might personally want for the good of the whole system. We are all in this boat together, so if it sinks, we all sink. If it floats, we all stay alive.

"As we have discussed, there are some goals that—much like our original goals—are for our safety and survival. Now most of us have been able to agree to these goals, including the goal of keeping the relationship with Tom. Tom has been good to us. Tom recognizes and cares for each of us individually, while taking very good care of Amanda. He is a strong Christian with strong beliefs. Yet he is gentle and considerate. He works hard and makes a good living. He has already sacrificed a lot of personal desires to be sure that Amanda, and all of us, are happy.

"He has proven himself trustworthy. He hasn't exposed us to anyone without our permission. He hasn't told any of our secrets. He hasn't even threatened to leave or abandon us over things from our past. He has turned the stress from the unexpected night with *Sabrina* into a solid friendship with her,"

Mitch says, careful to not offend *Sabrina* with his words.

"Tom is someone that we can trust. God has given him to us as a strong guiding hand that serves us with compassion. When he is unsure of what to do, he doesn't just guess—he gets input from professionals. But he doesn't just take their word for things, he prays and considers it before making his decision. And when he makes a mistake, he is willing to admit it and change direction as needed.

"This is one of the aspects of our lives that has changed. When we first moved out of our parents' house, we struggled to find our way. We had always gotten such strict and specific direction from 'the father'. When we left that environment, some of us felt lost and confused.

"*Everett*, that's when you showed up," *Mitch* explains, turning his attention directly to the person created to replace their father. "Someone felt that you could take the place of dad and give us that constant direction that we were used to.

This person felt insecure without it and needed to have it. And you did that for her. You became the voice of dad."

Turning his attention back to the rest of the group, *Mitch* continues, "It was done out of concern, making sure that we did things the way Dad wanted. See, it wasn't just any direction that you sought, it was Dad's. You wanted to be sure that we did things in a way that would please him," *Mitch* continues, careful not to look at any one person too long.

"But now, our dad is gone. We don't have to please him any longer. We don't have to guess at what he wants us to do. In fact, we don't have to worry about making him happy ever again. That goal has been removed from our lives. That is not something that we have to work toward any longer.

"Our new goal is to make Tom happy. Not because he threatens us, but because Amanda loves him and because we all want him to be part of our lives. He is good for us. He makes us feel good, not bad.

"So now, we can let go of the voice of our dad. In fact, having the constant pull to please a man who no longer exists can be a problem for us all. It will be a heavy burden for *Everett* and a distraction to us as a whole. *Everett* does not hold any secrets or special emotions that we could not handle. He doesn't hold any memories or any knowledge that needs to be kept secret. He hasn't been around so long that his absence would cause any issues.

"And I've seen this happen before, under different circumstances. I don't know if any of you remember *Janet*. She was older than the rest of us. Not like *Agnes*, but more like our parents' age. But shortly after she came into existence, things changed. We had been told that we were pregnant. Assuming that meant that we would need someone to care for the baby, *Dana* brought Janet into being. When we went to the doctor and had the abortion, *Janet* went back into *Dana*. It wasn't a painful thing for either of them. In fact, it was really quite natural given the short time that she was around and the change in our circumstances. It would have been more difficult to deal with the abortion if *Janet* had remained here, with no baby to care for.

"So you see, sometimes it is better to allow the reconnection between the one who creates you than it is to continue an existence that is harmful to others.

"Just as I helped Janet and *Dana* through the process, I can help *Everett* return to the one who created him. But I don't have to be involved in the process either. It is simple enough to be done on your own. This step is going to help us all move toward our future. It's a good thing to do and I'm so proud that you are willing to allow it to happen.

"And the last thing that I wanted to talk about," *Mitch* proceeds, not allowing for discussion about *Everett*, "is the house hunting process. Tom has asked that we each give our input into what we want in the 'together' house. This is a good sign that he wants us all to be happy and it's a good opportunity for you to have your voice heard. So I want to encourage each of you to take a few minutes over the next day or so to write Tom a note telling him what you want in a house. Now, let's keep it realistic, but go ahead and dream some too.

"Is there anything else that we need to talk about tonight?" *Mitch* asks, finally opening the floor for discussion.

As expected, the room is silent. "Okay then," *Mitch* concludes, "let's get some sleep so we can be ready for tomorrow."

As the others begin to leave, *Mitch* waits to see who will approach him. He anticipates that *Everett* will wait with him, either to get clarification or to move forward with the process. But he can't do that until he finds out who created *Everett*. It's been a mystery from the beginning and *Mitch* has never been able to uncover the truth. Now he hopes that he was able to convince whoever it is to step forward and talk about it at the very least.

As expected, *Everett* remained in his seat, tucked neatly into the corner. But to *Mitch's* surprise, both *Carol* and *Sabrina* stayed behind to talk. *Sabrina* told *Carol* that she could go first.

Pulling up a chair next to *Carol*, *Mitch* asks, "*Carol*, is there something you need to talk about?"

"Yes," *Carol* begins slowly. "I want to ask you a question."

"Okay, I will see if I can answer it," *Mitch* promises.

"What happened to *Janet* when she went back into *Dana*?"

"Well, it's not anything that we can see with our eyes so it makes it hard to explain. But I can tell you what I think happened."

Carol nodded her approval at his offer.

"I think that *Dana*, trying to find a way to make things better, took a part of herself and made *Janet*. It's like if one of *Dana's* teeth fall out. It was still *Dana's* tooth but it was no longer in her mouth. If her tooth stays out of her mouth for a very long time, it is more difficult to put it back into the right slot. But because *Janet* was only out for a little while, *Dana* was able to put her back, just as if she never lost her.

"So when *Janet* went back into *Dana*, it was like making *Dana* whole again. That part of her that was missing came back into her."

"What would have happened if *Janet* had been out of *Dana* for a long time?" *Carol* asks.

"Then I think it would be more difficult to put her back. The longer she is out, the more she takes on her own identity. When we have our own memories and our own emotions, I don't think we can fit back so easily."

"I see," *Carol* says softly.

"These are some pretty deep questions for such a little girl. Can you tell me what you are thinking about?" *Mitch* prompts.

"Well, it's just that I'm so tired," she explains as tears fall down her soft cheeks. "I do feel better now that daddy is gone, and Tom makes me very happy…but I'm all heavy inside. I was just wondering if I could go into someone and sleep like *Janet* did—I thought maybe it will feel better if I do that. But I don't know where I came from and if I'll still fit if I try to go back."

Mitch is taken back by her request. *Carol* endured many years of sexual abuse on behalf of the system. She has probably carried more emotional and physical scars than anyone. But no one has ever asked to go inside someone before. While he wants to help *Carol* and offer her some relief, he knows that what she is asking for is not the answer. She has gone through too much.

"*Carol*, I know you are very tired. I think you might be right, I think too much time has passed. But I tell you want I can do…I can help you go to sleep for a little while so that you don't have to feel heavy right now and I can ask Dr. Brown if he knows how to help you. He is a very smart doctor and I bet that he can help you feel better. How does that sound?"

"That sounds good, but can I write my note to Tom first?" *Carol* asks.

"Of course you can. Why don't you ask *Gerald* if this is a good time for you to do that and then let me know when you are ready to sleep for a while. I'll wake you back up in a few days, after I have a chance to talk with Dr. Brown. You just relax and sleep in the meantime, okay?"

"Thank you *Mitch*," *Carol* says, her energy renewed with the hope that she might not have to go on forever. "I'm gonna go see if I can write that note now."

"She's been around longer than I have," *Sabrina* says softly once *Carol* left the room. "I can't imagine this place with her gone."

"It would be strange," *Mitch* agrees. "But if that's what she needs, I'm going to do what I can to help her. She deserves nothing less."

"But she's talking about integration *Mitch*. That's death," *Sabrina* whispers her protest. "You can't let her kill herself. I mean, I understand wanting *Everett* to die, but *Carol*?"

"*Sabrina*, I don't want her or *Everett* to die. I'll admit that it is different with *Carol* than with *Everett*. *Carol* does have her own memories and her own emotions. She has existed far too long to try a 'take back' with her. But *Everett* is different. He doesn't hold anything yet. He still hasn't really taken on a shape of his own. As long as he is willing and you are willing, you can be fused back together with little effort and little problems."

"How did you know it was me?" *Sabrina* asks.

"Because I know you...and my description of why you brought *Everett* into being, wasn't 100% accurate. Was it?" *Mitch* asks.

"Just slightly...I also found that I missed him. But I was too embarrassed to say so. But I missed seeing him every day. I guess that—even though you tried to help me keep from it—I guess that I had some emotional attachment to him after all. So when I realized that, well...one night he was just there. I knew what I had done and I knew why. But I didn't want anyone else to know so I sent him away. I told him that all he had to do was to be like the presence of our dad so that he was with us all of the time. After he was gone, I felt better. I didn't miss the real Everett as much," *Sabrina* explains.

"And now? Now how do you feel about it?" *Mitch* asks.

"Well...I can see how his presence can be a problem. Everything you said makes sense. I know that he tried to interfere with Amanda's relationship with Tom, but...well, I wonder if that wasn't because he really wanted to keep Tom away from me," *Sabrina* thinks out loud.

"Sounds to me like you're thinking too hard," *Mitch* offers with a smile. "Why he did it doesn't really matter does it?"

"No, I guess it doesn't matter. It just matters what we do now. Right?" *Sabrina* asks for assurance.

"That's right. So what do you want to do now *Sabrina*? Have you talked with *Everett* about this?" *Mitch* asks.

"No, not yet."

"Then let's see what he wants to do about this situation. It's got to be a mutual agreement, something you both want to do. Let's see where he stands on the matter." *Mitch* suggests.

Talking with *Sabrina* and *Everett*, *Mitch* offers his observations. "It seems *Everett*, that your purpose in existing is different than I originally anticipated. I thought it had more to do with making sure that we do things according to our father's desires. As I have learned from *Sabrina*, it was that plus more. It seems that Sabrina needed you to be around because she missed seeing our father on a regular basis. You were made so that she would not be lonely for him. Is that a true statement *Sabrina*," *Mitch* asks to be sure that he has understood correctly.

"That's true," *Sabrina* says.

Mitch realizes that *Everett* was created more from an emotional need than a logical decision. He needs to focus more on *Sabrina's* feelings and *Everett's* feelings in order to determine if this re-fusion needs to move forward.

"*Everett*, how are you feeling about things?" *Mitch* asks.

"I don't know. I feel pretty strange. I feel like I should be dead because the guy I represent is dead. You can't imagine what it is like to see yourself in a coffin like that. It's really strange. Nobody likes me anyway. Not even you, *Sabrina*. I feel like I don't have the right to be here. And now this. It's obvious that everyone is eager for me to disappear," *Everett* states plainly.

"*Sabrina,* when you made *Everett*, how were you feeling?" *Mitch* asks, concerned by the depth of *Everett*'s feelings.

"I was lonely and scared. Like I didn't know where I belonged," *Sabrina* says.

"Then it sounds like *Everett* took those feelings with him when you created him. That also means that you might once again experience those feelings if he fuses back with you. Even though your circumstances have changed, those feelings have not gone away, they've just gone with *Everett*."

"I don't want those feelings back," *Sabrina* says, almost in a panic. "I've done too much with feelings lately. I don't want to relive feelings that I got rid of already."

"I can understand that," *Mitch* sympathizes. "*Everett*, what are you thinking that you want to do?"

"I don't want to cause any problems, but...I would like the chance to be part of something, part of this group. I want to really belong. I know that we couldn't change Everett on the outside, but is it possible for me to get a new assignment? Can't I do something besides represent him on the inside?"

"*Sabrina*, how do you feel about *Everett* taking on a different function? Are you ready for that?" *Mitch* asks, hoping to have the opportunity to be involved in the design of *Everett's* function at last.

"Yes, I'm fine with that. I don't really need him to represent *Everett* any more. I'm really doing good right now, which is why I don't want to bring those feelings back."

"Okay—we can do that. I can work with *Everett* to identify a new function for him and help him deal with the emotions that he has had all along. But there is one thing I want you both to understand...once we do this, *Everett* might not be able to go back into you, Sabrina. It seems that once a person has established their own purpose, this fusion thing might not work. I could be wrong because I've never really tried, but it just seems that way to me. I will ask Dr. Brown about that one too...

"Now *Sabrina*, I need you to think about this long and hard...If *Everett* takes on a new function, he might take on a new look, and even a new name. He will no longer serve the function that you created him to serve. I want you to be sure that you are ready for that because I don't want you to go and make another one to take his place."

"I understand," *Sabrina* says. "I'm okay with everything you have said. You don't have to worry about me making another *Everett*. My heart is sealed up in a box and the love that is there isn't for any Everett. I won't need to replace him. I promise."

"Then it's settled. I appreciate you both working together to find a solution that will help everyone. I'm proud of you both. You were both willing to talk about things even though you knew you didn't want what I was suggesting. Thank you."

Chapter Thirty

"So how did things go with the doctor yesterday," Travis asks as he kicks off the session with Amanda.

"Okay I guess. I'm glad we had the chance to talk before I went there. I had my list of questions ready like you suggested. That was a good idea because once I got there; I seemed to just go blank with what to say. Tom helped me come up with a few of the questions."

"So did you tell Tom what *Brooke* mentioned," Travis asks for clarification.

"Yes, it wasn't easy for me to do, but I did tell him. I was so scared that he would decide that I was just too damaged to be worth his time. People do that you know," Amanda says, as if needing to justify her fears.

"Yes, some people do that. But what did Tom do?" Travis asks.

"He held me and cried with me and told me that it didn't matter. Even when I told him that sometimes abortions can scar you so badly that you can't have children, he still said that it would be okay. He said that as long as he can spend the rest of his life with me, then he is happy," Amanda says, smiling at the security she feels in recounting the story.

"It sounds like Tom was able to help ease some of your anxiety before you even met with the doctor," Travis observes.

"Yes, he was. But it was still a very nerve racking experience," Amanda explains. "I did tell her that I wanted her to tell me if she could see anything that could prevent me from having children. After the exam, she said that she did see scarring but that most of the scarring seemed to be limited to the vaginal area with only small amounts of scarring in the uterus," trying to hide her embarrassment in talking about such personal details, Amanda continues. "She said that she doesn't think that any of it will prevent me from having children. Of course, she then gave me a long disclaimer about all the many things that can happen to cause someone to be infertile, you know, just to cover herself in case there is a problem."

"Of course," Travis nods. "That's probably a pretty standard response. So tell me how you're feeling about it this morning."

"Well…I'm relieved. I'm relieved because I really want to have children some day, and because Tom really wants to have children some day too. But I'm also relieved to know that *Brooke* wasn't lying."

"Tell me more about that," Travis prompts, curious with this reaction to learning the truth.

"When I began to talk with the others inside, I thought it was something I was making up in my imagination. I thought I was pretending or something. I don't know really what I thought, except that I thought it wasn't real. I've been listening to see if I can trust what I am experiencing. I need to know if the experience is real or not.

"Then you and Tom and Jessica all confirmed that the experience is real, I started doubting what I was being told by the others inside. When Brooke made such horrible accusations, I thought that maybe she was playing with me or with you—just telling stories for the scare factor.

"So while it is scary to hear these stories, at least I'm learning who I can trust to tell the truth. Things are complicated enough as it is, I don't need extra stuff added in there just for fun. And now, it sounds like I can trust *Brooke*. At least, I can trust this story from *Brooke*. It's just one less thing I have to worry about, I guess," Amanda concludes.

"That's good, Amanda," Travis agrees. "And what then is left on your plate to worry about?"

"Oh, the wedding plans…picking out a house…making sure that my mom is okay…being sure that chores are done…stuff like that." Amanda explains.

"That is a lot to have on your plate," Travis remarks. "It doesn't seem to leave much time for you to work through the new information you are discovering."

"I know—isn't it wonderful?" Amanda teases.

Travis shares a small laugh with her before pushing forward. "It is good that you have some distractions to keep you going. It will not be good if you allow those distractions to keep you from moving forward in your healing process.

"You have learned a lot of new information but you don't seem to be bothered by it. I'm not looking for you to roll around on the floor in agony, but

I was expecting a little more of an emotional connection to the information than I'm seeing. What are you doing with the feelings you have been having? And…don't tell me that you haven't had any feelings because I saw how you reacted to hearing *Brooke* last week. I know there were feelings and lots of them. So…what are you doing with those feelings?"

"I don't know," Amanda answers honestly. "I agree, I did have some strong emotions about what I heard and felt last week. But I don't feel that way now. It's like all of these stories are being told about another person. It didn't happen to me so why should I feel anything more than pity for the person it did happen to?"

"Okay good. This helps me understand how you are handling things so I know how to help you better," Travis explains. "Over the next few weeks, I'd like for us to explore some different ways to handle the stressors in your life. We'll just look at some of the principles and techniques that can be used to help you heal from emotional pain and trauma. Then you will be better equipped to own some of these experiences as your own. Does that sound like a plan?" Travis asks.

"I guess," Amanda says, unsure of what Travis is implying. "Are you saying that I'm doing something wrong?"

"No, not at all. You are using the same process to deal with this information as you have used all of your life. The problem with this process, with distancing yourself from the experience, is that the pain doesn't really go anywhere. It just sits there and continues to cause you pain. What I'm suggesting is that we can stop that cycle. We can stop and look at the pain—experience it—and heal from it. That way we aren't just moving it from one location to another, but instead we are receiving healing from the pain. It's a more permanent solution, and it's definitely more freeing," Travis adds with a smile.

"That sounds good," Amanda says. As she returns Travis's smile, the room begins to fade away into darkness.

Mitch spends the remainder of the session confiding in Travis and seeking his advice. He is pleased to have someone that understands the potential risks and benefits to the various paths he can take. The session ends with a mutual agreement: next session, barring any emergencies, Travis will spend the time working with *Carol* while *Mitch* stands close by—he needs to know exactly what is being said and what *Carol* wants to do so that he can help the process.

In the meantime, he has some corrections to make in the information he gave *Sabrina* and *Everett*. It seems that the rules are more flexible than *Mitch* had originally imagined. *Everett* is not required to go back into *Sabrina*, if he were to choose a fusion process. However, it is good for him to deal with his feelings first—otherwise the feelings get jumbled up with the other person's feelings and it becomes more difficult to focus on healing. This can help the three of them make a more informed decision about how to move forward.

Chapter Thirty-One

"Tom, can you come over right away," Amanda asks frantically.

"I was just turning off my computer, what's wrong?" Tom says as he picks up his pace, quickly grabbing his briefcase and jacket. "Are you okay?"

"I think so, but Tom I'm scared."

"I'm on my way…what happened?" Tom asks, trying to discern if she is in immediate danger.

"I don't know. I took a nap this afternoon and when I woke up, my apartment was turned upside down. Tom it looks like it's been ransacked," Amanda says, her voice trembling from fear and confusion.

"Is anyone in the apartment with you? Do we need to call the police?" Tom asks as he rushes out the door and into his car.

"I looked and I don't see anyone. The door is locked still, so I don't think that anyone is in here," Amanda says. "It just doesn't make any sense."

"Okay—I'm heading that way now. Just do me a favor and stay on the phone with me so that I know you are okay. Promise?" Tom asks as he speeds toward her location.

"Yes, I promise," Amanda says. "Just be careful. The last thing I need is for you to have an accident!"

"Okay—I promise," Tom says, trying to force a calm tone into his voice. "Is anything missing Amanda?"

"No, I don't think so. The television is still here, and the stereo. My jewelry seems to be all in place, I don't think anything was stolen," Amanda reports.

Beginning to think that the ransacking might have been the work of an insider, Tom changes the direction of his questions. "Amanda, what were you doing before your nap today?"

"I was talking with my mom. She was telling me about her session with the therapist that Dr. Brown recommended."

"So how did that go?" Tom asks as he races through the growing traffic.

"Well, she said that things are going fine. She said that she isn't going to dump on me any more because now she has a professional that can help her. She said that as she gets stronger, she will be better able to help me deal with the things that Dad did to us both," Amanda summarizes.

"Oh Tom," Amanda begins to sob, "Tom, the teddy bear you gave me is cut. It's cut to pieces and the stuffing is all over the place. Tom, how could I sleep through this?"

"Hang on Amanda, I'm pulling up to your place now. Can you meet me at the door? I'll be there in just a few seconds."

"Okay," Amanda says as she hangs up the phone.

Running to her front door, Tom is still unsure of what has happened. After giving her a quick hug, he tells Amanda to wait right by the door while he checks the apartment. Confident that the apartment is void of any gun slinging intruders, Tom retrieves Amanda and shuts the door.

Surveying his surroundings, Tom is leaning more toward believing that this is the work of an insider than a stranger. He knows that Amanda doesn't remember it happening, she's still shaking with fear. Stepping off into new territory, Tom decides that he must find a way to get *Gerald* to present and tell him what happened.

"Amanda, I think we need to know what happened while you napped this afternoon," Tom begins.

"I don't know what happened, Tom," Amanda interrupts. "I don't understand how I could have slept through this, but I did!"

Trying to calm her, Tom suggests, "Amanda, it could be that someone inside did this. That's why you would have slept through it. I have an idea of how we can find out for sure," Tom proceeds cautiously. "If I could talk with *Gerald*, maybe he can tell me what happened. He is usually standing by the door, right?"

"That's what he said," Amanda confirms.

"Then perhaps he saw what happened and can help us figure things out. Do you think I can talk with him?" Tom asks, unable to offer any suggestions on how to make that happen.

"I don't know," Amanda snaps, taken back by this new request. "It's not like I have any control over this, you know. It just happens whenever it happens. I'm sure that someone is controlling it, but it isn't me!"

"Okay—it's okay Amanda," Tom says trying to help her remain as calm as possible. "Perhaps he will be able to help you with that as well. And if not...we'll just see if we can find some clues out here on our own. Why don't you sit down on the couch for a minute and let me take a look around. Okay?"

"Okay," Amanda agrees, allowing Tom to escort her to the sofa. "Do you really think that someone inside did this?"

"I don't know, but I'm going to see if we can figure that out," Tom assures her as he begins looking around for clues.

"I can tell you what happened," *Marie* offers as she immediately stands to begin the cleaning process.

His head still spinning, Tom asks, "And you are?"

"I'm *Marie*—we met last week during that horrific scene at Mom's house, "*Marie* offers as she begins to fill in the blanks. "*Brooke* has thrown another one of her fits. I usually clean up after her, but I didn't get a chance to take care of things before Amanda came out this time."

Looking around the room she adds, "She isn't usually this destructive. She must really be mad today." Continuing the cleaning process, *Marie* doesn't stop to gauge Tom's reactions. She has a mission: bring order back to the chaos.

Dizzy from the rapid movements and developing information, Tom takes a minute to sit down at the table and watch *Marie* go about her chores. He considers helping, but is afraid of being run over by this ball of energy that is moving from place to place, cleaning as she goes. Instead, he decides to focus on information retrieval while allowing *Marie* to continue her seemingly well-rehearsed role.

"So what do you think set her off?" Tom asks.

"Oh, who knows with that girl. She is like a keg of dynamite with a very short fuse. But if I had to guess, it is probably something to do with Mom. *Brooke* absolutely despises her," *Marie* explains as she begins returning the books to the shelves, alphabetically. "She probably doesn't think that Mom needs to have any therapy or something. She looks for ways to blame Mom for her own stuff."

"And when she gets angry, she messes up the apartment?" Tom asks, still confused by this behavior.

Without missing a beat, *Marie* explains, "Yes, it is something that I've gotten used to over the years. You see, just as much as she hates Mom, she can't stand me. She knows that this kind of a mess is upsetting to me, so that's why she does it. She wants to hurt Mom, but instead she hurts me. The only way she knows to do that is to make a mess. The more anger she has, the more of a mess she makes." Stopping just a second to illustrate her next point, she adds, "This…this is a lot of anger."

"So because you care for your mom, *Brooke* is mad at you?"

"That about sums it up." *Marie* nods.

"But you don't seem to really be upset by the mess," Tom observes.

"No, not really. See, what *Brooke* might not understand is that I feel better when I'm cleaning. Even though it can be frustrating at times, it can also be relaxing for me," *Marie* smiles at the irony and continues her tasks.

"Well then, would you like me to help with the clean up, or do you want me to just stay out of your way?" Tom asks with a smile.

"Actually, I think I could use some help, Tom," *Marie* responds, grateful for the help and the connection she is beginning to feel with him. "Would you mind taking the bathroom? It's clean, but a mess, if you know what I mean. Can you put things back into the medicine cabinet and things like that?"

"You bet," Tom agrees.

Tom is surprised to see the bathroom in such disarray. The shampoo and conditioner bottles are opened and pouring their contents into the bathtub. The roll of toilet paper is stuffed into the toilet. Pills of all shapes, sizes, and colors decorate every flat surface available. The liquid makeup is poured into the sink and a message of hatred is written on the mirror with lipstick.

Stepping back into the living room, Tom asks for window cleaner, paper towels, and a plastic garbage bag. Supplies in hand, Tom begins the process of collecting the items that have now become trash. It will be easier to see what can be done once these items are out of the way.

An hour later, Tom emerges from the bathroom, exhausted and drenched in sweat. He is pleased to see that *Marie* has made faster progress and has already done most of the work in the bedroom.

"I've made a list of items that need to be replaced," Tom announces.

"That's a good idea," *Marie* says. "I'll be through here shortly."

"Are you getting hungry?"

"Oh, I'm sure I can eat something. I think that Amanda had planned on cooking something for you again tonight, but…well…*Brooke* had other plans apparently."

"Okay, then maybe *Brooke* should have to suffer right along with me. What do you think the chances are that *Brooke* will share a pizza with me?" Tom asks, completely unsure of how his offer will be received.

"I don't know," *Marie* says, surprised to hear that he would dare to reach out to *Brooke* after the mess he has witnessed.

"Well, I'm going to order the pizza now, so if she wants any input on the toppings, I need to have the answer," Tom teases, hoping to push a response from *Brooke*.

"But I'm not through cleaning," *Marie* protests.

"Oh, maybe *Brooke* and I can finish that up after dinner," Tom says, noticing that the majority of the work is already done. The only items that seem to be left are the clothes and the poor teddy bear that is spread out all over the bed.

"Come on, I really would like to talk with her. I'm not going to yell or anything if that's what she's afraid of," Tom assures.

"Afraid? I'm not afraid of anything," *Brooke* says. "You really going to buy me a pizza?"

"Yeah, I figure you must be starving with as much work as you put into this mess," Tom says with a grin. "So tell me, what are your favorite toppings?"

"Hamburger, mushrooms, and jalapenos," *Brooke* says as she moves to sit down.

"Wow, jalapenos? Okay, I'll order two pizzas then," Tom says. "So, while I'm ordering the pizza, do you think you could figure out which of those clothes need to be hung back up and which need to go into a drawer? I've never understood why, but I know that some people hang up jeans and t-shirts, but I put those into a drawer. Can you help me sort that out so I don't get into trouble?"

Without waiting for her response, Tom exits the room to place the order. *Brooke* knows that he's playing her somehow, but she doesn't know what his game is yet. Confused by his behavior, she isn't sure what to do. Deciding that the best course of action is probably to play along until she figures it out, she begins to slowly sort the clothes into two piles as requested. She'll give this some effort, but she isn't going to commit to doing what he says all the way yet. The way she figures it, she'll get some pizza out of the deal.

When Tom returns to the room he sits on the edge of the bed and begins folding the cloths to the best of his ability. "You know, I don't remember anyone ever ordering jalapenos on the pizza before. Is that because you haven't been out for their pizza nights?"

"Nah, they've been afraid that I'd scare you away or something. They don't like to admit it, but they treat me like some kind of hunch back that needs to be locked up in the bell tower or something. Every once in a while I manage to take control, but it's usually when they have their guard down, which is...when we aren't around people," *Brooke* explains, hoping to either intimidate Tom, or make him feel sorry for her—either way, it works for her purpose of avoiding any potential punishment Tom might send her way.

"Well...I'm glad you're having dinner with me tonight."

"Why?" *Brooke* asks.

"Well, because I can't fold clothes worth anything—now when *Marie* gets mad because things aren't folded right, she can blame you," Tom says with a chuckle.

Laughing with him, *Brooke* says, "Oh I don't care if she's mad at me at all. In fact, we can just throw these things into the drawer and she will come back later and fix them right."

"No, I want to try at least," Tom says. "I promised I would help her clean up so I'm going to do my best."

"Then let me show you how to do it," *Brooke* says, grabbing the wadded up t-shirt from him. "Here's how she will expect the t-shirts to be folded. Exactly like our mother folds them," *Brooke* explains while illustrating the correct method.

"So, is this right?" Tom asks as he makes another attempt at folding a t-shirt. *Brooke* laughs at his incompetence and patiently instructs him again. After the third t-shirt, Tom has finally mastered the art of folding them the "Victoria" method.

"I suppose there's a particular method for pairing up socks, too?" Tom asks.

"Of course there is," *Brooke* answers. "There's a method for everything—a rule for every action."

The lessons in proper cleaning and organizing continue well past their shared pizza. Tom never asks her to explain why she was angry, or why she was so destructive. He just spends time with her as a peer and a friend. It's the best time *Brooke* has ever had. Ending the evening, Tom promises that the next time she wants jalapeno pizza; all she has to do is ask. Tearing down the house is not required.

Chapter Thirty-Two

"Good morning, *Carol.*"

"Good morning, Dr. Brown," *Carol* says, happy to see that *Mitch* has kept his promise.

"Please call me Travis. I really prefer that name. Doctor just seems so stuffy, don't you think?"

"Okay…good morning, Travis," *Carol* smiles.

"*Mitch* tells me that the two of you have been talking, and that you have some questions for me."

"Yes sir, that's true," *Carol* says timidly.

"Well, before we start with the questions, let me tell you what *Mitch* and I agreed on. First, *Mitch* has promised to stay really close to you to make sure that you feel okay talking with me. He can also hear what I'm telling you so that he can help you on the inside if you want him to. Is that okay with you?" Travis asks.

"Yes," *Carol* says. She then shuts her eyes momentarily to see if she can see *Mitch.* Pleased to see that he is standing in the opened door, *Carol* nods her approval and opens her eyes to address Travis again. "Okay. He is standing there like he promised."

"Good. I've also asked that, if you agree to it, we will let Amanda hear and see what we are talking about. Now, *Mitch* tells me that there are a few observation rooms that Amanda can use to see what's happening, but that she will not be close enough to feel your emotions or interfere with our talk. *Gerald* is going to be sitting with her to make sure that she is okay.

"And let me tell you why I asked them to make these arrangements. When *Mitch* told me about your situation, I realized that you and Amanda will both be going through a similar process. You will be learning new things about how to deal with your feelings so they aren't so overwhelming. So if Amanda can hear us talk about these things, she can start practicing right away.

"I don't think we will talk in too much detail today, but if at any time *Gerald* feels like the information is too much for Amanda, he can always move Amanda to another room. So you don't have to worry about protecting Amanda from anything, *Gerald* is going to monitor that for us.

"Is that okay with you?" Travis asks, wanting her permission to share with others before moving forward.

"Yes, that's fine," *Carol* says.

"Perfect. Now, we've never spoken before, have we?" Travis asks, never sure when an alter has already presented, pretending to be the host.

"No sir, we haven't."

"Then can you tell me a little about yourself?" Travis asks, trying to find a way to make *Carol* more comfortable.

"What do you want to know?"

"Well, let's see. When I'm trying to get to know someone, I like to ask them about their favorite color and their favorite foods and their favorite things to do. Like my favorite color is blue. What's yours?"

"I really like purple," *Carol* offers. "But I thought your favorite color would be brown." She teases with a grin.

"Can you believe, that brown is really my second favorite color? I like to decorate with brown and blue. See?" Travis says as he points around the office at different items that have this special combination.

"That's funny," *Carol* giggles.

"So what is your favorite food?"

"My favorite food in the whole world is macaroni and cheese. My second favorite is Cheetos, the crunchy kind," *Carol* clarifies.

"Oh I like those, too," Travis says. "Now, tell me what you like to do most? What makes you the happiest?"

"The happiest?" *Carol* asks, buying herself some time to think.

"Yes. What is it that, when you do this thing, you feel really happy inside?"

"That's a harder question," *Carol* says as her demeanor begins to change.

"Okay—let me ask it a different way…Think about the last time you felt happy and tell me what you were doing."

"I was talking with Tom and with Jessica. They are my friends and they do nice things for me. Tom even gave me a big teddy bear," *Carol* says, throwing her arms open wide to show the enormity of the gift. "But that's not really me doing anything though Travis," *Carol* observes.

"It is, it is you spending time with your friends. That's doing something." Travis points out.

"Oh…then that's what makes me the happiest I guess. And what about you? What makes you the happiest?" *Carol* asks, enjoying the process of getting to know him, too.

"Oh there are lots of things that make me happy. I like to spend time with my wife and children. I like to go to church and to talk with Jesus. And I like to meet new friends like you," Travis shares.

"How many kids do you have?" *Carol* asks. She never thought about him having a family of his own.

"I have three kids," Travis brags. "Two boys and a girl. They are all three in high school now, and two of them are even driving."

"Oh wow," *Carol* says, matching Travis's enthusiasm.

"So you can see that there are a lot of things that make me happy. But I wasn't always happy."

"Why not?" *Carol* asks, with sudden concern.

"Well, life hasn't always been easy for me. There have been times when I felt hurt and sad. I didn't always know what to do with those feelings. So, I stuffed them inside and just let them grow. Each time someone hurt my feelings, did something bad to me, or just made me feel sad…well…I'd just stuff those feelings down with the rest of them. Before you knew it, I had a bunch of really bad feelings stuffed inside. It's kind of like a snow ball that starts off small and then grows bigger and bigger the more snow you add to it. That snow ball of feelings in me got to be pretty big before it was over. Do you know what I mean?" Travis checks in to be sure she understands his story so far.

"Yes," *Carol* says. "I do know what you mean."

"Do you have a big ball of bad feelings stuffed inside, too?" Travis asks.

Leaning toward Travis she whispers, "It's bigger than a house."

"Oh, then you definitely need to hear the rest of the story," Travis continues. "That big ball of feelings inside got so big that I couldn't really function any more. What I didn't know was that stuffing those feelings inside wasn't really good for me. It made me feel tired and grumpy. I knew that I had to find a way to get some relief."

"What did you do?" *Carol* asks, now on the edge of her seat.

"I asked Jesus to help me heal from those feelings. And he showed me something...he showed me that the only way to let those feelings out is to do three things: I had to really look at those feelings and acknowledge that they exist; I had to forgive the people that hurt me; and I had to let go of those feelings. When I did those three things, Jesus was able to take the feelings away and replace them with his peace," Travis nods his conclusion.

"Really? ...Did it hurt?" *Carol* asks.

"Well, I will say that it wasn't always easy. Sometimes I didn't want to admit that I had some of those really bad feelings inside me. And then, I had to learn what it means to really forgive someone. See...I thought that if I forgave that person that hurt me, well they would think that what they did was okay. But that's not what Jesus meant by forgiving them. He just meant that I wasn't supposed to hold onto the feelings I had against that person.

"Now, the last step didn't really hurt, but it can feel scary. I had those feelings inside me for a very long time and I was scared to think what it would be like without them. But I found out that Jesus never asks us to do things that are bad. He wants us to be happy and to have peace. He knows that the only way for that to happen is for us to let go of those nasty feelings. When I did that...man...I can't tell you how good it felt."

"Wow...I'm glad you feel better now," *Carol* says honestly.

"You know...that same process will work for you too, *Carol*," Travis says. "It's the same process for everyone. And I can prove it."

"How?"

"Do you believe the Bible?"

"Of course, Silly," *Carol* says.

"Do you believe that Jesus loves you?"

"I guess...I mean, He loves everyone right?"

"Yes, He loves everyone as a whole. But He also knows about you *Carol*, and He loves you."

"Really? You don't think that He just loves Amanda?"

"He loves Amanda. He loves every part of Amanda, including you. He knows what you have gone through and He wants to help you heal from that. Let me show you," Travis says as he picks up his Bible.

"Wait...I bet you know this first one already! Do you know John 3:16?" Travis asks.

"Yes! 'For God so loved the world that He gave His only begotten son, that whosoever believeth in Him should not perish, but have everlasting life.'"

"I thought you'd know that one," Travis says smiling at Carol. "Now, there's a few more that I want to show you. First, is Jeremiah 29:11. Here God is talking to his people and telling them that they have to turn away from doing bad things in order to receive His blessings. And then He says, 'For I know what plans I have for you, declares the Lord, plans to prosper you and not to harm you, plans to give you hope and a future.' So that says to me that God is interested in our future and He wants it to be good," Travis explains.

"But sometimes we make it hard for God to help us because of what we do. So I looked to see if God has any instructions on what to do with these feelings. And look what I found," Travis says as he turns to the next scripture. "In Ephesians it tells me to 'Get rid of all bitterness, rage, and anger…' Then it says, 'Be kind and compassionate to one another, forgiving each other, just as in Christ, God forgave you.'

"That tells me that I shouldn't hold onto these bad feelings, but that instead, I should let them go and forgive. And there are lots of other verses that tell us to forgive, too. And then, Jesus promises us peace. Look here…" Travis says, as excited about these truths as the first day he learned them for himself. "Here in John 14…Look what Jesus told his disciplines. 'If anyone loves me, he will obey my teachings. My Father will love him, and we will come to him and make our home with him.' And then see, here's the other part of the promise *Carol*. 'Peace I leave with you; my peace I give you. I do not give to you as the world gives. Do not let your hearts be troubled and do not be afraid.'

"Isn't that cool?" Travis asks.

"Yeah, it is. That peace sounds very nice," *Carol* says, still not fully convinced that she will ever feel that way. "But Travis, what if my bad stuff is too big? What if I never get to feel better?"

"Oh *Carol*, there is nothing too big for God. I know it feels overwhelming right now, but I promise that you can feel that peace as well. But *Carol*, it is going to be a journey. It will not happen over night."

With these words, *Carol's* heart and head sink. She had hoped that it would happen quickly and that she would be relieved of her pain immediately. It all sounds so good.

"I know that you are tired," Travis says, recognizing her disappointment. "That ball that's bigger than a house is exhausting to carry around, isn't it?"

"You have no idea," *Carol* says as tears begin to trickle down her face.

"I really want to be done. Can't I just go into someone like Mitch talked about?" *Carol* asks, desperate to find a solution to her pain.

"Once you get rid of that ball of feelings you are carrying around, we can talk about the option of you integrating. It sounds like it is a good option for you, but we first need to deal with that ball. See, if you integrate too fast, without taking care of those feelings, you still won't feel any relief. You'll just be taking those feelings with you. But I want you to see how well this process works so that you know there is hope. Can we go ahead and get started?" Travis asks.

"You mean we can start already?"

"Absolutely. Let's start with how you feel right now. You mentioned that you feel tired. But I bet that doesn't mean that you feel like you have been running around and now you're tired. Does it?"

"Not really. It's more like I've been running around with this big ball and now I need a nap," *Carol* tries to explain. "That big ball that we were talking about."

"What other feelings do you have about carrying around that big ball?"

"Hum…I guess I feel a little mad," *Carol* says quietly, not sure if that is an okay thing to say.

"I think I would be mad too if I had to carry around that big ball for so many years. It's okay to say that you're mad—even if you get mad at me, you can say it. I can handle it if you get mad," Travis assures her. "Do you have any other feelings about it?"

"I'm a little scared, too," *Carol* confesses.

"Okay—scared about what?" Travis asks for clarification.

"I'm scared that if I look too close at the ball, it will just open up and swallow me whole. Then I won't ever be able to get away from it."

"I see. Any other feeling you have about it?" Travis asks, not passing judgment on her fears.

"No, that's enough," *Carol* says.

"That is a lot, isn't it?" Travis agrees. "So now that you've admitted these feelings, let's look at them a little closer. *Carol*, tell me more about why you are mad."

****

With that question, the healing journey officially begins. Travis spends the rest of the session—and many more afterward—walking *Carol* through the process of replacing her ball of bad feelings with the peace that can only come from Christ's healing touch. With each step in the journey, *Carol* grows freer. Amanda and the others share in the process: learning how to recognize their own feelings; seek and give forgiveness; and accepting the peace of God's love.

Chapter Thirty-Three

"Are you sure you know what you're doing," Amanda teases Rick.

"Oh that's right. You haven't had the privilege of tasting one of Rick's smoked turkeys yet have you?" Jessica asks. "It was really pretty good last year."

Adding under her breath to Amanda, "And I'd rather he smoke it than try to fry it! I want to keep my house for a while." The two share a laugh at the imagined scene and move over to the outdoor table and chair set to take their place in the turkey smoking party.

"So let me tell you about the tradition," Tom offers.

"Tradition?" Jessica interrupts with a giggle. "This is only the second year we've done this."

"It only takes doing something two years in a row for it to become a tradition," Tom defends. "So, as I was saying...We have a tradition. The day before Thanksgiving, we all sit out here and watch Rick smoke the turkey. He has to add more woodchips every half hour, so Jessica serves as the time keeper."

Jessica smiles and waves her trusty watch, signaling her readiness to assume her role again this year.

"Last year, my job was to keep the music and coffee flowing. I thought maybe you could help with one of those tasks," Tom suggests.

"Sounds good, I'll pick the music...you can keep us warm with coffee," Amanda says, pleased with the opportunity to pick her part in this growing tradition. "Then what do we do?"

"You sit back and watch me work my magic on this bird," Rick says as they all laugh.

Amanda wastes no time in jumping into her new role of disc jockey. Picking a fun jazzy CD, she gets the music started. "Will that work?" she asks.

"Sounds good to me," Jessica says and the others agree.

As Rick takes his seat, indicating the first thirty minute break, the discussion begins. Amanda really enjoys their time with Jessica and Rick. It's great to have such wonderful friends who are also family. Over the last month, the four of them have grown accustomed to talking openly about Amanda's insiders as just a fact of life. It isn't a major part of the conversation, but a natural part of everyday dialogue. Today is no exception.

"So Amanda tells me that you two found a house," Jessica says to Tom. "Does it really have everything you were looking for?"

"Can you believe it?" Tom asks. "We had a lot of criteria. I think we just about drove Mary crazy trying to find a house with everything we wanted. But she didn't give up and neither did we."

"It's perfect," Amanda agrees.

"Does it have the laundry room that *Marie* wanted?" Jessica asks.

"You will not believe this laundry room!" Amanda exclaims. "It is huge! It has a built-in ironing board that folds into a cabinet when not in use. It has a folding table with storage underneath and a hanging bar above it."

"I'll never have another wrinkled shirt in my life," Tom laughs.

"Probably not," Jessica agrees. "And what was it that *Brooke* wanted? I can't remember."

"Oh, she wanted to be sure that we had some kind of a game room. She likes to play darts and pool," Tom says. "And *Sabrina* didn't want the house to have a basement, which is not an easy request around here. But the cool thing about this house is that it has an open basement of sorts. It's a multi-leveled house, so the 'basement' part is only about a half of a story down. And it's not closed off…the entrance to the lower level is actually about ten feet long. The steps go all the way across the entrance. There's no door! About half way down the room, it steps down one more time and turns slightly. So we could put the pool table in the first level and the noise will not really be bad for the rest of the house. But she still feels safe there because it isn't hidden or closed off.

"Then, the lowest of the lower level, the part that is kind of stuck behind everything…that's where we thought we'd put the media room for the guys. That, and a barbeque pit were their requests," Tom explains.

"Sounds awesome," Rick says.

"Oh yeah," Tom say, "and you will love the barbeque pit, Rick. It's hooked up to the gas line so you don't ever have to worry about running out of propane. It's built into the side of the house with this great brick frame around it. On one side of the pit is a burner to keep your sauce hot and on the other side is a little sink, complete with running water!"

"Oh man! You're living the high life for sure!" Rick says, genuinely impressed.

"Did you ever get *Agnes* to tell you what she wanted in the house?" Jessica asks.

"Yes, she did finally say that she wanted to have a nice kitchen for baking cookies. We don't see her very often, but I'm hoping that she will begin to feel well enough to do some fun stuff like that," Tom says.

"*Dana* said that she would like a place to read and write occasionally," Amanda reminds him. "There's a great spot in the master bedroom that is perfect for a little library type of area. Mary called it a parent's retreat. It already has some built-in shelves and there's plenty of room for a desk and a comfortable chair. I can't imagine that she wouldn't like it."

"And we all know what little Miss *Carol* wants," Rick says as they respond in unison.

"A puppy!"

"So is the backyard fenced in?" Rick asks.

"Yes, and there is plenty of room for *Carol* and a dog to run around in it," Tom says with a grin.

"It's time to check the woodchips Rick," Jessica says.

Amanda takes advantage of the natural break in the conversation to announce, "Speaking of *Carol*...we've been doing a lot of talking and...well...she has something that she wants to talk with you guys about. Do you mind?"

"Of course not," Jessica says as the others chime in.

Having practiced this maneuver dozens of times now, Amanda has become quite the professional switcher. With little obvious effort, Amanda is able to exchange places with *Carol*, allowing her to present while Amanda watches. *Carol* waits until Rick takes his seat before she starts.

"I have some news for everyone," *Carol* begins.

"What's up?" Jessica asks; her curiosity peaked.

"Our doctor, Travis, he said that I've done really good in letting Jesus heal my bad feelings from the past. He said that I should get a gold star in it in fact!" *Carol* brags.

"That's wonderful, *Carol*!," Rick responds.

Tom, aware of what *Carol* is going to talk about, nervously gets up from his seat and pretends to peek in at the turkey. *Carol* takes a deep breath and continues.

"It seems that I've done so good that I can now make a decision. I've talked about it with Travis, and I've talked about it with Amanda, and with Tom. Can I ask you for your ideas?" *Carol* asks permission before proceeding.

"Of course, Honey," Jessica says. "We're always happy to talk through things with each other. It's a smart way to make decisions."

Deciding that he might need to help explain things to Jessica and Rick, Tom returns to his seat and offers them a cautious smile.

"Okay, here's the thing. I've been helping Amanda and everyone else for a very long time. I worked really hard at it. And then, when I met Travis, I worked really hard at healing up that big ball of feelings inside. And now, well, now I get to make a choice. I can just be here, as *Carol*, with nothing really special that I have to do...or I can go back into Amanda." *Carol* nods as if agreeing with herself that she explained it all correctly.

Wanting to give Jessica and Rick a chance to think about things before they respond, Tom offers a more detailed explanation. "*Carol* has shared with me that she is really tired. She's not as tired any more, now that she has worked with Dr. Brown, but she feels like she is ready for a break...well, I guess you can say, she's ready to retire," Tom says, forcing a smile. "So for insiders, one way to retire is to integrate into Amanda. With her permission, I talked with Dr. Brown about the process. He said that, if *Carol* does integrate, she would still be around but would be more of a hidden part of Amanda. She wouldn't come out and talk to us as *Carol*, but we would see glimpses of her personality and strengths in Amanda."

Turning toward *Carol*, he says with a smile, "So I guess that means that Amanda would become even more adorable, more playful, and probably more ready to laugh at my silly jokes." In spite of his strongest efforts, Tom is unable to stop the feelings of sadness and grief that are welling up from inside.

"I see," Jessica responds, seeing her brother's struggle. "So *Carol*, Honey...what do you want to do?"

"I really think that I want to retire," *Carol* says while nodding her head.

Leaning toward Jessica she confides with a slight whisper. "I'm a little scared because everyone seems so sad about it, but that's what I really want to do. That's what feels right to me. Travis said that it's okay to do it now, and that's what I told him I want to do."

Wiping away her own tears, Jessica says, "Then my darling, it sounds like that's what you need to do. You know, we will miss talking with you. You're one of my best friends in the whole world. But it really isn't about me or anyone else. It's about what's best for you. And sweetie, you have gone through so much already. You have been such a brave little girl. I think it's wonderful that you have the chance to retire and just rest now."

Reaching over, Jessica gives her the most powerful hug she can without squeezing her to death. "I'm glad to hear that you will still be a part of Amanda. I know that I'll be able to spot your influence. It will be a good thing for Amanda, too. She will definitely benefit from having your positive and joyful outlook on life." Jessica adds.

"I agree," Rick says. "You're a great kid and you can't help but to make things better."

"But there's just one thing," *Carol* says. "I need you to promise me that you will make Tom buy that puppy still." She says with a smile.

"There's no need for anyone to back you up on that," Tom assures her. "I guarantee you that we will get that puppy. And I'll make sure that Amanda is out when we pick the puppy so that you get a say in which one we get. Deal?"

"Deal!" *Carol* say. "I feel better now. I'm so happy I have nice friends like you," she adds, talking to the whole group.

"I think you need to ask *Sabrina* to pick the music, Amanda picks that really old stuff," *Carol* says, changing the subject and making an excuse to go back inside.

Picking up on her cue, Tom says, "Well, I don't know, Amanda is pretty good at picking music. But if you think *Sabrina* will do better, then maybe we should let her give it a try."

As if playing her part in a well-rehearsed play, *Sabrina* makes her presence known. "Well, I don't know about the rest of you…but I intend to ignore the good doctor's advice and stuff my feelings about this integration down as far as they can go." Looking over at Tom she adds with a grin, "And don't even think about adding this as part of the Thanksgiving tradition!"

"No way," Tom says, smiling at his friend. "So do you really think you can pick better music than Amanda?"

"I have no idea, but I'm willing to give it a try," she says, trying to keep her tone light and playful.

"So *Sabrina*, how are the wedding plans coming?" Jessica asks.

"Oh don't even get me started!" *Sabrina* says, while sitting down to fill Jessica in with the latest developments.

****

"Are you ready then?" *Mitch* asks Amanda and *Carol*.

"Ready," *Carol* says.

"Me too," Amanda agrees.

"Good," *Mitch* says, giving them a reassuring smile. "This is going to happen very naturally so I don't want either of you to be worried or scared.

"So let's start by making you two comfortable. Do you think the two of you can share a bean bag chair, one of the larger ones?" *Mitch* asks.

"Of course we can, Silly, I'm not very big," *Carol* says with a smile. She loves to play around in the bean bag chairs. In fact, she's the main reason that they are all over the place on the inside.

As Amanda takes her seat, the chair naturally forms around her in a comfortable hug. *Carol* playfully jumps into Amanda's lap. "I'm not too heavy am I?" *Carol* asks.

"No, you're fine," Amanda assures her, hugging her in tight. In the last few weeks, Amanda has come to really love *Carol*. She has learned so much about her and enjoys her lightheartedness.

Mitch also sits in a bean bag chair next to them and waits for the wiggling to stop. "Okay, now just close your eyes and relax for a minute. I want to tell you a little about what to expect."

As the two follow his direction, *Mitch* begins talking them through the process. His instructions are a combination of his past experience with Janet and the information he received from Travis. He knows that *Carol* and Amanda could accomplish this task without his involvement, but he wants to help. He wants to make the transition as easy as possible for everyone.

"*Carol*, you have done such a good job over the years. Everyone is proud of you. But no one is more proud than I am. Anyone who has met you will remember you forever.

"That kind of hard work is so tiring, I understand. But now, it's a new day. You don't have to carry around any of those worries ever again. Now, you can put that all down and just rest."

Carol opens her eyes long enough to smile at *Mitch* and wave good-bye. As she closes her eyes again, her image begins to fade.

"As you begin to relax and let yourself melt into Amanda, you find that you know Amanda better than ever before. You are beginning to see her thoughts and feel her feelings. These become like your own thoughts…you still see the world as you always have, but now you share your thoughts and feelings with Amanda completely. You are no longer *Carol*, you are now Amanda.

"Amanda, as you open yourself to receive *Carol*, you are simply accepting her into yourself. You accept everything about her: her emotions, her thoughts, her joys, her sadness, her love, her playfulness, her strengths, and her weaknesses. You don't have to fear any of these things about her because she has already shared so much of it with you. You are both ready. She has always been a part of your life, but now she is blending herself with you.

"It's as if you have two colors of play dough, a blue and a dark pink. Then you begin to mix the colors together. And you keep mixing them, and blending them until you see a new color—light purple. The play dough hasn't changed colors, but the tiny pieces of dough have blended so closely together that it seems like the colors have changed.

"You are becoming a new color, a color of Amanda and *Carol* mixed together. The characteristics of Amanda and *Carol* remain. But as you mix together, the swirls of Amanda and *Carol* blend so tightly and are so close together, that it looks like a brand new color; a beautiful combination of two wonderful people, the perfect shade of purple."

As thoroughly as he prepared, as willing as he is to help, he is stunned at his own feelings of grief. As he watches *Carol's* image dissolve into Amanda, he remembers back on the many times that she willingly suffered at the hands of their father. Even with all of the horror she endured, she always remained childlike in her approach to life. He will miss her smile and how playfully she dubbed people 'silly' if they treated her like a baby.

As much as he will miss her, he is happy that she is doing this. She deserves to rest, to be free from the worries of fulfilling a function within the system. For only a split second, he allows himself to wonder what it is like for *Carol* and if he will ever have the chance to rest.

Returning his thoughts to the present, he sits and watches silently. The integration must move forward and conclude on it's own, in it's own time. Feeling as if Amanda is at her most vulnerable during the process, he determines to remain quietly by her side for as long as it takes.

Chapter Thirty-Four

"Can you believe it's finally here?" Amanda asks Jessica.

"It's very exciting," Jessica agreed. "Are you ready?"

"I am, I just hope everything else is ready. Did your mom get here with the groom's cake?"

"Yes, it's exactly like you wanted, Amanda! And the wedding cake is absolutely beautiful!"

"I know—it turned out so good! I can't wait for Tom to see it," Amanda exclaims. "And what about the flowers…who's making sure that the guys all get their flowers pinned on?"

"Mom's taking care of that. Your mom is making sure that the reception area is decorated like you told her and that the flowers are placed 'just so' in the church."

"Is the pastor here yet?" Amanda asks.

"Yes, but aren't you really wanting to know if Tom is here yet?" Jessica asks.

"Of course he's here, Silly, it's his wedding day," Amanda says. "Isn't he?"

"Yes, he is. I just couldn't help but tease you some. You know, I've never seen a wedding where something didn't go wrong at the last minute. But Amanda, I think this might be the exception," Jessica says encouragingly. "I've gone through your checklist twice just to be sure. Everything really seems to be in place.

"But we need to get you into your dress and ready to go. You've got about fifteen minutes before they start playing your song."

"Oh my goodness! Okay…I'm going to need help getting my dress on. I can't step into it with this silly petticoat on."

The two wrestle with the mounds of material, carefully placing it over

Amanda's perfectly groomed hair. Just as the last button is being fastened, Amanda spins around and announces, "Oh no!! I forgot the 'something blue'!"

"What do you mean you forgot it? I thought your garter belt is blue?"

"No…the one I bought was blue, but Mom made one for me. It's all white. I thought it was so sweet that she made it that I didn't think about the fact that I need something blue still. I was just thinking about the fact that I still need to put on the garter belt and that's when I remembered the blue rule," Amanda says in a full-blown panic.

"Oh—don't worry," Jessica says, trying to calm Amanda and thinking fast. "I've got an idea." Reaching into her purse, Jessica pulls out her cell phone.

"That's not blue," Amanda says, looking at the phone.

"No, I'm not thinking about my phone, Silly," Jessica says, borrowing Amanda's latest phrase. "I'm going to call my mom and ask if she is wearing her sapphire ring today. It would be perfect."

"Oh, thank you!" Amanda says, genuinely relieved.

"Do you have the something old and something new?" Jessica asks.

"Well, the dress is new…does that count?"

"I don't see why not," Jessica says after considering the rules as she learned them. "I never heard any criteria on what the new thing had to be."

"Good! The something old is the pair of earrings that my mom gave me. They used to be my grandmother's," Amanda says while showing Jessica the pearl earrings.

"They're beautiful Amanda," Jessica stops for only seconds to admire the heirlooms. "So then, if Mom has her ring on today, you'll be all set. You have all four items because your something blue is also borrowed."

"Right—that's good." Relieved to have the rules all covered, Amanda now focuses on getting the rest of her attire pulled together while Jessica contacts her mother.

Within seconds, both mothers come running into the room. "What's going on?" they ask in unison.

"Amanda needs something blue," Jessica explains. "Mom, do you have your sapphire ring on?

"No, I didn't wear it today," she explains.

Searching through her purse, Victoria timidly announces, "Okay, I think I have the solution. It's a little different…but it's blue." Holding up her key ring, she shares her idea with the others. Dangling from the chain is a small globe.

"I got this during one of our mission focuses at church," Victoria explains. "It helps me remember to pray for our missionaries around the world. Do you think it has enough blue on it?"

Considering this unorthodox solution, Amanda asks, "Where would I put it?"

"I can sew it to your petticoat in a matter of seconds. That way it will be out of sight and won't cause a bulge anywhere. What do you think?"

"I say go for it. You said that you wanted to share today with the whole world," Jessica giggles.

Nodding her approval to her mother, Amanda sits in front of the mirror to put on her veil while her mother sews.

"Thank you Momma," Amanda says as she reapplies her lip stick and blush. "I really appreciate you helping me out."

"Of course, Amanda! That's what mothers are for isn't it?" she asks with a smile. "I feel like I should be giving you some wonderful words of wisdom to help you start your life with Tom. I just don't know what to say," Victoria says as she fights back tears. "But I can tell you that I love you and I hope that you and Tom have an outstanding life together."

"Thank you Mom," Amanda says, stopping long enough to give her mother a hug. "I don't know what you're worried about…those words sound great to me—better than anything Dad would have said." Amanda laughs. "He never was very good at sharing emotions," she adds with a smile.

Unable to stop herself, Victoria asks, "Do you miss him?"

"Believe it or not, I do miss him, Mom. I wish that he could walk me down the aisle and give me away. I carry a daughter's love for her dad, I suppose I always will. But…I can't change any of that and I'm not going to let it get me down today," Amanda says as she dabs the tears off her cheeks.

"Thank goodness for water-proof mascara," Jessica says as she walks over to check on the progress.

"That's for sure! It was one of the criteria I had for today…don't mess up the makeup just because you cry," Amanda explains, grateful for her foresight.

"Okay—all finished," Victoria announces as she snaps off the extra thread. "Now you know you have to mean those vows, the whole world is watching," she teases.

"Thanks Mom…as long as they aren't looking up my dress we'll be good!" she teases back. "Now all I have to do is put on the garter belt and I'm ready as well," Amanda says, while taking care of that task.

"You two mothers need to be escorted to your seats so we can start the show," Jessica quips. Both mother and mother-in-law give Amanda a quick hug as they head out the door.

"Are you ready?" Jessica asks.

"Yes, I'm ready," Amanda says.

"Okay—one more check because I promised you and I promised Tom...who's out?" Jessica asks.

"It's Amanda," she says as she smiles back. "I got agreement from everyone to watch but not stomp all over me. I really think it's going to be a good day. Everyone is as excited as I am. But...thanks for checking."

"Good—I'm excited too! I've always wanted a sister! Now, let's get this show on the road," she says while pulling the veil forward over Amanda's face and handing her the bridal bouquet.

As they enter the foyer, Amanda can hear the music start, signaling that the bridesmaids are about to enter the church. Her soon-to-be father-in-law walks over and offers his arm to her. "You are positively stunning, Amanda."

"Thank you," she says bashfully. "And thank you again for walking me down the aisle."

"I consider it a tremendous privilege Amanda."

Before walking down the aisle herself, Jessica takes a minute to be sure that the train on Amanda's dress is properly fluffed and the veil is laying right. Satisfied that everything is ready to go, Jessica signals for the other two bridesmaids to begin the procession.

As the familiar cords of "Here Comes The Bride" begin to play, Tom's heart begins to pound with the rhythm. For just a moment, he can see Amanda as she begins her way into the church. Then, before he can process the scene, everyone stands in honor of his bride. While he's grateful for their respect, he's quickly becoming frustrated with them blocking his view.

Standing like a statue, Tom patiently waits for her to reappear. Although it lasts only a few seconds, it feels like an eternity. When he is able to see her again, she is much closer and he can actually see past the veil and the big white dress...he can see his beautiful Amanda. As soon as he is able, Tom gladly takes his bride's hand and escorts her up the steps to the waiting bridal party.

Lost in a universe of love and admiration, Tom and Amanda are only moderately aware of the others around them. Equally immersed in the joy of the moment, time looses all relevance. The pastor's words, the songs, the prayers…it all seems to be happening around them, as if their love has formed a protective shield that no sounds can penetrate.

Their participation in the process now required, the minister pulls them back to earth as he mentions that the couple has written their own vows. As the minister stops, he motions for Tom to go first.

Turning to face her, Tom takes both of her hands, looks into her eyes and shares his heart. "Amanda, from the moment I saw you, I knew God had brought us together. Since then, He has confirmed this belief over and over again, as our friendship has grown into a love beyond compare. Having you as my wife is so much more than I deserve, and is a privilege that I will never take for granted.

"I can't promise you that things will always be perfect, but through the grace and power of Christ I can promise you this: No matter what comes our way, whether we are having a great time or facing the most difficult struggles imaginable, I will always love and care for you without reservation, or regret. I promise to be faithful to you and to treat you with kindness and compassion. Everything that I am, and everything that I have, I willingly and gladly share with you for the rest of our lives."

Taking a deep breath, Amanda determines to push through her tears and make her vows heard by everyone, especially Tom.

"Tom, before I met you, my life was like an unattended rose garden after a storm. The blooms lay dead on the ground and the thorns threatened anyone who came near. That is until you came around. You brought light and color back into my life through the love that we share. It's with that same love that I freely and enthusiastically give myself to be your wife.

"I promise that I will always cherish our love and tend to it carefully. Deeply rooted in Christ, our love will endure the storms life throws at us. I will remain faithful to you forever. I promise to dream with you, laugh with you, and cry with you through all the seasons of life. Tom, my love for you will last through all eternity."

Moving toward the exchange of rings, the pastor asks, "May I have the rings?" Collecting both rings, he continues. "Let us pray. Holy Father, please bless the giving and receiving of these rings. May Amanda and Tom live in your peace and grow in their knowledge of Your love and Your presence. May the seamless circle of these rings become the symbol of their endless love. May they live together in Your grace forever. In Jesus' name, Amen."

Handing the ring to Tom, he says, "Now as a token of your love and of your desire to be united forever, you may place the ring on your bride's finger."

As he puts the ring onto Amanda's finger, Tom says, "Amanda, I give you this ring as a symbol of my love and faithfulness to you."

Turning to Amanda, the pastor hands her the ring and says, "By the same token Amanda, you may now place the ring on your groom's hand."

Amanda puts the ring on his finger, then looks back up at him, repeating the same pledge, "Tom, I give you this ring as a symbol of my love and faithfulness to you."

"By the power vested in me, I now pronounce you husband and wife. You may kiss the bride," the pastor says smiling at Tom.

Carefully lifting the veil from her face, Tom gently leans down and kisses Amanda. While strictly intended to communicate their affection to each other, it is obvious to all that the two are deeply in love and share a mutual respect for each other.

Motioning for them to turn toward the audience, the pastor announces, "Ladies and gentlemen, it's my great privilege to present to you, Mr. and Mrs. Tom Morris."

THE END